All rational thoughts dissolved into the tropical night under the provocative sensations his hands aroused as he began to caress her through the fabric of her gown. His touch kindled a deep yearning within her to feel his hands upon her naked flesh. The impulse was so intense it blocked all protest from her lips as his fingers unlaced her gown and slipped the bodice down to reveal the taut peaks of her breast.

Royale gasped with pleasure as his mouth covered one rose-colored nipple while he aroused its mate with his thumb. She wound her fingers in his long hair, pressing his head closer and arching her back to give him full access to her sensitive flesh. . . .

PRAISE FOR CORDIA BYERS'S
LOVE STORM

"A FAST, ALLURING ROMANCE ... A SATISFYING NIGHT'S READ."

Romantic Times

"Cordia Byers' plot has lots of action packed into it that will make LOVE STORM a favorite among readers."

Affaire de Coeur

Fawcett Gold Medal Books
by Cordia Byers:

CALLISTA

LOVE STORM

NICOLE LA BELLE

PIRATE ROYALE

Cordia Byers

FAWCETT GOLD MEDAL • NEW YORK

To my sister, Peggy, who left her pirate on an island so she could become a Registered Nurse.

Chapter 1

Witch's Cay resembled a crumpled piece of green velvet that had been carelessly tossed upon shimmering blue silk as the *Raven* neared the entrance to the small inlet where it would drop anchor. Until the captain of the twenty-gun frigate thought it necessary to make another voyage, it would remain moored there, safe and secluded from all eyes.

"Hold her steady, Tim," came the firm yet softly feminine voice of the ship's master as the *Raven* eased through the narrow channel to the cove.

"Lower the anchor, Fishbait; we're home," the captain ordered, watching as the seamen scurried to obey without question. A wry smile tugged at the corners of her supple lips as she reflected upon the crew's easy compliance with her commands. It had not always been that simple. Less than a year earlier the men who served on the *Raven* had adamantly refused to sail with a woman as their captain, even if she was Sir John Carrington's daughter and heir.

Royale's smile deepened as she watched the quartermaster, Fishbait Jones, give the order to release the heavy iron anchor. The *Raven* surged against the restraint before gently swaying to a halt in the still cove. Nay, Royale mused, it had not been an easy task to convince these seasoned sailors to sail with her at the helm. With some amusement she recalled the first day she had come on board the frigate and told them of her plans to continue sailing under her father's letter of marque.

She would never forget the expressions on their faces. At first they had gaped at her in disbelief, thinking she had lost her wits in her grief over her father's death. However, when they had realized that she actually intended to take Sir John's place as captain of the *Raven*, a rumble of protest had begun. It started in low whispers and grew in volume as the men rebelled at the thought of having a woman lead them. Their hostility was evident on their weatherbeaten features. They had been like a pack of dogs banding together with bristles raised to ward off an intruder encroaching upon their territory.

Royale had expected that reaction from them. She knew they would not meekly give in to the idea of having a woman usurp the authority they thought only a man could hold. She also knew it was left to her to change their minds. Her stomach had twisted itself into knots, but she let none of her feelings show as she faced them bravely. If she revealed any sign of weakness, she would never gain their respect and loyalty, and then she would be unable to fulfill the vendetta she had planned against the Spaniards. The damned Spaniards had caused her father's death, and she was resolved to retaliate against their gold-laden galleons with swift, unremorseful vengeance.

Knowing she would have only one chance to convince the crew, she cocked her head to one side, braced her hands arrogantly on her hips, and let a cool, challenging smile play over her lips as she said, "It seems you have doubts about my ability to lead you. You seem to forget that I was schooled at my father's knee. He taught me well, and I know as much about sailing as any man on board. Yet you refuse to sail with me.''

The quartermaster, Fishbait Jones, stepped forward as the crew's spokesman. ''Mistress, we'll not sail with a woman, no matter what she knows. We respected yer father, but having his daughter at the helm is another matter completely. A ship is no place fer a woman. We don't mean to be disrespectful to ye, but we have to think of our own necks. To captain a privateer, ye've got to have the guts and the strength to fight. Ye may have dressed yerself up in them men's britches and shirt, but ye don't look as if ye could fight off a mosquito, much less a full-grown man in battle.''

The men nodded in unison behind the quartermaster as he continued, ''We all know ye were taught good by Sir John, but there's more to being a privateer than just the running of the *Raven*. Ye have to be able to defend yerself and yer men. A woman could never do that.''

Without realizing it, Fishbait had provided her with the opportunity to force the men to give her a chance. That was all she needed. Once they filled the hold of the *Raven* with gold, she knew the sailors would finally accept her as their captain. Full pockets weighed much more heavily than superstitions about a woman's presence on board a ship boding ill luck.

''You mean you would sail under my command if I was able to show you that I could defend myself and the ship in battle?'' Royale asked as her hand slipped to the intricately carved hilt of the sword that hung at her side. It was a smaller replica of her father's. He'd had it made for her sixteenth birthday, two years earlier.

From the expression of relief that flashed across Fishbait's face, Royale knew he thought he had won the argument even as he answered, ''Aye.''

''So be it, then. I issue a challenge to any man on board

who thinks to best me with a sword. And I'll agree never to set foot on the *Raven* again if I am defeated.'' Royale watched the sailors look at one another and smile with confident superiority as they nodded their heads toward Fishbait. She had known he would be their chosen candidate. He was the most experienced and skilled with a sword of any of her father's men. Her next words dampened their glee slightly as she added, ''But there is one stipulation to our bargain. If I win the duel, then every man on board will sail with me for at least one voyage. After that, if anyone is not satisfied by my command, he will be free to leave my service.''

Royale watched Fishbait turn to the crew, his lined features flushed with annoyance as he asked, ''Do ye all agree to the young mistress's terms?'' She surmised from the men's faces as they nodded their agreement that they wanted to see Fishbait humiliate her by showing her that she could not best a man with his own weapon, and she smiled to herself, secure in her own abilities.

Fishbait released a long breath as he turned back to Royale and said, ''We agree to yer bargain. Now let this be a lesson to ye that a woman's place is in the home, raising her man's young'uns, and not at sea with him.''

''Perhaps for some women that is true, Fishbait, but I fear you have misjudged me,'' Royale replied as she drew her sword with such speed that her opponent's surprise was stamped on his leathery features.

The clash of metal against shining metal echoed eerily through the still afternoon air. No sound came from the sailors, who watched with bated breath as Royale and Fishbait parried each other's thrusts. Fishbait had gained his knowledge from many bloody battles through the years, but Royale danced lightly about her much larger opponent, nicking his shirt but never drawing blood and always keeping him on the defensive with her quick movements so that he could not use his size to his advantage.

She knew the quartermaster had forgotten that his opponent had been taught by an expert swordsman: Sir John Carrington. Since the age of six, when she had charmed her father into instructing her, she had trained in the art of fencing. The long, tiring hours of practice Sir John had demanded in return stood her in good stead in this duel.

Perspiration beaded and ran down both combatants' faces as Royale made her last move, forcing Fishbait back against the mast. With one last upward thrust she knocked his blade from his sweat-dampened grip. She smiled in triumph as she placed the tip of her sword at the base of the seaman's throat and asked, "Do you give quarter?"

Royale chuckled to herself now as she recalled the moment when the quartermaster had accepted his defeat at a woman's hand. He had regarded her with something akin to wonder as he'd said, "Aye, Captain."

No, it had not been easy to gain the crew's loyalty, but luck had been with her during the past months. She had been able to fill their pockets with gold from Spanish galleons, as well as to hold enough back to make their voyages profitable for England.

Tearing her thoughts away from the past, Royale rubbed the tired ache at the back of her neck as she glanced over her shoulder at the helmsman. "I've already divided up the men's purchase, Tim. Once they have made the *Raven* secure, give it to them and let them go ashore. They've earned their rest after this voyage."

"Aye, Captain," Tim O'Kelly said as he left the helm and moved to stand at the slender woman's side. "You want me and Fishbait to take the rest up to the cave?"

"Wait until the men have gone ashore first. There's a few here who might decide to get greedy if they discovered what we've stored inland," Royale said as she turned to look at the helmsman, her emerald eyes twinkling. "I'd hate to see all that gold used to buy women and rum."

Tim grinned, his young face lighting up with amusement at the thought. "I doubt that could ever happen. It would take more than one man to spend that much gold. He'd be long dead of exhaustion and gut rot before he got a quarter of the way through it, if he spent it in that manner."

"You could be right, but I bet there are a few who serve me who would love that type of death." Royale stretched her weary arms out in front of her. "Now it's time for me to go to Good Fortune. I've been away far too long this time. I wonder how well Adele has done in acting my surrogate through the past months. I suspect she's tired of pretending to be me. I know she detests riding through the village on horseback, veiled and dressed in my gowns. She hates horses."

"Aye, that she does," Tim chuckled as he recalled Royale's housekeeper's complaints about the ruse she perpetrated each time her mistress was away from Good Fortune. Adele moaned but continued to do as she was asked in order to protect Royale's secret life as a privateer. They all knew Royale would be cast out by polite society if her actions were ever known to her peers on Witch's Cay. They had always considered Sir John's daughter strange because of her love of the less feminine pursuits. If they ever learned of her captaining the *Raven*, it would ruin her reputation completely.

Royale glanced toward the tall cliffs where the lush foliage hid the path to Good Fortune. "I'm also anxious to see if any news has come from England. I might have received my letter of marque while we were at sea."

"Do you think the King will let you sail under England's marque?" Tim asked as he leaned back against the ship's rail, which was worn smooth by much use.

Royale regarded Tim thoughtfully for a long moment

before she answered, "He had best do so if he hopes to gain any of the gold we have taken this past year. I'll serve Charles loyally if he doesn't refuse me. He might think it unusual to have a female privateer sailing under England's marque, but he would find it even odder to have a woman *pirate* sailing the seas, taking and keeping what he thinks is his due."

Tim's face spread into a wide grin, revealing large, uneven teeth as he chuckled and said, "You learned much at your father's knee, Royale Carrington. Sir John would be proud of you. I think he would probably have made the same decision if he had been placed in your situation."

"I hope you're right. I've a score to settle with Spain, and if the King does not agree to my letter of marque, then I will not hesitate to take matters into my own hands. The bastards took my father from me, and I plan to see them pay for the deed," Royale said, her voice harsh with pent-up emotion as the vivid memory of Sir John's death came back to haunt her. He had died slowly, tortured by the gangrene that had taken hold in the wounds he had received in a skirmish with a Spanish man-of-war. He had caught several pieces of rusty shrapnel in his legs and chest, and that had been the beginning of the end. Royale knew she would never forget the sound of his anguished screams as his blood turned to poison and his fever soared.

Tim placed a comforting hand on Royale's shoulder. "You still miss him a great deal, don't you?"

"Aye, Tim," she said, and quickly looked away to hide the moisture that glistened in her eyes. "I owe it to Father to avenge his death. He was a good and generous man. There are few men born who are loved as well as John Carrington was."

Hearing the slight catch in Royale's voice and understanding her feelings for Sir John because he, too, had loved him, Tim nodded. He also sought revenge against those responsible for John Carrington's death.

Lifting one slender shoulder in an offhand shrug as if the action could push away her melancholy thoughts, Royale changed the painful subject. "It's past time I went ashore. I long for a hot bath and the feel of silk against my skin. When I'm on the *Raven* I don't mind wearing britches, but once I'm on land I'm afraid I quickly forget that I'm the captain of a ship, and I become the lady of the manor instead."

Relieved that the sad moment had passed, Tim chuckled as he glanced down at the long, shapely legs revealed by Royale's male attire. " 'Tis a shame to see such treasures covered by skirts.''

Royale's cheeks flushed a deeper rose at Tim's compliment. She found it strangely disquieting. Of late she had begun to wonder about her own future. Until now her life-style had suited her well. She had enjoyed the freedom that being master of her own vessel gave her, as well as the satisfaction of knowing she was avenging her father with each Spanish ship they took. However, she had begun to sense that something was missing from her life. She could not put a name to it, but Tim's comment had aroused the elusive specter that kept haunting her but would never come forward so that she could see it in the light. Hiding her feelings beneath her lighthearted banter, she said, "Tim, if anyone but you had said that to me I would have had to call him out for the insult. But we've been friends far too long, and I know you look at me as your sister."

"Aye." Tim grinned. "I'm beginning to believe that's a shame, too. You've grown into a beautiful woman, Royale, and had I not been around when you were nothing but arms, legs, and a mop of unruly chestnut hair, I most certainly would have other thoughts on my mind. Now I have to watch out for all the rest who look at you with heated eyes.''

"Heated eyes, Tim?" Royale said, and laughed. "I'm afraid the only men to look at me with heat in their eyes are the members of my crew when I give them an order they don't like."

Tim shook his head in wonder. Royale Carrington did not realize what a beautiful woman she had become. With her intriguing sea-green eyes fringed with thick, sooty lashes, her small, perfect nose, which tilted ever so slightly at the tip, and her provocative mouth with its gently full lips that gave her face a touch of sensuality, she was a beauty few men would be able to resist. At the age of eighteen the ungainly body he had spoken of had rounded into the soft, full curves of a woman. Seeing her, a man knew exactly where his hand would fit on her.

Putting that thought quickly from his mind, he said, "All right. If you refuse to believe me, I'll let you go on thinking you are a toad with warts all over your face."

Making a moue of disgust, Royale said, "I might not be the beauty you try to make me believe I am, but I don't think I'm a toad, either."

"All right, you're not a toad. But you are the mistress of Good Fortune, and the day is growing late. If you intend for me to carry out your orders before night sets in, you had best leave me to it. I'll be up to Good Fortune once we have everything stored away."

"Then I'll leave you to your tasks," Royale said with the authority of the captain of the *Raven*.

Tim saluted. "Aye, Captain."

Royale paused at the edge of the cliff overlooking the cove and watched as Tim ordered the remaining crew members to their duties. Satisfied that everything was well in hand, she turned toward the path that would lead her through the dense tropical forest to the two-story coquina house Sir John had built for her mother and named Good Fortune. The tall palms and thick vines overhead provided shade from the afternoon sun, but the humidity that was always present soon formed beads of liquid on her upper lip and brow. She wiped them away with the sleeve of her white muslin shirt as she followed the trail until it ended near the manicured gardens of her home.

A sudden burst of pride surged through Royale as she took in the beauty before her. Good Fortune had been built on the highest point of Witch's Cay, overlooking the sea. Its whitewashed walls made a striking contrast to the bounty of color from the bougainvillea, giant red hibiscus, and oleander that surrounded them. At the front of the house the rosebushes that her mother had carefully nurtured bloomed in profusion before the veranda. Smelling their heady fragrance upon the breeze, she smiled. It was good to be home. She loved the sea, but she loved Good Fortune more and was always glad to return, even when the voyage had been as profitable as this last one. They had captured two Spanish ships on their return voyage to Spain from South America. Their holds had been filled with gold and precious gems. The two prizes would add nicely to the King's coffers if, Royale mused as she crossed the garden and stepped upon the cypress veranda of her home, the King gives me my letter of marque.

"Adele, I'm home," Royale called as she entered the cool foyer. She took off the wide-brimmed hat that kept her thick hair in place and tossed it onto the intricately carved table, another of her mother's prized possessions. The legs were dark mahogany inlaid with mother-of-pearl, and the top was made of Italian marble. It sat in the middle of the foyer, where her mother had placed it so that it would be the focal point of Good Fortune's entry.

Hearing no response, Royale absently fluffed the rich

brown hair that cascaded about her shoulders as she called again, "Adele, I'm home." At last she heard steps on the landing at the top of the mahogany stairs and looked up to see her housekeeper and friend, Adele Johnson.

"Royale, it's good to have you home," Adele said as she swept down the stairs and embraced her. "It's about time you got back. I'd begun to worry about you and to wonder if I would have to ride that blasted beast for the rest of my life."

Royale gave Adele a big hug and smiled with pleasure as she said, "It's good to be home. I love the sea, but after so many months it does weary you. How has everything gone in my absence? Have I received any messages from England?"

"Yes, one came several weeks ago. I left it on your desk in the study. I hope it's what you have been hoping to hear," Adele said, inspecting Royale from head to toe to make sure no harm had befallen her.

"I do, too. Papa's been dead for nearly a year now, and I'd like to have his affairs finally settled. I have yet to understand the reason behind his solicitor's actions. I'm Sir John's heir, and he had no other living relatives in England, so I can't see the reason for that lawyer having to take everything before the courts in London. Perhaps this missive will grant me what is rightfully mine and that will be the end of it." Royale turned toward the study, eager to settle the matter. Pausing at the door, she said, "Will you have Pilar fill my bath and see that Rose lays out my emerald silk? I'm tired of sponge baths in cold water and the constant feel of salt in my hair."

"I can well understand that," Adele said as her young mistress strode into the study. She turned to do her bidding. The housekeeper couldn't imagine having to live on board a ship for three months with a bunch of rough men, much less having to do without her feminine apparel and warm baths. Her excursions into the village on horseback always required a steaming bath afterward as it was.

Royale crossed directly to the huge desk her father had used and settled herself in the large leather chair that had been constructed to fit John Carrington's immense frame. Propping her dusty boots on the desk's shining surface, her legs crossed at the ankles, she slit the wax seal that bore the King's insignia with the sharp edge of her dirk and began to read.

The peaceful expression faded from Royale's face as she read the missive from the King of England. A spark of ire glittered in her sea-green eyes, making them the color of storm-tossed waves as she sat up abruptly and slammed the paper down on top of the desk.

"Damn it to hell," she muttered angrily as she came to her feet and stamped across the study to the window overlooking the shimmering waters of the ocean. "It's not right, and I will not have it. John Carrington was my father, and no matter what anyone says I'll not meekly accept being a ward of the King. He can send anyone he likes to be my guardian, but that does not mean I will obey him," she ground out between clenched teeth, balling her fist against the wood of the windowsill. "Good Fortune and the *Raven* are mine." Fuming, she strode from the study and up the stairs to her chamber.

Her abrupt entrance caused the two young maids to start nervously until they recognized their mistress. Their faces lit with welcoming smiles, and they greeted her in unison, "Welcome home, Mistress Carrington."

"Thank you, Rose, Pilar. It's good to see you, too. Now, if my bath is ready, I'd like to be alone for a while. I'll call if I need anything further."

"Very well, Mistress," Rose said as she picked up the heavy wooden buckets and nodded for Pilar to come with her. She knew if she didn't make certain the girl left at the same time she did, Pilar would stay behind and annoy their mistress with tales of her latest beau. Pilar loved to talk about her love life to anyone who would listen. All the servants of Good Fortune and half the population of the village knew it, to the regret of their weary ears.

Royale saw Pilar wrinkle her nose at her companion, and as the door closed behind the two maids she could hear their heated squabble. A rueful smile curled her lips. Nothing had changed at Good Fortune while she was away, but since her return *everything* had changed. By King Charles's missive she was no longer in control of the household or of her own destiny, if she accepted his dictates.

"If," Royale mused aloud, pursing her lips into a firm, mutinous line as she began to jerk open the laces of her shirt. She drew it over her head and let it fall to the floor before she undid her britches and stepped out of them. Sent aloft by a swift kick that reflected her mood, they landed beneath the canopied bed to lie in a crumpled heap.

Stepping into the brass-bound tub, she eased herself down in the steaming water and leaned back against the curved side, letting the warm liquid soothe some of the tension from her muscles. Resting her head against the rim, her chestnut hair spilling over the side to touch the floor, she reflected upon the situation in which she now found herself an unwilling pawn.

The King had granted John Carrington Witch's Cay in return for his services as a privateer. Her father's death had ended their agreement, and everything—including her—had reverted to the crown.

Charles had also refused to grant her request for a letter of marque, stating in his missive that she needed a guardian to oversee her affairs as well as those of Good Fortune. It was unthinkable to him that a lady in his realm should even consider going to sea. He needed strong, capable men to captain his ships against the Spanish. Though he regretted having to deny John Carrington's daughter anything, he felt no woman had the strength or knowledge to rule a vessel, much less do battle with the heavily armed ships of Spain.

"I've heard all that before, your majesty; for all your great reputation with the ladies you know little of women, Charles the Second," Royale mused aloud, her tone reflecting her contempt as she sat up and lathered her body with a sweet-smelling soap that left a slight scent of lavender upon her skin. "Perhaps it's time you learned that women are not the weaklings your male vanity requires you to believe us."

An impudent smile curled her lips as she soaped her hair and rinsed away the salt that clung to each strand and made it stiff. It squeaked with cleanliness when she finished and stepped out of the tepid water.

Royale's supple body glowed with health and vitality after she toweled herself dry. She slipped on the soft, lacy undergarments Rose had laid out for her. Savoring the feeling of the silk after so many months of coarse linen against her flesh, she settled herself comfortably on the window seat to dry her long, chestnut-colored hair. The days spent under the hot Caribbean sun had streaked it with gold, and it curled freely about her shoulders and down her back, thick and luxuriant now that it was free of brine. She brushed the tangles from her unruly locks before pulling them back and tying a ribbon about them at the nape of her neck. Finished with her grooming, she slipped on the emerald silk gown.

Royale paused before the dressing table and eyed her reflection. Few would recognize her now as the captain of a frigate, just as they would not have known that the slender youth who commanded the *Raven* was actually a woman. When she was dressed in britches and a man's shirt, her hair concealed beneath her wide-brimmed hat, the truth of her identity was apparent only to the members of her crew. Royale gave her image in the mirror a jaunty smile and mused, ''I may not look like a privateer or a pirate now, but appearances are often deceiving, as our good King Charles will soon learn if I have my way.''

The sound of voices below brought Royale's thoughts back to the present, and she hurried from the room. She had immediately recognized Tim O'Kelly's deep voice, and at that moment she needed his reassurance that nothing would change in their future.

The light silk of her skirt floated about her in a shimmering cloud as she descended the stairs and swept across the foyer to the drawing room. She paused at the door to catch her breath and smiled at the sight of Tim's freshly scrubbed face and his hair, still damp from his bath.

''Tim, I'm glad it didn't take you all night to see everything put in order. We have to talk.'' Royale crossed the polished pine floor to where the tall, sandy-haired seaman stood near the liquor cabinet. She opened the door, which was inlaid with varying shades of wood in a flowery pattern, took out a crystal decanter of brandy, and poured a generous amount into a cut-glass goblet.

She handed Tim the drink, quickly dispensing of her duties as hostess, since more pressing matters held her attention. Settling herself on the sofa, she absently spread her skirts about her as she looked up at her friend, who was swirling the amber liquid around the wide bottom of his glass.

''I have heard from the King,'' she said.

Tim regarded Royale silently for a long moment, noting the pallor of her cheeks and suspecting it was useless to ask what had been the answer to her request for the letter of marque, but he did so anyway. ''Did the King grant your petition?'' He watched as her small chin came up in the air and jutted out at a pugnacious angle.

"No. He refused, but that is not the worst part. He has taken Good Fortune away from me and made me his ward. He is sending his minion to Witch's Cay to act as my guardian," Royale said, her eyes flashing with green fire.

Tim choked on the brandy and coughed. He had expected the King to deny her request, but nothing more. Wiping from his eyes the moisture that the fiery alcohol had brought forth when it burned down his throat, Tim uttered, "What in hell does he mean by doing that? Good Fortune is yours. Sir John wanted you to have it. Doesn't the King understand that?"

"From the missive I received today, he neither understands nor cares," Royale said, her anger rekindling as she began to tell Tim of the King's dictates and his estimation of her ability to oversee her own affairs. She nearly choked on the ire that built in her throat as she explained the situation in which she now found herself.

A bewildered expression played over Tim's features before he broke into a wide, toothy grin, threw back his head, and roared with laughter. His eyes were again damp, but this time it was with mirth, and he chuckled as he wiped them. "Damn me, King Charles doesn't know you as I do, if that's how he thinks. And from the look on your stubborn little face and the devilment I see flashing in your eyes, I suspect he's going to find out the hard way."

A tiny dimple formed in Royale's chin as she pressed her lips together, giving Tim an impudent grin as she nodded and said, "Aye, I fear you are right—much more so than our good King."

"I've a feeling King Charles will be eager to give you Good Fortune and anything else you desire before you are through with him," Tim said, already feeling slightly sorry for the monarch of England, who would be forced to battle against the beauty and charm of the girl-woman before him.

"If I have any say in the matter, he will," Royale said,

her mood lightening as she smiled up at her friend, knowing he would stand by her in any decision she made.

"When I go to London, I plan to have so much gold in the hold of the *Raven* that it will be too much of a temptation for a king who needs every sovereign he can get his hands on to finance his pleasures. He won't be able to reject my claims. but first I need to visit my father's solicitor in Gregory Town. Have the men ready to sail in two days. You can let them spend tonight with their rum and women, but by the day after tomorrow I want the *Raven* to weigh anchor," Royale said. She rose from the sofa and crossed to the wide windows overlooking the multicolored water of the bay.

Tim's brow furrowed with puzzlement as he asked, "Why do you want to visit that scoundrel? He has done you little good in the matter."

For a long moment Royale did not answer but gazed thoughtfully toward the straight blue line of the horizon. Her expression reflected the importance of her decision as she glanced over her shoulder at Tim and said, "I just want to confirm that there are no other avenues open to me before we set out on this venture. Once we sail openly without the King's letter of marque, we will be branded as pirates. I know we have spoken in jest about that very thing, but in truth, I'll be asking the crew of the *Raven* to become wanted men. If we're caught, it will mean the gibbet. I can't ask that of you or of the other members of my crew without first making sure there are no alternatives left."

Tim crossed to Royale's side, his own gaze sweeping over the shimmering expanse of water beyond the window before he looked down at her somber features. He could see the concern for the welfare of her crew reflected in her eyes, and his heart went out to her. She faced losing everything she held dear to her heart, yet she still considered the well-being of her men. That in itself made her a good cap-

tain. "You know you have our loyalty whether we sail
under a letter of marque or the Jolly Roger. I think the men
would follow you into hell if you asked," Tim said, stating
a truth they both knew.

"Aye, and for that very reason it is my duty to make
certain I've done everything possible before I ask them to
become outlaws who will be sought by every nation, even
their own homeland."

Taking Royale's hand into his own callused palm, Tim
gave it a gentle, reassuring squeeze. "We'll be ready to
sail in two days."

Royale smiled up at him. Her eyes were filled with gratitude as well as affection. Through the years the friendship
that had sprung up between two children playing on the
sandy beach below Good Fortune had developed into the
close bond of siblings. Though Tim's family lived in the
small fishing village on the southern tip of Witch's Cay, to
Royale he was her adopted brother, and she loved him as
such. Two years separated them in age, but Tim had been
her constant companion since she was six. He had taught
her to fish and swim in the cove where the *Raven* now lay
at anchor. He had been at her side when her father had
begun to teach her about sailing and had eagerly learned
as much as she had about the sea and ships. Fortunately,
he had learned his lessons well and had been ready to join
her when she took command of the frigate. Tim had stood
with her through the good times and the bad.

"Good," Royale said. "Now let's find Adele and see if
she has had a welcome-home feast prepared for us. Many
nights, after enduring one of Haskell's stews, I dreamed of
Mrs. Hogan's flaky pastry. Our ship's cook is a good man,
but he lacks much in the culinary arts." The two friends
laughed companionably as they strolled toward the dining
room.

* * *

The heat in her tiny room at the Gregory Town Inn was stifling to Royale as she paced its narrow confines, silently fuming over the length of time she had spent waiting to see Mr. Todd, the solicitor. The *Raven* had sailed into port two days earlier, and she had gone directly to the man's office, only to find that he had traveled to a nearby cay on business. The clerk who worked for Todd had told her the lawyer would return within the day, but so far he had not put in an appearance.

After the first day she had begun to suspect that Mr. Todd was avoiding her, so she had spent the entire morning and afternoon waiting for him in his dreary, mildew-scented office, hoping to catch him if he tried to sneak past her. However, to her great annoyance, he had not returned. Her patience had nearly reached its limit. If he did not come back tomorrow, she was determined to set sail.

After blowing out the candle to thwart any hungry mosquitoes that might be attracted to the flame, Royale threw back the wooden shutters of the window. She had hoped to catch a breath of fresh, cooling air, but her chamber faced inland, and the sea breeze could not reach it.

Disgusted by her lack of progress and irritable from the heat, Royale propped her elbows on the windowsill and her chin on her hands as she gazed out into the tropical night. It was late, and there were few lighted windows to be seen as the islanders sought their rest.

Glancing up at the dark, star-studded sky, Royale wished she had let Tim come ashore with her. Then at least she would have had someone to talk with to ease her boredom, and perhaps by voicing her suspicions about the solicitor's strange absence she could have rid herself of the restlessness that possessed her.

"Damn," she muttered as she turned away from the window. "If I stay confined here a moment longer, I'm sure to go mad." Lifting her discarded gown from the bed, she slipped it over her head. She had taken it off earlier in the evening because of the heat, and it still felt damp with perspiration, but she paid it no heed as she opened the door and stealthily made her way along the dark corridor.

All was quiet within the inn as she moved down the stairs toward the rear exit of the building. At the late hour she wanted no one to know of her nocturnal sojourn. While in Gregory Town she was the respectable Mistress Carrington, and it would do little good to her reputation to be found wandering the streets in the middle of the night.

Royale knew exactly where she wanted to go, and she turned in the direction of the beach she had noted as they sailed into port. It was separated from the busy quay by a small jut of land and would provide her with the privacy she needed to enjoy the peace and beauty of the night as she sought the cooling ocean breeze.

At the edge of the beach she slipped off her shoes and curled her toes in the sand. The gritty substance felt good beneath her feet and reminded her of the many times she had done the same thing as a child before scampering down to the waves.

For a moment she eyed the dark swells, listening to the gentle roar as they broke upon the shoreline. Then she smiled impishly, lifted her skirts, and ran toward the water.

The foamy waves lapped about her ankles and splashed the hem of her gown as she threw back her head and laughed with the pure joy of the moment. Gone were the captain of the *Raven*, the mistress of Good Fortune, and the would-be pirate. Royale was once more a child as she ran down the beach, the water beside her shimmering in the pale light provided by the scythe-shaped moon.

Enjoying her play and thinking herself alone, she kicked at the waves, sending sparkling spray into the air before racing away from each incoming swell of water. A gust of wind caught her hair and swirled its silken mass about her as she paused to gain her breath before challenging the sea again. She brushed absently at the long strands that webbed her face as she thought up a new game to play, failing to hear the soft crunch of a heavy foot crushing a small pile of shells behind her. She was completely unaware of the danger until a large hand clamped down over her mouth and nose.

She screamed in fright and protest, but the muffled sound was swept away on the sea breeze as a heavily muscled arm came around her waist and lifted her squirming figure from the sand.

As her feet left the ground she kicked out at her assailant with her bare heels but could find no place to do any damage. Her efforts were quickly halted as another pair of strong hands clamped down with bruising force on her ankles, their viselike grip making Royale think her bones would be crushed under the pressure.

The hand over her mouth and nose was suffocating her, and she struggled to breathe but gained little for her efforts. The world began to spin before her eyes, and she heard a gruff voice say, "Ye're killing her, Black Jack," before she fainted.

"I ain't kilt the wench, ye bastard. She's just passed out, and I'm grateful fer that," Black Jack said as he dumped Royale's limp body onto the sand at his feet. "I don't know how much longer I could have held on to her if she'd kept up all that fighting. This 'un is real feisty, she is," he muttered as he wiped the sweat from his brow.

"Ye must be getting old if a little thing like this can outdo ye, matey." Scrimshaw chuckled as he watched the other man's actions.

"Damn, ye say. I'd like to have seen ye try to hold her, as puny as ye are with no meat on that bony frame of yers. No wonder they call ye Scrimshaw. Ye ain't much more than a piece of whalebone at that,'' Black Jack growled as he eyed the smaller man.

"Well, at least I ain't the one sweating me guts out over carrying this wee thing, but that's neither here nor there. We ain't got all night to get this 'un back to the captain. Do ye think he'll be pleased by our small gesture to 'im?'' Scrimshaw asked as he glanced toward the dark silhouette rocking on the waves in the distance.

Black Jack scratched the coarse growth of beard on his chin and lifted one shoulder in a shrug. "Ain't no telling about 'im. I'd shore be pleased with such a one as this, but with El Diablo ye can never be certain as to what he's a-thinkin' and feelin'. I only wished we could have found one this comely fer us in the tavern.''

"True enough,'' Scrimshaw agreed as he bent and lifted Royale into his arms. "I ain't never seen a man who's so secretive before. No other pirate I ever heard of wears a mask when he takes another ship. He's a strange 'un, all right. I'd be able to understand it better if'n there was somethin' wrong with his face, but he's nearly purty enough to be a woman.''

"Aye, ye're right there. I've been with 'im now going on two years, and I still ain't figured 'im out. I'd give all the gold I earned from our last prize to know where he disappears to sometimes,'' Black Jack said as he held the small boat steady for Scrimshaw to board with his light burden.

"That I would, too,'' Scrimshaw said as he laid Royale in the bottom of the skip and picked up the oars. "But I guess I'll keep me curiosity to meself. That's one thing I do know about the captain. He don't like nobody messing around in his affairs, and as far as I'm concerned, that's his right. He can stay a puzzlement as long as he keeps us in gold from them Spanish galleons. I ain't goin' to complain when me pockets jingle every time I go ashore. I've sailed under many and ain't never seed the likes of 'im before; he seems to smell gold when it's near.''

"Aye, that he does," Black Jack agreed as he bent to the chore of rowing.

The small boat bumped against the side of the twenty-gun frigate known as the *Wicked Mistress*. Hoisting his burden unceremoniously over his shoulder, Scrimshaw climbed the rope ladder with the agility of a monkey, paying no heed to the swaying of the vessel. He grinned at the curious, wide-eyed sailors as he stepped down onto the deck. Patting Royale on her round bottom, he winked at the cabin boy and boasted, "I brought the captain a little somethin' from yon cay." Dumping his burden on a pile of canvas, he turned and came face to face with the scowling first mate.

"What in hell is the meaning of this?" Reed Barton demanded. "El Diablo will have you both strung up to the yardarm for this infraction."

Having the crew's full attention, Scrimshaw dug his thumbs into the waistband of his britches as he grinned up at the first mate. "I ain't so certain about that as ye seem to be, Mr. Barton. This bit of fluff might be just what the captain is a-wanting after such a long voyage. Why don't we let him decide how he feels about it?"

"I agree," came a deep male voice from the shadows behind him. "But what is it that you think I should decide about, Scrimshaw?"

The bony sailor's eyes bulged, and he tried to swallow the uncomfortable lump that had formed in his throat when he heard the silky smooth and deceptively congenial tone of the ship's master. Scrimshaw had not been aware that his cocky display before the first mate had been witnessed by the captain of the *Wicked Mistress*. He cast a nervous glance over his shoulder at Black Jack to reassure himself that his friend would back him up before he turned to the

tall man who ruled the pirate vessel with an iron fist. "I—
I mean we—thought ye could use a little diversion, since
ye didn't have time to go ashore. We found this bit of flesh
on yon beach."

The sailors seemed to dissolve from El Diablo's path as
if a huge wave had suddenly washed over the deck and
swept them away. He strolled forward with the grace of a
man much accustomed to living at sea. Taking the brass
lantern from the cabin boy's hand, he bent to inspect
Scrimshaw's and Black Jack's gift to him.

The expression in El Diablo's eyes as he turned his cold
regard back to the two men made the other members of his
crew feel as if they were looking at the devil himself. His
dark eyes reflected the light from the lantern, and in the
minds of the superstitious crewmen it only served to en-
hance the illusion. On any ship other than the *Wicked Mistress* the sailors would have feared the presence of a girl
on board more than they feared the man they served, but
after sailing under "the devil," as the Spanish had named
him, one small female was little to be alarmed about when
compared to the wrath of their captain.

"Take the girl to my cabin while I deal with these two,"
El Diablo ordered, his eyes never wavering from the guilty
faces of Scrimshaw and Black Jack.

The two men who had El Diablo's full attention felt the
cold prickle of fear race up their spines. Sweat popped out
and beaded their upper lips and brows while they nervously
awaited El Diablo's retribution for their folly.

"I—uh—Captain," Scrimshaw began, but his words
were abruptly cut off by El Diablo's sharp command.

"Quiet."

He eyed the two sailors speculatively for a few long,
nerve-racking moments, and they suspected that behind his
dark, assessing gaze he was devising ways to make them

suffer. Their anxiety made them tense with anticipation, and their eyes flew wide when El Diablo began to speak.

"You try my patience too far. It is my right to have you both lashed for bringing the wench on board my ship, but since you did it out of ignorance and the desire to please me, I will let you off this time."

Scrimshaw and Black Jack visibly relaxed as their captain paused. They released a long sigh of relief in unison, but their moment of reprieve was short-lived. His next words caused their hearts to tremble in their chests.

"But remember this. If I ever catch either of you stepping over the line of my authority again, you will not be let off so easily. When I need something I will order it. It is not your duty to attend to my comforts or pleasure. You are here to see to the welfare of the *Wicked Mistress*. Your orders were to get fresh water, not to visit the taverns of Gregory Town or kidnap a wench for my bed. I suggest you heed my warning well this time. In the future your backs will pay the price if you do not." With that El Diablo turned and strode from the deck, leaving all to share a sense of relief.

Scrimshaw and Black Jack glanced uneasily at the scowling first mate before hurrying once more over the side of the ship and down the rope ladder to the small boat. In their excitement and rum-fogged state they had completely forgotten about the barrels of water they had left on the beach.

Chapter 2

A *circle of golden lamplight illuminated the bed as El Diablo* bent once more to look at the unconscious girl. His thick blue-black hair flowed freely, almost brushing his silk-covered shoulders as he leaned forward and, with one well-manicured finger, traced the slender curve of her cheek. His action served to partially appease the desire that had seized him while gazing at her on deck. Softly he mused aloud, "Ah, my little gift, your beauty is bewitching. I can see why Scrimshaw and Black Jack thought I would enjoy you."

The sound of his voice seemed to draw Royale from the darkness that blanketed her mind. Her lashes fluttered gently for a moment before she opened her eyes and blinked several times in an effort to focus her gaze.

El Diablo, remembering who he was, quickly stepped into the shadows beyond the ring of light. He pulled a piece of black silk from his pocket and masked his features, leaving only the lower half of his face exposed to view. Without making a sound to alert the girl of his presence, he watched as she stared groggily up at the dark timbers over the bunk. He knew from the puzzled expression she wore that the last shreds of her faintness were still clinging tenaciously to her mind. After a few moments he saw her eyes grow wide, and he suspected from the look of fear that flashed into their mysterious sea-green depths that she had finally recalled her abduction.

"Welcome on board the *Wicked Mistress*, my lady," he said from his vantage point.

Royale bolted upright in the bed, a startled gasp bursting from her lips as she swung about, clutching the sheet tightly against her breasts.

She peered into the inky shadows but could discern nothing of the owner of the voice. Moistening her lips, she fought to hide her mounting trepidation as she asked, "Who are you, and why did you bring me here?"

Her heart drummed against her ribs as she waited breathlessly for the man's answer. When her captor stepped into the light, her throat seemed to clog up, choking off her air completely. Contrary to her belief that she would fear nothing that she could see, the sight of the man did little to ease her fright. If anything, her apprehension grew as he neared the bunk and she saw the sparkle of his dark eyes through the slits in the black silk.

It was not only his masked features that made him appear so sinister. His clothing added to the illusion as well. His large, muscular body was clothed entirely in black, from his wide shoulders to the tip of his polished knee boots. Looking up at him, Royale would have sworn that she was facing a demon instead of a mortal man, had not his square chin and shapely lips been visible below the mask.

Drawing in a deep, steadying breath, she clung to that thought—he was only a man, not a satanic specter sent to carry her into hell. Never having been a person to let her fear control her, she stiffened her spine as she stared up at him and said, "Sir, I demand that you release me at once."

"Demand, my lady?" he said, his lips curling at the corners as he casually folded his arms over his chest. "I'm afraid you do not understand exactly where you are. You're on board the *Wicked Mistress*, and I am the only person who makes demands on this vessel.''

A faint memory niggled at the back of Royale's mind, but the mockery in his voice stung too much for her to pay attention to it. Raising her chin in the air, she said, ''Then, sir, I would ask you to return me to Gregory Town. I will forget this unfortunate episode, and I can assure you that I will not report your behavior to the authorities.''

''Authorities?'' El Diablo said, and chuckled, enjoying the girl's spirit. ''Surely you jest, my lady. We are at sea, and I'm the only authority here.'' A ghost of a smile still touched his lips as he turned a chair around and straddled it. Propping one elbow across its back, he studied her lovely face. Under his intense gaze, the last of the color drained from her features, leaving her thickly fringed eyes even more startlingly beautiful.

''You can't keep me here,'' Royale said with an assurance she did not feel. Her fear was biting away her bravado in great chunks, and even as she spoke she was searching for a means of escape. Spying the door, she bolted from the bed toward it, but before she could reach it El Diablo blocked her path. She squealed in protest as his hands went around her waist and swung her off her feet. She squirmed and kicked but could do no damage.

''Let me go!'' she demanded, and found to her amazement that he freed her. The action was so swift and unexpected that she was unable to keep her balance, and fell to her knees before El Diablo.

''Far be it from me to deny a lady's request,'' he said, and chuckled as he stood over her, his arms once more folded across his chest. ''Now, if you think you can behave yourself, we shall begin again. I am El Diablo, captain of the *Wicked Mistress*.''

Furious and humiliated at finding herself in such a position, Royale felt her breast rise and fall rapidly as she breathed. Her face was flushed with mortification as she came to her feet, ready to do battle.

"How dare you!" she spat, and before El Diablo could thwart her she drew back her hand and slapped him across the face. The blow echoed eerily through the cabin; then a deadly silence settled over them.

Lightning seemed to crackle in the air as El Diablo's hands snaked out and captured her in their brutal grip. His fingers bit savagely into the flesh of her upper arms as he drew her against his hard body and ground out between clenched teeth, "Wench, I think you need a lesson in manners."

Royale's temper flared even hotter, fanned by El Diablo's cruel actions. No man had ever handled her thus, and she would rather die than give way to the searing pain that raced up her arms. She would not cower to the beast even if he killed her. Her nostrils flared as she drew in a deep, angry breath and glared up at her captor. "Take your hands off me, you bastard," she said, and flinched against the new pressure from his fingers.

El Diablo gazed down at her through narrowed eyes. A cold little smile curled the corners of his mouth as he said, "It seems, my little wildcat, that you need someone to tame you as well as show you the proper way for a lady to behave. I assure you that I will be the one to do it if you insist on acting like such an uncivilized little heathen."

"Uncivilized heathen! At least I don't prey on defenseless women," Royale spat as she stared up into the glittering orbs behind the silk mask.

"Defenseless as a viper," El Diablo said softly, his gaze sweeping over her face, tracing each lovely feature. "If your actions are those of a defenseless female, then I'd hate to encounter one with weapons."

"I wish I had a weapon right now. I'd slit your throat

so quick that you'd be in hell before you knew you were dead.''

"My, aren't we a bloodthirsty little wildcat? Pull in your claws, minx, or I'll have to trim them for you. I'm sure you wouldn't like my methods," he said, enjoying their verbal combat.

Royale felt his hold slacken during their exchange and took advantage of his moment of carelessness. Balling her hands into fists, she brought them up against his chest with all the force she could muster. The blow made him release her, but her freedom was only momentary. In one swift motion he recaptured her, and before she could comprehend his intention he swung the chair around and forced her down into it. With his free hand he jerked the silk lacing from his shirt and bound her hands behind the back of the chair.

"Now, my little minx, let's see you get free of that." He smiled with satisfaction as he watched her strain against her bonds.

"Do you think you can behave now and try to act at least a little civilized?" he asked. He braced his palms behind him on the tabletop and leaned back against its edge. He smiled with amusement at the mutinous light that glimmered in her eyes as she glared up at him.

The minx, he mused, deserved more than she was getting. His stinging cheeks attested to that fact. However, he had to admire the girl's spirit. She was a welcome respite from the women he usually encountered. They eased the ache in his loins but held little interest for him otherwise. He had never before encountered a woman who stared defiantly at him, as if daring him to do his worst. She was definitely a challenge, but one he sadly had to forgo.

A rueful smile touched his lips as he bent and cupped her small chin in the palm of his hand. Tilting it up so he could peer into her fascinating eyes, he said, "You are a bewitching little thing, and I regret that I do not have the time to enjoy your company. It would be interesting to see if your passion is as hot as your temper.''

Royale jerked away from his touch and regarded her captor warily as he leaned closer, his arms encircling her to untie her bonds. Noting her reaction to his nearness, he chuckled as he lifted her from the chair and set her on her feet before him. Releasing a resigned sigh, he said, ''I fear I will have to grant your request and free you. That was my intention all along, and had you not been such a termagant you would already be back in Gregory Town in your own bed.''

Relief coursed through her until the indignity she had suffered at his hand hit her like a bolt of white-hot lightning. It whipped her volatile temper into an inferno of fury. ''You bastard! How dare you kidnap me and then abuse me in such a manner just to play out some sadistic game?''

El Diablo cocked his head to one side, eyeing her coolly. ''My lady, it seems as if the idea of freedom does not give you the pleasure I expected. If you prefer, I can always change my mind and keep you as a gift, as you were intended.'' Seeing a flicker of bewilderment cross her face, he continued, ''You see, *I* did not bring you on board my vessel. Two of my men found you on the beach and thought I would enjoy having you to break the tedium of a long voyage. Since you don't appreciate the thought of being returned to Gregory Town, out of consideration for my men's concern for their captain's pleasure I should accept their gift.''

Royale instinctively took a step backward as she shook her head and forced the words past the sudden constriction in her throat. ''No. I want to go back to Gregory Town.'' Even to her own ears her tone was tinged with the fear she had been desperately trying to hide, and she knew her captor had also heard it.

One corner of El Diablo's mouth curved into a wry smile as he regarded her speculatively for a few long, tense moments. "At what price?"

"What do you mean?" she asked, suddenly wary of his answer.

"Since the *Wicked Mistress* is a pirate ship, a ransom is usually paid for the freedom of its prisoners," El Diablo said, and watched with interest as his words sank in and made her blanch.

The memory that had been lurking in the dark recesses of her mind now sprang vividly into the light of her consciousness. She moistened her suddenly dry lips and said, without realizing she spoke aloud, "Pirate ship; El Diablo." Her eyes grew wide as she stared at the man before her. She had often heard the grisly tales of his exploits. By all reports, he was one pirate that few had the courage to face.

Her heart seemed to do a rapid flip-flop in her breast. She felt like a fool for not having comprehended her situation earlier, when she had first set eyes on the man. His manner of dress should have instantly told her his identity, but she had thought little of it. Living in the islands all of her life, she had seen all manner of men whose costume was unusual. Men who lived their lives at sea often took small bits from every culture they encountered on their voyages. A few of her own crew sported colorful silk scarfs from the Orient, exotic feathers from Africa in their hats, and gold jewelry from South America.

Abruptly understanding her predicament, Royale was also aware of the fact that she could raise no ransom without giving away her own identity. If the pirate found that she was John Carrington's daughter, he would demand such a high price that it would take all the gold she had plundered plus everything else she owned to cover it. Upon the heels of that thought came another: she owned nothing beyond the clothes upon her back since the King's missive had arrived at Good Fortune. She spoke the truth when she said, "I can't raise any ransom. I own nothing of value to exchange for my freedom."

Casually settling his lean frame in the chair she had vacated a few minutes earlier, El Diablo tilted it back on two legs and folded his arms over his chest as he said, "Then what do you suggest I do with you?"

"Please let me go. I have no money nor anything of value to you," Royale said again, her eyes glistening with tears of frustration.

Her stricken expression touched El Diablo, and he released a long sigh. He was tired of the game and wanted to find a few hours of rest before dawn crept over the horizon. He had much to do in the next weeks. Each hour in the following days would be long and tiring, and he had no time now to dally with a wench, no matter how beautiful she might be.

"Since you have no money, I think a kiss will suffice for the ransom. Do you think the price too high?"

A surge of relief washed over Royale as she shook her head. She had been expecting anything but his simple request. One kiss: she would eagerly pay that to be free of this nightmare that had descended upon her during her waking hours. No, the price was not too high if it meant getting away from this sinister, masked pirate. His appearance and presence disturbed her too much. She didn't like the sense of helplessness she felt when confronting him. It was a foreign emotion to her, one she had rarely experienced before and one she knew she could do without.

Her relief fled, however, as she watched the pirate rise from the chair and approach her. Without realizing her action, she took a step away from him. She captured her lower lip between her teeth and worried it nervously as she stared up at him, her eyes resting on his sensuously molded mouth.

She was eighteen years of age but had never been kissed by a man. When Tim was fourteen and she was twelve they had experimented with kissing but had found little to interest them in pressing their lips together. They had quickly abandoned the experiments in favor of things that offered more entertainment: fishing and digging for clams.

The thought of the pirate's lips upon hers was unsettling, and she swallowed convulsively as his lean brown fingers captured her chin and tilted it up so that he could gaze down into her wide, apprehensive eyes.

Puzzled by her expression, El Diablo said, "The ransom is a small one, and you have nothing to fear once it is paid."

Royale remained frozen and unable to speak.

Assuming her silence meant her consent, El Diablo lowered his lips to hers. He was not surprised to feel her lack of response, and he raised his head. He regarded her curiously for a long moment before saying, "My lady, if you intend to gain your freedom, I suggest you put a little feeling into the kiss. I could get more warmth from the lips of the wooden figurehead on the prow of the *Wicked Mistress*. Relax; they may call me the devil, but I promise not to steal your soul with one kiss."

Royale's heart fluttered wildly in her breast as he spoke. She wanted nothing to interfere with her chance to escape this man, whose voice was like a velvet caress, which was more frightening to her than his appearance. She drew in a deep breath and forced herself to relax in his embrace as he enfolded her once more in his arms.

Strangely, and to her surprise, she found the feeling of his lips against her own not unpleasant. When she felt his tongue gently probing, seeking entrance, she opened her mouth to him. She felt a fiery current ripple along every nerve in her body as the kiss deepened and his tongue caressed hers enticingly. The sensations the kiss created in her were new and intriguing and made her forget that it was the price of freedom. The unfamiliar feelings were intoxicating, and without realizing her own actions, she molded her body against his sinewy frame, her arms slowly creeping up around his neck, her fingers entwining themselves in his dark hair.

She savored the warm furor that was beginning to course through her entire being, making the firm muscles in her belly quiver as her dormant passion blossomed into life like a seed under a spring shower. Royale was unprepared for all the new sensations that swept over her, and she innocently enjoyed the pleasure they brought, completely unaware of the effect her response was having on El Diablo.

His blood raced hot and scalding through his body and settled with an agonizing intensity in his groin. He felt himself swell with desire for the young woman in his arms. He had not meant to let himself become aroused, and had only intended to enjoy a brief kiss before sending her on her way. However, the innocence of her lips pressed against his own was his undoing. It was the spark that ignited his passion, and her caress was the fuel that fed its fire.

Under the onslaught of his throbbing desire, all his good intentions fled. He lifted her easily into his arms and carried her to the bunk. In one swift motion he blew out the lamp, leaving them in darkness. He tore away his silk mask and tossed it to the floor as he once more sought the tantalizing sweetness of her lips.

Royale stiffened momentarily as he left her, but when his mouth reclaimed hers the moment of doubt was forgotten. All rational thoughts dissolved into the tropical night, banished by the provocative sensations his hands aroused as he began to caress her through the fabric of her gown. His touch kindled a deep yearning within her to feel his hands upon her naked flesh. The desire was so intense it blocked all protest from reaching her lips as his fingers unlaced her gown and slipped the bodice down to reveal the taut peaks of her breasts.

His lips left a heady trail of fire along the smooth curve of her cheek and down to the hollow at the base of her throat. He lingered there, lapping her softly fluttering pulse with his tongue before lowering his head to the satiny mounds below.

Royale gasped with pleasure as his mouth covered one rose-colored nipple while he aroused its mate with his thumb. She wound her fingers in his hair, pressing his head closer and arching her back to give him full access to her sensitive flesh.

With the care of one much experienced with women, El Diablo disrobed her with his caresses. He explored her virginal body with the hands of a connoisseur of love, rousing her with each touch. Under his sensual assault she opened to him, her thighs spreading of their own volition as his hand sought out the moist warmth at their junction. He teased the rosy buds of her breasts with his tongue and teeth, nibbling and suckling as his fingers found her silken passage and stroked rhythmically there, urging her to follow. Her body obeyed, instinctively seeking more than her mind could comprehend. Their breathing grew heavy as their desire rose. Like a budding flower beneath the sun, she began to bloom into womanhood under his impelling hands and lips.

Royale returned to reality for one fleeting moment as El Diablo rose from the bed to discard his clothing, but before she could consider the folly of her actions he rejoined her on the bunk and recaptured her mouth with his own. All reason fled her once more as his tongue thrust into the velvety cavern and his hands molded her body against his naked form. Nothing existed within her now except the heat of her newly discovered passions.

With a tenderness that belied his name, El Diablo took Royale. He entered her gently, trying to minimize the pain he suspected she would feel. From her innocent and sometimes awkward responses he believed her to be a virgin, and his feeling was confirmed when he found the tight shield of her virginity intact. With one sharp thrust he broke through the barrier and made Royale Carrington his.

She winced from the sting but soon forgot the tiny pain as El Diablo began to move. She gave herself up to the pleasure his thrusts built within her, following eagerly where he led, savoring the delicious furor of his lovemaking. Heady rapture washed over her in a breaking wave that made her tremble as she clasped his tanned shoulders and arched her hips against his. A moan of pleasure escaped her lips as her entire body seemed to explode with fulfillment. It was such an intense sensation that she felt she would faint from the vehemence of her release.

Feeling her shudder of ecstasy as the silken passage pulsated about him, El Diablo could no longer withhold his own pleasure. His sun-browned fingers captured her shoulders and held her tightly as he spilled his seed deep within her. A moan of passion escaped his lips, echoing hers of a moment before.

The languid euphoria left by their lovemaking cradled them softly as they lay with limbs entwined and bodies damp with perspiration. For a long while they savored the contentment found only by lovers who have reached the magic plateau of pleasure. No words passed between them to destroy the moment as El Diablo nestled his head against her breasts and listened to the steady rhythm of her heart as she gently traced his finely sculpted features with her hand. A contented sigh escaped his shapely lips as he lay snuggled against her warmth, feeling the caress of her fingers against his skin.

Still pressed to his hard, muscular body, Royale, too, knew only contentment as she touched his supple skin, exploring the planes of his face with the tips of her fingers. She followed the line of his high cheekbones up to his wide brow and across it to the narrow bridge of his nose. She moved her fingers along its slender length and down to the lips that had given her so much pleasure. Suddenly dissatisfied with her exploration in the dark and yearning to view the features of the man who had taken her to such heights of rapture, she said, "Let me see your face."

For several long minutes the only answer to her request was the tensing of his muscles beneath her hand. Then she felt him draw in a deep breath before he said, "No."

Royale felt the chill of the night air against her warm flesh as El Diablo moved away from her. A shiver passed along the entire length of her body. It was caused not by the sea breeze that came through the open porthole but by the coldness that settled in the pit of her stomach as reality stamped the mellow glow of their lovemaking beneath its iron heel. It left her suddenly feeling the fool for having given herself to the masked stranger.

El Diablo retrieved the piece of black silk from the floor and once more masked his features before he jerked on his britches and lit the lantern. His wide shoulders and back were still dewed with perspiration and gleamed a shining bronze in the golden light. He did not speak as he turned to gaze down at Royale.

Ashamed of her nakedness under his silent regard, she pulled the sheet up to cover her body. She clenched it tightly against her breasts as if the thin material could protect her from the realization that was descending upon her with brutal force. Cringing inwardly, she looked up into his masked countenance and flushed with mortification at her own wanton behavior. She had willingly given herself to a man who cared nothing for her beyond the heat of the moment. Unabashedly she had surrendered her honor to him, knowing he would sail out of her life, never to look back at the woman he left behind. Her throat clogged with the need to cry, but she refused to give way to it. She had already humiliated herself enough without shaming herself further by bursting into tears.

A muscle worked in El Diablo's lean jaw as he settled himself on the edge of the bunk at Royale's side. His dark hair shimmered with glints of deep blue-black in the lantern light as he slowly shook his head. With the tip of one finger, he gently traced the outline of her kiss-swollen lips and said, "Tonight was beautiful, and for that I thank you, but I cannot let you see my face."

Royale jerked away from his touch. Her eyes were glassy with unshed tears and looked like polished jade as she sat up and glared at him, humiliation and rage boiling through her veins at his casual attitude. She had given all she possessed to him, and he had the audacity to thank her for it. Yet for all that, he still refused to let her see his face.

"Keep your thanks, El Diablo. I have no need of them. I paid your ransom well over the price you set, and now I feel I should receive some recompense," she spat furiously.

Before El Diablo could stop her, she reached up and jerked the black silk away from his face to reveal the most devastatingly handsome features she had ever seen on a man. She drew in a sharp breath as she looked at him. She had suspected from the feel of his finely sculpted bone structure that he was handsome, but nothing had prepared her for the beauty before her. Her gaze swept over the smooth planes of his forehead to the black brows that arched symmetrically above his deep brown eyes, eyes that in the lantern light looked like shining onyx in their darkness.

They were heavily fringed with curling black lashes. His nose was thin, with slightly flaring nostrils that gave his face an animal quality, as if he were the hunter seeking his prey. She let her eyes drift down to his sensual lips, now thinned into an angry line, before she looked once more into his eyes.

The breath froze in her throat at the expression she saw in the flashing orbs. The piece of black silk floated unseen from her hand to the bunk as El Diablo captured her wrist and jerked her against his chest.

"You should not have done that. Now I fear I can't let you go," he ground out between clenched teeth.

"You can't keep me here," Royale said as she tried to free herself from his harsh grip. The look he bestowed upon her sent a chill of apprehension racing down her spine.

"I beg to differ with you. I can keep you here for as long as I want," he said, and he showed her a smile, but there was no warmth in it.

Royale paled and shook her head rapidly back and forth. Her long hair swung about her naked shoulders in wild disarray as she said, "Please, no. I won't tell anyone I've seen your face."

"You should have thought of that a little earlier, my beauty. It's too late now. Too much depends on my identity remaining a secret for me to let you go and perhaps someday identify me as El Diablo to my enemies. And since I can't let you go, all that is left is for me to decide what to do with you." El Diablo's voice was dangerously soft as he gazed down into Royale's ashen features.

The smell of her drifted into his nostrils, cooling his ire and reminding him of the passionate moments they had shared. His gaze lingered on her soft mouth before traveling down to her bare shoulders, then returned to her wide, frightened eyes. Her beauty was the flint that again sparked the flames in his blood, heating his loins and making his decision for him.

Royale watched the play of emotions cross his face. Fearing the worst, she again tried to plead for his mercy. "Please, let me go. I swear I'll never tell anyone I've seen your face."

" 'Tis too late, as I said. Your fate has been decided. You'll remain on board my ship as my mistress. The matter is settled." The thought of having her to grace his bed lightened his mood, and he cocked one curious brow at her as he asked, "By the way, what is your name? I'm afraid things happened so swiftly earlier that we failed to properly introduce ourselves. As I recall, I got as far as telling you my name before other, more pleasant things interrupted us."

Royale felt her cheeks grow hot with his reminder and quickly averted her eyes, ashamed of her own response to him. Even now, when she despised him, she was still drawn to him as if against her will. He possessed a powerful magnetism that seemed to pull her into a maze from which she knew there would be no escape if she did not resist to the very limit of her willpower. Unconsciously, she jutted her chin out at a pugnacious angle and silently resolved to fight against the pirate's allure. She would not meekly let him do with her as he pleased. He would soon learn that she was not just a piece of flesh to be used by king or pirate. She was Royale Carrington, the captain of the *Raven*, and would take orders from no man.

Unable to read the fleeting expressions that passed over her face, El Diablo forced her to look at him. Tipping up her chin with his thumb and forefinger, he said, "Your name, mistress? Since you will be sharing my bed, I would know your name."

"You can go to hell," Royale spat, her eyes glinting with rage. "I have no intention of telling you my name nor of becoming your mistress. I would rather die than suffer that horrid fate.''

El Diablo chuckled as he gazed down into her sparkling eyes. They reminded him of those of a tigress he had once seen on his travels in India. She, too, had been snarling and spitting in the hunter's net before he had freed her. This spirited young minx's fate would not be the same as the great noble beast's, however. He could not afford to give her the freedom she sought. There was too much at stake to risk anyone's learning of his activities during the past two years. He wasn't fond of the idea of forcing her to do his bidding, but there were more lives to be considered than just that of one young woman. It was also a shame to have to put a damper on her spirit, but it was necessary.

Releasing her, he stood and crossed to the table that held a decanter of brandy. Pouring himself a liberal·dose, he turned once more to look at her. His eyes swept along the sheet that covered but did not hide her naked body. No, he mused to himself, it would be no hardship on him to have her as his mistress, but she had to be brought under control first.

''As I see it, you have no choice. Either you become my mistress or I will have to take you to Tortuga and put you on the auction block. Your beauty would bring a high price among the brethren of the coast. And it would not matter there if you have seen my face, for no one on Tortuga cares about anyone's identity. They have too many secrets themselves.'' He downed the last of his drink and put the glass aside. ''We set sail for Tortuga within the hour. I'll leave you now to ponder the alternatives I have given you. I will expect your answer by the time I return.'' He strode across the cabin, opened the door, and then shut it behind him.

''You bastard,'' Royale screamed as she bolted from the

bed and tried to stop him from locking her in his cabin. She was too late; the latch would not give under her hand. Furious, she banged on the door with her balled fists until she realized the futility of her actions.

"El Diablo, if it's the last thing I do, I'll kill you for this. I swear it," Royale muttered as she leaned her cheek against the smooth surface of the door, her hands falling limply to her sides. "I'll see the *Wicked Mistress* at the bottom of the sea before I'm through with you."

Pushing herself away from the door, she wiped at her stinging eyes. At present she had no time to plan her revenge, but she would have in the future. For now, she had to find a way to escape the pirate vessel before it put out to sea. She knew she would have to swim back to shore, and that would be an impossible feat once the *Wicked Mistress* weighed anchor. The distance would be too great even for an experienced swimmer like her.

Knowing she would have to depend on her own ingenuity if she was to make her escape, she scanned the dim interior of the captain's cabin, searching for something to use as a weapon against El Diablo. She found nothing that would work on the shelves that lined the wall, nor on the desk where the ship's log lay open. At last she spied the crystal decanter of brandy and moved swiftly across the cabin to it. Lifting it, she weighed it in her hand. She smiled. It would do nicely if it was brought down with enough force. She set the decanter back on the table and pulled the chair directly behind the door. When El Diablo returned he would have the answer he sought from her.

Satisfied with her own inventiveness, she retrieved her gown from the floor and slipped it over her head. She was already lacing it before she realized that the garment would hamper her efforts in the water. Caring little about the damage done to the fine material, she tore it off and kicked it into the corner before she began to search the pirate's cabin for something more suitable to wear. She rummaged through El Diablo's footlocker until she found a pair of britches and a shirt. They were much too large, but she managed to make the necessary adjustments to fit them to her before she heard the sound of footsteps in the passageway beyond the door.

Royale grabbed her crystal weapon and climbed up onto the chair. She stood braced and ready as the door swung open a moment later and El Diablo stepped into the cabin. He paused at the sight of the empty bunk, and in that same moment she struck him with all the force she could muster. However, her precarious perch toppled beneath her, offsetting what she had meant to be a lethal blow.

Stunned, El Diablo sank to his knees and clasped his head. A bright stream of blood flowed from the gash in his scalp, wetting his probing fingers and trickling down his forehead.

Royale heard his agonized moan and saw the scarlet rivulet but did not pause in her flight to freedom. She raced up the steps and onto the deck, and before anyone could guess her intention or stop her, she dived overboard. Her dive was perfect, her slender body knifing through the water and then arching back upward to the surface. She treaded water for only a few moments to ascertain the right direction, and then, with smooth, even strokes, she made for shore.

She was a strong swimmer. The years of playing and swimming in the ocean now stood her in good stead as she sliced through the waves. However, the distance was far greater than she had first surmised, and that took its toll on her strength. She was gasping from the exertion when her feet finally touched the sandy bottom.

The muscles in her legs quivered and would not hold her erect as she tried to stand. A wave hit her behind the knees and knocked her feet out from under her, making her fall backward into the swell of another, much larger wave, which washed over her head.

Coughing and spluttering, she came to the surface and managed to crawl the last few feet to dry land before collapsing facedown upon the beach. Her heart pounded against her ribs, and her lungs burned as she drew in deep breaths of air in an effort to regain her strength.

The sea breeze carried the sound of the commotion on board the *Wicked Mistress* across the water to her, and she knew a search party had been sent out to find her. Though exhausted from her swim, she forced herself to her knees and brushed the sand-matted tangles of hair back from her face as she glanced toward the pirate vessel. The moon had set, and the darkness obscured the small boat that had been lowered for the search, but she could hear the sound of the oars and knew she did not have time to linger if she was to make good her escape.

Staggering to her feet, stumbling as she tried to run, Royale made her way back along the path she had taken from the inn just hours before, though it seemed a lifetime ago. She found her slippers where she had left them but did not spare the time to put them on. The pirates were in hot pursuit, and every second counted.

She paused only briefly at the crossroads that would lead her back to the inn or take her to the quay and the *Raven*. She chose the latter direction. Her breath came in ragged gasps as she ran toward safety and home.

Relief washed over her at the sight of Fred, the *Raven*'s cabin boy, snoozing in the small boat by the pier. She suspected Tim had ordered him to stay on shore in the event that she chose to return to the *Raven*, and she was grateful for his forethought.

"Fred, wake up. We've got to get to the *Raven* immediately," Royale said as she clambered over the side and into the boat, the motion rousing the young man with a start.

He blinked at Royale several times before he recognized her in her bedraggled state. "Captain?" he murmured groggily as he wiped the sleep from his eyes. "Do you want to go out to the *Raven* at this time of night?"

"Blast it, Fred. Why else would I be here?" Royale said as she glanced anxiously over her shoulder. "Now row, damn it, like our lives depended upon it."

Fred bent to the task without question, though Royale's actions baffled him. He'd never seen her in such a disheveled and agitated state before. She kept glancing over her shoulder as if the devil were in pursuit.

The dinghy had no more than bumped against the hull of the frigate before Royale was scurrying up the rope ladder and onto the deck. She did not pause to draw in a deep breath of relief until her feet touched the smooth, scrubbed surface.

"Royale?" Tim asked from behind her as he lifted the ship's lantern to get a better view. His eyes grew wide as he took in her appearance. "What in hell has happened to you?"

Taking in a tremulous breath, she pulled at the silk shirt in an effort to straighten her appearance before she looked up at her friend. "I'll tell you about it in the morning, Tim. For now all I want is a bath and my bunk."

"Captain?" Tim asked again, but Royale shook her head, forestalling his questions.

"Not tonight, Tim," she said as she glanced about the deck, noting the lone watchman on duty. "Double the watch tonight. There are pirates in the area, and it would be easy for them to take the ship with only one man on guard."

"Pirates?" Tim said, his brow furrowing in bewilderment.

"Don't argue, damn it. Just do as I order," Royale ground out as she turned away and strode toward her cabin. The events of the night were beginning to take their toll upon her composure. Her nerves were taut, making her feel as if she were a coiled spring ready to burst at any moment. She had to get away from everyone to try to think things out.

At the moment she could not contend with Tim's questions, nor could she give any explanations until she settled the matter in her own mind. She had to have time to think rationally and put her life back into perspective. If she had done so earlier in the night, perhaps her world would not have been suddenly jolted from its orbit by a masked pirate with a velvet voice.

Against her will, Royale felt her pulse quicken at the thought of El Diablo and the passion his touch had aroused within her. She ground her teeth together in a vain effort to suppress the memory as she murmured beneath her breath, "Damn you, El Diablo. You will pay for this night's work."

Chapter 3

The crisp breeze molded the white lawn of Royale's shirt to her lithe body as she stood on deck, her feet splayed for balance, her hands folded behind her back as she stared out across the broad expanse of blue water. Her wide-brimmed hat, its red feather plume dancing gaily in the air, shaded her features from the sun, yet tiny lines fanned the corners of her eyes as she squinted against the bright reflection of the rays upon the waves.

The *Raven* dipped and swayed, slicing through the sea toward Witch's Cay. By late evening they would be anchored in the cove around the point from Good Fortune. Royale glanced up at the taut, wind-filled sails overhead, satisfied with the time they had made since sailing from Gregory Town the previous day.

Gregory Town, she mused to herself as she unconsciously pressed her lips into a rueful grimace. Her venture there had gained her nothing but had cost her a great deal. She feared she would never be able to put the events of their last night there from her mind. She had tried unsuccessfully to do so for the past two days. Every waking hour—and her dreams as well—had been filled with thoughts of El Diablo and her growing desire for revenge against him. No matter how hard she tried, she had been unable to come to terms with herself about her own actions or the humiliation that lay smoldering beneath the calm exterior she presented to the world. Like a venomous snake it lay coiled, waiting to strike out at her in her unguarded moments and make her experience again the shame of knowing that she was not the strong, independent woman that she thought herself to be.

El Diablo had found a weakness within her that she had not known existed and because of it she could not forgive him or herself. The realization that she had fallen eagerly into man's oldest trap without making an effort to fight against it shook Royale's confidence as nothing in her life had ever done.

Leaning against the rail, her hands balled into fists, she stared pensively down into the foaming water that lapped the *Raven*'s hull. "I won't let you do this to me, El Diablo," she ground out between clenched teeth.

I have been used for one night's sport by a masked pirate, but I won't let it ruin the rest of my life, she vowed silently as she tried to rebuild her shattered pride. Her father had often told her that the sea of life presented many tumultous storms that were not easily navigated, but you had to be strong and fight against the currents that threatened to pull you beneath the dark waves of despair. Remembering Sir John's words, Royale stiffened her back and raised her chin in the air. She would heed his advice. She would not let one mistake destroy her. She had made her plans for the future and would let nothing stand in the way of her regaining what was rightfully hers. That goal was her paramount concern, but there would also come a time when she would repay El Diablo for his one night of pleasure at her expense.

Her eyes stung with the need to cry, but she staunchly refused to give way to the urge. Once the pitcher was overturned it was too late to cry over the milk, but one could always look for the culprit whose callous actions had knocked it over and make him pay for the mistake.

The corners of her mouth curled upward with the thought. Within the month she planned to have the *Raven* refitted and sailing toward Tortuga. If she had her way, El Diablo would live to regret their few hours together. She might not find him in the pirate stronghold, but she knew his face, and that was a major factor in her favor. Someday their paths would cross again, and she would be able to recognize him even without his mask.

Unaware that she was no longer alone, she gave an involuntary start when Tim said, "Royale."

Drawing her thoughts away from El Diablo, Royale glanced up at her friend. Noting the look in his eyes and the fine lines that etched his wide brow, she knew that he was concerned for her. For the past two days she had been avoiding this moment, but now it had come. They had been friends far too long; Tim was too attuned to her moods not to know when something troubled her. She had hoped to postpone any discussion till a much later date, because at the present moment she could tell no one, not even her beloved Tim, of El Diablo.

"Tim, we'll be home soon," she said, and forced a smile to her lips, hoping to forestall the questions he wanted to ask.

"Aye, we'll reach Witch's Cay by evening, so don't you think it's about time you told me what happened in Gregory Town?" Tim said, his gaze holding hers.

"I don't know what you mean," Royale bluffed, and quickly turned her eyes toward the distant horizon, unable to look at him and lie.

"You know damn well what I'm talking about. You came scurrying aboard the other night looking like a drowned rat with a cat hot on its tail and then tried to tell me nothing happened while you were ashore. Royale Carrington, I've known you too long to believe that. I've seen few things that could put a fright into you, but when you boarded the *Raven* you were afraid. Now I want to know why.''

Again Royale tried to smile as she said, ''All right, Tim. If you must know, I'll tell you. When I was on my way to the quay I was approached by several drunken sailors. Since I was alone, their indecent suggestions frightened me, and I ran from them. To my embarrassment, I ran in the wrong direction and ended up falling over the sea wall into the bay. I didn't tell you what happened because I was too ashamed and knew you would laugh at me. Now are you satisfied?''

Tim eyed Royale dubiously. Her story did not ring true at all. The girl he knew would hardly have been frightened by a bunch of sailors. She would have flayed them alive with her tongue or taken a sword to them. Nor had she explained why she had wound up dressed in oversized men's clothing when she had worn a gown to shore. However, he would let the matter rest for the moment. She was safe now, and when she chose to tell him the truth, he would be there to listen.

''Yes, I'm satisfied, but in the future I intend to see that you have an escort no matter how much you argue against it. Far too often you forget that you are a beautiful young woman,'' Tim said, his tone firm with resolve.

Royale was about to tell him she could take care of herself, but she bit the words back. She had not fared so well in Gregory Town. ''All right, if you insist, my great mother hen,'' she said, and wrinkled her nose at the helmsman. She knew the gesture would have the desired effect, as it had done since she had used it the first time on him at the age of six.

''Good,'' Tim said, and grinned as he folded his arms across his chest. ''And I promise not to laugh at you.''

"You'd better not, if you know what's good for you, helmsman. I'm still the captain of this vessel, and that would be insubordination." Royale chuckled, but then her expression grew serious. "It's time we discussed our course of action once we reach Witch's Cay, Tim."

"You've come to a decision?" he asked.

She leaned back against the rail, her eyes scanning the deck below them before she looked once more at her friend. "Aye, that I have. If you and the crew are with me, we go a-pirating. I could learn nothing in Gregory Town, since the solicitor never returned to meet with me, and I doubt it would have changed anything if he had. Have you spoken with the men?"

Tim nodded. "Aye, they're with you. They say you're their good luck charm, and where you go, they'll be right behind."

"I'm relieved to hear it," Royale said, and, for the first time in two days, smiled without having to force the gesture. "There'll be much for us to do in the next few weeks. After the men have had a couple of days' rest, I want them to refit the *Raven* from stem to stern, scrape her hull, and paint her black."

"Black?" Tim asked, puzzled by her odd request.

"Aye, black. I want her as black as the devil's soul. From now on we sail under the Jolly Roger and not England's colors. I want my enemies to know my vengeance is as dark and abiding as the color of the *Raven*'s hull," Royale ground out through clenched teeth, and her thoughts turned once more to El Diablo.

Hearing the underlying note of hatred in her voice, Tim could not help but wonder where such vehemence came from. Even after Sir John's death she had never spoken with such rancor, nor had her eyes held such a hard, implacable look as they did now. Feeling a sense of relief that her enmity was not directed at him, Tim did not question her motives further but remained quietly at her side. He suspected that Royale had her own private demons to slay, and he would be at her side when she did so, as he had been since their childhood.

The sultry aroma of rose and camellia filled the veranda in the balmy twilight. The sweet fragrances lay gently upon the warm air that enveloped Royale and Adele as they sat in the deepening shadows, enjoying the peace of the evening.

The only sound to disturb the tranquility was the creak of the wooden rockers moving back and forth upon the cypress floor. It was a restful time, one Royale needed after the labors of the past weeks. She had had little chance to relax since her return to Good Fortune. Her days had been spent overseeing the work on the frigate.

Laying her head back and closing her eyes, she savored her last hours at home. With the morning tide she would no longer be the mistress of Good Fortune but an outcast from society. She had set her course and would not look back, and if all went as planned, when she returned to her home it would truly belong to her once and for all.

"Royale," Adele said, breaking the stillness, "I wish you would reconsider this scheme of yours."

Royale's fingers curled about the chair arms as she slowly turned to peer through the shadows at the housekeeper. Releasing a long, tired breath, she said, "Adele, let's enjoy my last night at home without arguing further. I've heard all of your misgivings for nearly a month, and you know they have not changed my mind."

"For God's sake, Royale, this is ridiculous. You are a gently bred young lady, not a pirate. You are supposed to marry and have babies, not go sailing the oceans in search of the Spanish and their gold. That kind of life has already taken your father from you; don't let it take you from us as well," Adele said in exasperation.

"We've been over this time and again. This is something I have to do. Please try to understand why I can't just sit by and accept what has been dealt out to me," Royale said, her tone firm and unyielding.

"I do understand. I've been with you all of your life and have loved you as my own. You are driven by needs that you are not aware of yourself. Since the day you learned that Sir John was not your father by blood, I've watched you go to every extreme to prove your worth to him and to yourself. But there was truly no need. Sir John could not have loved you more had he sired you himself.

"I didn't object to your adventures before because I knew you were working out your grief and hoped that you would finally come to terms with yourself and settle down. What you are proposing to do now is the same thing you did years ago, but this time it is the King of England with whom you are dealing, not an adoring father. Charles has been generous in his dealings with you. Don't tempt the Fates by going against him, Royale, I beg of you," Adele pleaded, her tone reflecting the compassion she felt for the child she had watched grow from a gangling girl into a beautiful, troubled woman.

Adele's words hit too close to the mark; she'd voiced things Royale refused to admit even to herself. She pushed herself abruptly from her chair and crossed the veranda. She leaned against a coquina post with her arms folded across her chest and turned her face up to the sky. Gazing at the stars without seeing them, she said softly, as if she were speaking to herself, "Adele, perhaps you are right in some small way about me. I don't have to prove that I was Sir John's daughter; I *was*, and because of that I will show those who attempt to use me that I am more than a lump of flesh fit only to breed. I may not have Sir John's blood, but he gave me his pride. Father would approve of what I do now to regain what he wanted me to have. No man, be he king or pauper, has the right to take away my home. I love this land. It is part of me, and I intend to keep it."

Glancing over her shoulder at the housekeeper, she said, "Wish me well, Adele, for on the morning tide I will be at the helm of the *Raven*."

Dabbing at her tears with her handkerchief, Adele rose and moved to Royale's side. She hugged the young woman close, and her voice was husky with emotion as she said, "I love you, Royale Carrington, for all of your hardheaded ways. If you must go, then do so with my love and blessing."

"Thank you, Adele," Royale said as she returned the housekeeper's hug.

The peaceful moment between the two friends was disturbed by the rapid approach of a lone rider. His horse galloped up the sandy drive and skidded to a halt in front of Good Fortune. He had already dismounted and was hurrying up the walk, breathing heavily from his haste, before Royale recognized her helmsman.

"Tim, what's wrong? Has something happened on the *Raven*?" Royale asked as she hurried across the veranda to meet him.

Wiping the nervous sweat from his brow, he shook his head rapidly. "No, the *Raven*'s fine. I just came from the village to warn you that he's arrived."

"Who's arrived? What on earth are you talking about, Tim?" Royale asked, bewildered by her friend's behavior.

"Your guardian, that's who. A British frigate sailed into port today, and he was on it. I just found out a short while ago when I was at the Rum and Gullet. He came in with another man and I overheard them talking about coming up to Good Fortune in the morning," Tim said, then he drew a long breath to try to calm his pounding heart.

Though the night was warm, a chill swept over Royale. The king's man had come to take control of her life. Warding off the alarm Tim's words had inspired, she smiled as she looked at her two friends. "Well, I'm afraid he's going to be disappointed if he thinks to find me here. Our plans have not changed. We sail in the morning."

"Royale," Adele said, her tone reflecting her worry over having to explain the girl's absence when the king's man arrived at Good Fortune, "what will I tell him when he finds you gone?"

"Tell him anything you like, Adele," Royale said before cocking her head to one side and regarding the housekeeper thoughtfully for a long moment. An impish grin tugged at her lips as she said, "Tell him I'm dead. That explanation should serve the purpose of keeping my whereabouts a secret."

Adele rubbed her arms as if to rid herself of a sudden chill. "I can't say that, Royale. If I did, I'd feel as if I were placing a curse on you."

Royale laughed at the housekeeper's superstitious nature. "You have nothing to fear by telling him that, because Royale Carrington *will* be dead until she returns to claim Good Fortune as her own. From this day forward I will be known as El Diablo."

Tim's eyes seemed to nearly pop from his head, and he had to swallow several times before he could utter, "El Diablo! Royale, you've gone completely mad." Suddenly Tim froze. He eyed Royale suspiciously, a knowing look coming into his eyes. "You've had this in your mind since the day you ordered me to paint the hull of the *Raven* black, haven't you?"

"Aye, Tim, and I have my reasons, though you may think me mad." Royale's tone indicated that she would stand for no opposition in the matter.

Tim thumped his forehead with the heel of his hand and

rolled his eyes heavenward. "I should have known you had some scheme brewing in that head of yours. But Royale, for the love of all that's holy, reconsider this matter. El Diablo is not called the devil for nothing. He earned his reputation. The man is feared by some of the most ferocious cutthroats who sail the seas."

Annoyed by Tim's reaction, Royale turned and left Adele and her helmsman on the veranda. She strode into the house and went to the drawing room, where she poured herself a small glass of fine Madeira. As she lifted the wine to her lips she turned to find that her friends had followed her. Exasperated, she downed the ruby liquid in one gulp and set the glass on the table none too gently as she said, "In this, Tim, I'm firm in my resolve. I will not change my mind, no matter what you or anyone else says to the contrary. From now on there will be two El Diablos raiding the gold-laden Spanish ships, but only one will be accused of it. If all goes as I have planned, we will not have the stigma of piracy placed on us."

"El Diablo will hunt you down. He'll not stand meekly by while you use his name and grow rich," Tim said.

"I suspect you're right. But when our paths cross, I am determined to see that only one of us remains afloat," Royale said, her voice icy.

Adele threw up her hands in despair and slumped into a chair as Tim asked, "Why, Royale? What brought on this mad scheme of yours?"

Suddenly furious with the world, worn out by the constant badgering from Adele and now from Tim, Royale picked up the crystal wine glass and threw it against the fireplace, shattering it. The night with El Diablo, the king's edict taking Good Fortune from her, and now the arrival of Charles's man all combined to rip away the veneer of calm she had managed to build around her emotions during the past weeks. It disintegrated like the glass, fragmenting into a thousand little pieces, leaving only the rage that had been smoldering for so long.

"Damn it, Tim, I have a score to settle with the man. If you have any qualms about it, then I suggest you stay here. I want no one sailing with me who fears his own shadow or who will not obey my commands," Royale spat, her fury unappeased by the hurt, bewildered expression on her friend's face.

"Make your decision now. Either you follow me without question or you stay on Witch's Cay. It is your choice," she said. She had been pushed too far. Everything was crowding in on her, and she refused to retreat anymore.

The silence in the room lengthened. Royale and Tim stood regarding each other as if they were seeing each other for the first time. Finally Tim released a long, resigned breath and nodded. "You know I'm with you, no matter how foolhardy I think you may be." A muscle worked in his jaw as he glanced at Adele and then back at Royale. "I just hope for all our sakes that the *Raven* will not be the one to end up at the bottom of the ocean."

"She won't be," Royale said as she poured three glasses of wine. "Shall we drink to our success?"

"Aye." Tim grinned as he took the proffered glass and raised it in salute to his captain. "To our success, now and in the future."

Adele's hand shook as she took her glass and looked from one young face to the other. "To your safe return," she said before raising her glass to her lips.

Royale smiled as she sipped her wine. She loved Adele and Tim and knew they argued against her venture out of concern for her, but she had set her course and would not change it. She would have Good Fortune, and while on the way to achieving that goal she would also be striking out at the man who had taken something else precious to her—her honor.

A knock on the door interrupted their farewell toast. For a long moment they stood frozen, each sensing that the time for Royale's departure and her guardian's arrival had come much sooner than they had expected.

Another impatient knock sounded at the door and sent them into action. Tim moved to the window and peered out. As he turned back to the two women his grim expression told Royale all she needed to know. Giving the housekeeper a quick hug, she said, "I love you, Adele. Try not to worry too much." Glancing toward the door, she continued, "I know you don't like to lie, and I'll not ask you to, but it would help us if you could avoid telling him all of the truth." Brushing her lips against Adele's cheek, she hugged her once more before motioning for Tim to follow her through the French doors and out into the garden.

Near the entrance to the clifftop path Royale paused and turned back toward her home for one last look. The light from the drawing room drew her attention, and she watched as a tall, white-wigged figure strode inside. She could not make out his features from this distance, but she could hear the faint rumble of his deep voice as he spoke with Adele. Something in his tone made her heart give a slight twist in her breast before she resolutely turned her back on the scene, putting it from her mind. Taking the path that led to the *Raven*'s isolated cove, Royale mused to herself, "For now I leave Good Fortune in your care, but soon I will return to reclaim it. Be assured of that."

Sir Bran Langston eyed the housekeeper suspiciously. "You say that my ward left Good Fortune over a month ago, and that you have been living here alone since that time?"

"Yes. Mrs. Hogan, the cook, comes during the day, as do the two maids who live in the village," Adele said nervously as she watched the man's dark gaze settle on the three partially filled wine glasses.

"That is strange, Mrs. Johnson. I could have sworn I heard several people mention my ward today, and none seemed to know that she had departed Good Fortune."

Adele glanced down at her tightly clasped hands. "Mistress Royale may have gone to visit friends on another island. She often did that when her father was alive. I saw no reason to tell anyone of her absence."

"I find that even more unusual, Mrs. Johnson. It seems to me that Mistress Carrington would have told you of her plans or at least left you a note. Since she is only a young girl, I'd think you would take your responsibility for her welfare more seriously." Bran crossed to the table where the decanter of wine sat and poured himself a drink.

Adele's head snapped up at the reprimand. "Sir, I am only the housekeeper at Good Fortune, not Mistress Royale's bodyguard. She is a young woman grown and does as she pleases. I have no control over her actions. I am sure she is safe, and when she decides to come home she will do so. Sir John placed few restrictions upon her, and as a paid member of her household it is not my duty to limit her in any way."

Bran swirled the Madeira in his glass, studying it thoughtfully for a few moments before his eyes swept once more to the three glasses on the table and then settled on Adele. "Is it your duty to tipple while the mistress is absent?"

Adele's face flushed a deep scarlet at the insult, and she came to her feet in a huff. "Sir, I do not tipple. Now I will bid you good night. I'm sure you can find your way to your room at the top of the stairs." With that she spun on her heel and stamped from the room. The sound echoed back to the drawing room when she slammed her chamber door shut.

Bran chuckled as he settled himself in a chair and stretched his long legs out before him, crossing them casually at the ankles. Relaxing back in the chair, he mused aloud, "Damn, but I'm tired." Draining the glass of wine, he set it on the table at his elbow.

He clasped his hands over his hard stomach and gazed about the elegantly appointed room. The housekeeper had aroused his curiosity. Why had the woman lied—for lie she had, and not very well at that. After all the years that his life had depended upon his ability to judge people accurately, it was easy for him to discern the woman's guile. Unable to answer the question, he sat up and rubbed his hand across his face. A yawn escaped him as he pushed himself out of the chair.

It was too late to solve the riddles of Good Fortune that night. The morning would be soon enough to unravel the housekeeper's falsehoods and set about finding his missing ward. After that he would begin to bring some sense of order to the household, which seemed to him to have little organization if no one could keep tabs on one young girl.

He had to admit that Charles had been right in one respect. From what he had observed so far at Good Fortune, the girl did need some supervision and a firm hand to keep her in line. No young woman should have the freedom to go about and do as she pleased; even married women did not have that right.

Blowing out the candles with the exception of one to light his way, Bran climbed the stairs to what he hoped would turn out to be his bedchamber. Opening the first door at the top of the landing, he was relieved to find that it seemed to be the master bedroom.

He kicked the door closed behind him and set the candle on the dressing table. Shrugging out of the deep blue velvet jacket, he tossed it on a chair near the fireplace, then worked his cravat loose. Tossing the lacy neckcloth onto the table, he pulled the white wig from his head and absently ran his fingers through his own dark hair. He winced as he touched the tender place on his scalp and muttered, "Damn," bending to inspect the still-healing wound in the mirror.

At the same moment, his eyes came to rest on the painting reflected in the glass. They grew wide with shock before he swung about to stare into the face of a young woman with eyes the color of the sea and chestnut ringlets framing the lovely features he would never forget.

Though he suspected the painting had been done several years earlier, there was no mistaking the identity of the image rendered upon the canvas. It was the girl from Gregory Town. As if drawn to it against his will, Bran moved across the room and stared at the name engraved on the tiny plaque at the bottom of the heavily carved frame. It read *Royale Carrington, 1666.*

"Royale Carrington, my ward; the girl from Gregory Town," Bran said aloud, dumbfounded at the discovery. "No, it can't be," he protested, but even as the words left his lips he knew it was.

Unconsciously, he rubbed his knuckles across his furrowed brow as he stared up at the painting, recalling what the housekeeper had said earlier. Royale Carrington had left Good Fortune a little over a month earlier, about the same time his men had brought the beautiful girl on board his ship.

Turning abruptly away from the painting, he strode across the chamber to the decanter of brandy that rested on a mahogany table near the French doors. He poured a liberal amount into a glass and downed it in one gulp, hoping the fiery liquid would ease some of the tension that gripped his gut.

The girl from Gregory Town had jumped overboard, and his men had searched the waters for more than an hour trying to rescue her, but they had failed. The watchman on duty had seen her go under but had not seen her resurface. Since they had not been able to find her body, they had assumed she had been caught by the undertow and it had swept her out to sea. To his regret, he had just solved the riddle of his missing ward.

Bran slumped into a chair and covered his face with his hands. It had been hard to face the fact that because of him a young girl had jumped to her death. His dreams during the past weeks had been haunted by her specter accusing him of murder. He had tried to reconcile the incident in his own mind by telling himself that he had no other recourse, that his actions had stemmed from his loyalty to his king and country. He had sought to convince himself that her death was like all others that happened in war. It was a cold-hearted way to justify anyone's death, but it had been the only way for him to live with himself.

He had been unsuccessful, however, in his attempt to keep the memory of their moments together at bay. To his chagrin, he found that each time he looked across the rolling waves of the sea its color reminded him of her eyes and of the expression in their depths as her passion rose to meet his.

"Damn," Bran muttered again as he leaned back in the chair, his hands falling limply to the armrests. He stared blindly at the ceiling as he recalled the girl he had made love to, who had vowed she would rather die than become his mistress. She had been his ward, his responsibility; the duty given to him by his king, a man who cared greatly about her welfare, for some unknown reason.

The guilt he had been trying to deny now riddled him like a termite in a piece of wood, gnawing away, leaving the insides hollow, though the exterior looked as if nothing had transpired within. He could not even dredge up his loyalty to Charles and England to help abate the turbulent waves of pain that were washing over him as he finally recognized the fact that in the brief time he had spent with Royale Carrington, she had affected him more than any woman had ever done in the past. Her beauty and spirit had appeased the restless beast that lived within him. In her arms he had found peace to fill the void inside himself that kept him roaming the seas in search of some elusive entity that he could not identify. For years he had known that he sought something without a name, and for one brief moment he had thought he had found it in Royale Carrington. He feared he would never be so fortunate again.

"It's too late," Bran said as he pushed himself lethargically from the chair. His steps seemed weighed down by his heavy thoughts as he crossed to the French doors and threw them open. Stepping out onto the balcony, he stared out across the dark landscape of Witch's Cay.

Gazing into the quiet night, he knew he could not stay there. Everywhere he looked he would be reminded of the fact that it had been his callous disregard of an innocent girl's feelings that had cost Good Fortune its mistress.

Tomorrow, when Miles Granville arrived with their luggage from the *Dolphin*, he would leave his friend in charge of the estate and he would set sail back to Tortuga and the *Wicked Mistress*. From there he would resume his life as El Diablo and hope that either a cannon ball or time would help him to forget the feelings one fiery-tempered girl had aroused within his pirate's heart.

A muscle worked in his jaw as he gripped the lacy wrought-iron railing that enclosed the balcony. In the last few minutes something had died within him. The future did not hold the prospects it once had. He would again fill England's coffers with his ill-gotten gains, but this time he feared his actions would not be tempered by his heart—the heart that now lay heavy and cold in his chest because of the guilt he felt over one night's pleasure in the arms of the beautiful girl-woman he now knew as Royale Carrington.

Bran turned back to the bedchamber, resigned to the fact that fate had granted him one chance to catch something very precious and he had arrogantly misused it.

Chapter 4

*T*he Raven *swayed gently at anchor as Royale stood with* legs splayed wide and arms folded over her chest, gazing at the busy quay of Tortuga, or Turtle Island. She had to agree with the island's name, for its hilly, somewhat barren terrain did look like a huge turtle rising out of the ocean. However, the busy docks dispelled further resemblance to the slow creature from which the island got its name. The harbor was filled with ships that were being relieved of their ill-gotten gains. The French governor had no scruples about how the goods were obtained, and he lined his pockets with the proceeds. Trading with the pirates also helped his own political reputation in France. The healthy profits he sent back to Louis XIV eased the burden of France's finances, since its king's love of war and extravagance had placed the nation in nearly as dire financial circumstances as those his cousin's England was in.

"There be the pirate stronghold, Captain," Fishbait said as he came to stand at Royale's side, "and from the look of it the other ships there have been more fortunate than we have."

"Aye, but our luck will change, Fishbait," Royale said as she glanced at the quartermaster. "Once I've finished my business on shore, then it will be our turn to line our pockets. The hold of the *Raven* will soon be filled with Spanish gold—or that of anyone else who sails across our path."

"I don't doubt it, Captain. Ye've never failed us before," Fishbait said, rubbing a callused hand across the salt-and-pepper stubble of his beard.

"And I'll not fail you this time," Royale said as she scanned the nearby ships, searching for one in particular, the *Wicked Mistress*. Failing to find it in the harbor, she glanced back at Fishbait. "I want you and Tim to come ashore with me. The sooner we finish our business here, the sooner we can be seeking fat galleons to plunder."

Fishbait frowned at Royale as he pulled the flat-crowned sailor's hat further down on his head. "Uh, Captain, I don't mean to be disrespectful, 'cause I know ye've shown us what yer made of in the past, but do ye think ye should go into Tortuga with just me and Tim?"

"Don't you think I'm able to take care of myself?" Royale said, smiling at the quartermaster.

"Aye, ye can take care of yerself in a fair fight, but this here is Tortuga. The cutthroats here don't fight fair, and should they realize that ye're a woman, it'd take more than just me and young Tim to protect ye," Fishbait said, his already ruddy complexion deepening in hue as he recalled his own defeat at the young woman's hand.

"Then we'll just have to make sure that they don't find that out. I appreciate your concern for me, but I am the captain of this vessel, and it is my duty to rout out any information that will benefit us." Glancing once more toward the busy quay, she continued, "When I chose to become captain of this frigate, I did so with the knowledge that I would often find myself placed in danger. Now that we're sailing without England's letter of marque, we will have to do business here. We can't sail into just any port and sell our goods. Tortuga is the only place where we'll be welcome from now on.''

"Aye, ye're right there, but I still don't like the thought of ye going ashore with just me and Tim,'' Fishbait said, still uneasy. During the past months he had grown fond of Sir John's daughter, and though he knew her ability with the sword, he could not stop himself from worrying about her.

"Since the men can't go ashore on this visit, break out a barrel of rum for them to share after they lower the dinghy. That should appease them this time. They can celebrate when we return and they have their pockets full of gold,'' Royale said, dismissing Fishbait's concern. Turning her back on the view of the island, she strode from the poop deck and went to her cabin to ready herself for their first excursion to Tortuga. The pirate haven would be their main port of call from now on, and she wanted to become familiar with it.

Fishbait gave a long, resigned sigh as he watched his captain stride away. Shaking his head, he reflected on their conversation. She was much like Sir John had been. Both were stubborn to the bone, and once they set their minds to something, nothing could dissuade them from the course they had chosen.

The sun was sinking slowly into the west as the small boat scraped against the sandy bottom. Tim jumped over the side into the knee-deep waves to pull it further up the beach and secure it. The evening shadows stretched out from the hills, shading the quay as Royale stepped from the boat. The water lapped at her boots as she paused to take in the sight of the coquina structures clustered on the hillside along the narrow, winding road that ran from the bay up through the village. Even at that late hour the sandy thoroughfare was teeming with people, many garbed in outlandish costumes or in clothing that had been stolen from some unfortunate merchantman that had happened to sail across their path.

Strands of music and laughter floated on the air as the pirates celebrated their successful voyages. The pleasant sounds mingled with the curses and grunts of those who still labored. Occasionally a scream would rend the air to mar the illusion of harmony the tropical setting created. That alone was a clear indication that Tortuga was a place that was merciless to those who showed any sign of weakness. They soon became victims who suffered at the hands of cutthroats—the brutish men who gained a sense of power from inflicting pain upon others.

A chill rippled up Royale's spine at the idea, and she shook her head, resolutely pushing the thought away. However, her hand rested protectively upon the hilt of her sword as she made her way up the beach with Tim and Fishbait at her side.

As Royale began to ascend the steps that led to the road above the seawall a gust of wind whipped her hat from her head. Her long chestnut hair spilled over her shoulders in wild disarray, and a cry of dismay escaped her lips as she tried to grab the fleeing headgear. Fortunately, Tim managed to catch her hat before it was lost in the waters of the bay, and he returned it to her. She quickly secured her heavy mane of hair beneath it once more as Tim and Fishbait shielded her from the view of those who passed on the road above them.

"That was a close 'un," Fishbait grumbled as he glanced about to see if anyone had noticed the sudden transformation of the young pirate captain into a beautiful woman. Seeing that no one was paying any attention to them, he relaxed and said, "No harm's been done this time. Let's just hope our luck holds."

"Aye," Tim muttered as they continued up the steps to the edge of the busy road.

Enjoying the coolness provided by the shade of the sea-wall, Scrimshaw hefted the bottle of rum to his lips and took a healthy swig, letting a small stream of the sweet liquor drizzle down his stubbled chin. "Ah," he said with satisfaction as he wiped his mouth on his sleeve, then poked Black Jack in the ribs, rousing him from his alcohol-induced slumber.

"Do ye see that, Black Jack?" he asked, and pointed toward the bay.

Weaving back and forth, Black Jack blinked to clear his vision as he peered in the direction Scrimshaw indicated. "Aye, 'tis a ship, ye bag of whalebones. Ain't nothing unusual about seeing a ship when there's an ocean nearby, ye fool." Hiccuping, he grinned a foolish, lopsided grin at his mate. "Now, if ye were in the middle of England, it might be slightly odd to see one." Chuckling at his own wit, he reached for the dark brown bottle of rum.

"That ain't what I was talking about, ye ole piece of shark bait," Scrimshaw grumbled, and withheld the bottle from his bleary-eyed companion.

"Then what in the 'ell were ye a-blabbering about?" Black Jack growled, reaching for the bottle again.

"Her color, ye bilge maggot. If I didn't know the *Wicked Mistress* to be anchored up in yon cove, I'd swear that was 'er," Scrimshaw said as he braced his back against the seawall and forced his wobbly legs to push him upright so he could get a better view of the ship anchored in the bay.

Scratching the dark growth on his chin and rubbing his face, Black Jack did likewise, though he had to keep himself precariously balanced against the wall to stay erect. Swaying, he squinted his eyes and forced himself to concentrate over the effects of the rum.

"Aye, I see what ye be a-blabbering about now. She do resemble the *Wicked Mistress* all right, but from here I can't read her name. She must be new in Tortuga, 'cause I don't ever recollect seeing 'er before." Black Jack peered intently at the ship.

"Read her name! Ye son of a she dog, ye can't read in the first place," Scrimshaw said as he took another swig from the bottle of rum.

"I can too read—at least a few words. That's more than ye can say." Black Jack gave his companion a dark look through narrowed, bloodshot eyes.

"Well, ain't we the well-educated gent all of a sudden? Ye've let the rum addle yer wits, Black Jack. If ye can read, then I'm the King of England, and ye're the Lord High Admiral." Scrimshaw laughed as he handed the bottle to his friend and sank back to the sand.

Black Jack slumped down beside his friend with knees bent and head braced against the wall, his eyes once more on the ship in the bay. "I wonder where she come from and who be her captain."

"Can't answer that, but it looks like we'll soon see. They're lowering a dinghy."

"I can see that, ye fool. Tell me something I don't know," Black Jack muttered before taking a long swallow of rum and then belching loudly.

The two pirates remained quietly in the shadows, watching the small boat approach the beach. When the three passengers stepped from it, they glanced at one another, their faces mirroring one another's curiosity about the strange trio.

"That's the weirdest bunch of buccaneers I've ever seed before. And if that's the captain in the middle, he sure is puny," Scrimshaw said as he poked Black Jack in the ribs and grinned.

Black Jack grunted from the pain inflicted by his mate's

sharp, bony elbow and growled, "If ye don't quit poking me, ye're going to be a mite punier yerself."

Rubbing his battered ribs, Black Jack gazed at the three men who were striding toward the steps of the sea wall. He opened his mouth to speak, but no words passed his lips as he watched the crisp breeze catch the small man's hat and sweep it from his head. Black Jack gaped at the long chestnut curls that fell about the small figure's shoulders, and when he turned to take the hat from his companion, the pirate saw the features of the man—rather, the woman—for the first time. The big sailor's eyes widened in shock and his jaw went slack as he watched her coil the heavy mass of hair back beneath the hat.

Noting his companion's expression, Scrimshaw followed the direction of his mate's gaze with his own. It was the girl from Gregory Town—the girl they all thought had drowned.

"Damn me if it ain't 'er. And all along we been a-thinking she was food for the fishes," Scrimshaw said, scratching absently at his matted head.

Black Jack snapped his mouth closed, the quick movement rattling his few remaining teeth. "Ye sure it is 'er?"

"Damn right it is. It'd be hard to forget a face like 'ers. I got a good look at it that night. That be 'er all right, just as sure as I'm standing 'ere." Glancing down at the sand, he grinned a little sheepishly and said, "Sitting here, I mean."

"Won't the captain be surprised with this bit of news when he returns? He be a strange 'un anyway, but when he thought the wench had drowned he seemed to go mad there fer a while. I was beginning to wonder if he hadn't lost his mind, the way he was acting." Black Jack lifted the bottle to his lips and, finding it empty, tossed it toward the water's edge.

"Reckon we should keep an eye on 'er so we can report

back to the captain?'' Scrimshaw asked as he staggered to his feet.

"Good idea, but first we'd better find us another bottle to keep up our strength," Black Jack said as he, too, rose unsteadily.

The two pirates stumbled along the seawall and managed to climb the steps without mishap. However, by the time they reached the top, their commitment to follow the girl and her companions had dwindled as their thirst had grown, overpowering their good intentions. Making their way to the nearest tavern, they bought several bottles of rum to quench their dry throats and settled themselves in the corner to fortify themselves with the sweet, potent brew. Soon both were snoring with their heads flat on the table and arms hanging loosely at their sides, their mouths gaping as they snored noisily.

Flanked by Fishbait and Tim, Royale, acting the part of the buccaneer captain, swaggered into the smoky interior of the Pieces of Eight tavern. The stagnant odors of unwashed humanity, spilled ale and rum, smoke, and other things that she did not like to consider made her gorge rise. Swallowing several times to force the bitter bile from her throat, she strolled across the litter-strewn floor to the bar, which was made from several ships' hatches placed end to end on overturned wooden barrels. Feigning a casual air, she deepened her voice to perpetrate her ruse and ordered a bottle of rum from the wiry little man behind the bar.

The barkeep eyed Royale and her companions suspiciously for a long moment before turning to move with a crablike gait to the rack of bottles that lined the wall behind him. Taking one brown clay bottle down, he spat on the neck and wiped it with his sleeve to remove the dust before setting it on the bar with a bang. "Ye're new here, ain't ye?" he asked as he pulled the cork free. He poured the liquor into three tankards and then shoved them across to Royale and her companions.

"Aye," she said as she lifted the tankard to her lips and leaned negligently against the bar. Unconsciously, she scanned the interior of the Pieces of Eight, searching each rough-faced customer for any sign of familiarity.

"Well, who be the captain of yer ship?" the bartender asked, curiosity overwhelming his normally taciturn disposition.

"I am," Royale replied gruffly as she took another swallow of rum. Though she did not relish the taste of the sweet liquor, it helped to settle her churning stomach and ease the tension that had been mounting in her since she'd set foot on Tortuga.

The barkeep's eyes widened as he looked at the young man. He assessed the youth's smooth features, accurately judging that a razor had never touched his cheeks, and wondered how one so young could captain his own vessel. Putting his curiosity aside, he returned to his work. It was not his business to question any man's word.

The barkeep, known to all as Billy because of the billet club he used whenever trouble started in the Pieces of Eight, made it his policy never to ask too many questions about his customers. It was best that he know nothing about them. In that way, when trouble erupted, he felt free to bash any head without feeling remorse for his actions. As long as he was ignorant of them as people, he considered them nothing more than animals. Giving a mental shrug, he bellowed at the barmaid, "Chiquita, show these gents to a table and see they're made comfortable."

A voluptuous black-haired woman strolled across the tavern, her wide hips swinging invitingly, her ruby lips spread in what she considered a sensuous smile, her heavy breasts nearly spilling from the white peasant blouse she wore, her pink nipples visible through the thin, worn material.

She was of about the same height as Royale and had to cock her head to one side so as to appear smaller as she paused in front of the captain of the *Raven*. Her eyes sparkled with invitation as she said, "I'd be glad to show ye to a table, and if there's anything else ye desire, I'd be most pleased to accommodate ye."

Glancing at Tim and Fishbait for the first time, she bestowed a flirtatious smile upon them as well. "All three of ye would pose no hardship for me. I can assure ye of that. Ye all be handsome brutes." She fluttered her dark lashes provocatively as she looked at Royale once more. "But I do like 'em young and handsome like ye are, me fine gent."

Royale felt like laughing and weeping at the same time. She could feel the heat of her embarrassment rise to her cheeks, though she knew no pirate captain would blush over the attentions of a whore. She glanced at Tim and Fishbait and saw mirth shimmering in their eyes at her predicament. That did little to help her composure as she followed Chiquita to the table.

Hoping to relieve the situation and be rid of the woman, Royale dug into her pocket and retrieved a coin. Tossing it to the barmaid, she said, "For now, my fine beauty, I'll enjoy my rum. The evening is still young." Without waiting for the woman's reply, she pulled out a chair and slumped down in it, propping her feet up as she had seen the other patrons do.

Thinking she had everything in control, she jerked up with a start as she felt the barmaid's fingers under her chin. Glancing into the woman's worn, made-up features, she saw a hot look of desire shining brightly in Chiquita's dark eyes. Her red lips were only inches from Royale's as she whispered huskily, "I'll be awaiting yer pleasure." The barmaid winked and then returned to her duties. Though she tried to ignore the woman, Royale often felt Chiquita's gaze rest expectantly upon her as she moved about the room bantering with the rough men.

Tim looked as if he were about to burst as he settled his lean frame in the chair across from Royale. Noting the look he gave her, she narrowed her eyes at him, daring him to laugh at the situation, then bestowed the same silent warning upon Fishbait.

The men glanced at each other, their eyes shining with mirth. They knew their young captain had been ready for anything except being seduced by a woman. It took every ounce of willpower they possessed to keep from laughing out loud.

"If we're to learn anything here, we'd best have something other than rum and women to occupy our time," Royale said with asperity to the two men before taking a deep swallow of rum and setting the tankard on the table. They were enjoying themselves at her expense, and she found little humor in the situation. Slamming her feet down, she withdrew a deck of cards from her pocket and began to deal them out.

"Tim, I'm warning you," she muttered as she heard him choke. She looked up to see him hurriedly down his rum to stifle a guffaw. Glancing at Fishbait, she saw a muscle twitch near his mouth also, though he sat straight-faced and picked up his cards.

"That goes for you, too, Fishbait," she said.

A few moments later the episode with the barmaid was forgotten as several sailors entered the Pieces of Eight and took the table to their left. "Chiquita," one pirate with a black eye patch called, "bring us rum to celebrate with. We're going to be privateers."

Chiquita glanced at Royale before strolling across to the new arrivals. "Scully, ye sound as if ye've already had a fair amount of the brew. Ye're talking out of yer head, lovey. Ye and yer mates are pirates, not privateers. Do ye recall who ye are now, love?''

The one called Scully wrapped his beefy arms around the barmaid's hips and pulled her down onto his lap before bestowing a hearty kiss upon her red mouth. "Now, Chiquita, yer Scully hasn't lost 'is mind. We're a-taking Morgan up on his offer. Aye, we're goin' to sail under letters of marque like all of them h'oity-toity privateers of the King's.''

Royale's hands froze mid-deal at the mention of letters of marque. She had to force herself not to openly eavesdrop on the pirates' conversation. Shaking herself mentally, she finished dealing the cards as if she had heard nothing that was being said.

Chiquita noted the slight pause and smiled to herself, her spirits soaring at the thought of the young pirate's jealousy. Playing the game to the hilt, she draped her arms around Scully's neck and laughed. "Ye're drunk, me love. Ye're talking nonsense.''

"Nay, me hot little Spaniard. 'Tis true what I say. Henry Morgan done come to Tortuga and made us the offer. He said that any buccaneer who wants to join him when he sails will get their letter of marque from the governor of Jamaica himself.''

"Ye've seen the great Henry, and ye plan to join him?'' Chiquita said with awe, her dark eyes widening in amazement.

"Aye, wench. We sail in two days' time to give him his answer, so ye'd best give me all yer loving while ye've got the chance,'' Scully said as he dipped a callused hand down the front of her peasant blouse to free one large-nippled breast for all eyes to see. He flicked the rose tip until it hardened beneath his thumb. "See, yer body already wants me hard and hot between yer thighs.'' Scully's voice had grown husky with desire, and all thoughts of sailing with

Morgan had left his mind as his manhood swelled with the heat of his passion.

"Hold on there, lovey," Chiquita said as she pushed his hand away. "I be spoke for tonight."

A look of cold fury replaced the hot light of lust in the pirate's good eye as he growled, "Who be the bastard who thinks he can oust me from that hot place between yer legs, wench?"

"Oh!" Chiquita squealed and a grimace crossed her face as Scully's fingers bit brutally into the breast he recaptured and squeezed. "Him." She pointed at Royale.

With little consideration for the woman he was about to fight over, Scully dumped the barmaid to the floor, rose to his feet, and turned toward Royale. His scarred face was twisted into a violent mask as he kicked the chair out of his way and snarled, "So ye think to steal me woman, do ye? Well, I can take care of any such thought as that." Withdrawing a needle-sharp dirk from the wide red sash around his waist, he said, "When I get through with ye, ye little whelp, ye won't have nothing between yer legs to pleasure her with."

Royale felt her blood run cold at the suppressed violence in the pirate's voice, and it took every ounce of courage she possessed to look calm and unaffected by the man's threats. She sensed the tension mounting in the air and knew that if she did not take control of the situation her friends would die trying to protect her. Casting a swift glance around the tavern, she noted the eager expressions on the other pirates' faces. She and her men would receive no help from that quarter. It would be their three swords against the entire group, since they were the newcomers.

Slowly and with a forced air of calm deliberation, Royale turned to face the one-eyed pirate. She eyed him coolly as he stood towering over her, ready to strike at the least provocation. Her gaze flickered contemptuously over the painted whore at Scully's feet as she calmly said, "It seems there's been some misunderstanding here. You are welcome to the wench. I have no need for her."

Chiquita gave a squeal of protest and scrambled to her feet, the action serving to make her blouse slip further down and expose both large globes of flesh as she pushed her way past the furious pirate and threw herself into Royale's lap.

"Ye don't mean what ye say, handsome. Ye want Chiquita as bad as she wants ye. I'll show ye that ye do, and Scully can't stop me. I'm not his woman."

Before Royale could protest or react to the woman's weight, the barmaid grabbed her face in both hands and pressed her red mouth to Royale's. Revulsion swept over Royale in a tidal wave, giving her more strength than she normally possessed. In one swift motion she came to her feet and shoved the woman away. She wiped her mouth with the sleeve of her jacket, and a visible shiver of disgust rippled over her.

Tim and Fishbait came to their feet at the same time, protectively flanking Royale as she again faced the pirate. Without realizing that he did so, Tim placed his arm around Royale's shoulders.

Scully eyed the trio for a long moment before a knowing look crept across his scarred face. He grinned contemptuously at them and said, "So that be the way of it, then?"

"Aye, that be the way of it," Tim said, feigning a simpering little smile as he sensed the man's train of thought.

A deathly silence filled the tavern as Royale looked at Tim, then back at the smirking Scully, puzzled.

"Yer right, ye have no need fer me wench when ye've got yer own. I've served under men like ye before and know how they find their pleasure," the pirate said with a chuckle.

"You enjoy your type of pleasure and I'll enjoy mine.

To each his own is my way of thinking. Now take your wench and let us return to our rum,'' Royale said, finally grasping Scully's meaning, which left her both embarrassed and relieved.

She held her breath as she awaited the pirate's decision, wondering if he would want to continue the argument or go off to enjoy the ripe body of the whore. The lustful expression on his face as he looked down at the cowering Chiquita indicated his choice. Slowly releasing a long breath, Royale withdrew a gold coin from her pocket, tossed it to the pirate, and said, "Enjoy a dram of rum with the wench. It'll help warm your blood."

Scully caught the coin and tucked it into his pocket before gripping the barmaid roughly by the arm and jerking her to her feet. "Get up them stairs, ye bitch, and I'll show ye what a real man can do." Casting one last sneer of disgust in Royale's direction, he shoved the whore toward the narrow flight of steps that led to the second floor, where she took her customers nightly.

"I think we've enjoyed enough of this company for one night," Royale said as she turned back to Tim and Fishbait.

"Aye, ye're right," the quartermaster muttered as they turned toward the door. "If we don't hurry, we may have to fight off a few others. I suspect from the looks ye've been receiving from more than one of these cutthroats that they'd like to try a hand at seducing ye, since they now think ye're of their persuasion."

Glancing warily around the tavern, Royale saw several pairs of lust-filled eyes focused on her and realized with a start that Fishbait was right in his assumption. She had to restrain herself from breaking into a run as they strode through the maze of tables and, leaving behind the smelly interior of the Pieces of Eight, walked out into the balmy night.

The fresh air was welcome to the three who strolled toward the harbor by the light of the full moon. Royale drew in several long, cleansing breaths to rid her lungs of the smoke and stench of the tavern. When they reached the sea wall, she paused and glanced out across the glistening water toward the *Raven*. The conversation between the pirate and the barmaid kept replaying itself in her mind. She had learned that the governor of Jamaica was willing to give letters of marque to those who joined Henry Morgan, though for what reason she didn't know.

Thoughtfully she gazed at her ship as she considered her reason for having come to Tortuga. If she chose to sail to Jamaica and join Morgan, she would have to set her vendetta against El Diablo aside for the moment. However, if she could gain her letter of marque, she would be free to pursue him and able to sell their booty at ports other than Tortuga. Her moment of reflection past, she glanced up at Tim, who stood grinning down at her.

"We're bound for Jamaica, right?" he said.

"Aye, it's to Jamaica for the *Raven*," Royale agreed, and smiled.

Fishbait looked from one young face to the other as he cocked his head to one side and said, "Then ye're giving up yer pirating?"

"Nay, Fishbait. For now we are still sailing under the Jolly Roger. We're going to Jamaica, but until Morgan accepts us and guarantees our letter of marque, we'll continue to plunder vessels as planned," Royale said as she descended the steps to the sandy beach.

With the morning tide the *Raven* slipped quietly from the bay and out into the Windward Passage, sailing southwest toward Jamaica and Port Royal—Henry Morgan's home port.

The weather was good. No clouds marred the blue sky

that merged with the turquoise waters of the sea on the horizon as the frigate sliced through the choppy waves. A crisp southerly breeze filled her white canvas sails, holding them taut as it pushed the vessel speedily toward its destination.

From her place on the poop deck, Royale stood with her hands loosely clasped behind her and her face turned into the wind, musing over the strange turn of events. For the first time since she'd read the King's edict denying her petition and making her his ward, she felt as if she had a chance to put her life back on the right course.

Recalling the episode in the tavern, she knew she would have few regrets over leaving her brief career of piracy. She had no desire to be one of the vermin who skulked about the stronghold on Tortuga. However, she was candid enough with herself to realize that if things did not go as she planned with Morgan, she would have no other course but to return to that low type of life-style. Piracy would be the only means left for regaining what was rightfully hers, no matter what legal questions were raised by her bastardy.

The word caused her to wince inwardly, and she unconsciously raised her chin at a defiant angle. John Carrington had been her father, whatever anyone else said. He had loved her as if she was the product of his loins, rather than an accident from her mother's unfortunate love affair before their marriage.

Royale's expression softened as she thought of the man she considered to have been her father. There were few men born as good as John Carrington. He had accepted his wife's two-year-old bastard as his own upon their marriage and had raised her with love and pride. Though he had not legally adopted Royale, he had given her his name when he had moved his family to Witch's Cay. From the day of their arrival, no one ever knew that she was not in truth Sir John's daughter by blood.

It had been Sir John himself who had reinforced the strong bond between them after her mother had told her the truth about their lack of kinship. He had cradled her in his arms as he explained to her that people often made mistakes in their lives, but that he had never considered her birth one of them. Barring the small matter of her conception, she was his daughter, and no one had the right to say differently.

It had been his love and understanding that had seen her through the most devastating moment of her life, and ever since she had forced herself to forget that they were not actually father and daughter. It had been only during the year since Sir John's death that the question of her true sire's identity had begun to creep into her conscious thoughts. Against her will, she found herself wondering who the man was and if he still lived. However, that mystery would never be solved. Her parents had guarded the secret of the man's identity well, and it had died with them.

As the question again arose in her mind, her features reflected the tension it created within her. She pressed her lips into a firm line as she valiantly sought to be rid of it. No, she mused with asperity, I don't want to know. Sir John was my father, no one else. He is the one who loved me and worked to ensure my future, and because of that love I'll fight to have Good Fortune, as he intended. I owe that to his memory, and I'll not betray him.

"You're thinking of Sir John, aren't you?" Tim said softly at her side.

"Aye, Tim, I was thinking of Father. How did you know?" she asked as she tried to slam a mental door on her painful reverie.

"You had that faraway look in your eyes that you always get when you muse upon the past." Folding his arms across his chest, he leaned back against the rail and studied her. "And when you do so, your thoughts usually end up with Sir John."

"Do you always know what I'm thinking?" Royale asked, wanting to change the painful subject.

"Not always. It's only when you're not aware that anyone is watching you that I can see your feelings upon your face. Most of the time you're able to hide them from the world, but I've been with you too many years not to be familiar with your moods. I know Sir John's death still hurts you."

Royale regarded Tim thoughtfully for a long moment before turning her eyes once more to the horizon. He knew her well—often too well for comfort. He shared all of her secrets, with the exception of the night in Gregory Town and the fact of her bastardy. The only person left who was privy to that was Adele. She had been with Royale the day she had gone to her mother's sickbed to learn that she was not her father's daughter. Royale had feigned a calm acceptance of the news so as not to bring more pain to her dying mother; it had been in Adele's arms that she had wept out her pain after the door to the sickroom had closed behind them.

"Aye, Tim, I miss him greatly," Royale said at last, her throat suddenly growing tight with unshed tears.

"Sail ho, due south, starboard side," cried the lookout from the crow's nest. His warning halted further conversation between the two friends.

Tim watched Royale's expression change as she locked away her thoughts of the past and once more became the captain of the *Raven*. He, like the rest of the crew, admired the strength and courage she had learned from her father. They were as alike as two people could ever be; both were stubborn, brave, and proud. They would ask nothing of anyone that they would not do themselves. Tim's esteem for Royale grew with each passing day.

She raised her hand to shade her eyes as she squinted against the bright sun and peered in the direction the watch had indicated. From her position she could only discern a small speck on the horizon that told her little about the approaching vessel. Cupping her hands around her mouth, she shouted, "Can you see her colors?"

The brass spyglass flashed in the sun as the lookout raised it once more. After several moments he called, "She flies Spain's flag, and from the way she sits in the water, her hold is full."

"It's about time," Royale said as she turned to Tim. "To the wheel, helmsman. El Diablo has found his next prize."

Cocking one sandy brow at Royale, he asked, "You're still planning to use that ruse? I thought you had forgotten all about that when we set out for Jamaica."

Royale grinned up at her helmsman. "It seems, Tim, you can't read my mind as well as you thought. Nothing has changed, nor will it, for that matter."

Recalling the last time he had ventured to voice an opinion contrary to hers, Tim swallowed back the argument that rose to his lips. She had issued her ultimatum at Good Fortune, and he had accepted it. Now he could not protest her actions. She was his captain, and he would obey her orders without question. Though he said no more as he turned and strode back to the helm, his face reflected his apprehension.

Noting his expression, Royale gave a mental shrug as she strode from the poop deck and gave the order to make ready to attack. She didn't like there to be any disagreement between herself and Tim, but she would no more change her mind about using El Diablo's name than she would about regaining Good Fortune. She owed that to Sir

John, just as she owed herself a debt of revenge that would be paid in full by the time she finished with the masked pirate.

The *Raven*'s crew scurried to obey their captain's orders. They loaded cannon, filled fire buckets with coals to light the fuses, and scattered sand upon the deck to ensure secure footing when the time came to board the other vessel, or in the event of blood being spilled if their quarry chose to fight. They armed themselves with several pistols each and short swords for fighting in close quarters; each man knew his duty and carried it out with efficiency.

Seeing everything was well in hand, Royale strode to her cabin and stripped off her fawn-colored britches and white shirt. For her plan to succeed, she had to look the part of El Diablo. She had prepared for that before leaving Good Fortune. Adele had not questioned the motive behind her request to have a black silk shirt and britches made. Had the housekeeper suspected at the time the way Royale intended to use them, she no doubt would have been horrified.

Royale smiled at the thought as she bent over the footlocker and opened it. Her costume lay on top of her other clothing, where she could easily find it when it was needed. Lifting the duplicates of El Diablo's garments from the brassbound chest, she slipped them on before coiling her hair up beneath a black, wide-brimmed hat. To complete the disguise, she masked her features with a piece of slit black silk. Securing the knot, she turned to observe her image in the mirror above the washstand.

The reflection in the glass brought back painful memories. It awakened the feelings she had sought to forget since the night in Gregory Town. She did not want to remember the touch of El Diablo's hands on her flesh nor the passion he had kindled in her heart nor her response to his lovemaking. All she wanted to recall of her experience with the pirate was the pain and humiliation she had suffered at his hand. She could let nothing else intrude upon her thoughts if she intended to carry out her vendetta.

Annoyed with herself for letting her mind wander back to the tender moments they had shared, Royale buckled on her sword belt and strode purposefully from the cabin. She was eager to encounter the Spanish vessel and set into motion her revenge against the man who aroused such tumultuous and contradictory emotions within her.

As she took the steps up to the poop deck two at a time, Royale's face was set with her resolve. Her eyes glittered with a cold, hard light, and her full lips had thinned into a narrow line. Today would be her first strike at El Diablo, but it would not be her last. Once she reached Jamaica she would have to curtail her reprisals in order to gain her letter of marque, but until then she would play out her ruse and hope that in time it would bring the pirate to her. She would then give full retribution for their one night of passion. The corners of her mouth curled upward, but there was no warmth in the smile that touched her lips as she stood at the rail and watched the distant speck grow until she could see its colors waving in the crisp sea breeze.

True to the lookout's word, the Spanish ship rode low in the water, a sure indication that her hold was filled with cargo. After their disappointing voyage from Witch's Cay to Tortuga, Royale hoped it would be valuable. Her men needed something to lift their spirits, and she had learned that pockets filled with gold always had that effect upon them.

An air of tension seemed to fill the *Raven* as the Spanish galleon neared the frigate. Royale lifted her chin in the air, and her nostrils flared as if scenting for any unexpected danger from their quarry. Raising the spyglass, she peered at the galleon and smiled. The vessel carried only twenty guns. Though the ships were equal in firepower, she knew her ship could easily outmaneuver the much heavier galleon, making it an easy conquest, if no other Spanish ship came to the rescue.

Sir John had taught Royale never to take any unnecessary chances, and, heeding his advice, she scanned the horizon for other sails. Often a galleon would be protected by a Spanish man-of-war, and it would be disastrous for the *Raven* to be caught in such a trap. Pleased to see no sign of an armored escort, she lowered the spyglass and ordered, "Raise the Jolly Roger. Let's let the devils know whom they are dealing with.

"Bring her about, Tim. Fishbait, prepare to fire a warning shot over her bow," Royale commanded as she glanced over her shoulder at the two men.

The *Raven* reacted smoothly to Tim's touch, and she came about, her guns prepared for a broadside if the Spaniards refused to give quarter. The frigate swayed from the concussion of the cannon blast as Royale's order was carried out. The warning shot sailed harmlessly over the galleon's bow, landing in the ocean and spraying water over the deck of the vessel.

The tension mounted as Royale and her crew awaited the Spaniard's answer. When none came, she shouted, "It seems they are hard of hearing, Fishbait. Take out their rigging. Perhaps they'll understand that."

Again the *Raven* was jolted by the explosion of the cannon as it sent a crossbar shot toward the galleon. The two half balls connected by an iron bar sliced easily through the Spanish vessel's rigging, making her sails sag limply toward the deck and crippling her, as Royale had intended.

At last the white flag of surrender inched its way up the galleon's mast. Royale watched its slow progress with a wary eye. The Spaniards had given quarter without firing a shot in their own defense. Instinctively sensing danger, she placed her hand on the hilt of her sword as she ordered Tim to bring the *Raven* alongside the galleon.

The deck of the Spanish ship was suspiciously quiet as the two vessels swayed next to each other. Only a few members of her crew were visible, and Royale cautioned her men to remain on the frigate until she gave the order to board. She suspected that the Spanish captain had realized that his vessel could not outmaneuver her much lighter and smaller ship, so he had decided his best option was hand-to-hand combat. In that manner he could hope to overpower the pirate crew and save his ship and cargo from any further damage.

Tension seemed to crackle in the air as the captains and crews of the two vessels eyed one another, playing out the cat-and-mouse game, each one assessing the other's strength.

"Señor, I suggest you order your crew on deck," Royale shouted in fluent Spanish—another lesson well learned from her father. She knew the other captain could be stalling for time, hoping his escort would arrive to ward off the attack. That was not a chance she was willing to take.

"It seems, señor, that we are at a standoff," the Spanish captain shouted in return, his thin black mustache curling upward at the tips as he sneered.

Royale smiled and shook her head. Her voice was low and filled with determination as she said, "No, señor. We are not at a standoff. Your ploy has failed. I will give you three minutes to have your entire crew on deck or I will give the order to fire."

"But señor, if you fire, you will go down with us. We are too close for you to escape damage. From this short distance your cannon would set off our powder magazine, and the explosion would surely destroy your vessel as well," the Spaniard said, smirking.

"Aye, perhaps my vessel would suffer a minimum of

damage, but I will take that chance to see you at the bottom of the sea if you don't do as I order, and quickly. Your time is running out. El Diablo is known for his daring. Do you wager your life and that of your crew on the chance of seeing us sink with you?'' Royale held her breath. She knew the Spaniard had accurately appraised the situation, but she hoped he would not have the courage to call her dare.

She watched with satisfaction as he mopped his heavy features with a white handkerchief and said something to his second-in-command. The man argued briefly, and then, with a shrug, he gave the order. The hatch opened and a large group of men filed onto the deck, their swarthy faces mottled with anger at having to give quarter to the pirate vessel.

''Now, señor, have your men put all their weapons in the center of the deck,'' Royale ordered as she made ready to swing across the short space between the two ships to board the galleon.

It took only a few moments for the heavily armed boarding party to make the Spanish ship secure. In their search for booty they found only two chests filled with jewels and gold; they brought them on deck to be hoisted over to the *Raven*. The rest of the cargo was equally valuable, but the spices and hardwood bound for the rich houses in Spain were not as easily exchanged.

Eyeing the profusely perspiring Spanish captain, Royale smiled coolly and said, ''Spike their cannon, Fishbait. I doubt our brave captain here would try the same trick twice. The next time he might decide to have the nerve to stand and fight.''

''Aye, Captain,'' Fishbait said with a grin as he motioned several members of their party to the task.

''Señor,'' Royale said as her gaze settled once more on the galleon's flustered captain, ''El Diablo has gone easy on you today, but in the future I may not be so lenient. I suggest you do not try such subterfuge again, or you will pay the price at the end of my sword.''

To emphasize her words, she pressed the tip of her blade against the Spaniard's bulging paunch and watched as his swarthy features paled. With a smile, she bowed from the waist and said, "El Diablo thanks you, señor. Now we will bid you good day and a pleasant voyage.''

She could not suppress her laughter as she grabbed the boarding rope and swung agilely back to the *Raven*'s deck. Revenge tasted sweet—all the more so, since no shots had been fired and no lives had been lost. With her spirits soaring, she ordered Tim to set their course for Jamaica.

Chapter 5

The Raven *sailed past Lime Cay, with its white sand* beaches, and into the wide bay of Port Royal, the buccaneer haven that had gained the reputation of being the wickedest city on earth. Fort Charles, Morgan's headquarters since the king had recalled the fleet in 1662 and disbanded much of the army, sat on the western tip of the Palisadoes, a narrow strip of land that edged and protected the deepwater harbor that made the city so attractive to privateers and pirates alike. The government of Port Royal turned a blind eye to their means of making a living and welcomed them with open arms, seeing in them a force that would defend the city against the Spanish, since they could not rely on the British navy to give them support.

Fort Charles, which had begun as a single round tower, had been enlarged during the past year under Henry Morgan's supervision, and two smaller forts had been built— Fort James and Fort Carlisle. The tax levied by King Charles on brandy had provided the revenue for their construction. The two new forts were located on the harbor side of the Palisadoes, while Fort Charles guarded the channel and bay to ensure the safety of the city against attack from the Spanish.

A treaty had been signed in Madrid in 1667, nearly a

year earlier, between Spain and England, but the Spanish still refused to recognize British possession of Jamaica; because of the continued Spanish claim, the inhabitants of Port Royal were constantly on guard against reprisals.

Eager to settle the business that had brought her to the island, Royale paid little heed to Jamaica's verdant hills, from which the Blue Mountains rose majestically in the distance. She felt only a sense of restlessness that made her pace the *Raven*'s deck as the frigate eased through the channel and around the tip of the Palisadoes to drop anchor in the harbor of Port Royal.

For several long minutes Royale observed the busy quay. Wharfs lined the shore for more than a half mile. There was much activity, but, as she would soon learn, there was little loading or unloading of cargo, since it was already afternoon. Due to high wharfage costs, captains moored their vessels at the docks for only short periods of time, and most were loaded and unloaded at dawn to save on the fees.

The quay was lined with warehouses. The largest was the King's warehouse, a two-hundred-and-thirty-four-foot structure that fronted Thames Street just behind the King's wharf, where an agent of the crown levied its ten-percent charge on the merchandise unloaded from the ships before letting it be stored in the warehouse.

Looking beyond the busy quay, Royale gazed at the thickly clustered buildings of the city. From her vantage point they seemed a solid mass, with some structures towering two to four stories high. They varied in color, and she suspected that the more prosperous of Port Royal's residents built their homes from brick, while the less fortunate settled for stucco and wood.

Port Royal is a thriving city, she thought as she glanced at the many ships that lay at anchor in the harbor. She could well understand England's determination to keep Jamaica from the Spanish. The plunder brought in by the pirates and privateers helped fill the King's coffers.

"The King's coffers," Royale mused aloud. It had been for that reason that she had chosen to sell her booty in Tortuga. It would have been preferable to use Port Royal but for the fact that it was held by England and Charles II profited from each transaction that took place there. In her opinion, the King had already gained enough from her and would get no more if she had her way.

Royale frowned and turned her mind to her own reason for coming to Port Royal. Ordering Fishbait to make the boat ready to take them ashore, she looked at her helmsman, who stood silently at her side.

"Tim, I'll leave you to see that the *Raven* is secure before you let the men go ashore."

Tim frowned and clamped his lips tightly together. He didn't like the idea of Royale going ashore with only Fishbait as her escort, but he knew from past experience that it was useless to argue the point.

"No, it won't do you any good to try to talk me out of it," Royale said. She laughed at the look of surprise that flickered over his features. "You aren't the only person who can read minds, Tim. Especially when your face mirrors the thunderclouds that are building on the horizon."

"Aye, so it would seem. But at least you know how I feel in the matter. I just hope Fishbait can keep you out of mischief," Tim said, a slow smile easing the rigid line of his mouth.

"I shouldn't run into any trouble as long as there are no buxom wenches who want to seduce me," Royale said, and laughed, now able to see the humor of the situation in Tortuga.

Tim chuckled at the memory. He would never forget her expression when the whore had kissed her. Indignation, revulsion, and shock had passed across her lovely face as she bolted from the chair like a streak of lightning. Had the encounter not been so dangerous because of the pirate, Scully, it would have been hilarious. Grinning, Tim said, "Aye, but it's not always the women you have to guard against. As I recall, it was the opposite sex that caused you to end up looking like a drowned rat the night you came aboard from Gregory Town."

Royale's smile faded and her eyes took on the color of a stormy sea as her light, bantering mood fled. The mention of Gregory Town brought back too many unwanted memories.

"Don't ever mention that night to me again. I'm tired to death of your mother hen attitude toward me. During the past year I've proven my ability to take care of myself, and I see no reason for you to constantly hover around me as if I were a child. I'm your captain, not your charge, and it's high time you realized that fact. I thought I had made that point clear to you before we set sail from Witch's Cay. If I didn't, I'll reaffirm it now. I'm the captain of this vessel, and I'll do as I damned well please. Not you nor anyone else has the right to say me nay when I make a decision. Is that understood?"

Startled by her rapid change of mood and her sharp reprimand, Tim furrowed his forehead in bewilderment as he looked at Royale from beneath lowered brows. He could not understand what had changed between them in the past weeks. Until recently they had always been able to banter back and forth without any hostility developing between them, but now her actions hurt and confused him, and he could say little more than a gruff, "Aye, it's understood, Captain," before he turned away.

Royale was immediately contrite over her abrupt manner with Tim. She sensed his hurt and wanted to ease it. She reached out to stop him, but before her hand could touch his arm she let it fall back to her side. It was best to let it be. She couldn't explain her outburst to him any more than she could understand her violent reaction to the mere mention of the night she'd spent in the masked pirate's arms.

Her emotions of late seemed to be precariously balanced on the edge of a deep, unknown chasm that threatened to engulf her if she didn't fight with all her willpower to stay above it. Because of the strain she was under, she had become a vindictive, quick-tempered shrew who could not control her fits of fury when they erupted, often with little or no provocation.

"Damn," she muttered under her breath as she gripped the ship's rail, her knuckles white. She had thought when they had captured the galleon in El Diablo's name that she could appease the demon who gnawed unmercifully at her insides, but that had not been the case. Her triumph had lasted only until that night when she lay alone in her bunk, trying to find in sleep escape from the memories of the passion she had shared with the masked pirate. She had tossed fitfully, slumber eluding her as the ghostly specter of her conscience raised its head, mocking her with the knowledge that she had given herself of her own free will to a man who had carelessly used her innocence to slake his lust without thought of her feelings.

Her humiliation had burned away the small satisfaction she had gleaned from plundering the Spanish vessel and had left her more staunchly determined to pursue her revenge upon El Diablo. She knew herself well enough to know that until she met him face to face she would find no peace to calm the tempest that raged within her.

"Captain," Fishbait called from the deck below, "the boat is ready for us to go ashore."

Royale gave herself a mental shake and glanced one last time at Tim before joining the quartermaster at the rail. She followed Fishbait down the rope ladder and into the dinghy. As it pulled away from the side of the *Raven*, her eyes rested briefly on the ship's black hull. She pressed her lips firmly together and her eyes glittered with ire as she thought, El Diablo, you will pay for every sleepless night I've had and every harsh word I've uttered because of the turmoil you've created in my life.

Fishbait's heavily muscled arms made swift work of rowing them the short distance to shore. The aroma of the fish market filled the air as he secured the small craft on the sandy beach. It was a smell he remembered well from the days when he had come to Port Royal with Sir John as his captain.

Recalling the blond giant who had been his late master, he glanced at the silent figure at his side, marveling at the similarity between the two, though strangely she lacked any physical resemblance to her father. In fact, he would have wondered who her father was if she had not possessed the same stubborn pride and determination as Sir John. Fishbait smiled to himself as he led the way up the steps to Thames Street, the thoroughfare that fronted the harbor and traversed the entire length of the quay from Fort James to Fort Carlisle. His young captain was Sir John's daughter, all right; no one could ever deny that, he mused as they reached the ballast-cobbled street.

Noting the bewildered expression on Royale's face as she paused and glanced about the busy street, he was glad that she had chosen him to escort her into the city. As he had done when he'd first visited Port Royal, she would soon learn that the city drew its immense prosperity from the ships that arrived from Europe. They traded wine, silk, and other commodities that were unavailable on the island for locally produced sugar, indigo, and spices. The city teemed with people engaged in carrying out that exchange.

Fishbait scanned the many faces that passed them. Jamaica was a buccaneer haven, but unlike Tortuga, its populace varied from pirates to rich English plantation owners who grew the indigo and sugar further inland, where the land was fertile. The city drew every type of humanity, each seeking a share of the wealth that poured into it. Everyone believed the legend that fortunes were made in a day and lost in a night there. However, each man thought he would be the one who could retain his wealth, if he was lucky enough to obtain it.

Fishbait knew great sums of money were squandered in Port Royal. He had seen it happen far too often when men came into port with the attitude of easy come, easy go. Many a sailor entered the taverns with pockets lined with gold and left the next morning empty-handed, having spent it all on rum and women. Every vice was available for a price, and it was this that had gained Port Royal its reputation as a godless city where profligacy, drunkenness, and wantonness overflowed into the crowded streets.

Aye, he was glad he had come with his young captain. He could steer her away from some of the unsavory parts of the city and guard her against its noted vices. However, there was one thing he couldn't help her with, and that was locating Henry Morgan. It had been several years since his last visit to Port Royal, and at that time the army had still been in charge of it, rather than the privateers.

Royale felt lost as she gazed at the maze of brick-walled buildings with their red-tiled roofs. It seemed that finding Henry Morgan would not be as easy as she had first surmised. She glanced at her quartermaster, hoping he would know where to go, but his shrug killed that hope before it was completely born.

Seeing several men smoking long-stemmed clay pipes as they sat on barrels playing a game of dice in the shade of the cooper's shop, Royale crossed the street and paused before them. They eyed her and her companion curiously for a moment before turning back to their game without speaking. New arrivals in Port Royal were an everyday occurrence, and only a moment's interest was taken in any of them.

"Can you direct me to Henry Morgan's headquarters?" Royale asked.

The men paused in their play and turned to regard the young captain thoughtfully for a long moment before one took his pipe from between his black stubs of teeth and said, "Aye, fer a price."

Digging into her pocket, Royale drew out a coin and tossed it to the spokesman. "There's your price. Now, where is Morgan located?"

The man bit the coin, testing its value, before he dropped it into his pocket and pointed toward the west. "At Fort Charles," he said before returning to his game of chance.

Royale was relieved to see Fishbait nod when she glanced at him. She suspected that she would never find her way through the city, much less reach Fort Charles, without her quartermaster's knowledge of Port Royal. She was even more grateful for his help as they traversed the narrow maze of streets. It was not an easy task even for someone who knew where he was going. The siesta hour was over and the streets were crowded with people. On several occasions their progress was delayed when they had to detour around brawls that had begun inside the taverns and then spilled outside to embroil the passersby who were unfortunate enough to be nearby. Maneuvering through the section where the merchants' stalls were located was nearly as hazardous. Each sought to sell more than his neighbor, at times forcibly dragging customers to his booth.

Port Royal throbbed with life. Taverns and brothels were plentiful, well patronized by the varying assortment of merchants who came to the city to become rich. They succeeded in a short span of time by trading not only with the European captains but with the pirates and privateers who disposed of their spoils in Port Royal. No one questioned any man's business, and because of this reticence, the city and its people prospered.

By the time Royale and Fishbait had made their way through the sandy, winding streets to reach Fort Charles, the heat of the afternoon had beaded their brows with perspiration. Their discomfort was little eased when they stepped out of the bright sun into the dim interior of Morgan's headquarters. The roof was arched and high, but because of the thick brick walls, the constant heat, and the dampness from the sea, the humidity was suffocating.

Royale paused upon the threshold to let her eyes adjust to the gloomy interior of the fort before crossing the chamber to stand before the rough-hewn table where one of Morgan's men napped with his chin resting on his chest. Giving the table a sharp rap with the hilt of her sword, she roused the man from his slumber and said, "I'm here to see Henry Morgan."

The man yawned widely as he peered up at the young captain before him. "That's too bad, 'cause he ain't here."

"Then where is he?" Royale asked, exasperated that they might have come this far only to be disappointed.

"Now, I ain't supposed to just tell everyone that asks about him where he is, even if I could remember," the man said as he sat up and scratched his chest.

"Perhaps this will help your memory," Royale said as she dug into her pocket and slapped several gold coins down on the table. The man reached for the coins, but the hilt of her sword blocked his way before he could touch them. She shook her head and smiled. "No, you'll not get paid until I know the whereabouts of Henry Morgan."

The man gave her a sullen look, his ruddy features flushing a deeper hue as he said, "He's at Littleton's tavern, near Fort James."

"Then we'll bid you good day," Royale said, lifting her sword off the coins, which the man quickly pocketed.

Though seeking out Morgan at Littleton's tavern meant another hot walk through the city, it came as a welcome relief to Royale. She was used to close quarters on her ship, but the fort's heavy atmosphere was stifling. The walk would be uncomfortable, but at least they might catch a small breath of air blowing in off the sea.

As Royale and Fishbait stepped back into the bright sunlight of the drill yard the quartermaster released a long breath and wiped his damp face with the back of his work-roughened hand. "This heat is hell. I'd be better off with a large tankard of cool ale." Glancing up at the grayish, cottony clouds that were boiling overhead, he continued, "It's as hot as Hades here, and I suspect the weather is going to play the devil from the looks of them clouds. There's a storm a-brewing in the west."

Royale paused outside the thick wooden gates and looked toward the horizon. It was already dark and foreboding, indicating that the quartermaster's prediction would soon prove true. She smiled. The thought of a storm seemed to bring her renewed energy, erasing the fatigue brought on by their long walk in the heat.

It had been so all of her life. Even as a child, when others at Good Fortune had trembled from the loud explosions of thunder and the jagged streaks of lightning, Royale had loved turbulent weather.

Storms seemed to give her strength, and she savored them, much to Adele's frustration through the years. The housekeeper could not keep her young charge from leaving the safety of the house and often found Royale on the balcony outside her room, standing with her face lifted to the raging tempest as the wind and rain whipped about her.

Thunderstorms could not be harnessed to man's will, and that had been their fascination for Royale. She felt an affinity with them, more so now than at any other time in her life. Men sought to dominate and mold her to their will, and she was resolved to show them that they would fail with her as they did when they stood against the forces of nature.

As she breathed in the cool air that blew off the bay, the last vestiges of fatigue evaporated from her body. She raised her chin in the air, boldly defiant once more.

The storm moved swiftly across the open sea, and by the time Royale and Fishbait had made their way back to the harbor by way of Fisher's Row, the sun was totally obscured by dark gray-green clouds. The first heavy drops of rain pelted them as they reached the entrance of Littleton's tavern. The wind whipped the wooden sign over the doorway that proclaimed the name, and it squealed in protest on its rusty hinges as the two strode into the dim, smoky interior.

A deep, angry rumble of thunder shook the building, rattling the onion-shaped bottles of rum and wine that lined the shelves behind the long, rough-hewn bar. From the ceiling, brass ship's lanterns swayed with nature's jarring impact. Their light cast elongated shadows over the tavern's patrons as they sat guzzling the dark Jamaican rum while they gamed and regaled one another with stories of their voyages. Interested only in their own affairs, they paid no heed to the slender youth and his weatherbeaten companion as they made their way through the maze of tables and chairs.

A large man with one ear stood behind the bar, polishing pewter tankards. The lantern light shimmered on the gold earring that dangled from the heavy lobe of the lone appendage and shone on his bald pate. He showed little inclination to serve the newcomers until Royale slapped a silver coin down on the rough wooden surface of the bar and ordered two rums in a deep timbre, so as not to arouse suspicions about her sex.

With a grunt and nod the barkeep poured their drinks and set them down with a thud before picking up the coin and dropping it into the leather pouch that hung from a cord about his obese waist. With another grunt he returned to his task, blowing on the shining metal before buffing it with a cloth.

"A friendly gent, ain't he?" Fishbait mumbled as he lifted his tankard to his lips. He took several long swallows before releasing a loud belch and wiping his mouth with his sleeve. "That does me old gullet good," he said with a satisfied grin, then drained the contents of the tankard and set it back down. "I kin use another dram of that, me good man."

Royale leaned negligently against the bar as she, too, lifted her tankard to her lips. She might detest the taste of rum, but she would drink it. She had to act like a sailor fresh in from a voyage if she was to succeed with her ruse. Casually, as if enjoying her drink, she surveyed the tavern's customers, her gaze taking in each rough face, as she hoped to discern the famous Henry Morgan among the patrons.

Spying a group of men sitting toward the rear of the building, she surmised from the cut of their clothing that they were not just ordinary sailors celebrating a successful voyage. After taking a deep swallow of rum to fortify her courage, she set the tankard down with an air of determination and strode purposefully toward the group, who conversed quietly among themselves.

The brass lantern hanging over their table cast a warm glow upon the four men. Its soft light gentled the harsh features of three of them while emphasizing the dark good looks of the fourth.

Royale came to an abrupt halt at the sight of his features.

The ebony eyes and hair, combined with his arrogant expression, vividly recalled to her mind another pirate whose sensual good looks haunted her nights and days.

The involuntary sound that escaped her lips as she gazed at the man halted their conversation and drew their attention to her. They regarded her with eyes filled with varying degrees of interest, but it was the dark man who spoke first as he leaned back in his chair, tipping it carelessly onto its two back legs, the motion making the muscles in his thighs bulge as he balanced his weight. A slow smile spread over the shapely mouth beneath his dark mustache as he examined her from head to toe.

"Do you have some business with us, boy, or did you just come to stare?"

Collecting her wits and forcing her thoughts away from El Diablo, Royale said, "Aye, I've come to see Henry Morgan. I was told he was here."

"Henry Morgan?" the dark man mused aloud, touching the tips of his mustache as if trying to recall the name. "Now, what would a young man like you be needing with an old pirate like him?"

"I've come to join his expedition. I was told in Tortuga that he was looking for men and ships. Do you know of his whereabouts?" she asked, suddenly feeling as if she were the butt of some unspoken jest of the men. Unconsciously, she lifted her chin in the air as she glared at the spokesman.

The man's three companions chuckled, and the sound grated on her nerves. Their mirth at her expense irritated her unreasonably. She flashed each a hostile look before letting her eyes rest once more on the dark-haired man. The twinkle she saw in his eyes further served to increase her ire. The heat of her anger rose steadily as he sat casually regarding her, his long, tapering fingers rubbing thoughtfully at his lean jaw and square chin as if he was considering whether or not to answer her question. She had to clamp a firm hold on her temper. She knew it would serve little purpose to vent her ill humor as she longed to do. Drawing in a deep breath, she awaited his answer.

"Aye, I know his whereabouts, and since I'm closer to Henry Morgan than any man alive, I can already give you his answer and spare you the trouble of searching him out," he said at last. After another nerve-rending pause, he continued, "He'll not have a young pup like you serving under him. I suggest you tuck your tail between your legs and go home to your mother until you've gained a few more years. Morgan needs men, not boys."

"I prefer to hear Morgan's answer from himself, not some drunken cur," Royale said as she glared at the man. "I've come to see Henry Morgan, and I don't intend to leave Port Royal until I do."

"Then you've seen him and heard his answer. Now get yourself gone. I've no time to waste on young boys pretending they're men," Henry Morgan said, and he slammed the chair down on the floor, the loud sound suddenly silencing the entire room.

Royale found herself momentarily speechless as she realized with whom she spoke. She gaped at Morgan, her face reflecting her shock at finding the man she had called a drunken cur to be in fact the one whose favor she sought. Seeing her chances of gaining her letter of marque slowly fade into obscurity, but still unwilling to give up, she braced her hands on her hips, eyeing Morgan with hostility. The angry light that flashed in her eyes matched the lightning that ripped through the tropical air, followed by a deafening roar of thunder that rumbled like a huge cannonball across the sea and land.

"It seems that your reputation for being a fair man to serve under has been much exaggerated. A fair man would at least give me a chance to prove my worth without judging me by my appearance," Royale spat, her eyes raking insultingly over Morgan. "Aren't you fortunate that *your* first commander did not react in the same manner?"

"For one so young and small, you speak very foolishly," Morgan said as he rose to his feet, his lean body uncoiling like that of a lithe, savage animal. His height made Royale appear even smaller as he towered over her, his swarthy features flushing with annoyance.

"I suggest you get out of my sight if you want to live to be an old man. Go home, boy, and gain some wisdom before your reckless tongue offends someone who is less lenient than I."

Undaunted and letting her own temper have free rein, Royale eyed Morgan belligerently. "I may be small, but that does not mean that I can't fight as well as any man present, and that includes you."

"Damn me, boy, but you are stubborn," Morgan said, and laughed, but there was no humor in it. "I have need of men on my expedition into Cuba. Were I to take you along, the Spaniards would have you for breakfast and still go hungry."

"Cuba?" Royale asked, momentarily forgetting their quarrel.

"Aye, Cuba. Since the British fleet can no longer protect Jamaica because of their damned treaty with Spain and their lack of funds, Governor Modyford fears an invasion and needs every man and ship I can commission to join me in an effort to thwart the Spaniards before they can launch an attack here. That's why he chose me, boy. He knows I can give him the men and ships he needs. Now, I'm telling you for the last time, go home, boy, until you can at least grow a beard."

"You're in need of ships," Royale said quickly, seeing the opportunity she needed to convince Morgan to let her sail with him, "and I captain the *Raven*; she's a twenty-gun frigate. I've come to volunteer her services, if you agree to assist me in getting a letter of marque from your governor.''

Morgan chuckled at the youth's bravado. He had to grant him persistence, if nothing else. His offer of the frigate was a temptation hard for the privateer to resist, but he still could not accept it. He needed seasoned men to go against the Spaniards in Cuba. Giving a rueful shake of his head, he said, ''I've given you my answer. Now be off with you. Come back when you are full-grown, and then we can talk.''

''Damn you, Henry Morgan,'' Royale spat in exasperation. ''I may be young, but I'm as good a captain as any man who serves you. You have no right to question my abilities.''

Morgan had begun to turn away, thinking the conversation at an end, but at these words he slowly faced her once more, his eyes flashing with a deadly fire that made the men at the table hold their breaths. No one cursed Morgan and came away unscathed. He was well noted for his violent temper, and many had paid with their lives for saying less to him than the youth had done. The boy seemed to dare the privateer to put an end to his life.

The air in the tavern was laced with tension as Royale and Morgan faced each other. Silence lay like a heavy mantle over the group of spectators as they waited for Morgan's wrath to fall on the foolish boy who stood facing him bravely, with no trace of fear upon his young features.

All eyes were centered on the pair, and no one noted the one-eared barkeep as he moved to the rear of the building and slipped quietly into the adjoining room to meet with the dark-skinned, dark-eyed Spaniard. ''It's as you thought,'' the barkeep whispered. ''Morgan is bound for Cuba.''

The Spaniard nodded and dropped a pouch that jingled

into One Ear's hand. "Gracias, señor," he said softly before climbing through the window and dropping silently to the wet sand outside.

One Ear hiked up his britches as if he had just heeded nature's call as he reentered the taproom to watch the tense drama between Henry Morgan and the youth unfold. His mission was complete, and now he could enjoy seeing the boy take his whipping.

"I have every right to question your abilities," Morgan was saying. "I lead this expedition, and it is my responsibility to ensure that we lose as few lives as possible to the bastards on Cuba. Now, I've had all the guff I'm going to take from you. If you value your life, you'll heed my warning."

Refusing to cower before the cold, deadly glare Morgan bestowed upon her, Royale said, "If you doubt my abilities, then test them. If I fail, I will say no more. However, if I win the contest, then you will agree to let me sail with you, and once the mission is complete, you will help me gain my letter of marque." Royale's eyes reinforced the challenge of her words as she stared unflinchingly into Morgan's rage-flushed face.

Feeling like a large bone the pup would not release without a good whipping to show him who was master, Morgan spoke, his tone indicating his exasperation. "Blast it to hell! If that's the only way to be rid of you, then I'll take up your foolhardy challenge. But I give you fair warning— it may cost your life. Are you prepared for that event?"

"Aye, I'm prepared. Are you?" Royale said, secure in her own abilities with the sword.

"Captain," came the shocked, strangled cry from Fishbait as he shoved his way to Royale's side, "ye cannot do this thing. Give it up. Morgan will run you through without a thought."

"You forget that I won the duel between us, Fishbait," Royale said, and smiled with confidence.

"Aye, Captain, that you did—" The quartermaster's words were abruptly cut off as Morgan drew his sword.

"Now we'll separate the men from the boys," he said, smirking.

"Aye, we will," Royale said as she, too, unscabbarded her sword and kicked a chair out of the way before making the first thrust; the tip of her blade aimed directly at Morgan's heart. She felt a thrill of exultation as a rumble of thunder shook the building. It gave her a renewed surge of confidence, and her laughter rose above the sound of nature at the surprised expression Morgan wore as he deflected the blow.

"So you're determined to play a man's game, are you?" Morgan said as his blade sliced downward, its movement so swift that the air seemed to sing with the vibration.

The storm intensified outside as the duel between the two grew in ferocity within the tavern. The thunder boomed loudly as the steel of their blades met and clashed, sending shimmering sparks into the smoky air. Again and again they met in fierce combat, their struggle overturning tables and chairs in their paths as each sought to win the contest.

Too late Royale realized what Fishbait had been trying to warn her about. As a swordsman Morgan was far superior to the quartermaster or even her father. For all her training and agility, she soon knew that the English privateer had all the advantage in size and speed. He moved like lightning, and she was hard pressed to counter each thrust from his deadly blade. She suspected from the little smile that curled his lips that he was only toying with her, wearing her down until she could fight no more.

The thought infuriated her, but there was little she could do to change things. For the moment she was fighting for her life, and she knew that she was nearing the limit of her endurance. Her arm ached, the muscles burning from the strain. The weight of her own sword sapped her remaining strength as she parried each heavy impact of Morgan's blade. Her breath came in labored gasps, and sweat beaded her brow, running in tiny rivulets down her cheeks as she fought on valiantly. She knew her defeat would soon come, but she refused to give quarter until all hope was completely gone and her life had drained from her onto the sandy floor; for die she would. Morgan had made that clear.

Her heart felt as if it would burst from the exertion as she evaded Morgan's blade time and time again. She felt the muscles in her legs quiver and watched as a triumphant light entered her opponent's eyes. She knew he meant to end the contest at last.

Drawing in one last searing breath as she watched his blade whistle through the air, its target her shoulder, she managed at the last moment to twist to one side to avoid the deadly blow. Then Morgan's sword slashed upward once more, and the tip caught the rim of her wide-brimmed hat, jerking it from her head. A cry of dismay escaped her as her long mane of chestnut hair tumbled over her shoulders in wild disarray.

Time and space seemed to freeze around Morgan as he gaped at the boy, turned suddenly into a girl. He was stunned and wide-eyed with astonishment to find that he had been dueling with a woman. He paused, trying to let his mind register what his eyes saw.

His moment of confusion was the advantage Royale had been seeking, and before he could act, she swung her blade upward, the impact knocking his sword from his hand. With one swift motion she brought the tip of her blade to rest threateningly at the base of his throat.

Her breast rose and fell rapidly as she drew in several deep, ragged breaths. Her hand shook unsteadily from her exertion, and her voice quavered from the effort it took to speak. "Will you keep your word and honor the terms of our agreement?"

Morgan's dark gaze traveled the length of the steel before moving slowly up to the face of the most beautiful woman he had ever encountered. As he met her sea-green gaze a slow smile curled his lips up at the corners, making the tips of his black mustache quiver slightly. Damn if she had not bested him where few men could, he mused, and found the thought as well as the situation ludicrous. Throwing back his dark head, he roared his mirth until his dark lashes were damp with moisture. The girl's beauty and courage restored his good humor and made him look forward to the weeks ahead. He'd keep the bargain he'd made with the slender youth and anticipate as well the pleasurable moments with the young woman he'd turned out to be.

Puzzled by his strange reaction, Royale let down her guard. Before she could make a move to avoid him, he captured her in his powerful embrace and bestowed a hearty kiss upon the soft lips that had formed an "oh" of surprise. The bargain was sealed, more thoroughly than Royale Carrington realized.

With the exception of one man who sat silently frowning at the tableau being played out before him, the tavern erupted into a den of noise more deafening than the thunder from the storm. The spectators clapped and cheered their appreciation at Morgan's handling of his beautiful adversary. His actions served to strengthen his already immense reputation with the fairer sex. There were few women in Port Royal who would not mortgage their souls to spend one night in his bed.

However, unbeknownst to the men who laughed, winked, and slapped one another rowdily on the back as they watched one of their own show the young beauty who was master, Royale Carrington was not among the women who felt honored by Morgan's attention.

His kiss stunned her momentarily, and she stood unresisting in his arms as he devoured her lips, to the wild approval of the other men. But her shock was soon replaced by white-hot rage. With a muffled squeal of protest she brought both fists up against his chest and, with one quick movement, freed herself. Gasping for air, she backed away from the privateer, her eyes shooting fiery sparks.

"How dare you!" Royale spat as she wiped her mouth with the back of her hand. She made to unsheath her sword but realized too late that her weapon lay where it had fallen during the kiss, at Morgan's feet.

Henry Morgan stood with his arms akimbo and his legs splayed as if he still commanded the swaying deck of his ship. Cocking his head to one side, he regarded her with amusement, his lips curling up at the corners, his grin that of an impish little boy who has stolen a sweet and has no regrets about the act.

"I only sought to seal our pact," he said with a chuckle, unable to suppress his mirth at the sight of Royale's infuriated expression.

Giving an angry toss to her gold-streaked mane, which hung in a soft cloud around her face, she glared at him, raising her chin haughtily in the air. "Do you seal every bargain you make with a kiss?"

With the knowing smirk of one who is sure of the effect that his good looks have upon the opposite sex, Morgan glanced around the room, his gaze scanning the crowd, who had grown quiet once more as they watched this new development between the young woman and the privateer. Winking at his audience, he grinned wryly at Royale. "Nay, I can assure you that I do not make it a habit of kissing every captain who joins me."

Several spectators gave a loud hoot of laughter at the mental image his words conjured up. They could just imagine what would happen if Morgan tried to kiss their captains.

"Then, sir, I suggest that from now on you treat me as you do all the others. I am the captain of my own vessel and expect the same respect meted out to me as you give the men who follow you. The fact that I'm a woman does not give you the right to manhandle me," Royale said with a defiant glance at Morgan as she bent to retrieve her weapon.

His fingers clamped down on her wrist and pulled her once more against his hard body. His ebony gaze held hers prisoner as a slow, seductive smile spread over his shapely mouth. "Perhaps I should make it my habit to kiss all my men, if that is the only way to taste the sweetness of *your* lips, Madame Captain."

"Then I suggest you keep yourself well armed at all times. I doubt your men would appreciate such a display," Royale retorted as she glared up at him unflinchingly.

The tavern erupted again in raucous laughter, and Morgan himself could no longer contain his own. He threw back his dark head and roared until once more his lashes glistened with tears of mirth.

"Damn me, Madame Captain, but you're going to make this voyage interesting. You've wit as well as beauty, and that is a rare find." Morgan released her and wiped the dampness from his eyes before retrieving her sword and handing it to her.

His good humor was contagious, and Royale had to hide the smile that tugged at her own lips as she scabbarded her weapon and picked up her wide-brimmed hat. She stuffed the heavy chestnut curls back beneath it, then asked, "When do we sail?"

Morgan's dark gaze traveled appreciatively over her trim form. For the first time in his life he had found a woman he could admire outside the boudoir. She had shown courage and determination in the face of nearly insurmountable odds when she had challenged him. And he did not regret the bargain he had made with her. He knew she would show the same courage when it was required of her in the future. And it *would* be required, once they reached their destination—Puerto Principe, Cuba.

"We sail within the week."

"The *Raven* and her crew will be ready," Royale said, and started to turn away, her business completed. Morgan's hand on her arm stayed her steps, and she cocked her head to one side as she looked up at the privateer. "Is there something else you need?"

"Aye," Morgan said, a slow grin playing over his lips as he noted her finely arched brow raised in question. "What is your name? I can't keep calling you Madame Captain."

Royale smiled for the first time since entering the tavern. It served to make the breath freeze in Morgan's throat. He could feel the heat rise in his loins as he gazed down into her exquisite face.

"Madame Captain suits me well, but my name is Royale Carrington."

"Royale Carrington," Morgan said, rolling it over his tongue several times as if tasting it. "It is fitting. Now let us drink to our success." Lifting the two-quart silver tankard that was reserved for his use only, he ordered, "One Ear, bring my new captain an ale."

Within moments the barkeep had shoved the tankard into Royale's hand, and she was lifting it in toast.

"To our success against the Spanish and to the fairest captain that has ever sailed under my command," Morgan said as he lifted the heavy tankard and took several long swallows. Wiping the excess ale foam from the edge of his mustache with the back of his hand, he glanced once more at the crowd. His keen eyes missed little, and they soon came to rest on the man still sitting at his table.

"*Mon ami,* will you not drink to our success?" he asked pleasantly.

Uncoiling his slender frame from the chair, the Frenchman stood but did not make the effort to raise his tankard to join in the toast.

"*Non,* I will not drink to such foolishness. Surely you do not mean to let this female sail with us, Morgan? Our venture will be doomed from the beginning if you do this thing."

"I have given my word," Morgan said. His swarthy features flushed a darker hue as he eyed the Frenchman.

"Your word?" Pierre LeCruel said, waving his hand in the air, the gesture indicating the insignificance of the matter. "What does it matter if you give your word to a woman? They are fit for nothing more than to warm your bed."

Royale drew in a sharp, angry breath at the insult and opened her mouth to retaliate, but Fishbait's warning hand on her arm made her snap it shut. Behind her she heard the quartermaster breathe a deep sigh of relief.

"My word when given, LeCruel, is my bond. She sails with us," Morgan said, his tone firmly indicating he would brook no question of his authority.

The Frenchman, who had been born Pierre LeCrosse but who now was known as LeCruel because of the vicious way he treated his prisoners when he captured a ship at sea, regarded first Morgan and then Royale through narrowed eyes. He held his thin lips in a harsh line as he said, "I will accept your decision, *mon ami,* but do not think I agree with it. She is trouble. I see it written all over her lovely face. There is no place for anyone on this expedition who cannot carry his own weight. She may have proved she is adequate with the sword in a duel, but that is very different from what we have planned. I will not see her weakness endanger any of my men. Should it become necessary, I will slit her throat myself. The life of one of my men is worth more than ten females. Do I make myself clear?"

"Aye, you've made yourself clear," Morgan said as he eyed the Frenchman. He suspected that it would not be the beautiful captain of the *Raven* who would cause trouble, but Pierre LeCruel.

"To our success," he said, and again raised his tankard as he forced a pleasant smile to his lips.

"To our success," Royale echoed, and smiled with relief. For one fleeting moment she had feared Morgan would change his mind in the face of LeCruel's open hostility toward her. She gazed up at the privateer over the rim of her tankard and saw him wink at her. That small gesture seemed to confirm that it would take more than one Frenchman for him to break their bargain.

The burden that had weighed upon her spirit since she'd received the King's missive seemed to evaporate under Morgan's regard. She sensed that she had found a friend in the privateer. He would help her gain her letter of marque, and then she could set about regaining her home. Once that was done she would deal with the last shadow on her horizon: El Diablo.

Chapter 6

The storm moved swiftly over Jamaica and out to sea, traveling northeast toward Hispaniola. It overtook the *Wicked Mistress* as she sailed southward along the Windward Passage. Fortunately, it did little damage to the frigate beyond drenching the crew as they worked. Nor did it hinder the ship's progress. Since setting sail with the morning tide, she had made good time and had passed the northwestern tip of Hispaniola before the storm struck. Her course was set for Jamaica, and she did not falter as she sailed through the tropical tempest and on into calmer waters.

Drenched to the skin, El Diablo left Reed Barton in charge of cleaning up the decks and made his way to his cabin. He wiped the rain from his face as he strode in and kicked the door closed behind him. His mood was gray—neither happy nor sad but somewhere between the two more distinguishable emotions. Tiny drops of rainwater scattered in a circle around him as he shook his head, freeing his dark hair of the excess moisture before toweling it dry. It curled damply about his shoulders as he shrugged out of his wet clothing and donned a set of garments identical to those he had just discarded. Since the black britches and shirt were the trademark of El Diablo, his wardrobe on the *Wicked Mistress* was limited.

To finish his toilet he pulled his hair back and tied it with a velvet ribbon at the nape of his neck before turning his attention to ridding himself of the chill caused by the rain-cooled wind.

Pouring himself a brandy, he settled his lean frame comfortably in the large leather chair behind his desk. He took several long sips, hoping the fiery liquid would warm him. Finally feeling the effects of the liquor, he relaxed and picked up the missive that he had received the previous night upon his return to the *Wicked Mistress*.

He propped his feet upon the desk as he leaned back and reread the message from his friend Henry Morgan.

Greetings to you, El Diablo,

As you and your highly placed friends are aware, Spain refuses to recognize England's possession of our fair Jamaica. It has been reported to Governor Modyford that they are planning an invasion in the near future. Due to that fact and out of his concern for England's position in the West Indies, our esteemed governor has granted me a special commission to organize the English privateers to go against the Spanish and to take prisoners in an effort to confirm the reports he has received. I need men such as you if this endeavor is to succeed and would be honored to have you join my expedition to attack the Spanish in Cuba. We sail within the month.

Captain Henry Morgan

El Diablo frowned as his eyes rested on the date scribbled at the top of the page. It had been dated three weeks earlier.

"Damn," he muttered aloud as he tossed the missive

upon the desk, "we've less than a week to make it to Jamaica before Morgan sails."

Drinking the brandy down in one gulp, El Diablo—Sir Bran Langston—leaned his head back against the chair and stared up at the beamed ceiling as he reflected upon Morgan's message.

Officially, England was at peace with Spain, and—by taking this venture upon themselves—Morgan and Sir Thomas Modyford could bring the wrath of the crown down upon their heads. Their actions could easily start another war.

Bran gave a rueful smile. He did not blame Morgan or Modyford. He knew that if he were placed in the same situation he, too, would do as they were doing. Spain sought to monopolize the West Indies in their effort to keep all the wealth of the New World to themselves. But men like Henry Morgan and him were just as determined to see that they did not succeed.

Bran's smile deepened as he realized he was looking forward to setting out on this new adventure with Morgan. If he was lucky, it would be the very thing for him to help rid himself of the unrest that kept chewing at his insides since his leaving Good Fortune. With his days filled with battling the Spaniards, his nights might be free of the haunting dreams of the girl from Witch's Cay. So far nothing else had managed to ease his mind. His late-night sojourns on deck, restlessly pacing its scrubbed surface, and the bunk that was often not slept in were proof of the turmoil that possessed him.

"Damn it to hell. She's dead and it's over," Bran cursed softly. "Why do I let the ghost of one young girl torment me?" He found no answer to his question in the silence of the cabin.

Bran welcomed the knock that interrupted his musings and called, "Enter."

Scrimshaw poked his head in the door and grinned. "We've sighted a ship and she's a-flying Spain's colors."

Bran smiled as he once more became the pirate El Diablo. Picking up the piece of black silk from the desk, he said, "Good. It's been too long since our last prize."

"Aye, Captain, it's been a while. It'll be good to feel gold in our pockets agin. None of us had a penny left when the whores and barkeeps got through with us on Tortuga," Scrimshaw said, and chuckled as he followed El Diablo from the cabin up onto the deck.

"Mr. Barton, when we're in range, bring her about for a broadside," El Diablo ordered before glancing at Scrimshaw. "Get the gunners ready. We'll fire a warning shot over her bow first to see if they will give quarter or stand and fight."

"Aye, Captain," Scrimshaw said, and turned away to hurry down the steps that led to the gundeck below. The gunners were already busy bringing powder and shot from the magazine as he stepped through the doorway to the gunnery, where the ten cannons were lined up in a row before the open gunports.

"Look lively, mateys. Our pockets are a-goin' to jingle when we reach Port Royal. Ye'll have the whores a-begging ye fer it when they see yer gold."

"Aye, they beg ye fer it and then leave a little somethin' behind to remember 'em by," Black Jack growled as he scratched at his crotch.

Scrimshaw grinned at his friend's obvious discomfort. "I kin take care of that fer ye," he said as he picked up a pair of tongs and carefully lifted a glowing coal from the fire. "Drop yer britches, Black Jack, and I'll singe the little buggers to death."

Black Jack eyed first the hot coal and then Scrimshaw before he grabbed his crotch protectively with both hands and backed warily away. "I think I'll just keep the little buggers. I've got to where I think of 'em as family."

"So be it, then," Scrimshaw said as he dumped the coal back into the grate. "I was just trying to help a friend."

"Aye," Black Jack muttered as he lifted one of the iron balls and began loading the cannon, "some friend ye are when ye want to burn off a man's jewels."

The breeze ruffled El Diablo's black silk mask as he stood on the poop deck and watched the white flag of surrender inch its way up the mast of the galleon.

He smiled at the sight. The Spaniards were giving quarter without even attempting to fight to save their cargo. The captain of the vessel was either a fool or a coward. El Diablo didn't care which as long as the booty taken from the galleon helped fill his own coffers.

He led the boarding party himself, swinging agilely across the short space that separated the two ships. He landed with feline grace upon the deck, and with sword drawn and ready, he confronted the heavy-jowled Spanish captain. Giving the man a gallant bow, the gesture mocking the man in his defeat, he smiled.

"Señor, pardon us for hindering your voyage, but we have need of your cargo. If you will surrender it, then we will be on our way and detain you no longer," El Diablo said, his Spanish fluent, his tone congenial, as if they were friends who had just met in passing.

"Señor," the Spaniard stuttered, "as you well know, we have no valuables left on board."

"Come now, señor, I have little time to spare and would have your cargo."

The Spaniard threw up his hands in exasperation. The pirate must be mad if he could not remember attacking them less than a week earlier. Wiping the sweat from his brow, he said, "Señor, you do not listen. You know there is nothing left of value on board my vessel. Have your men search the ship if you cannot believe what I say."

"If that is your wish—but I'm warning you, if this is some sort of trick you will pay with your life," El Diablo said. The set of his lean jaw indicated his resolve to follow through with this threat if anything untoward happened. To reaffirm his intentions, he rested the tip of his blade on the Spaniard's bulging abdomen before ordering the ship searched.

"Señor, please, I give you my word. You took everything of value that we possessed last week. Do you not remember?" the Spanish captain asked, his jowls quivering visibly as he mopped his forehead.

El Diablo stared at the man through thickly fringed, narrowed eyes. The man had to be mad as well as a coward. He kept saying they had already taken his cargo. Either he was crazed with fear or this was some new ploy—one he would not get away with, if El Diablo could help it.

"Captain," the bosun shouted as he came running across the deck, "he told ye the truth. There ain't a thing worth taking on this vessel. All that's in the hold is some kind of dark wood and spices."

The Spaniard rolled his eyes heavenward as if seeking divine guidance to help him convince this madman that he had already taken all their gold and jewels.

"See, I do not lie, señor. Less than a week has passed since you attacked my vessel and took everything. Please, señor. I'm sure if you try hard enough you might remember it."

Pressing the point of his sword against the man's belly, El Diablo said impatiently, his voice hard, "I've had enough of this. You keep raving that we attacked your vessel last week, but I can assure you that we did not. If you have hidden your valuables, I suggest you find them at once or be ready to forfeit your life and the lives of your crew.''

The Spaniard's eyes bulged with fright as he glanced down at the sharp blade pricking his middle. His chin trembling, he said, ''How can I convince you? I have no way if you can't remember it yourself.''

''Señor, you are either a madman or a good liar,'' El Diablo said, lowering his sword.

''I am neither,'' the Spanish captain said, suddenly showing courage as he lifted his chin at the affront. ''I know what my eyes tell me. You wear the same black mask and sail the black ship. Those are not easy things to forget. Perhaps, señor, you've had a bump on the head and do not remember, but I have total recall. It was you who attacked my vessel and made away with two trunks of gold and jewels bound for their majesties of Spain.''

''Damn it, man, I've never set foot on your ship before this day. Have you lost all your reasoning?'' El Diablo growled, infuriated that he could not get the man to change his insane story.

''Señor, all I know is what I saw. If it was not you, then perhaps it is another who also wears a black mask and sails a black ship.'' The Spaniard held up his hands, palms upward, pleadingly.

El Diablo released a long breath in disgust, then ordered, ''Spike their blasted cannons, Scrimshaw, and then get back to the *Wicked Mistress*. We've wasted enough time here with this lunatic.''

A few minutes later Scrimshaw poked his shaggy head out of the hatch that led down to the gundeck. ''Captain, they be already spiked. I checked every one of 'em meself, and there's not a working gun on this ship.''

Regarding the Spanish captain speculatively for a long

moment, El Diablo began to wonder at the man's story. Their cannons were useless; that had been the reason no attempt had been made to stand and fight. Obviously, someone had already attacked the galleon. It had not been him but someone who had the audacity to imitate him. Curious to know more, he asked, "Did this so-called masked pirate perhaps give you his name, señor?"

"The last thing the pirate said to me was, 'El Diablo thanks you, señor.' "

"Are you sure he said 'El Diablo'?"

Nodding his head vigorously, the Spaniard said, "Most sure, señor. Those were his exact words."

"Then again, El Diablo thanks you, señor," El Diablo said as he bowed to the captain of the galleon. They had lost valuable time in this unprofitable endeavor, and he could spare no more in trying to find out about the impostor. Ordering the boarding party back to the *Wicked Mistress,* he grabbed the thick hemp rope and swung back to the deck of his own vessel.

"Put her back on course, Mr. Barton," he ordered, and watched as the distance between the frigate and the galleon grew. The *Wicked Mistress*'s white sails filled with the crisp breeze, billowing taut, carrying them swiftly southward toward their destination—Jamaica.

Once the galleon was left behind, Bran untied his mask and stuffed it into his pocket. Tiny lines knit his dark brows as he pondered the strange conversation he'd had with the Spaniard. His chiseled features hardened into an angry granite mask as he stared out across the choppy blue waters. Someone was masquerading as El Diablo, using his reputation to his own advantage and taking the booty that should now be filling the *Wicked Mistress*'s hold.

He had to admit that it was a clever ruse. By doing so

the unknown pirate got away with the booty while El Diablo took the blame.

"Damn," Bran muttered, his hands balling into fists at his side. "He had best pray that he never finds himself crossing my path, or he will find my reputation is well deserved. I'll slit the rogue's throat without a qualm."

"Captain," Scrimshaw said, coming up to him. "I heard what that Spaniard told ye about the black ship."

"What about it?" Bran said, one brow lifting quizzically as he glanced at the man.

"Well—uh—ye see, me and Black Jack spied it in Tortuga, and fer a little while we thought it was the *Wicked Mistress*," Scrimshaw finally managed to stutter. He always found his usually quick tongue thick with apprehension when he had to speak with his commander.

"Did you see who captained her?"

"Nay, we never did because we got interested in the woman who came ashore."

"That sounds about normal for you and Black Jack," El Diablo said, dismissing the sailor.

"Captain, it weren't like that at all. This woman was special. She was the same one that we brought to the *Wicked Mistress* in Gregory Town," Scrimshaw said, and watched as his captain tensed visibly. "She didn't drown like we thought."

"That's impossible. The girl drowned when she jumped overboard," Bran said, forcing his voice to remain calm while his heart fluttered strangely in his chest.

"Nay, we seed her just as plain as day. It was her, all right. We was enjoying our rum in the shade of the seawall when she come ashore with two men. We tried to follow 'em, but—uh—me and Black Jack got a little sidetracked and lost 'er," Scrimshaw said nervously, crushing his seaman's hat in his hands.

The hope that had momentarily sprung to life within Bran

faded as he realized that Scrimshaw and Black Jack had been in their cups. In their inebriated state any woman could have looked like his ward. Feeling a strange emptiness well up within his chest, he said, "The girl you saw couldn't have been the same one from Gregory Town. Now, that will be all, Scrimshaw."

Dismissed and lacking the courage to continue the conversation further, the sailor returned to his duties, all the while grumbling under his breath, "It was her, all right. Damn right it was, even if the captain don't believe what me eyes saw."

The morning shed its gray coat and donned one of gold as the sun crept over the horizon, robing the new day in brightness. It cast long shadows across the *Raven*'s deck as she swayed gently against the restraint of her anchor. Along with the eleven other ships that had joined Morgan's expedition, she lay hidden among the cays off the south coast of Cuba. She was manned only by a skeleton crew; the majority of the men who served on her had rowed to the beach to join the rest of Morgan's men. Including the crew from the *Raven*, he had seven hundred men under his command.

The dozen ships could not be called a grand flotilla, nor could Morgan's recruits be considered an army; but among their ranks were men toughened by years of hard life at sea. Unlike the military, they had not been trained for battle but had learned their skills as a means of self-preservation. Having little to lose beyond their lives and not being bound by a gentleman's code of honor, they would fight savagely to gain the booty on which their livelihoods depended.

From her vantage point atop a sand dune dotted with tawny sea oats, Royale observed the activity on the beach below. Her crew, along with the crews from the other ships, had been working since before dawn, preparing for the thirty-mile trek across the country to Puerto Principe. They would travel on foot through the tropical forests, following the San Pedro River to their destination. It would not be an easy journey for men accustomed more to sailing the seas than to traversing the land, but you could not see any misgivings on their weatherbeaten faces. They joked good-naturedly among themselves about what each would do with his share of the prize that they would find in Puerto Principe.

Royale smiled as she listened to their banter. It was odd to realize that she had grown fond of these outcasts from society who lived their hard, dangerous lives in such a reckless fashion. They had accepted her as one of them, seeming to have no qualms about the fact that she was a female.

Royale frowned. Well, nearly all of Morgan's men had accepted her, she mused to herself as she scanned the beach for the French privateer, Pierre LeCruel. He and his crew had kept their opinions of her to themselves and kept their distance as well. She didn't need a reaffirmation of the objection to her presence the Frenchman had voiced in Port Royal; she saw it often enough in his beady eyes when she chanced to find his gaze resting upon her. The look he gave her made his feelings plain. She could easily read his hatred in his rodentlike eyes.

"Do you not think it would be wise to give up this folly before it causes the death of some of your own men as well as those from the other ships? Take my advice and sail away from here now."

Royale jumped with a start and swung around to find the object of her thoughts regarding her with hostility. Her chin automatically rose in the air at his obvious antagonism.

"I see no reason to change my mind, nor do I have need

of your advice, LeCruel. If you fear for your life, perhaps it is you who should have second thoughts about going on.''

''You bitch,'' LeCruel ground out. He took a threatening step toward her, his eyes flashing with rancor, his fists tight at his sides. ''You think if you smile and swish your hips invitingly that every man will let you have your way, no matter how foolish it may be. I'll not be drawn into that trap, even if Morgan falls for it. I'm warning you, if one of my men dies because of you, you'll live to regret it.'' With that he swung angrily about and stamped away down the dune.

''Royale,'' Tim called as he passed the Frenchman on his way up the dune, ''Morgan's given the order to move.'' Noting for the first time her angry expression, he glanced back at the Frenchman before once more looking at Royale. ''What did LeCruel want?''

''Nothing, Tim,'' Royale said, her voice tight as she swallowed back the rage that bubbled in her throat.

''From the look on your face, I'd say it was more than nothing,'' Tim mused aloud as he turned his attention back to the privateer, who strode briskly down the beach, snapping orders to his men.

Royale's gaze rested briefly on her enemy before she glanced up at her friend. ''It's nothing to be concerned about. I just don't like that man. He makes me feel uneasy every time he comes near me. He reminds me too much of a poisonous snake or a large rat. I can't decide which fits him better, but either one makes a shiver run up my spine.''

''Aye, I know what you mean. He does resemble them both in many ways,'' Tim said, chuckling.

Smiling at their assessment of Pierre LeCruel, Royale and Tim walked back to where the *Raven*'s crew awaited them.

"Morgan's given the order to move. We'll follow his lead, and by tomorrow at dawn we should reach Puerto Principe. It's going to be rough going, but if we're to surprise the Spaniards at first light, there'll be little rest for any of us. We can't let anything slow us down," Royale said to her men.

"Then why are we standing here a-jawing?" Fishbait chimed in as he settled his seaman's hat firmly on his head. "Let's get the move on, mateys, 'cause we don't want to be the last ones there. We can't let them Frenchies get there first and steal all the booty from us."

A rumble of agreement went up from the crew, who had already armed themselves like walking arsenals. Some carried as many as eight pistols strapped across their chests, plus daggers and swords at their waists. It was not an unusual display of weapons. All of Morgan's men were similarly armed. Men who lived at sea and made their living the way pirates and privateers did often fought at close quarters and had little time to draw pistols from holsters when they were needed. Instead they hung them from small loops on their belts and strapped them over their chests for easy access.

Royale buckled her sword around her waist before hanging several pistols from the loops on her belt. Like her men, she would go into the Cuban city well armed. She was their captain, and as such she accepted the responsibility of her position. Sir John would have led his men into battle, and she would do no less.

Settling her wide-brimmed hat more securely on her head, she said, "Since we're all in agreement, 'tis time to move."

The night was black when Morgan's force paused to make camp. The city of Puerto Principe lay sleeping, unaware that beyond the verdant hillside overlooking the town were seven hundred men who had traveled for over eighteen hours on foot to attack at dawn. Their bellies would be filled with biscuit and hardtack; no fires would be lighted to warn the Spanish of their presence. Each man would make his bed upon the hard ground and take from the pouch at his waist his meager meal. When his hunger was appeased, he would seek his rest and dream of the riches to be gained in the morning.

Too tired to even consider eating the stale biscuits and hardtack, Royale slumped to the ground at the base of a tall palm. She was weary to the bone. Her legs and arms ached from the long hours spent walking and cutting her way through the dense undergrowth. Folding her legs up to her chest, she wrapped her arms about them and rested her forehead on her knees. She meant only to close her eyes for a few moments, but as soon as her heavy lashes fluttered down against her cheeks she slept.

She was startled from her exhausted slumber when a large hand clamped down on her arm and jerked her roughly away from the tree. Even in the inky blackness she could see the glimmer of steel as it slashed downward. Instinctively, her mind still drugged with sleep, she reached for the dagger sheathed at her side. The identity of the night-shadowed face of her assailant did not penetrate her mind until she heard his blade strike the bole of the palm and he muttered, "I'd advise you to be a mite more discriminating in your choice of bed partners, Madame Captain."

Morgan used the tip of his sword to flip the two still-squirming halves of the snake into the underbrush as Royale blinked up at him, still recovering from her abrupt awakening, her dagger poised and ready to defend herself from attack.

Seeing her, Morgan chuckled and said, "Damn me, woman. It seems every time I get near you, you are determined to try to stick a blade in me.'' Scabbarding his sword, he continued lightly, ''Even when I'm saving you from a fate worse than myself.''

Royale let her hand sink slowly to her lap as she realized that Morgan had probably saved her life. A snakebite, even if it was nonpoisonous, could easily become infected in the hot climate, and that could lead to a death as horrible as the one her father had suffered.

''You have my thanks, Captain Morgan,'' Royale said, and drew a deep breath in an effort to still her pounding heart.

'' 'Tis not your thanks that I want, Royale, but for now I'll settle for them.'' Morgan hunkered down beside her and cupped her chin in his wide palm. He peered into her shadowed face as he gently traced the delicate line of her jaw with his thumb.

''No, Royale, 'tis not your thanks I want,'' he murmured again.

His innuendo was not lost on her. She felt her mouth go dry as her heart did a rapid tattoo in her chest. She didn't like the feeling his subtle caress aroused within her, nor the memories it revived of El Diablo's touch. Moving away from his hand, she said, ''You have them nonetheless. I could have died from a snakebite, and I'm grateful to you for seeing my danger.''

''Cuba has snakes, scorpions, alligators, and an occasional iguana that lie just waiting for the unwary. 'Tis best to always be on guard,'' Morgan murmured softly as he lifted her hat from her head and let the silken mass of chestnut-colored curls fall around her shoulders. Winding one long strand around his finger, he smiled his pleasure at the feel of its rich texture.

The familiarity of his simple gesture disturbed Royale even more. Without touching his hand, she pulled her hair away from his fingers and scooted further from his side.

She fought to remain calm so that her voice would not reflect the uneasy feelings his actions aroused within her. Seeking to remind him of her position as one of his captains and to turn their conversation to the reason they were camped in the dark glade, she said, "Do you think we will have any trouble taking Puerto Principe?"

"I doubt there will be any, but I've sent LeCruel with several men to check their fortifications. If Puerto Principe is like most Spanish settlements, it will be weakly defended."

As he spoke Morgan made no further effort to follow Royale. He rested one arm indolently over his bent knee, and a self-assured smile curled his lips. For now he would press her no further. He was a firm believer in the old adage that all things come to those who wait. And come she would; he was positive of that. He had decided that he wanted Royale Carrington, and once he made a decision, he would let nothing stand in his way until he gained his desire. And he had wanted her since that first night in the tavern when he'd tasted the honeyed sweetness of her mouth. He had begun even then to gain her trust, and once he accomplished that, Madame Captain would be his for the taking. No woman in the past had been able to withstand his sensual seduction, nor would the young captain of the *Raven*.

Rising in one fluid motion, Morgan handed Royale her hat and said, " 'Tis time you rested. Tomorrow will be another long day. Good night, Madame Captain."

"Good night, Captain Morgan," Royale said, relieved that she would no longer have to abide his unsettling presence. She watched his dark form disappear into the night before she lay back and curled on her side, pillowing her head on her arms.

She tossed from side to side in a futile effort to find a comfortable position upon the hard earth. She could get no rest on her primitive bed, haunted by the memories Henry Morgan's touch had rekindled. His long, gentle fingers had brought back with vivid clarity the moments of passion and desire El Diablo's touch had ignited within her innocent body.

She managed to doze several times during the dark hours of the morning but finally gave up the effort to sleep as the gray light of dawn began to chase the stygian night across the sky toward the west.

Low mumbles and curses floated on the morning air as the camp slowly came awake around her and the men began to make preparations to meet the Spanish just over the hill. Like her comrades in arms, she breakfasted on stale biscuits and hardtack. The coarse fare did not appeal to her, but she forced herself to eat because she knew she would need all her strength in the coming hours.

Feeling somewhat better after her less-than-palatable meal, she rearmed herself with sword and pistols. With her own preparations complete, she stood quietly at the edge of the encampment, regarding the men who served her. Though each knew that some of them would not come back from their encounter with the Spanish, every weathered face seemed to reflect the excitement that she herself felt. It flowed through her veins, overriding her fatigue and apprehension, turning them into the heady sensation that warriors through time had experienced before going into battle.

The feeling was like a stimulant in her blood; it gave her confidence and made her eager to meet the enemy. During the past year she had often experienced the same elation when she had captured another vessel. Her steps reflected her state of mind as she strode purposefully toward her crew. There were no thoughts of the past or the future. All of her energy was centered on the next few hours as they awaited Morgan's orders to take Puerto Principe.

Chapter 7

*S*weat, *gunpowder, and grime smudged Royale's face as* she braced her back against the stucco wall for protection and reloaded her pistols. Around her, musket fire and the screams of the wounded and dying filled the air. Morgan's assumption that Puerto Principe would be an easy conquest had proved misguided. The residents of the city had been forewarned of the invasion and were armed and ready to defend their homes.

For the past three days the battle to take Puerto Principe had been intense. Morgan's forces were slowly winning, but the price for each foot of land they gained was high. They had paid with their blood and their lives. The lead balls of the Spaniards' muskets had also taken a heavy toll on the crew of the *Raven*. Ten of the men who had followed Royale into battle had fallen.

The excitement she had felt that first morning had dissipated within the initial hour of battle. In her innocence, she had expected to find the same thrill in combat that she had felt when capturing a vessel at sea. She soon found she had no taste for watching a man fall dead at her feet, the bullet that ended his life shot from her gun. In the past three days of watching men die she had often wondered what had led her to believe that this would be an easy way to gain her letter of marque.

Royale did not relish killing, but she fought on, as did all of Morgan's men. She had to fight or die. She had chosen to join his expedition, foolishly bragging that she could fight as well as any of his men. Those words had come back to haunt her during the fierce fighting.

Fortunately, she had managed to hold her own, but she did not know how much longer her strength would hold out. She was tired to the bone and wanted nothing more than a place to lay her head down and sleep.

Glancing up into the haggard face of her friend Tim as he stood guard, giving her time to reload her pistols before they made a dash for the house across the street, Royale knew that she would already have been cut down by a Spaniard's musket or sword had not he and Fishbait been her constant companions. On several occasions they had come to her rescue in the nick of time. She was grateful for the friendship that had kept them close to her side at all times.

"I'm ready if you are," Royale said as she hooked two of the loaded weapons to her belt and held one firmly in her hand. She looked stealthily around the corner of the building to make sure their passage was clear.

Only one section of Puerto Principe remained under Spanish control, and Morgan was determined to take that part of the city before nightfall. Over the bloody bodies of several of his men he had vowed to make the Spaniards pay dearly for the lives they had taken. Recalling the demonic light that had entered his eyes as he spoke, Royale could not control the shiver that passed along her spine. She, too, wanted to extract full recompense for the men from her crew who had died, but her revenge seemed a small thing compared to the maniacal vengeance of the privateer.

"I'm as ready as I'll ever be," Tim said, and he waved to Fishbait, who, with several Frenchmen, had been guarding the other end of the alleyway in which they stood. "Fishbait and the Frenchies will guard our rear."

Glancing once more into the street, Royale gave a quick nod as she made to dash into the shadows between the two houses across the sandy thoroughfare. Her flight was cut short as several musket balls splattered the sand at her feet. She jerked to a halt, firing at the two Spaniards who stood on the roof of one of the houses. Her aim was true, and one crumpled as the lead ball ripped into his chest, but his companion had already reloaded his musket and had it aimed directly at Royale. She had no time to reach for another pistol and knew at that moment that she looked her own death in the face. She heard the report of the Spaniard's gun and felt herself knocked to the ground.

Dazed from the impact, her mouth filling with sand from the street, she wondered if death could be that gentle. Another explosion nearby jolted her alert once more, and she pushed herself to her knees, wiping the gritty soil from her eyes and drawing her pistol at the same time.

An eerie silence seemed to hover over the street as her gaze cleared and she saw the Spaniard who had shot at her lying in a bloody heap a few yards away. A strange gurgling sound broke the stillness, and she turned to find Tim lying beside her, his blood gushing from a wound in his chest. Her cry rent the air, her heart pounded with fear, and her pistol fell from her numb fingers as she bent over her friend, raising his head. She cried, "Tim, my God, Tim."

Large tears trembled on her lashes as she pulled her shirt from her britches. She tore a long strip from it and then folded it against the helmsman's chest. Ragged sobs broke from her throat as Fishbait and the Frenchmen lifted Tim's body and carried it to the safety of one of the vacant houses.

The battle for Puerto Principe was forgotten as Royale worked to save her friend's life. She managed to stop the steady trickle of blood from the gaping wound, but beyond that there was little she could do. The only chance she had to save Tim was to find a surgeon to remove the musket ball.

Fishbait did not have to be told what was needed, and as soon as Tim was carried into the elegantly decorated master bedchamber the quartermaster went in search of a surgeon. It was not until early evening that he returned with the haggard physician. For the past three days the man had worked night and day seeing to the wounded.

During the intervening hours Royale had worked feverishly to keep Tim alive. She protested vehemently when Fishbait and the surgeon insisted she leave Tim's side until after the man had extracted the musket ball. Fishbait had to physically force her out the door, telling her she needed a break and that what the physician had to do was not a pretty sight. He knew from experience that even in the helmsman's condition his screams of agony would rend the air once the surgeon started to probe for the piece of lead. His young captain had bravely endured much during the last days, but he was afraid that seeing her friend in such anguish would push her to the breaking point.

Exhausted and unable to make the quartermaster change his mind, Royale stumbled out the door. Her face was drawn with fatigue as she staggered to a halt, wondering where she should go to wait. Hearing the sound of revelry, she moved toward it.

The last man to be felled by the Spaniards of Puerto Principe had been the *Raven*'s helmsman. While Royale had waited for Fishbait to return with the surgeon, Henry Morgan had claimed the city. To the privateer's dismay and anger, there was little to be found. The residents of

Puerto Principe had hidden their valuables after receiving warning of Morgan's intention to attack.

Enraged, Morgan gave his men free rein in the city, letting them loot and destroy as they chose. The smell of smoke permeated the air as the privateers tossed expensive furnishings into the street and set them ablaze, making huge bonfires to celebrate their victory. Donning the finery of the city's residents, they danced with the female captives and ate and drank the best the town had to offer.

With her mind still on her friend, Royale was unaware of the events taking place or of the seamen in her path until she came to the edge of the circle of men who surrounded Henry Morgan and a short, plump Spaniard whose wide eyes looked as if they would bulge from his head as he gazed up at the privateer.

Brushing a straggly, sweat-begrimed strand of hair from her face, she watched as Morgan heated his dagger in the flames of the bonfire. The steel of his blade glowed red as he lifted it from the fire and slowly moved it beneath the Spaniard's chin, the heat of it sizzling the man's pointy beard, making it kink at odd angles.

"Now, you bastard, I want to know how you learned of my plans," Morgan growled, his dark eyes reflecting the light from the bonfire and making his face look satanic as he spoke to Puerto Principe's mayor. "I've been in no Spaniard's company, so I know it has to be a man who is either English or French who spied for you. Now, out with it, damn you, or my blade will slit your throat."

"It—it was the man at the tavern in Port Royal," the mayor stuttered, his eyes riveted to the searing steel.

"That's not good enough, you bastard," Morgan said as he caught the man by the throat and shook him like a mongrel. "I want his name, or you're a dead man."

Trembling visibly, his fat jowls quivering as if they had a life of their own, the mayor nodded. "It—it's the bald

man with only one ear. My informant, uh, never told me
his name, Señor."

Giving the man a brutal shove toward two burly, vi-
cious-faced pirates, Morgan said, "Lock him up." Turning toward the other captives who watched the city's mayor
being dragged away, he growled, "Since you were forewarned of our coming and had time to hide your valuables,
I'm going to give you twenty-four hours to ransom your
homes, or Puerto Principe will be burned to the ground.
Tomorrow night at this time I expect to have your gold in
my hands, or I'll see the city leveled and one member of
each household strung from the gibbet. The choice is yours
to make. I also suggest that you remember that all of you
will be well guarded tonight. Don't try to escape, or your
sentence will be carried out immediately. Is that understood?"

The heads of the frightened assembly bobbed up and
down in unison, then Morgan said, "Take them away before I remember how many of my men have died because
of these bastards." The prisoners eagerly followed their
guards, wanting to put as much distance as possible between themselves and the English privateer whose dark
countenance reminded them of the devil himself.

Noting Royale at the edge of the crowd, Morgan smiled
and crossed the few feet that separated them. Draping his
arm around her shoulders, he led her toward the long, intricately carved table that had been carried into the street
from the mayor's residence. Dragging a gilded leather
monk's chair across the sand, he seated her in it before
pouring her a glass of fine Madeira. Handing her the crystal
goblet, he leaned against the edge of the table, quietly
studying her dirt-smudged features. His smile faded as he
watched her hand tremble in lifting the glass to her lips.
She gulped down the ruby liquid as if it was water.

"Well, Madame Captain, the day—or should I say

days—is ours at last. We hold Puerto Principe,'' he said, bending to refill her glass.

Thinking only of Tim, Royale did not reply as she again drained the goblet, her eyes turning in the direction from which she had just come.

Noting her distraction, Morgan took the glass from her hand and set it on the table. Then he hunkered down in front of her chair so that he could peer into her care-worn face. A frown etched a crooked path across his brow at what he saw there.

''Madame Captain, 'tis not like you to be so quiet. You should be celebrating with my men. Today insures the letter of marque you wanted so desperately.''

Again she did not respond.

''What's wrong? Can you tell me?'' Morgan asked, suddenly worried that the young woman had been pushed beyond her limit by all the death and destruction she had witnessed.

Before Royale could form a reply, a heavily accented voice came from the crowd. ''I can tell you what's wrong with the bitch. She's feeling guilty that her helmsman is dying because he took the lead ball that was meant for her. Had she been a man, she'd have known what to do instead of freezing in the middle of the street like a fool. Captain LeCruel tried to warn her that this was no place for a woman, but she wouldn't listen, and now she's paying with her own man's life. I wonder how many more men are dead because of her.''

With a growl Morgan swung about to face the Frenchman, but before he could make a move toward the man, one of the men from the *Raven* rose in her defense. ''You bloody Frenchy, shut yer lying mouth. Me Captain ain't at fault. She fought as well as any two of ye bastards.''

''You English sea slime, you take up for her because she probably services all of you on the long voyages when you can't get another whore. You think more of what's between your legs than you do of the men who sail with you," the Frenchman said, and he spat upon the ground.

Before anyone could stop the *Raven*'s crewman, he withdrew his dagger and threw it at the Frenchman. It struck its mark, landing between the man's ribs, just left of the center of his chest, piercing his heart and killing him instantly.

Even before his man slid limply to the ground, his blood soaking into the porous sand, Pierre LeCruel stepped forward. "Captain Morgan, I demand immediate justice. I will have my men prepare a rope."

"You call that justice, LeCruel?" Morgan said, and he shook his head. "I'm afraid not. The man will be taken back to Port Royal and tried for murder. If the courts find him guilty, then he will be hanged, and no sooner."

"Morgan," LeCruel said menacingly, his cold gaze sweeping from the privateer to Royale and then back again, "I warned you in the beginning about letting that bitch sail with us. I told you there would be trouble. She has already cost men their lives during the last three days, and now one of my crew is dead because of her. I will not abide any more of this foolishness that you permit because you want to lie between her thighs. I want justice now, and I will have no less."

"LeCruel, I've made my decision. The man will go back to Port Royal for trial. As for Madame Captain, she proved her courage well during the fighting, and you will apologize to her for your words. She does not deserve such slander, as you well know," Morgan said, his eyes glittering dangerously.

"Apologize to that bitch? Never! I spoke the truth," LeCruel spat.

"You will beg the lady's pardon, LeCruel, or you will

live to regret it,'' Morgan said, his hand resting on the hilt of his sword.

A rumble of support rose from the English privateers, making LeCruel glance about warily. His face flushed an ugly red as he realized that his small force was outnumbered two to one. He narrowed his beady eyes as he glared at Morgan and said, ''If you think I will apologize, you are wrong, Morgan. As for your justice in Port Royal, I spit upon it.'' To emphasize his remark, he spat at Morgan's feet. ''I will have my justice in the future. Rest assured of that. But for now, my fellow countrymen and I will leave you and your herd of swine. After today we will sail no more with Englishmen. We leave for Tortuga. But beware, Henry Morgan. You might one day find yourself under our laws and have a taste of our justice.'' With that he strode away from the angry group, the French contingency following in his wake.

''Why'd ye let the bastard get away, Captain?'' one of the English crewmen asked.

''He's not worth the trouble it would take to skewer him, and at the moment we've more important matters to attend to,'' Morgan said. Then he added with a grin, ''And if the Frenchies aren't here tomorrow, there'll be more to divide among good Englishmen.''

''Aye, I kin see yer way of thinking,'' the man said, and he laughed, appeased. The remainder of the group saw Morgan's point as well, as the low grumbles were replaced by laughter, their greed a balm to their wounded pride.

Satisfied that his men would not go after the Frenchmen, Morgan turned his attention back to the white-faced girl who sat with her head bowed and hands clasped tightly in her lap.

''Royale,'' Morgan said, his voice gentle as he tipped up her chin and peered down into her begrimed little face, "you're not at fault. LeCruel spoke out of malice. We all know you fought as well as any man here."

Royale bit into her lower lip as she fought to control the hot tears that stung the backs of her eyelids. Her eyes were large, glistening pools as she looked up at Morgan, trying to believe his words but finding that it was one of the hardest things she had ever tried to do. Tim was fighting for his life, and had it not been for her, he would not have been wounded.

"I understand that you're trying to comfort me, and I appreciate it. But if Tim dies, I'm afraid that LeCruel will have spoken truthfully," Royale managed to say after swallowing back the tightness that clogged her throat.

Morgan regarded her for a few long moments, knowing from his own experience over the past rigorous days that she was near the point of exhaustion. He paid little heed to her words. He knew her spirit had been momentarily beaten down, and when she was well rested he'd see the sparks in her eyes again. In her weary state of mind she had accepted the French pirate's accusations without even attempting to fight back. He knew that would change, but until it did he would goad her into dredging up a tiny bit of her fighting spirit to see her through the next trying days.

"Madame Captain, you disappoint me. After all we've been through, you're now going to turn into a weeping woman. Tsk, tsk, I should never have allowed you to join my expedition. There's no place for weakness here. We've still much work to do. We've all lost men, but I don't see any of my other captains crying into their wine. The living are our responsibility, not the dead."

"Damn you, Morgan," Royale spat as she came abruptly to her feet, her face ashen, her eyes haunted. "Tim's not dead, so don't speak of him as if he was. I know my responsibilities and will see to them." With that she stiffened her back and stalked away.

Morgan smiled as he folded his arms across his chest and leaned back against the edge of the table. For now, she would survive. Turning his thoughts back to the matters at hand, he said, "Purnell, tell my captains to meet me in the mayor's house within the hour."

"Aye, Captain," Purnell said, and he hurried away to do Morgan's bidding.

Lifting the crystal decanter, Morgan poured himself a drink and downed it before smashing the glass into the bonfire. There was business to attend to, and he couldn't worry about the woman. He had no time for celebration, either. There was the matter of the ransom for Puerto Principe, as well as the one-eared barkeep who must be taken care of once he returned to Port Royal. That business would be a pleasure to conclude. The man's death would not be easy. He would suffer as much as or more than the men who had died because of his traitorous actions.

Royale's hand trembled in midair as she reached for the latch on the heavily carved door. She was afraid of what she would learn on the other side. Pausing, she drew several long breaths to help her find the courage to open the door and walk through. Morgan's words seemed to hover about her, challenging the weakness that made her legs quiver. Before her fear could master her once more, she pressed her lips into a firm line of resolve and slid back the brass bolt.

The door swung open on well-oiled hinges to reveal the foyer. A lone candle illuminated the entrance, its flame flickering erratically in the breeze, throwing distorting shadows over the man slumped in a large leather chair. He sat with his head in his hands, his elbows propped on his knees as he stared down at the tiled floor.

"Fishbait?" Royale called, her voice hoarse with apprehension as she hurried across the foyer and knelt in front of the quartermaster.

Fishbait let his hands fall limply between his parted thighs as he raised haggard eyes and looked into the frightened young features of his captain. A slow, tired smile briefly touched his lips, but his eyes still held their worried expression.

"He lives. The surgeon managed to remove the lead from his chest but Tim's still weak from all the blood he lost. There's little we can do fer him but hope."

"And pray, Fishbait," Royale said as she clasped the quartermaster's hand between her own. "Tim can't die. He's too young and good."

"Aye, he's young, and ye can't beat him when it comes to being a friend, but that ain't never stopped the reaper from taking his due. I've lived a long and hard life, and I ain't never been one fer getting down on me knees, but if I thought prayers would help the boy, I'd wear the floor out," Fishbait said tiredly. He glanced in the direction of the stairs that led to the room where Tim lay unconscious, burning with fever.

"Well, this time the reaper will just have to go away empty-handed. He's not going to get Tim, if I have my way." Royale got to her feet and started up the stairs.

Wearily, Fishbait rubbed his face with both hands, and then he forced the aching muscles in his legs to work as he followed Royale to the luxuriously appointed bedchamber.

During the next two days, while Morgan extracted his ransom—fifty thousand pieces of eight and a thousand head of cattle—Royale and Fishbait did not leave Tim's side. They worked tirelessly, catching only brief naps and snatching bites of food to keep up their own strength.

On the third day Morgan ordered the privateers back to

the beach, where he intended to slaughter the animals to provision the ships for the next invasion he had planned into Spanish-held territory. Royale didn't want to move Tim in his condition, but she knew he would be in more danger staying in Puerto Principe after Morgan's contingency left. Resigned to the fact that they would have to carry him the thirty miles back to the bay, Royale had several of her men construct a makeshift stretcher from two long-handled wooden spikes and a blanket. It was not the best way to travel, but it was far better than leaving him in the hands of the Spanish.

The journey that had taken them less than a day and a night now required days of hard travel. The wounded and the herd of cattle slowed their pace. To Royale's relief, Tim seemed to hold his own, though his fever did not abate. The majority of her time was spent caring for her friend, but when Fishbait spelled her she also tried to relieve some of the suffering of the other wounded men. She fed them, wiped their fevered brows, and changed their bloody bandages. Beyond that, there was little anyone could do for them.

When they finally reached the beach and made camp she had several lean-tos hastily constructed to shade the wounded from the sun until they recovered or died. She never ventured far from the makeshift infirmary during the following two weeks. And as Tim grew weaker Royale grew gaunt from all the work and worry. Dark circles shadowed the soft skin beneath her eyes, and her skin was stretched taut over the delicate bones of her face. Instead of ruining her loveliness, it gave her a haunting beauty, emphasizing the sea-green eyes that seemed to reflect the mental anguish she suffered. Love and guilt drove her, and she worked tirelessly to keep her friend alive. She paid no heed to the stench of festering wounds, a scent so nauseating that even the most stoic of the hardened seamen could not bear it. She sat in the fly-infested lean-to and watched helplessly as Tim's fever ate away his life.

Tim O'Kelly left life as gently as he had lived it. He did not thrash about and cry out as many did but slipped quietly across the delicate line that separated the living from the dead. He moved silently into the other world, as if he followed the sun as it sank below the horizon in a blaze of gold and scarlet.

Royale sat for a long while staring at her friend's pale, still face. Tim was gone, and she could never bring him back. Because of her foolish determination to show everyone, including the King of England, that she was Sir John's daughter and deserved to be treated as such instead of as the bastard that she was, Tim was dead.

She accepted the blame entirely. Tim had given his life protecting her, as he had done all through the years, each time she ventured into trouble. Never, when she had dreamed of her success, had she envisioned the tragedy that would strike the men who had followed her so faithfully.

She had promised to lead them and had done so—to their deaths. Eleven of her crew had paid with their lives for trusting her decision to seek her letter of marque by joining Morgan's expedition. Now, too late, she realized the folly of her own willful conceit. Nothing was worth the price of her men's lives. Neither Good Fortune, gold, nor a letter of marque would do them any good.

"I'll see to him now, Captain," Fishbait said as he placed a gentle hand on Royale's shoulder.

She looked up at the quartermaster without truly seeing him. Her eyes were wide, grief-filled pools that did not take note of her surroundings as she suffered under her mental self-flagellation. She rose unsteadily to her feet and stumbled into the night. The exhaustion she had held at bay through the days of caring for Tim settled over her in an oppressive cloud, weighing down her limbs and making her stagger as she slowly walked along the moon-shadowed beach.

She wandered aimlessly, giving no thought to the direction in which she traveled, chastising herself with each step. At last, when her tired body would go no further, she collapsed to her knees on the sand and hid her face in her hands, not wanting even the night to see her guilt and shame. Sobs shook her shoulders as she wept for her friend and for the other men who had died because of her. Her tears cascaded over her fingers and sparkled in the moonlight as they dropped to the sand. When no more would come, she lay on the damp beach, drained of every emotion, staring blindly into the night.

Morgan found her hours later, huddled in a ball, her arms clasped tightly about her knees. She did not move or respond as he knelt and said, "Royale, I'm sorry about your helmsman. I know you were close friends."

The life Morgan had lived, first as an indentured servant and then in the British navy, had left little time for tenderness, but his heart went out to the grief-stricken young woman. Lifting her gently in his arms, he cradled her against his chest. Her head rested beneath his chin as he rocked her to and fro, comforting her as if she was a hurt child and he the father trying to ease her pain.

He held her for a long while, murmuring soothing words against her tousled chestnut hair, trying to find the right thing to say to console her. In that moment he wanted to share his strength with her, to mend her broken spirit and bring back the courageous girl that he had grown to admire during the past weeks.

He understood what she was suffering. He remembered well the guilt he, too, had felt after leading men into battle for the first time and having to watch helplessly as they died around him. It was not easy for a man to endure such ugliness, but from childhood men were bred to defend themselves. They were taught to accept death and to go on without letting it destroy them. But even then, men who led others into combat and saw them die felt the same debilitating guilt that Royale was experiencing. If it affected trained men in that fashion, the effect upon a woman who knew nothing of such brutality must be devastating.

Morgan knew he had to find a way to make her understand that she was not at fault, or she would never again be the high-spirited creature who had the power to make his blood run hot through his loins.

Tenderly, he placed his hands on her shoulders and moved her so that she still sat on his lap but he could look into her face as he spoke.

"Royale, 'tis well to grieve for a friend, but you can't let one man's death shadow the rest of your life."

" 'Tis not Tim's death alone that I'm responsible for," Royale said, her voice filled with anguish, her pale features reflecting the misery in her soul.

"You killed no one except those who would have taken your own life. That was self-defense," Morgan said as he cupped her chin in his hands, his fingers framing her face.

He watched as she pressed her lashes tightly together and several crystal droplets trickled down her cheeks into his palms. Her lips trembled as she shook her head between his hands.

"Look at me, Royale," he demanded softly. "I won't let you castigate yourself this way. If anyone is responsible for the deaths of your crewmen, it is the Spaniards in Puerto Principe. They are the ones who fired the musket balls that killed your men, not you."

"But they would still be alive if I had not wanted that damned letter of marque. They believed in me, and I let them down—at the cost of their lives," Royale said as she stared up into Morgan's shadowy face.

"They were grown men who made their own decisions.

You did not force any of them to follow you. None were chained and dragged to Puerto Principe. They knew what to expect much better than you did, and yet they still chose to go. You cannot blame yourself nor go through life feeling responsible for the choices others made for themselves,'' Morgan said firmly.

"I know what you're trying to make me believe, but Tim''—her voice faltered and she had to swallow back a new flood of tears that threatened to choke her—"Tim took the ball meant for me.''

"Aye, but that was his choice also. He chose to save your life though it cost him his. In battle men are often placed in situations such as that. Some react instinctively to save their fellow man, while others think only of themselves. That is what makes the difference between the hero and the coward, but that is still their choice. No one can make another person place his life before anyone else's. Cease this feeling sorry for yourself and be grateful for Tim's bravery. He wanted you to live. I doubt he would have made such a sacrifice if he thought he would be ruining the rest of your life. Don't let his death be for nothing. You can avenge him if you don't let yourself wallow in self-pity and guilt,'' Morgan said.

"Avenge him? My need for revenge was one of the things that led me here, and see what it has cost,'' Royale said as she pulled away from Morgan's hands and set her lips in a grim line.

"Revenge?'' he asked, cocking one dark brow. "I thought you wanted your letter of marque.''

"Aye, I wanted the letter, but I also wanted revenge against the Spanish for my father's death, revenge''—Royale quickly stopped herself from uttering El Diablo's name—"against a king who would take what was rightfully mine because I'm not the issue of Sir John's loins.'' Giving a rueful laugh, she shook her head. "And now that I've had a taste of it, I find I don't want it as much as I thought. The price is far too high.''

"My poor Madame Captain," Morgan murmured as he captured the back of her head with his hand and drew her against his chest. Running his fingers through her long hair, he continued, "You're far too young and beautiful to have suffered so much. But your experiences have given you a strength that few possess. I've known men who would not have challenged the fates as you have done.''

"But to what advantage? My conceit has availed me nothing but the deaths of the men who followed me," Royale said, leaning back to gaze up into Morgan's sympathetic eyes.

"I've heard enough of this foolishness." He took her firmly by the shoulders and shook her lightly. "You've accomplished what many men could not do. Grieve for your friends, but put away this incessant guilt. It serves no purpose.''

Royale was too weary to argue further with him, but she knew in her heart that she would never be able to free herself completely from feeling responsible for Tim's death, no matter what argument Morgan made. Tim would have followed her to the ends of the earth because of the bond that existed between them, and he had died because of it. That knowledge would be with her for the rest of her life.

"Now, Madame Captain, 'tis time to return to camp," Morgan said as he set her on her feet and dusted the sand from their clothing. He smiled as he draped his arm protectively over her shoulder and said, "The men have spitted a beef to celebrate the fact that they no longer have to play the butcher. They slaughtered the last of the cattle today and now can return to being seamen again. You'll feel better once your belly is full.''

Royale didn't comment but walked silently back to the encampment with the privateer. A large fire blazed in the center of the camp, its flames popping and sizzling from the grease that dripped off the side of beef. A lively sea chanty filled the air from the homemade flute of one seaman while another sang along with his own version of the words to the song. The laughter produced by his risqué lyrics made Royale halt at the edge of the circle of men. She could not join in their celebration while Tim's still body lay only a short distance away.

"I'm not hungry," she muttered, shaking her head. She tried to pull free of Morgan's arm, but he held her firmly.

"No, Madame. Tonight you will eat and rest. Tomorrow will be time enough to attend to your friend's body." Morgan took her hand and drew her into the circle of light. He led her across the encampment to an uprooted tree bleached white by the sun. Seating her on its wind-smoothed trunk, he left her long enough to fill two tankards with rich, sweet rum from a large keg that had been brought ashore for their celebration.

"Drink," he ordered as he came back and placed the tankard in her hand.

Royale obeyed and found to her surprise that she was thirsty. Though she did not like the taste of rum, she drained the tankard and set it aside as Morgan settled himself on the sand next to her legs. He relaxed back against the bole of the tree, stretching his long legs out before him. A satisfied smile curved the corners of his mouth as he gazed up at Royale and sipped his rum.

To those who observed him, Morgan appeared to be a man who had fulfilled all of his desires. The tender expression on his face and the warm light in his eyes as he looked up at the girl seemed to be substantial enough evidence of what had gone on between the two before they entered the camp.

To the tall, dark-haired man standing in the shadows across the bonfire from Royale and Morgan, it was taken as such. The muscles that ridged his stomach contracted sharply, making him draw in a sharp breath as he recognized the girl sitting and drinking rum with the privateer.

"That be her, Captain. I told ye she was alive, but ye wouldn't believe what me and Black Jack had seed in Tortuga," Scrimshaw said as he pointed at Royale.

At that moment Bran could not answer Scrimshaw. He felt as if his guts were being twisted and pressed in a steel vise as he stared across the sand at the chestnut-haired woman. The girl he had thought dead, his ward, was still alive; from the look on Morgan's face, very much so indeed.

For one fleeting moment he felt a heady sensation of relief, but it was quickly replaced by the more violent emotion of rage. It swept through him like a bolt of searing lightning as he recalled all the torment he had suffered because of the bitch who enjoyed whoring for pirates. For the past months he had been castigating himself with a mental whip tipped in guilt, and it had been all for nothing. Like an eraser on a chalkboard, his fury wiped out all of the tender memories of his moments with Royale on the *Wicked Mistress*. His jaw set in a rigid line, his dark eyes flashed with fire, and his fingers tensed at his side as he fought to suppress the urge to throttle her. He stepped into the circle of light to make his presence known.

Royale saw El Diablo step from the shadows, and her face paled. Her eyes widened in shock as she stared up into the dark orbs that glittered behind his mask and held her transfixed. The flames from the fire made his eyes glow, and a shiver of fear passed along her spine, for at that instant she felt she was looking not at El Diablo but at the one he was named for.

Her startled expression alerted Morgan to the newcomer's arrival; following the direction of her gaze, he saw his friend. A warm smile of welcome came to the shapely lips beneath his mustache as he laughed and said, "Damn me, El Diablo, that black-masked visage of yours has near frightened the wench to death."

"I doubt my appearance could frighten her after she had already seen you. How have you been, Henry?" El Diablo said, strolling across the encampment to where Morgan sat beside Royale. A sardonic smile played over his lips as he glanced at her, his eyes lingering briefly on her mouth. He gave no sign of recognizing her as he extended his hand to his friend.

"Better now that you're here," Morgan said. "What in the devil took you so long? I expected you before we left Jamaica." He clasped El Diablo's outstretched hand and shook it exuberantly.

"There were a few small matters that needed my attention before I could join you," El Diablo said, his gaze sweeping once more over Royale. "We also ran into some heavy weather before reaching Port Royal and had to make repairs on the *Wicked Mistress* once we anchored there."

"Well, you've come at last, and you're needed. I've only a few hundred men left since the French bastards tucked in their tails and sailed back to Tortuga. I'll need every man and ship when we set sail for Panama," Morgan said, and he watched as El Diablo arched once dark brow quizzically. He chuckled. "Aye, did you think Puerto Principe's small offering would satisfy me? I intend to finish the task Mansvelt started in '66. It should be simple this time, since there will be no spies who can alert the inhabitants of Puerto Bello of our intentions. Fill your tankard, my friend, and we can discuss our expedition." Morgan indicated with a nod of his head the keg of rum across the way.

As El Diablo strode away Royale made to rise. His sudden appearance combined with Tim's death was nearly too much for her to cope with at the moment. She was grateful that he had not recognized her. It gave her a grace period to rebuild the defenses the last exhausting weeks had depleted. In her present state of mind she knew it would take little for her to explode into a raging frenzy. Her temper had always been her source of protection when she was forced into situations she found intolerable. El Diablo's presence had placed her in that position once again, and she knew she had to get away. When she dealt with him, she wanted to handle the encounter without any emotional interference. She was too weak physically and mentally to meet him on equal footing, and she needed time to rest and plan for their inevitable confrontation.

"No, Madame Captain, I want you here. This concerns your vessel and crew as well," Morgan said, placing a firm hand on her shoulder and forcing her once more to her seat.

Earlier Morgan had tried unsuccessfully to revive Royale's flagging spirits. Where his soothing words had done little good, now his domineering manner succeeded. With her temper flaring, she jerked away from his hand.

"I see no reason for me to be here. The *Raven* will not be joining your expedition to Panama," Royale said as she came to her feet and started to walk away.

"What do you mean?" Morgan rose quickly and grasped her wrist none too gently. Pulling her around to face him, he continued, "You know I need the *Raven* and her men."

"Captain Morgan, I agreed to come to Puerto Principe but not to go on to Puerto Bello. I fulfilled my end of the deal we made at the expense of the *Raven*'s crew. We'll be lucky to make it back to our home port with so many of the crew lost," Royale said, straining against the hand clamped about her wrist, her face flushed with anger.

"Damn it, Royale, you can't think of leaving now. I thought you wanted revenge against the Spanish," Morgan said, releasing her arm.

Rubbing her bruised flesh, the imprint of his fingers having left red streaks on her skin, Royale spat, "I did want revenge, but as I told you, I've found the taste is not so sweet when the price is the lives of my men. Even if I felt differently, you know as well as I that the *Raven* can't sail without a full crew. Would you have me watch the rest of my men die because of another foolish decision?"

Neither Royale nor Morgan noted El Diablo as he stood silently listening to their verbal combat. His eyes glittered with surprise and interest behind his mask as he sipped the sweet, dark rum in his tankard. There was more to the situation than he had first surmised. If what he had gleaned in the past few moments was true, his ward was not a harlot traveling with Morgan but captain of her own vessel, and her wild actions stemmed from her need to avenge herself upon the Spanish.

A tiny line creased his brow as he pondered this new bit of information about the girl his King had sent him to oversee. She was a fiery bit of fluff if she sought to take on Spain's heavily armed ships, he mused, unconsciously touching the spot where she had hit him with the brandy decanter. Aye, the girl had spirit, but if she was not careful it would be the death of her. And it was his responsibility to ensure her safety.

El Diablo regarded first Royale and then Morgan, trying to decide where his duty lay. If he took his ward back to Good Fortune, he would be leaving Morgan without enough men to take Puerto Bello, and the ensuing defeat would encourage the Spanish to think England's defenses in the West Indies were too weak to protect Jamaica. If he saw her home and then returned to join his friend, it would leave her free to carry out hare-brained schemes against the Spanish. There was only one decision he could make to solve the dilemma facing him. She would have to sail with Morgan so that he could keep an eye on her, and in that manner he could also aid his friend.

El Diablo opened his mouth to speak, then abruptly closed it as he recalled the scene he had witnessed upon his arrival in camp. Again his gaze swept over the privateer's features before it moved to his ward's face. Uncertainty swept over him. He'd made a mistake about Royale's position with Morgan, but he had not misconstrued the look on his friend's face as he had gazed up at the young woman. Morgan wanted the girl, and if they were not already lovers, he knew the privateer was only waiting for the right moment to seduce her.

With that thought a sudden flash of jealousy singed El Diablo, but he ignored it, telling himself that the reason he didn't like the idea of Royale and Morgan together was because it was his duty to protect her against men like the privateer. His King would not abide such a relationship for his ward.

Settling the matter in his mind, El Diablo said, "It would seem you both have a problem, but I think I have the answer."

The two turned in unison to face him. He gave them his most charming smile and said, "Morgan, you need the lady's ship, and she in turn needs men to man her vessel. What I propose is that we come to a mutual agreement. If she'll agree to sail to Puerto Bello, I'll send enough of my own men to man her vessel."

"No," Royale said with a quick shake of her head. "I don't want or need your assistance."

"Madame Captain, I suggest you seriously consider El Diablo's offer. Either you accept his proposal, or I will commandeer your vessel and leave you and your men here. I doubt you would find Cuba a hospitable place once the Spaniards learned of your presence," Morgan said, smiling triumphantly.

"You wouldn't," Royale said, flashing El Diablo a hostile look before bestowing the same upon Morgan.

"Aye, I would and will. I have the right. I am in command of this mission, and if I have to take your ship to ensure its success and the safety of Jamaica, I will have no recourse but to do so." Morgan folded his arms across his chest and leaned back against the bleached bole of the fallen tree.

Royale could hear the blood pounding in her temples as she stood speechless with rage. After all she had gone through to escape the tyranny of a distant king, she was now confronted with a similar situation by Morgan. She knew he would take the *Raven* from her without any qualms, just as the king had taken her home. The force of the fury that possessed her was so powerful that she felt faint. She swayed unsteadily and needed to grasp a broken limb to support herself as she faced the two men. She had to find a way to deal with the new and unexpected threat from the privateer. But at the present moment she was too harried to plan how to outmaneuver him. She drew several deep breaths to ease the tightness in her throat.

"It seems I have little choice but to consider El Diablo's suggestion; however, that's all I'll agree to at the moment. For now, there are other more pressing matters that need my attention," Royale managed to say at last.

"Aye," Morgan agreed. "See to your friend's burial tomorrow, because I want your decision by the following morning."

Royale stared at him as if she was seeing him for the first time. How could she have deluded herself into believing he was her friend? How could the man who had held her so tenderly only a short while before speak so callously to her now?

"How generous of you to allow me to bury my helmsman while deciding to risk the lives of the rest of my crew," she spat, her voice laced with sarcasm. Giving El Diablo one last caustic glance, she turned on her heel and strode in the direction of the infirmary, leaving the two men staring after her.

"Damn," Morgan said as he lifted his tankard and took a deep swallow of rum. "That one small girl has more fire than all the women I've ever met rolled into one. From what I know of our little Madame Captain, she'll not meekly accept your offer nor my dictates."

"Aye, I suspect you're right," Bran murmured as he raised his own tankard, a thoughtful look on his face. Gazing in the direction Royale had traveled, he mused that she'd not be acquiescent, if her actions in the past served as any indication of what she would do in the future. And for that reason he was determined to keep a close eye on his wayward ward.

Chapter 8

*The cry of a gull was the only sound to disturb the still-*ness of the afternoon as Royale bent and placed a bright bouquet of red, heart-shaped anthuriums upon the mound of dirt. Her long, gold-streaked mane fell over her shoulder, shielding her features as she whispered, "Forgive me, Tim," before rising and brushing the shining hair back from her face. Dry-eyed, she turned to stare out across the blue water. Her tears had been spent early that morning when the men had buried her friend, and now there were none left to shed as she said her final goodbyes and forced herself to put the past behind her. In her heart she would never forget Tim, but as the captain of the *Raven* she had to think of the present—and of the immediate future that loomed dark with Morgan's ultimatum.

Her eyes narrowed thoughtfully as she stared at the shining expanse of water. Today, well rested, she had to admit that the privateer had been right about one thing: her responsibility lay with the living; and because of that, she was even more firmly determined not to succumb to his demands. Glancing over her shoulder at Fishbait, who stood quietly awaiting her, she said, "I want the crew to meet me on the beach at sunset. Tell them I want no one except

the men from the *Raven* to know of our meeting. Is that
understood?''

"Aye," Fishbait said, scratching the gray-speckled stubble on his chin, " 'tis understood about the secrecy, but I
ain't quite certain as to the reason behind it.''

Royale twisted her hair into a coil on top of her head
and secured it with her hat as she glanced about the area
to ensure their privacy. Seeing no one, she said, "We set
sail tonight. Morgan has threatened to commandeer the *Raven* if I don't agree to sail to Panama. I agreed to come to
Cuba, but no further. I'll be damned if I let him or anyone
take my ship from me.''

"That do prove to pose a dilemma of sorts, Captain. We
haven't enough crew left to fully man the *Raven*," Fishbait
said. The lines in his weathered face deepened as he
screwed it up thoughtfully. "I was hoping we'd be able to
recruit a few men from some of the other ships before we
set sail agin.''

"We'll have to make do. If the weather holds fair, we
should have no problem.'' Royale once more scanned the
area around them. It would not do for Morgan to hear of
her plans and have time to thwart them.

"Captain, the weather wasn't what had me concerned.
If we should happen across a heavily armed man-of-war,
we'd not have a chance. Without the manpower to use our
guns, we'd be like ducks out of the water. We'd have no
defense,'' Fishbait said. He watched as Royale's narrowed
gaze came to rest speculatively upon him. He shifted
uneasily from foot to foot under her intense scrutiny.

"Fishbait, during the past year I've come to know you
well enough to see that you're not telling me everything.
Out with it, man, before someone overhears us and we
have no chance to get away,'' she ordered, bracing her
hands on her hips, her stance reflecting her annoyance.

"Well, Captain, the men have been grumbling of late

about the small amount of purchase from Puerto Principe. They be a-wanting to feel the jingle of gold in their pockets and are a-wondering what you intend to do about solving their problem. If we set out now with so few men, even if we come across a rich prize, we couldn't take it."

"Damn it, Fishbait, I'm the captain of the *Raven*, and it's my decision when and where we sail. Do I have a mutiny on my hands?" Royale watched as the quartermaster rapidly shook his head.

"Then that settles it. We set sail tonight."

"Aye, Captain," Fishbait said as he clamped his seaman's hat firmly on his head and strode to the beach.

Royale had turned to follow the quartermaster when the sound of soft laughter froze her steps. Swinging around, her hand automatically going to the hilt of her sword, she ordered, "Damn you, come out, if you place any value on your scurvy hide."

Another deep chuckle floated out from behind the tall palm, stilling the breath in her throat as she recognized its owner even before he stepped into view. Her heart seemed to do a rapid flip-flop in her breast, and she felt the blood drain from her face as she stared at El Diablo.

"It seems, Madame Captain, that you are beset by problems," he said as he folded his arms across his chest, leaned one shoulder negligently against the tree, and arched a brow quizzically at her.

"I have no problems, with the exception of you and Morgan," Royale said, her hand still resting defensively on the hilt of her weapon.

"That's not the way I heard it. I suspect you will have a mutiny on your hands if you try to sail away without giving your crew a chance to make their own decision about going to Puerto Bello," El Diablo said, as if it were of little import to him.

"Damn you, I'm not asking your opinion. I'm trying to

decide how best to keep you from telling Morgan of my plans. It seems my only alternative is to skewer you where you stand," Royale said furiously, meaning every word she spoke.

"My, you are a bloodthirsty little wench, aren't you?" El Diablo said, raising his hands in the air, palms upward. "As you can see, I'm unarmed. Since you intend to kill me, do you plan to come over here, or would you prefer that I run at your sword to save you the trouble?"

"I don't appreciate your brand of humor, El Diablo. Nor do I like the thought of killing any man, much less an unarmed one, even if he is a worthless pirate. But I can't let you and Morgan prevent me from sailing. I've led my men into one disaster and am determined not to do so again." Royale unsheathed her sword and began her wary approach.

El Diablo's smile never wavered, though it grew more guarded as he watched her move closer. He knew she meant to kill him. He could read his fate in her eyes, and the only way to prevent it was either to hurt her or to convince her that she should sail with Morgan. He chose the latter.

"I think, my bloodthirsty little vixen, that you are being as irrational now in your decision as you were the night you jumped off the *Wicked Mistress*," he said, and he watched as Royale came to an abrupt halt, her eyes widening. His smiled deepened. "Ah, you thought I did not remember you or the little love tap you gave me as a going away present?"

"I wish I had killed you then so I would not be faced with this problem now," she said, her face drained of all color.

"Your intention was quite clear that night, but—fortunately for me—your aim was bad. But that is neither here nor there. We can settle that matter between us at a later date. At present we are discussing your plans to sail tonight.''

"There you are wrong, El Diablo. There is nothing to discuss about my plans. They are already made. I intend to sail tonight. I won't let anyone take my ship from me,'' Royale said, her voice taut with tension.

"There lies the flaw in your decision. No one will take your vessel from you unless you keep up this scheme of mothering your crew instead of acting like their captain. Playing the mother hen will do you little good. Your men want gold in their pockets and are willing to risk their lives for it. They chose you because they thought you were capable of leading them. Once they realize you cower at the sight of a little blood, they'll mutiny, and you'll lose the *Raven*—or perhaps even your life." El Diablo smiled to himself as he saw the flicker of uncertainty that passed over her features.

"I'm the captain of the *Raven*, and I make the decisions," Royale said, though she did not feel as confident as she had a few moments earlier.

"Aye, you're their captain, but for how long? At least give your men a choice in the matter. It would be a much wiser decision. Sailing with a dissatisfied crew is more dangerous than swimming in a school of barracuda."

Royale regarded El Diablo through narrowed eyes as she considered all he had said. She abhorred the thought of admitting that he was right about anything, but in this instance she knew that he had spoken the truth. Cocking her head to one side, she eyed him skeptically for a long moment before she said, "If I should decide to let my men choose whether to sail with Morgan or not, do you agree to abide by their decision and let us leave tonight if they elect not to go on to Panama?"

"Aye, my word as a gentleman."

"Then it seems that I have no choice but to kill you, El

Diablo. We both know you are no gentleman,'' Royale said as she raised her blade and pricked at the laces of his black silk shirt.

El Diablo tensed, thinking her serious until he saw the glimmer of a smile tugging at her lips. Relaxing, he gave her a rakish grin and said, ''Aye, I'm no gentleman, nor are you the proper lady, so I suggest we each just take the other's word. That would be much easier than trying to figure out exactly what we are, don't you think?''

''I think we both know already,'' Royale said as she scabbarded her sword and gave him a scathing look before turning on her heel and leaving him to ponder her words.

At ease, El Diablo lounged against the tree and watched as she strode away, his eyes resting on the shapely curves of her hips. A satisfied smile played over his lips as he mused to himself, aye, we both think we know, my dear ward, but you're in for a number of surprises in the near future.

Royale regarded the sullen, obstinate faces of her crew and felt a sinking sensation in the pit of her stomach. There was no sign of approval upon their set features, and she knew she had no alternative but to accept El Diablo's advice and let them decide their own fate.

''Since it seems none of you support my decision, I'll let you decide whether we sail for home or join Morgan's expedition to Puerto Bello. But I'm warning you now, should you choose to go with Morgan, I'll hang the first man I hear complain if we find as little in Panama as we did in Puerto Principe. Is that understood?'' Royale said, her throat tight with anger. It galled her to have to give way to her crew's dictates. Had her father still been at the helm, they would not have attempted to question his orders.

''I'll give you an hour to decide our course,'' she said,

forcing the words past the bitterness that rose in her throat to choke her. With sudden clarity she realized how tenuous her position as captain actually was. Suddenly feeling as if she had been betrayed by her men, she turned and strode down the beach, no longer able to remain in their company and listen to them talk about the riches to be had in Puerto Bello.

With thumbs hooked in her belt and shoulders hunched, she paused on a deserted stretch of beach and gazed at the dying sun. Her mind wandered back over the year she had spent as the captain of the *Raven*, and she could find no reason for her crew's defection. Until the disaster of Puerto Principe, she had kept their pockets filled with gold, and they had suffered no loss of life while capturing their prizes. The only rationalization she could make for their present actions was that they still had not fully accepted her as their leader because she was a woman. That thought stung her deeply and made her aware that she had not escaped the cage of male dominance as she had imagined only a few short hours before. The unfairness of it was like a slap in the face. It made her feel as if they had only been letting her play out a fantasy until they chose to regulate her back into the position they felt proper for a woman.

Her face flushed with humiliation at the thought of how ridiculous she must have appeared to them during the past months of going about her duties and thinking herself in charge. She could imagine the merriment they had enjoyed at her expense. A sudden burst of anger deepened the rose in her cheeks, and her eyes sparkled as the sun slipped slowly below the horizon.

"Damn it, I've served them as well as any man could, or better. They should accept me for that reason alone," she mused aloud, completely unaware that she was no longer alone.

"It has nothing to do with you, Royale. 'Tis their greed," El Diablo said close by her side.

Royale gave a start and swung around to face the masked pirate. Her heart raced in her breast and it took a moment for her to regain control over her voice as she stared up into his handsome face. Taking a deep breath, she managed to say, "Greed?"

"Aye, greed. I could easily find myself in the same situation if my men had to choose between obeying my commands or filling their pockets."

Royale's laughter was tinged with sarcasm as she shook her head in denial. "I doubt that very much. I've seen how your men jump to obey you. They would follow your orders without thought or question even if their stomachs were gnawing at their ribs."

"Aye, they serve me well, but it's because they stand to gain more by doing so than by not. On board the *Wicked Mistress* I rule, but that command is given to me by my crew. How long do you think I could stand against sixty dissatisfied crewmen? Granted, it seems I hold all the power, but a pirate ship is not like a ship of the British Navy. I command because my men allow it. They know I have the knowledge to gain them what they desire," El Diablo said, trying to make Royale realize that it was not her abilities the men questioned but their lack of purchase. There were only two things the hardened seamen lived for, and that was women and rum. Both had to be paid for with gold.

Seeing the dubious light that still lingered in her eyes, he continued, "You'll see that I'm right when you have their answer. They'll choose to go to Panama, but you'll have no more trouble from them. You've gained your men's respect, but they will always think of themselves first."

"You heard?" Royale asked.

"Aye, and I saw one small woman surrounded by a

group of rough seamen who could have throttled her with little effort, had they chosen to do so. You were like a tiny minnow in a pond of sharks, but you held your own and did not let them gobble you up. You're still the captain of your vessel, Royale. Every man you have would fight to prove it.''

Royale gazed up at El Diablo, wondering at him. At that moment he was so much like the man she had first met on the *Wicked Mistress*, who had shared such tenderness and passion with her. There was little resemblance to the pirate who had callously threatened to sell her in Tortuga.

Royale gave herself a sharp mental shake. She could not let herself remember their moments together, or she would find herself caught once more in the silken web of his allure—the same trap that had caused her to give her innocence to him. Slamming the door on such thoughts, she raised her chin in the air.

''If what you have said holds true, then it is my duty to lead my men into Puerto Bello, no matter how I feel about this new mission of Morgan's.''

''Aye, you're their captain, and they expect it of you. With luck, Puerto Bello will be more profitable, so you will not have to hang any of them,'' El Diablo said, with a slow smile tugging at the corners of his shapely lips and his eyes twinkling.

Royale's cheeks flushed a becoming rose, and she quickly averted her eyes from the pirate's. ''It was an empty threat. I doubt that I could hang any of the scoundrels after all the death I witnessed in Puerto Principe. But as long as they don't know I didn't mean every word I spoke, perhaps the *Raven* will be safe from mutiny even if this expedition gains us as little as the last.''

''I suspect, Madame Captain, that you have no taste for fighting. Why did you join Morgan's expedition, if that's the way you feel?'' El Diablo asked. He needed to know the reason she had left her comfortable existence at Good Fortune for the rough life on the high seas. He desperately wanted to understand what drove his young ward to take such drastic measures. From what she had just said, he could not believe it was her need for adventure.

"It was better to join Morgan than to turn to piracy. I extracted his promise to help me gain my letter of marque from Governor Modyford if we succeeded in Puerto Príncipe. Now I find I'm bound for Panama as well," Royale said as she again looked at El Diablo, her own curiosity blooming. "Why did you join Morgan?" she asked in turn.

"Gold, a great deal of it."

Toeing a large shell loose from the sand, Royale bent and picked it up before sending it sailing back into the waves. Dusting the grit from her hands, she said, "Then it seems we have the same purpose on this mission."

"I thought you told Morgan you wanted revenge against the Spanish," El Diablo said. She flashed him an angry look.

"Do you make it a habit to eavesdrop on every conversation?"

"Only when I think it will benefit me. You haven't answered my question, Royale," he said, folding his arms across his chest as if he was the father of a recalcitrant child.

"Gold, a letter of marque, revenge. Why should my reasons for joining Morgan concern you?" Royale said, turning away. Her life was her own, and she owed no man an explanation of what lay behind her decisions. Especially El Diablo. He deserved nothing from her but her contempt, and she'd be damned if she'd tolerate his using her again for any purpose.

Before she could move away, El Diablo caught her firmly by the wrist and pulled her back to face him. "Everything about you concerns me, my fiery-tempered little privateer.

There are matters between us that need to be settled," he said, but before he could add, "because I'm your guardian," Royale jerked free of his hand.

"I settled the matter between us that night on the *Wicked Mistress*. My only regret is that I didn't finish the job. We're committed to this mission, but beyond that there is nothing to bind us. Had I met you before now, I would have taken great pleasure in sending you and your ship to the bottom of the ocean, where you deserve to be," Royale said, her voice harsh with pent-up fury.

"You still haven't learned when to pull in your claws, have you, wildcat? As I recall, I managed to trim them neatly that night and will do so again, if you insist. My memory serves me well as to how you purr under my taming hand." El Diablo's dark eyes kindled with desire as the unforgotten image of her lying naked upon his bunk flashed into his mind. The heat of it was so intense that it singed away the thought of his guardianship and rushed through his veins to settle achingly in his loins.

He took a step toward Royale, and she warily backed away from him. Her own mind feasted upon the memory his words served up, and she was suddenly aware of the danger she faced from her own traitorous body, as well as from El Diablo.

"You bastard," Royale ground out, fighting to remain composed but failing miserably as all the humiliation and pain she had suffered swept over her. Tears burned her eyes, and she blinked rapidly to keep them at bay. "You took my innocence that night and now seek to further humiliate me by reminding me that I was too ignorant to realize I was being used. You! I can't find a word vile enough to call you." Royale choked on the sob that rose in her throat and—with no thought other than escaping him—fled down the beach.

Her words slammed into Bran. The muscles in his chest

contracted painfully as he fully comprehended the wrong
he had done her. He had been plagued with guilt over the
thought of her death, but he had never considered the consequences of their passionate encounter. The women in his
past, ladies of Charles's court, had been experienced and
thought little of flitting from one lover to the next. As long
as they took a step upward on the social scale they thought
nothing of sharing a man's bed. They had been pleasure
seekers as well and enjoyed their carnality to the fullest.
The King set the morals at court, and they followed his
example, tasting forbidden fruit without fear of condemnation.

He had been Royale's first lover and had ignored the
fact of her innocence, thinking only of his own selfish desires. He had felt no real remorse over his taking her virginity; his guilt stemmed from the belief that she had died
because of it.

"Royale," Bran called as he raced after her, his long
legs eating up the distance between them. He caught her
in his arms and dragged her to a halt, wrapping her tightly
in his embrace to still her squirming body.

She fought him. She twisted from side to side, pounding
on his chest with her fists and shaking her head so that her
hair flowed about them in a silken wave as she cried, "No,
please, no."

"Royale, listen to me," he said as he tightened his hold
on her and brought her against his hard body. One bronzed
hand buried itself in her hair as he captured her head to
still her movements so that he could gaze down into her
moonlit face. Noting the crystal path of tears that stained
her cheeks, he murmured softly, "Royale, I'm sorry. I
didn't mean to hurt you."

"Don't you think it's far too late for apologies? Why
can't you just leave me alone and stop tormenting me?"

Royale said, her lower lip trembling, her eyes shimmering with moisture.

"Strangely, my little wildcat, I find I can't just leave you alone. Since that first night I have not been able to rid my thoughts of you. I look across the waves and remember the color of your eyes when they are soft with passion. I touch a piece of silk and recall the feel of your skin." El Diablo's voice was husky with the desire aroused in him by the pressure of her body against his.

His voice was a gentle caress, wrapping itself around Royale and drawing her into its silken net. It made her heart flutter in her breast as it tugged at her, urging her to reach out to him. Unaware of her own action, she placed her hand against the bare skin that was revealed by the deep V opening of his shirt. She felt the sinewy muscles contract at her touch, and a thrill of excitement raced through her veins. It was a heady sensation to know that he was also affected by the contact of their bodies.

"Damn it, Royale," El Diablo breathed sharply as he placed his hand over hers, pressing it more tightly to his flesh, "I'm the one who's tormented. Tormented by the memory of your body warm against mine. During the past months I was tortured day and night by the knowledge that I had caused your death, and now that I've found you again I don't care what has transpired between you and Morgan— all I know is that I still want you with every fiber of my being."

Through the haze of pleasure she felt in touching him, Royale managed to grasp the meaning of his last words. She stared up at him, unable to believe that he could think such a thing of her.

"You think that Morgan and I are lovers?" she asked, stunned that he had come to such a conclusion about her.

"That's all in the past. Nothing else matters now that I

have you once more," El Diablo said softly, unaware of the brewing storm.

"How beneficent of you," she retorted. He seemed to turn to fire beneath her hand, and she jerked it away, unwilling to let herself be scorched again by succumbing to his attractions. Her eyes sparkled with ire as she glared up at him.

"In one moment you apologize and in the next you insult me. How dare you to believe that Morgan is my lover or ever has been! You think because I gave myself to you that I will eagerly fall into any man's bed. I can assure you that nothing has ever happened between Morgan and myself. I'm one of his captains, not his whore. No man has ever made love to me but you. You are the only man to use me to appease his momentary lust, and you will be the last. My innocence is gone now, and I'll never let myself be used as a plaything again. Of that you can be sure."

Royale's fury mounted with every word, and before El Diablo could move out of her way she brought up both hands, palms flat against his chest, and used all of her strength to shove him from her path. Without a backward glance she stalked down the beach, her head held high, her back stiff with indignation.

Caught off balance by her abrupt push, Bran teetered precariously for a moment before toppling over backward. He landed with a hard, humiliating thump upon the sand. A bemused expression played over his face as he watched her stamp away. Finally seeing the humor in the situation, he threw back his head and laughed.

He was still chuckling as he lay back and braced his hands behind his head. Staring up at the star-studded sky, he unconsciously picked out the different constellations as he reflected upon Royale's heated outburst. A smug smile curled his lips, and he felt his spirits soar up into the night with the realization that he alone had tasted the sweetness of her body.

"Royale Carrington is like a potent brew; once she's in your blood, it is hard to dispel the heady intoxication she creates," Bran mused aloud as he lay contemplating his young charge. She was an intriguing mixture of beauty and spirit. She was like a breath of fresh air to his jaded senses. She had the power to arouse thoughts and emotions within him that he had long ago relinquished as futile dreams of youth. And he wanted her.

In Bran's eyes, the pampered beauties of Charles's court paled in comparison to Royale. Their painted, perfumed bodies clothed in expensive gowns and jewels seemed tawdry next to her lithe form in britches and a shirt. She needed no artifice to heighten her loveliness. Her own natural vitality added color to her cheeks and made her eyes sparkle. If he were to take her to court, she would be like a vibrant wild rose in the midst of wilting lilies.

At the thought of Royale surrounded by the backstabbing greedy pack that curried the King's favor, Bran shook his head. No, Charles's court was no place for his beautiful ward. It would stifle her as assuredly as it had done him. All the petty intrigues that were as constant there as the rising sun would strangle her vivacious spirit.

From his observation of Royale thus far, he suspected she would detest that life as much as he did. He was considered one of the King's favored courtiers, but he disliked the thought of being counted among the retinue of noblemen who did nothing for the crown but fawn upon Charles for their livelihoods.

He much preferred sailing as El Diablo. At least he found some satisfaction in knowing he was helping his King and country with the booty he captured. Charles needed the gold he secured from the Spanish galleons to help ward off bankruptcy, but the King could not afford to antagonize his enemies by openly giving letters of marque to English privateers. Instead he had sent out one of his favored courtiers in the guise of a pirate to obtain the much-needed coin. However, if Bran's actions were known, it could mean war with Spain. That would devastate Britain's fragile economy. Charles's subjects would remain loyal until hunger began to gnaw at their bellies. When that happened, their loyalty would swiftly turn into anger. That event Charles could not chance. He had no desire to follow in his father's footsteps to the gibbet.

Bran was satisfied with his mission, but even that had not fully appeased his own restless soul. He had sought one adventure after another, hoping to quench the craving that he could not name. It was a yearning for something that always seemed to be just beyond his reach. He knew himself well enough to know that until he found what he was seeking he would never find contentment and could not settle down and be the proper nobleman his heritage required.

Bran stirred restlessly and sat up. Looping his arms over his knees, he stared at the white froth of the breakers that rolled onto the beach and receded in a spill of bubbles. A slight frown knit his dark brows beneath his mask as his thoughts turned to the mission his King had delegated to him.

He was responsible for the welfare of the fiery beauty he desired. The thought made him press his lips into a narrow line. He had been determined to protect her from Morgan—and now found he would also have to guard her against himself.

Charles would look no more favorably on an affair between Bran and his ward than one between Royale and Henry Morgan. Royale Carrington's welfare was of great interest to the King. He had said it was because of his friendship with her father and mother, but he would elaborate no further upon the subject. From the King's reticence Bran suspected that there was more that Charles was not telling him.

Shaking his head at the situation in which he found himself, he raked his fingers through his hair, disgusted at trying to solve all the mysteries that surrounded Royale Carrington. He knew nothing for certain except that he had been placed in charge of an alluring young woman who made him forget his duties to King and country when he held her in his arms.

"Damn," Bran muttered into the night as he lifted a shell and threw it violently into the incoming waves. He was faced with a choice between his King and the woman he desired. He feared the latter would be his choice because he did not think he had the strength to resist, even if he wanted to do so, and his body made him achingly aware that he did not. He admitted freely that he wanted Royale and had wanted her since the first moment he had seen her. He also accepted the fact that he felt for her as he had for no other woman; she had found a place in his heart, though at that moment he was still unprepared to call it love.

Feeling an overpowering need to go after her and try to right things between them, Bran pushed himself to his feet and strode purposefully back to the privateers' camp.

Chapter 9

T*he night was unusually quiet as Royale approached* Morgan's camp. His men had all retired early. They had abandoned their games of chance and tankards of rum to get the rest their tired bodies needed. They faced another grueling day's labor of readying the ships to sail as their leader had ordered. Only their snores and an occasional grunt disturbed the stillness as she made her way through the maze of bodies, carefully stepping over the sleeping men whose outflung arms and legs often blocked her path.

Pausing in the shadows just beyond the circle of fire-light, she studied the man she had come to see—Henry Morgan. As was his custom, he sat enjoying his nightly tankard of rum before seeking his own bed and sleep. For several long minutes she regarded the privateer, dreading the moment she would have to face him and admit that she had no choice but to sail with him to Panama.

As she had expected, her men had made their decision in favor of Morgan's expedition. Fortunately, they had not gloated over it. Her crew had been subdued when they had told her of their decision. That and the fact that they still considered her their leader were the only bright spots in the whole affair. However, her crew's faith in her did little to lighten her mood. Her encounter with El Diablo and the success of Morgan's threats combined to make her feel like one of Adele's teakettles set over an open flame. It would take little to make her scream.

Drawing in a deep breath, she stepped into the light and watched as Morgan's face lit with something akin to surprise before he rose to his feet and bowed graciously to her, as if she was a great lady at court.

"Madame Captain," he said as a charming smile curled his lips beneath his dark mustache, "I hope the honor of your presence means that you have considered our conversation from last night and have come to give me your answer."

"Aye," Royale said as she crossed to stand before the privateer. She held her head high and her back straight, giving no indication of the inner turmoil she was experiencing. Her expression reflected none of her feelings as she faced Morgan, determined that she would show no sign of subservience to the man. She was still the captain of her vessel and would meet him on equal ground.

Morgan arched one dark brow quizzically as he peered down into her set face. "Your answer, Madame?"

"The *Raven* sails with you to Puerto Bello," Royale stated flatly, and she turned away. Having delivered her answer, she had no more to say to the privateer.

Morgan's hand on her arm stayed her steps, and she looked first at his lean brown fingers before letting her gaze travel up to the swarthy face of their owner. Her eyes were cold as she regarded him, but she did not speak.

"Royale," he said, his voice tinged with remorse as he turned her to face him, "will you forgive me? I didn't like what I had to do last night, but I need the *Raven* and her crew. This mission is too important for both England and Jamaica. Spain has kept her greedy stranglehold on the West Indies far too long. Right now England has her problems with the French and Dutch, so our small force is all that keeps the Spaniards at bay. England also needs gold; she's nearly bankrupt since the fire two years ago and can do little to defend herself, much less think of her colonies. We are Jamaica's defense and Charles's hope to rebuild England with the gold we take.''

Royale pulled her arm free of Morgan's hand as she looked up at him. Her face was empty of emotion, but her eyes sparkled with fiery lights as she said, ''I know from firsthand experience of our good King's need for gold. He took everything that was rightfully mine and sent his man to ensure that he received each precious coin that he deemed his due. Why should I feel obligated to a king who is thousands of miles across the ocean, when he felt no loyalty to my father's wishes?''

''Then why did you choose to sail to Puerto Bello? Is it your need to avenge your father's death, or is it your own greed for gold?'' Morgan asked, wondering at the complexity of the young woman.

Royale gave a harsh little laugh and her voice was laced with bitterness as she said, ''You gave me very little choice in the matter, as I recall. But I assure you that your threats were not the deciding factor. Had my men not wanted to join your expedition, we would already be far from here. As for my revenge, I think my need for that died with my friends. It now rests with their cold bodies beneath the sandy soil of Cuba. I admit I have need of gold, but it's not to appease any greed I feel. I need it to regain what my father wanted me to have, though English law says I don't deserve it. Call that a bastard's pride, if you will, but until I accomplish that I will not rest. You protect Jamaica's and England's interests, but once the *Raven*'s hold is filled with enough gold to exchange for my home I will sail no more.''

''Then you may have your wish when we reach Panama, Royale. Puerto Bello is a rich city. The treasures from the mines in Peru are brought by mule train to the city to be shipped back to Spain. You may be grateful to me for coercing you into this mission once you've seen the wealth we find there," Morgan said, and he smiled. He wanted to mend the rift he had unthinkingly created between them. He wanted Royale. The ache in his groin was evidence of the weeks he had patiently waited to have her. If he could not end the hostility between them, all his patience would come to nothing.

"Grateful, Captain Morgan? Surely you jest. How can you even think that I would ever appreciate your domineering manner? I am a woman, not a child, and I find little consolation in knowing I have to abide by your dictates instead of making my own decisions."

Morgan placed his hands gently on Royale's shoulders as he bent to peer into her flashing eyes. His face was only inches from hers as he spoke softly. "I know you are a woman, Royale. I've known it since the first night in the tavern. I've reminded myself time and again that you are one of my captains, but it does little good when my body craves to have you pressed against it and my lips long to taste the sweetness of your mouth again. Aye, Royale, you are a woman; too much of a woman for any man to resist."

The tight leash Morgan had held on his desires slowly unraveled like a worn hemp rope under the pressure of the ache swelling his loins. Before Royale had time to comprehend his intentions and disengage herself from his hand, he drew her against him, his lips capturing hers possessively as his large hand trapped the back of her head in his palm, holding her captive as he devoured her mouth.

Patience be damned, Morgan thought as he wrapped one strong arm about her, his hand spreading wide at the small of her back, forcing her even closer to his hard, eager body. The taste of her mouth and the feel of her slender body obliterated all else from his mind except the pleasure he was experiencing.

As on the previous occasion in Port Royal, Royale was caught completely off guard and found that she could not even make an effort to fight against his advances because her arms were trapped between their tightly pressed bodies. She moaned her objection, but he did not release her mouth as his tongue darted into its moist cavern. She squirmed, trying her best to avoid the invasion, but found to her distress that he had lifted her off her feet, making her as helpless as a rag doll.

A deep guttural sound in Morgan's throat gave proof of his appreciation of the delicacy he was enjoying. Her movements only served to inflame his passion further, and his breathing grew heavy as he deepened the kiss. He did not free her mouth as he slid his arm down her body and beneath her knees, lifting her as if she weighed no more than the froth upon a wave. With no thought to her feelings, letting his own searing desire dictate his actions, he strode toward the darkness beyond the campfire.

Royale managed to collect her wits enough to put up some resistance. She pushed futilely against his muscular chest and heard Morgan chuckle at her efforts as he reached the edge of the ring of light.

Frantic now that only a few steps separated them from the dark blanket of the night, Royale began to beat against him with her fists. She knew that once they were enshrouded by the blackness, concealed from curious eyes, there would be no turning back for Morgan.

He seemed not to feel her blows but held her prisoner so that she could not free her mouth to call for help. A moan of despair escaped her as she realized that soon she would find herself the prey of Henry Morgan. There was no one to come to her aid. Even if she managed to call for help, her men would be unable to hear her over the sound of the waves. Nor would any of the privateer's crew come to her rescue. They would not put their lives in jeopardy to protect her virtue. Instead they would probably encourage their captain to do his worst while enjoying the spectacle of her struggles.

There was only one man who would be brave enough to dare Morgan's wrath, and if he witnessed the scene, he would assume she had run back to her lover after rejecting him. Feeling completely helpless against Morgan's strength, she still sent a silent plea of help to El Diablo.

"It would seem, Henry, that the wench either does not want your attentions or she has a strange way of showing her ardor," El Diablo said as he stepped from the shadows.

Morgan's muscles went rigid with tension as he slowly released Royale's mouth and turned to face his friend. His dark eyes glittered with a mixture of passion and anger as he glared at El Diablo.

"This is none of your affair. It's between Royale and myself."

"At first that's what I thought also. Then I remembered a small matter concerning a twenty-gun frigate that we need to take Puerto Bello. Do I have to remind you that if you finish what you've started, it may cost you the entire expedition? How eager do you think her men will be to sail with you once they learn what you've done to their captain? I agree that she is a lovely woman, but to them, she is their leader. They will not stomach anyone, not even you, harming her in any way," El Diablo said, his own body tense and ready if necessary to fight Morgan to save Royale. He had heard and seen the entire affair between Morgan and his ward but had remained in the shadows, hoping that she would find a way to extricate herself without his assistance. He had not wanted to confront Morgan; their mission was too important to have any dissension between them, but he could not let the man harm Royale. He'd also had a more intimate reason for not interrupting them earlier. He had wanted to see his ward's reaction to the privateer's advances, just to confirm what she had told him on the beach before stalking away.

He knew now that she had spoken truthfully, and that in itself made it even harder for him to face Morgan calmly when all he truly wanted to do was to throttle the man for laying a hand on her.

Slowly—at what Royale considered to be the pace of a sea slug—Morgan let her slide down his lean body to her feet, though he did not release his hold on her for several long, agonizing minutes. At last his hand dropped away, and he smoothed his mustache with his thumb and forefinger as he looked from El Diablo to her and said, "Forgive me, Royale. I apologize for letting myself get carried away. I did not do it intentionally."

He paused and drew in a shaky breath and said in a voice too low for El Diablo to hear, "But damn it, it's not finished between us. I want you as I've never wanted another woman, but I won't jeopardize this mission. Our time will come later."

A chill swept up Royale's spine at the firm conviction in his tone. For the time being she was safe, but after Puerto Bello she would have to make certain that she was far from Henry Morgan before he remembered his threat. El Diablo might not be nearby to save her the next time.

"I accept your apology, Captain Morgan, because I have no other choice but to sail with you. However, should anything such as this happen again, no threats under the sun could make me sail with your fleet. If you value my ship and crew, you will stay far away from me in the future. I warned you once before that I don't like to be manhandled. The next time I will be prepared, and you'll find my blade in your ribs," Royale said, marveling at her own calm voice when she felt her insides had turned into a mass of trembling jellyfish. She could feel the muscles in her legs quiver and knew that if she did not get away from the two men quickly, she would humiliate herself further by crumpling to the sand at their feet.

Inching her chin up in the air, she moistened her bruised lips and said, ''Goodnight to you both.'' Holding her head high and her back stiff, she managed to give the appearance of a person in complete control as she stalked from the encampment. Her brave front lasted until she reached a deserted section of the beach. Then her legs suddenly turned into boneless appendages, her knees buckled beneath her, and she stumbled to the sand.

She did not cry. She was too relieved to have escaped Morgan to shed any tears, but she shivered violently, as if possessed by a severe chill. Hugging herself, she bowed her head and squeezed her eyes tightly closed as she mentally relived her terror-filled moments with the privateer.

At no time with him had she experienced the feelings she had with El Diablo. Where the pirate's kisses had inspired her passion, the privateer's had only roused her fear. There had been no deep, quivering sensation in the pit of her belly when Morgan had touched her, nor did his lips make hers tingle with excitement or make her yearn for more of their intoxicating caress. She had felt thrilled when pressed against El Diablo's lean, sinewy body, but Morgan's had only repulsed her.

Slowly she raised her head to stare out across the dark water streaked with ivory moonlight. She caught her lower lip between her teeth and held it pensively as she reflected on her reaction to El Diablo, whose very presence seemed to stir a response in her. She could curse and rage against him, but even then she wanted to reach out and caress the lean line of his jaw or run her fingers through the thick, dark hair that lay so carelessly on his wide shoulders. Her passion for him seemed to lie like a tiny ember deep within dead ashes, just waiting for his voice or touch to ignite it once more.

Bemused, she sat and tried to understand her obsession with the pirate. She compared him with Morgan, wondering why the privateer did not cause her to react the way El Diablo did. The two men were much alike in appearance. They were of the same stature, and both possessed dark eyes and hair. Each had an aura of strength about him, but only one, El Diablo, had the power to stir within her something so primitive that her body instinctively gravitated toward him as if he was a lodestone for flesh and blood.

She had vowed to see him pay for their one night of passion, yet when he was near all she wanted was to be held in his arms and to feel his mouth hot against her own. In one moment he would infuriate her to the point of madness, but in the next her heart would pound against her ribs with the anticipation of his touch. He aroused no mild emotions in her. Each one she experienced was as intense as the next. He was her persecutor and her savior, her lover; her enemy, her demon, and her god; and he was an enigma, a mystery she could not fathom any more than she could understand her own feelings toward him.

Bran stood quietly watching Royale as she sat staring out across the waves. A thoughtful frown creased his brow as he reflected upon the purpose that had led him to follow her back to Morgan's camp. His intention to tell her the truth had evaporated into the night when he'd heard her conversation with Morgan.

He had wanted to know the reason behind her decision to leave Good Fortune, and now that he did he realized the futility of revealing his identity to her. Learning that the same man who had taken her innocence had come to take what she considered her rightful inheritance would only serve to deepen the hostility between them into hatred.

A cold hand seemed to grip his heart at the thought. At present he was unprepared to face such a fate. There was something between them that he could not name, and he was not willing to destroy it by telling her the truth.

The sultry night breeze whipped his hair back from his face as he gazed past Royale toward the horizon. If all she had told Morgan was true, then he could well understand her animosity. Beyond what Charles had told Bran, he knew little about the events that had led up to his becoming her guardian. He had assumed it had been her parents' wish that she be made a ward of the crown, but from what he had overheard that seemed not to be true.

Bran's frown deepened as he unconsciously pursed his lips and tried to reconcile all he had learned of the King with the man he knew. It was hard for him to believe that his friend, Charles II, could be so generous with his cast-off mistresses and then take away one young girl's home. Such an action did not seem possible for the man he had known for over ten years.

Looking once more at the lone figure on the beach, Bran realized he had solved one piece of the intricate puzzle surrounding her, but there were still too many questions left unsettled. The words "bastard's pride" flashed into his mind, seeming to illuminate the dark tunnel of his thoughts as he recalled Royale's statement to Morgan. That could be the only reason for Charles's actions; the spirited young woman with the flashing green eyes was not the legitimate heir of Sir John Carrington. By English law, everything Sir John owned would revert back to the crown at his death if he did not have legal issue to inherit his estate. The King, the Charles Bran knew and admired, did not want to toss the girl aside like unwanted baggage, so he had generously made her his ward out of respect for the man who had served him faithfully over the years.

The harsh lines that etched Bran's face softened as he

looked at Royale with new understanding. His heart went
out to the brave young woman whose lineage might not be
as pure—though her spirit was as noble—as the King's own.
She would not meekly give over the inheritance she thought
belonged to her, just as Charles would not surrender the
kingdom he had fought so hard to regain.

Suddenly feeling the need to comfort and protect Royale
from the harsh realities life had dealt her since Sir John
Carrington's death, Bran silently made his way to her side.
He knelt on one knee and gently brushed a gold-streaked
curl back from her forehead as he said, "Royale?"

When she did not respond, he cupped her chin within
his hands and forced her to look at him. For a long moment
no words passed between them as he gazed down into her
solemn face, noting the wary light that flickered in the
shining depths of her eyes.

"Royale, you've nothing to fear from me," he said, his
voice a soft caress in itself as he lightly brushed his thumb
along the line of her cheek, stroking the pliant flesh.

Royale gazed up into his masked countenance, wondering if her thoughts had conjured him to her side. Her heart
seemed to tremble in her breast as she moistened her lips
and asked, "Why did you follow me?"

"I had to, Royale," he said as he slipped one hand
through her silken hair and captured the nape of her neck,
drawing her toward him. He peered into her shimmering
sea-green eyes as if searching for the secrets she kept hidden behind them.

"Please, no more tonight. I'm too weary for any more
battles. Can't you just leave me in peace?" she said, her
eyes pleading as she strained against his hand.

"Royale, I'm not Morgan. I won't force myself on
you," he murmured huskily, his mouth only inches from
hers. He could feel her tense at the mention of the privateer, and he instinctively drew her against his chest, gently

smoothing her hair away from her face, needing to shield her from any more pain.

Holding her protectively against him, he gazed over her head toward the distant horizon as he began to speak. His voice reflected the longing he felt.

"I admit I've wanted you since the first moment I set eyes on you, but I want all of you, Royale, not just a piece of unwilling flesh beneath me to ease the ache in my loins. I want you to come to me without fear, as you came that night on the *Wicked Mistress*. I want to feel your response to my lovemaking and see your face softly flushed with desire for me and only me. I don't want your hatred; I never did."

His velvety voice combined with his gentle caress loosened the tight control Royale held on her emotions. She fought to keep her own voice steady but failed as she asked, "Then why did you threaten me? I thought we had shared something beautiful, but then you made it ugly and humiliating with your—" Her words faltered and a sob rose in her throat as the vivid memory resurfaced to haunt her.

"There is much I can't explain to you at the present moment. I can only ask that you believe that I never meant to hurt you," he said, recalling the callous remarks he had uttered to her after she had unmasked him.

At the time his only thought had been to protect his identity. His mission for the King required the utmost secrecy, and had anyone ever learned that El Diablo and Sir Bran Langston were one and the same, they would have made an immediate connection between the pirate and the King of England. It would have caused irreparable damage to the shaky peace that existed between Spain and England. That was the reason he wore the mask. It prevented anyone from recognizing him when he by chance encountered someone from one of the Spanish vessels he had captured. All would be ruined if even one nobleman from Spain visited England's court and learned that he was behind the attacks on Spain's gold-laden ships. Too much depended on his keeping his features masked.

"Royale, look at me," he said as he removed the piece of black silk that shielded his features from her. Lifting her away from him, he tipped up her chin with his thumb and forefinger. "I spoke out of anger that night, as well as from my desire to keep you to myself. Once you saw my face, I had a reason not to release you. We shared something that night that few find in their lives, and I did not want to lose it. That is why I went through the agonies of hell when I thought you had drowned after jumping overboard. There is a fire between us, Royale, that neither of us can deny, no matter how hard we try. We are thunder and lightning. Each separate, but joined by the storm of our passions. They rage within us, and like nature's own tempest they cannot be conquered once unleashed."

"I don't know what you mean," Royale said, trying to draw away from him. She was afraid of her own responses, fearing they would lead her down a path from which there would be no return.

"Tell me you don't feel it," Bran said as he lightly placed his fingertips against the pulse in her throat. Taking her hand, he pressed it to the opening of his shirt.

"Does not your heart beat in answer to mine? You can try to deny it, but don't think to negate your body's response to my touch. It echoes what I feel when you are near. Your words may refute what I know to be true, but don't deceive yourself."

Wrapped in the warm glow his voice and touch aroused, Royale drew in a shaky breath as she gazed up into his dark, penetrating eyes. She saw her own emotions reflected in their shining depths and could no longer contradict the truth of his words. She craved his touch as the addicted sailors she had seen craved the poppy. They knew the dan-

gers that lay in their paths but could not refuse the intoxicating drug. He was in her blood like opium in the blood
of the sailors who smoked it.

She recognized the chance she was taking in believing
in him. She could easily find herself in the same humiliating situation as she'd been in after their first encounter.
Once Morgan's expedition was over, El Diablo would be
free to sail out of her life once more. However, at that
moment, with his hands touching her, that possibility
seemed far in the distant future, and as her gaze rested on
his shapely lips her mind recalled the taste of him, and all
her doubts faded into obscurity.

Bran's breath caught in his throat and his heart began to
pound violently against his ribs as he saw the look in her
eyes. Reflected within their entrancing depths was a desire
equal to his own. The muscles that banded his flat abdomen
contracted sharply and an intense heat settled in his loins
in answer to the soft expression on her face.

"Royale, my beautiful Royale," he murmured huskily
as he laid her back on the sand and his mouth claimed hers.
He feasted upon the sweetness of her lips before his tongue
sought entrance to the delicacy that lay beyond. He savored
the taste of her as he moved his hand up to caress her breast
through the material of her shirt.

Royale arched toward his caress before moaning in protest and pulling free of his questing lips. She pushed him
away and sat up.

For one heart-wrenching moment he thought she meant
to leave him until she reached for the hem of her shirt and
began to draw it over her head. He smiled with pleasure
as he quickly assisted her efforts. Once free of her garments, she lifted her arms to him, but he chuckled and
shook his head.

"Nay, my little beauty, you'll not receive all the pleasure," he said as he too disrobed, throwing his clothing off without a thought to where it landed.

The hardened rose-tipped peaks of her breasts beckoned his lips as he came back to her, and she arched against his mouth, her arms encircling his shoulders, her hands pressing his head closer. He took the aroused buds and suckled them, his tongue playing its erotic game until Royale could no longer sit up. She moaned with pleasure as his hard body pressed her against the sand.

The muscles in her belly quivered with anticipation and she felt a warm, dewy sensation at the junction of her thighs as his hand found its way to the shadowy valley. She opened to his questing fingers and savored the gentle exploration as he delved into the hot passageway that led to the core of her womanhood. Her hips moved with his hand, urging him on, willingly offering all to him and wanting his lean belly pressed to hers as that male part of him entered her to appease the fiery hunger that was tearing at her insides. Rolling her head from side to side, she murmured huskily, "Take me, El Diablo."

He needed no further invitation. He had meant to make their lovemaking long and leisurely but found that he, too, knew only a burning urgency to possess her lovely body. He had been denied that pleasure far too long.

His mouth found hers once more as he covered her alabaster body with his tanned, hard flesh. Her hips arched upward to receive him as he thrust into her velvety sheath of love. A moan of pleasure escaped him as he began to move, savoring the moist warmth of her encasing his aroused maleness. Each thrust carried them higher upon the turbulent wave of passion until they reached the crest and exploded into a heady froth of ecstasy. It left them gasping for breath, and their bodies glistened with perspiration in the moonlight.

For a long while they lay without moving, their limbs

entwined, their bodies still joined intimately. Neither wanted to destroy the beauty of the moment by word or action. What they had shared was too precious.

Bran rested his head upon Royale's breast, listening to the steady beat of her heart. At last he was able to come to terms with his feelings for her. Until that moment he had not been willing to admit that she brought forth emotions within him that he'd never known existed. She was the embodiment of all that his soul craved to make his life complete.

In her he found beauty, strength, adventure, and passion, and if it was in his power, he would never venture from her side again. He had wandered the seas, always seeking some elusive thing to satisfy the yearnings of his spirit. Now he recognized what he had been seeking all along; love. He loved Royale Carrington, and he would fight to his death to keep from losing her again.

A prickle of apprehension tingled its way up his spine, and he tightened his arms protectively around her. He could lose her. They were setting out on a dangerous adventure, one in which they could lose their lives. He feared for her safety, yet he felt secure in his own ability to protect her from physical harm. However, he was much less certain of the outcome he would face when she learned that he was the man sent by the King to oversee her affairs. He was afraid that when she knew the truth, all the love he felt for her might be of little consequence.

He knew it was his responsibility to tell her his secret, but lying so close to her made it impossible. For now he would keep his own counsel and pray that he could gain her love before telling her that he was in fact Sir Bran Langston, her guardian.

"Royale," he said as he leaned upon one elbow and gently traced her lips with the tip of his finger, " 'tis growing late, and if we tarry here much longer, someone is bound to stumble over us. Though I dislike the thought of being separated from you, I doubt that either of us would like to be found in such a situation. It might help my reputation, but I doubt it would do yours any good.''

Royale's cheeks flushed a becoming rose as she arched one shapely brow at him. Her eyes twinkled with mischief, and she fought to keep from laughing.

"I wouldn't be so smug if I were you. It could do your reputation little good if the rumor was circulated that you were found making love to one of Morgan's captains.''

"You minx," he said, and he laughed as he tweaked her nose before getting to his feet. Grasping both her hands, he pulled her to him and said, "I'll race you to the water.''

"I do need a bath," Royale said, and she made a moue of disgust as she brushed at the gritty sand on her back and bottom. She gave him an impish grin and said, " 'Tis strange I didn't notice the discomfort until now.''

Bran threw back his head and laughed before he swept her up into his arms and dashed for the waves. A large swell of water washed over them, knocking them beneath it. They came up spluttering in the salty brine before beginning a water battle that left them limp with mirth in each other's arms. The touch of their wet, slippery bodies soon made them forget their play and rekindled the embers of their passion as they emerged from the water like Zeus and Aphrodite rising from the waves. The dawn pearled their sleek bodies as they stood with limbs entwined and let the gentle ocean waves caress their heated flesh.

Royale felt El Diablo's arousal against her belly and knew again the need to have that male part of him deep within her. She clung to his damp shoulders as his hands cupped her buttocks and lifted her out of the surf to impale her eager flesh once more on his throbbing member. Wanting all of him, she wrapped her legs around his hips and pressed her breasts to his furred chest as she sought the salty taste of his lips.

Their mouths devoured each other as their bodies moved in the ocean current, heightening their pleasure until Bran felt his legs quiver and knew he could no longer stand erect. Still intimately joined, he held her tightly as he walked toward the beach. However, as they reached the edge of the surf he could bear it no longer and crumpled to the water-lapped sand. He cushioned their fall with his body, bringing Royale on top of him. He savored the beauty of her dawn-pinkened body as she rode him with head arched back and breasts thrust forward for his caress. He accepted the invitation and molded the satiny mounds to his palms while he further inflamed her passion by rubbing the hardened nipples with his thumbs.

She moaned her pleasure as he began to move beneath her, and her fingers curled into the thick mat of hair upon his chest as ripples of ecstacy washed over her. Again a moan of pleasure escaped her lips as the muscles in her belly quivered with fulfillment and a shudder shook her from head to toe. She collapsed over him with a deep sigh of contentment, her long wet hair wrapping itself about them like a fine web of silk.

Knowing that she had experienced the bliss shared by lovers throughout eternity, he, too, sought his piece of heaven. He grasped her hips and moved her against him as he arched upward, thrusting deeply within her moist warmth. His cry of pleasure echoed hers and his body trembled as he found the release he sought.

"Never leave me again," Royale murmured as she clung weakly to him, savoring the last sensations of ecstacy that rippled through her belly in response to the throbbing hardness of her lover; her love.

The words "her love" seemed to run through her mind over and over in shock waves as she realized that she did love El Diablo. All the confusion she had felt before this had been for that reason alone. She had begun to love him the first time he had made love to her, and until now she had refused to recognize what she felt for him. The words, "I love you" trembled unspoken upon her lips. Too many things from the past rose up to haunt her and make her wary of voicing her innermost feelings.

El Diablo had said he desired her, but he had never uttered any words of love. At the present time she feared her own vulnerability. The tiny seed of love was just sprouting its tender roots in her heart and was far too fragile for her to voice her new-found emotions. Only time and trust would nurture it and make it strong enough so that she would feel confident to tell him of her love. For now she would savor their passion and hope that someday he would come to love her in return.

"Never, Royale, I'll never leave you," El Diablo murmured against her ear as he lifted her from the water and carried her back to where their clothes lay scattered on the sand.

Chapter 10

*T*he Raven *shuddered beneath Royale's feet like a great* animal awakening from a long sleep. The white canvas flapped lazily as it unfurled before catching the breeze and billowing taut. The ship reacted as if it had a life of its own; it trembled and surged forward once it was free of the restraint of the anchor. The vessel seemed to reflect the mood of her crew. Both were tired of being moored to land for so long and eager to be on their way across the hundred and twenty miles of open sea to Puerto Bello.

From her position on the poop deck Royale listened to the men bantering good-naturedly among themselves as they went about their duties. She understood their feelings well. It felt good to be back on the *Raven*. Until the moment when she felt the ship move, she had not realized how much she had missed its gentle sway and the sounds of the creaking timbers as it sliced through the turquoise waters. It gave her a sense of freedom that she had not experienced since dropping anchor in late March. Now, in the last week of June, she agreed they had tarried far too long in Cuba.

Raising her face to the wind, she leaned back against the rail and folded her arms over her chest as she cast one last glance toward the swiftly receding shoreline. There she had left many of her friends, but no amount of grief or remorse would change the fact. It had been a hard reality to accept, especially where Tim was concerned, but now she had managed to come to terms with herself and to realize that it was time to put the tragic events behind her and look toward the future.

She felt the prick of tears at the backs of her lids at the memory of her beloved Tim. It was still hard for her to think of never seeing that smiling, boyishly handsome face again. He had been like a brother to her, and she'd loved him as such. Drawing a deep breath, she blinked rapidly to stay the moisture in her eyes as she silently mused, Goodbye, Tim. I may leave your body here on Cuba, but in my heart you will always be close by.

Turning her back on Cuba and the past months, she stared out across the blue waters, searching out the black hull of the *Wicked Mistress* among Morgan's small fleet of ships. Had anyone told her a few weeks earlier that she would one day look toward the pirate vessel, eager for a glimpse of its master, she would have called them every kind of fool under the sun. Nothing would have made her believe that her feelings for El Diablo could change so drastically.

Spying the frigate, she scanned its deck for the tall, dark-haired man who commanded her. At last she saw him standing with arms folded and feet splayed wide for balance. Even from the distance she could see the flash of his white teeth beneath his mask as he smiled in her direction and raised one hand in salute. She returned the gesture and felt her heart swell with love for the handsome pirate. It had only been a matter of hours since they had lain in each other's arms, but she already missed him.

Recalling their lovemaking of the previous night, her cheeks flushed a deep rose. They had sated themselves with each other, knowing it would be their last chance to be together until they reached Puerto Bello. It would take ten fair sailing days to reach their destination, and she suspected they would be the longest she had ever spent.

With a sigh of resignation upon her lips, Royale turned back to the duties at hand. She would throw herself into her work and pray it would help make the hours and the days pass swiftly.

An Englishman who had once been a prisoner of the Spanish in Puerto Bello led Morgan's small contingency of four hundred and fifty men. Packed into the twenty-three piraguas they had confiscated from the local Indians, they sped along the shoreline of Panama toward the Spanish stronghold.

When it was necessary to convey an order they spoke in muffled tones, but beyond that they traveled in silence. The only sounds to break the stillness of the predawn hours were those of the wooden oars striking the sides of the canoes as they paddled through the dark waters. They made swift progress in their light craft, and an hour before dawn was due to lighten the sky in the east they landed on the beach south of the Spanish city.

El Diablo stayed close to Royale's side as Morgan's men moved stealthily toward the town. She was grateful for his presence, but it did not quell the trepidation that gnawed at her insides like some ferocious beast, taking great chunks out of her courage with its sharp fangs. She thought she had managed to put the past behind her, but as they neared the city too many memories of the disaster they had experienced in Puerto Principe rose to haunt her. It did little to help her feelings when they reached Puerto Bello and found that, unlike Puerto Principe, it was a heavily fortified town with three reputedly impregnable forts. Two of the stone battlements protected the harbor entrance, while one guarded the city from attack from the landward side.

However, when Morgan's order came at dawn to storm the harbor forts she did not let her apprehension control her but led her men as she had done in Cuba. It was a quick assault. Their surprise attack caught the garrison off guard, and before most of the Spaniards could be roused from sleep the privateers had seized the forts—and, to Royale's great relief, without losing the life of a single Englishman.

The July sun rose higher in the sky, heating the day as the privateers secured the forts and locked the Spaniards in their own dark, humid dungeons. They found and freed eleven Englishmen who had been held captive for over two years. They were also pleased to find that both forts were well supplied with ammunition and provisions. That made their position much more secure, and they could concentrate their efforts on holding the city and capturing the landward fort.

Morgan had commandeered the Castillano's headquarters as his own base of action and was already busily making plans to take the third fort as Royale sank wearily into an embossed leather monk's chair. She was exhausted from their journey in the canoes and the ensuing battle to take the fortifications. Through smoke-reddened eyes she watched as Morgan and El Diablo bent over a crudely sketched plan of the city and its three forts, mapping out their strategy.

A commotion outside drew her attention away from the two men, and she watched as two burly-looking members of Morgan's crew dragged a slender youth roughly into the room and shoved him before their captain and his friend. The expression on the young man's ashen features clearly indicated the terror he felt at facing them. Royale could easily sympathize with his plight. Each man was intimidating, and together they were a terrifying force to reckon with.

"We caught this 'un just outside of the gates, Captain," one of Morgan's men said, giving a quick nod of his head toward the youth.

"Good, now we'll have some answers," Morgan said as he stepped around the table to confront the youth. He regarded him for a long moment, his keen eyes taking note of the stark terror in the Spaniard's eyes. Morgan sensed the young man's fear even without it being reflected upon his face; he could smell it emanating from the youth through every pore. He smiled to himself. The Spaniard's fright would make his job much easier.

"Señor, I have had you brought here to offer you a choice. You can either tell me how many men hold yon landward fort, or you can die. Which do you choose?"

The youth swallowed several times, his Adam's apple bobbing up and down nervously. He moistened his dry lips and wiped the beads of perspiration from his brow as he cleared the tightness from his throat so that he could speak.

"I choose to live, Señor. There are only a hundred and thirty men in the garrison with the governor of Puerto Bello."

"I thought you looked like a sensible youth," Morgan said, his tone congenial. "Now that you have told me what I need to know, I have one more duty for you. You will take a message from me to your governor ordering him to surrender the fort immediately if he wants to keep his life."

Already pale, the Spaniard turned a deathly white and his dark eyes seemed to bulge as he said, "Señor, he will have me killed."

"It is your choice. You can risk your governor's putting a musket ball into you or be certain that I will if you don't obey my orders," Morgan said, his voice edged with steel.

Royale watched as the youth nodded and then bowed his head, resigned to the fact that he had no real choice in the matter. Compassion for the young man rose within Roy-

ale's heart. He might be her enemy, but she well understood what he was feeling at that moment. She, too, had
found herself in circumstances in which she'd had no real
alternative but to do as others bade. Her being in Puerto
Bello was the result of such an instance.

"Here, drink this," El Diablo said, thrusting a crystal
glass into her hand. "You look as if you've seen a ghost."

"Perhaps I have," she murmured as she lifted the glass
to her lips and sipped the rich Madeira they had found in
the Castillano's private wine cellar.

Bran seated himself opposite her and stretched his long
legs out before him, taking a few well-deserved minutes to
rest as they awaited the governor's answer. He drained his
glass and set it aside before arching a curious brow at her
and asking, "How so?"

Royale set her unfinished wine aside. Its taste had suddenly turned sour in her mouth as the old bitterness rose in
her throat. Leaning back in her chair, she lay her head
against the soft leather and stared up at the high, arched
ceiling. When she began to speak her voice was soft with
introspection, as if she was speaking to herself.

"I saw myself in the young Spaniard's place. He had no
more control over his life than I have had over mine. I was
so bold as to think I could take my destiny in my own
hands, but look where it has gotten me. I'm no closer to
accomplishing what I set out to do than when I began this
foolish mission."

Bran felt the need to comfort her. He wanted to go to
her and take her in his arms and tell her that everything
she desired would be hers; that he would see that it was.
But before he could make a move or say a word, the sound
of cannon fire shook the fort.

Across the room, Morgan smashed his glass against the
wall as he came to his feet with a low growl. His face was

set in grim determination, and his dark eyes were hard with anger.

"It seems we have the governor's answer," he snarled as he strode from the chamber and up the stone steps to the parapet overlooking the city.

Their conversation forgotten, Royale and El Diablo followed quickly upon his heels. They found him standing, arms akimbo, eyeing the distant fort. The wind ruffled his black hair as he glanced at them before turning his attention to the streets below.

"Damn it to hell," he cursed. "If we don't do something soon, this expedition will turn out just like the one in Cuba." Pointing to the crowded streets, he growled, "Look, they're taking their valuables and fleeing into the woods in every direction. I'm in no mood to go away practically empty-handed, as we did in Puerto Principe."

Morgan's face was dark with fury as he swung about and started shouting orders to his men in the drill yard below. "You, Purnell, take a group of men and stop those bastards from getting away." Pointing to Scrimshaw and Black Jack, he ordered, "You two from the *Wicked Mistress*, get several men and start constructing ladders. We're going to scale their damned walls."

The diabolical look on Morgan's face as he turned back to El Diablo would have chilled the strongest of hearts. His mouth was set in a grimace and his eyes were coldly calculating shards of ice.

"I want you and Madame Captain to take a group of your men and go to the priory to round up all of the nuns and friars. I intend to let their precious holy people put our ladders against the walls of the fort. The bloody Spaniards hold such reverence for anyone associated with their church that they wouldn't dare fire on them for fear of sending their own souls to hell."

A look of horror and indignation crossed Royale's face

as she gaped up at Morgan, unable to believe that he could even contemplate such an atrocity.

"You can't do this," she uttered as she looked from Morgan to El Diablo, seeking his confirmation.

"Ah, but we can and will," Morgan said, and he smiled at his ingenuity in using the Spaniards' own religion to defeat them.

"El Diablo, you can't mean to go along with what he is proposing to do?" Royale asked.

"I can see Henry's reasoning, Royale. They will be safe enough. The Spaniards hold too much respect for their faith and those who serve it to fire on their clergy."

"I won't let you do this," Royale spat, and she withdrew a loaded pistol from her belt, aiming it at Morgan's heart. "I'll see you both in hell before I go along with murdering innocent men and women."

"Put your weapon away, Royale. No harm will come to anyone. I'm only doing this to save the lives of our men," Morgan said as he held out his hand, palm upward, for the gun. "Trust me, Royale. I know what I'm doing."

"Trust you? I trust you only to appease your own greed and lust, Henry Morgan. I trusted in you once, but never again. I've gone along with all of your orders in the past, but in this I'm firm. I won't allow you to harm those people."

Morgan kept Royale's attention centered on himself as El Diablo eased stealthily behind her. When she cocked the pistol, ready to fire if necessary, Morgan shouted, "Now!"

El Diablo gave Royale no time to comprehend the privateer's meaning. He knocked the gun from her hand and wrapped his arms around her, imprisoning her against his lean body, the sound of the exploding pistol reverberating as it struck the stone parapet.

"Damn you, El Diablo, I'll never forgive you for this

villainy. You deserve your name because only the devil would condemn men and women of God to death out of his own greed," Royale swore as she struggled to free herself.

"Take her to the Castillano's residence and lock her up. She'll be comfortable enough there and out of harm's way until we finish what we set out to do," Morgan said as he disarmed Royale. "You won't be needing these, my dear," he murmured, stripping her of her sword and remaining pistols. Dismissing her with a smile, he turned and shouted for several men to go to the priory to collect the Spanish clergy.

"El Diablo, I'll hate you for the rest of my life if you let him murder those people in cold blood," Royale squealed as the pirate lifted her off her feet and carried her down the narrow steps back into the fort. She fought futilely against the strong arms that kept hers pinned to her sides but could do little more than squirm about to make his task more difficult.

Her screams of rage echoed off the high stone ceiling as he crossed the main room of the Castillano's headquarters and took the stairs to the late Spaniard's luxuriously appointed living quarters.

By the time he reached the heavily carved door to the Spanish commander's apartment, El Diablo was breathing heavily from the effort it took to handle the wriggling, screeching female. He kicked the door open with the heel of his boot and thrust her inside. Before she could regain her balance and turn to attack, he slammed the portal and locked it securely. Dropping the iron key into his pocket, he released a long sigh of relief.

Perspiration beaded his brow as he leaned against the door frame to regain his breath. He wiped his forehead absently as he listened to Royale beat against the door and curse, "El Diablo, damn you! Let me out of here."

"Royale, calm down and listen to me. I'm going to try to stop Morgan, but I won't let you out. You're far safer where you are," he said, and he strode away, leaving her banging furiously from within the chamber. Satisfied that his ward and lover was safely out of harm's way, he now had to try to persuade Morgan to change his mind about using the Spanish clergy in such a ruse.

Royale kept beating upon the door until her hands were bruised and sore from the abuse. Her unabated fury made her blood pound in her temples as she strode across the richly furnished drawing room. Needing to vent her ire upon something, she kicked the solid wooden leg of a satin-upholstered chair. The moment her toe came into contact with the inanimate object she regretted her action.

"Damn you, El Diablo," she muttered, her face screwing up with agony as searing pain raced up her foot and into her leg. She limped over to the settee and eased herself down before tugging off the soft leather boot and rubbing her mistreated toes.

Tears of frustration brimmed in her eyes, but she quickly wiped them away. She'd be damned if she would cry over the man. She'd known from the beginning that he was nothing more than a pirate who had earned his name of the devil. Today had only removed the blinders she had been wearing where he was concerned. He and Morgan were of the same breed. Both were murdering savages who tried to pretend to be civilized human beings. They dissembled very well. Their sensual good looks and masculine charm disguised their true natures from those who were easily deceived, like herself.

Recognizing her own gullibility, a new ache formed in her breast that had nothing to do with the pain of her bruised foot. It twisted and tore at her heart as she realized she had known the type of man El Diablo was after that first night on the *Wicked Mistress*, but she had let her desire for him delude her into believing otherwise.

"I won't care," she murmured as she buried her face in her hands and propped her elbows on her knees. Her shoulders drooped under the weight of the misery that rested upon them. "I won't let myself love you, El Diablo," she whispered, but she suspected from the agony welling in her breast that it was much simpler to say than to do.

The sound of musket fire and the boom of cannon drew her away from her painful reverie. It sent her into action, and she shot off the settee and hobbled across the room to the velvet-draped windows. From her vantage point she could see the landward fort and the massacre that was taking place. Even from such a distance she could clearly make out the black robes of the clergy upon the ladders, and she watched in horror as they fell. Helpless to change the events taking place before her eyes, Royale hid her face in the heavy drapes and wept openly, her sobs shaking her slender shoulders.

Wearily, Bran rubbed his hand over his powder-smudged face before massaging the aching muscles in his sword arm. The battle was over, and Morgan had taken the day. The governor of Puerto Bello had vowed that he would fight to the death before surrendering, and he had kept his word. Out of the hundred and thirty Spaniards who manned the garrison, seventy-four had died with the governor.

From the ramparts of the fort, Bran surveyed the carnage wrought by the fierce fighting. Among the shining armor and brightly colored uniforms of the Spaniards lay the black robes of the clergy. At that moment he was glad that Royale could not see the slaughter that had taken place. She had said Morgan would be murdering the innocent men and women of God, and he had done nothing less.

Morgan had miscalculated the Spaniards' spiritual obligations. They had chosen duty over piety and had kept up a steady stream of musket fire as the holy people were forced to carry the ladders to the walls and climb them ahead of Morgan's men. Their bodies had shielded the privateers, who had carried fireballs and pitchers of powder to throw at the Spanish on the other side of the stonework. Morgan had been surprised by the governor's reaction, but that had not stopped him from using the nuns and friars to achieve his aims.

Bran had to give Morgan credit for being a brilliant strategist. With only a small force of men, he had taken three reputedly impregnable fortifications, and his use of the clergy had minimized the casualties among his own men. They had lost only eighteen and had thirty-two wounded. But no matter how brilliant Bran thought the English leader, that did not make him agree with the way Morgan had accomplished his goals. It turned Bran's stomach to view the sprawled, bloody figures lying in the dust, still clutching their rosaries even in death.

He had tried to stop Morgan from carrying out his plan, but the privateer would not listen to him. He had been convinced that only such a desperate measure would see them victorious, and he had firmly believed that the Spaniards would not fire on their holy people.

Bran shook his head sadly as he strode down the stone steps to the drill yard. He tried to ignore the stench of death that rose from the bodies littering the ground as he made his way from the fort back into the crowded streets of Puerto Bello, where the victors were already enjoying the spoils of their conquest, raping the city and its female inhabitants.

Tired to the bone, Bran pushed his way through the throngs of people. Many had filled carts with their belongings and were still trying to flee the city, while others had already fallen into the hands of Morgan's men and were suffering the consequences. Sporadic gunfire, screams of pain and terror, and raucous laughter filled the air. He knew the men from the *Wicked Mistress* and the *Raven* were also celebrating at the expense of the natives of Puerto Bello, but there was little he could do about it. It was the expected and accepted way of things in war, and he could change nothing.

At the sight of the stone battlements of the fort where Royale was secured he breathed a sigh of relief. It had been looted earlier, and now all was quiet within its thick walls as the privateers ventured into the city seeking much richer booty than ammunition and provisions. His steps rang loudly upon the stone floors as he made his way up the stairs to the Castillano's residence. Unlocking the door, he pushed it open.

"Royale," he called as he stepped into the quiet chamber, "it's over. Puerto Bello is ours at last."

When no answer came his first thought was that his ward had somehow managed to escape him once more, but as he glanced toward the windows he saw her. She stood clutching the drapes, silently staring in the direction from which he had just come.

"Damn," he muttered beneath his breath as he realized she had witnessed the slaughter that had taken place. "Royale, I tried to stop it, but Morgan wouldn't listen."

Slowly she turned to face him. Her pale features were set with resolve and her eyes were the shade of a storm-tossed sea as she glared up at him.

"Do you think I will believe any more of your lies? I saw what happened today, as well as the part you played in it. I could easily recognize your black garments amid the rest of Morgan's brightly-colored band," Royale said, her voice hoarse with suppressed rage.

"Damn it, Royale, I don't like what happened today any more than you do, and if I could have changed it, I would

have. But it's done, and no matter how much you hate me
for it, nothing will alter that fact.''

"You're right. We can't alter the events that have taken
place, but that does not mean I have to accept them, either.
Nor does it mean that we can go back to the way things
were before they happened. The only thing that I'm grateful for is that it has made me realize what a fool I've been
and what a bastard you are. Now get out of my sight. I
want nothing to do with you or your evil comrade, Morgan,'' Royale ground out, clenching her fists tightly at her
side in an effort to keep from flying at him and trying to
tear him apart with her bare claws.

"Royale,'' El Diablo said softly as he took a step toward
her. He wanted desperately to mend the rift between them.

"No,'' she said, her voice firm with her resolve. Raising
both hands to keep him at a distance, she shook her head.
" 'Tis over. I want no more of Morgan's plans or of the
type of life you have chosen. I'm tired of blood and death.
I'm leaving this horrid place as soon as I can gather my
crew.''

"Neither you nor your crew are going anywhere, Madame Captain,'' Morgan said from the doorway behind
them. "I've just learned that our battle is not yet over. The
President of Panama is now marching on Puerto Bello with
three thousand men. We've no time for your childish fits
of temper if we intend to save our own necks. It will take
all of our efforts to survive against such a force.''

"I've had enough. I'll fight no more of your battles,
Henry Morgan,'' Royale said as she turned to glare at the
privateer.

"You'll fight or you'll die, Madame. At this moment
you have little choice in the matter. The President of Panama is not coming here to have a polite cup of tea with us.
You'll return to your duties, and if I have any more insubordination from you, I'll have you shot for it.''

"Damn it, Morgan," El Diablo swore as he turned on his friend, "I won't allow her to be placed in more danger. She's already been through enough."

"Allow, El Diablo? I'm in command of this expedition, and she'll do as I order," Morgan growled, his face flushing with anger.

The two men stood glaring at each other, each tensed and ready to do battle if necessary. Since the night in Cuba when El Diablo had come between Morgan and Royale, an underlying current of antagonism had developed between the two men. Both knew that there was much more to their quarrel than merely Royale's responsibilities as a member of Morgan's force. Each man wanted her, and their jealousy was eating away at the foundation of their long-standing friendship.

Royale didn't understand the exact nature of the tension between them, but she knew it left her feeling like a battered toy being fought over by two small boys. Neither man really cared what happened to her, but each was determined to try to control her life. The thought stoked her fury to a higher degree of heat. It blazed within her in a searing current until she felt her blood boil as it pounded in her temples.

With her hands braced on her hips, she came between them. Her green eyes flashed with fiery glints of rage as she looked from one deeply tanned face to the other.

"Damn you both to hell. I know my duties and will fulfill them, but it is not because either of you will allow or order me to do so." She tilted her chin haughtily in the air, spun on her heel, and stamped to the door, pausing only briefly to look back over her shoulder at the two dumbfounded men.

"You can stay here and fight over which one of you is my master while I go out to meet the President of Panama.'' With that parting comment she stalked from the room.

The two men stared at the empty doorway for a long moment before looking at each other once more. Both felt as if a hurricane had passed through, leaving them without wind to fill their sails. Their anger faded and their lips began to twitch before both broke into laughter.

''Damn me. That wench has more pluck than anyone I've ever met. You can knock her down, but she comes right back up fighting with bared claws,'' Morgan said, and he chuckled again as he wiped the dampness of mirth from his eyes.

''Aye, she has spirit, Henry, but it could get her killed.''

Morgan's smile dimmed, and a look of uncertainty crossed his face. ''You don't think she really meant what she said, do you?''

''Aye, I'm afraid she did. One thing I've learned about Royale is that she's stubborn and has a devilish temper. Once she sets her mind to something, she'll do it or die trying,'' El Diablo said as he made for the door.

''Oh, hell!'' Morgan muttered beneath his breath as he, too, raced in the direction Royale had taken.

Chapter 11

It was over at last. Henry Morgan's boldness helped his men to victory. After turning the Spanish governor's cannon against the President's troops, maiming and killing a great number of them, he sent his buccaneers out against the remaining Spaniards and put them to flight with such heavy casualties that the President was willing to ransom Puerto Bello from the privateer for a hundred thousand pieces of eight. That ransom, combined with the booty they had collected in the city, had made his expedition as profitable as he had predicted.

The buccaneers' celebration of their triumph had begun soon after Morgan had announced that the negotiations had been finalized and the Spaniards were willing to pay for the return of their city. Bonfires blazed in the streets, illuminating Morgan's men as they danced to the music of the Spanish guitars that was just becoming popular in other European countries.

The sound was as sultry as the Panama night. It drifted up to Royale, who stood alone on the parapet of the fort. It curled its sensual strands about her as she gazed down at the revelers in the street. A pale moon inched across the star-studded sky as she looked out across the city Morgan now claimed, and her mind wandered once more to those celebrating their victory in the Castillano's apartments. She clenched her jaw against the raw pain that gripped her heart and strove to keep anger at the forefront of her emotions.

She had managed to avoid El Diablo and Morgan during the battle. She had kept herself busy tending the wounded and had thought little about the two men who now sat in the Spaniard's luxurious quarters with several Spanish ladies of noble birth.

When she had stumbled upon the small party, her only thoughts had been of finding a moment of rest and of easing her hunger and thirst. It had been a shock to find El Diablo and Morgan entertaining the beautiful women.

The two men had been dressed in lace and velvet, their finery rivaling that of their female companions, who were sumptuously attired in bright silks and satins and adorned with pearls, rubies, and diamonds.

Her face smudged with grime and her clothing torn from battle, Royale had suddenly felt very much like a scraggly urchin who had accidently found herself before royalty. Embarrassment had burned her cheeks before reality once more struck her as she realized that the women were their prisoners, yet they had lost none of their finery to Morgan or his men. Her gaze had raked over El Diablo and Morgan, her contempt toward them made obvious by her snort of disgust as she turned on her heel and left the room.

The sound of the women's soft laughter had floated after her like a mocking specter as she had sped back down the stairs. Her hunger had been forgotten as a mixture of emotions raged tumultuously within her. She had run out into the night, only to come to an abrupt halt in the drill yard, unable to decide where to go. At that moment she'd had no desire to see anyone and feared that her face would reflect all the turmoil in her heart. She knew she needed to be alone to reconcile her feelings and had sought out the stone steps that led up to the parapet overlooking the city.

"How can those women be so heartless and disloyal?" she fumed. "They are enjoying themselves with the very men who perpetrated such atrocities against their own people, just to keep their finery." Royale shook her head again in disgust. She knew she could never forgive El Diablo or Morgan for what they had done, no matter what the Spanish ladies chose to do.

"No, never," she muttered into the night as she propped her elbows on the rough stone and placed her chin in the palms of her hands. Even as she made her vow, the image of El Diablo in the dark velvet jacket and the fawn-colored britches that hugged his corded thighs, outlining each powerful, sinewy muscle and leaving little else to the imagination, rose to haunt her thoughts. She could not erase from her mind the way he had bent seductively close to one of the beautiful, dark-haired women before he'd noticed her presence.

She could not stop the hard, cruel hand that seemed to grip her heart and squeeze. She swallowed several times to force back the tears that rose in her throat and drew in a deep breath in her effort to keep hold of her anger and push away the pain.

"Damn him," she cursed under her breath, vexed at her own reaction as well as at El Diablo's actions.

"Why should I let the sight of him with another woman bother me?" she questioned the warm night. "I don't care what he does or who he does it with. I don't give a bloody damn if he beds every hussy from here to Hades," she spat, yet she could not rid herself of the intense pain that stabbed at her and belied her words.

"Royale," El Diablo said softly at her side.

Royale gave an involuntary start at the sound of his voice but managed to compose her features into a cool, haughty mask as she turned to face him.

"What do you want?"

El Diablo removed his mask, and she could see his dark brows come together in a frown.

"I came to see why you bolted from the room as if the devil was after you. Are you ill?"

Royale gave a harsh little laugh and shook her head. "No, I'm not ill. The only thing that sickens me is the sight of you. Now, if your curiosity is satisfied, don't you think it's time to return to your lady friends and your celebration?"

"Damn it, Royale. What in blazes has gotten into you?"

"Perhaps I'm finally growing up and realizing that the world is not as I had first imagined it in my girlish fantasies. I'm seeing things now as they really are and not as I want them to be."

Bran gazed down into her moon-drenched face, seeing there a look that frightened him more than a dagger pressed against his heart. He knew from her expression that nothing had changed since their earlier argument, and if he could not make her understand, he would lose her forever.

"If you are finally growing out of being a spoiled, impetuous child, then you'll know that life is not black and white. It is colored with varying shades of gray. Often there are things that happen that we don't approve of, but that does not mean that they are completely wrong. I'm not defending the action Morgan took to gain the city, but it did save many of our men's lives. Have you even considered that point in your pious condemnation? If he had listened to our objections, how many of our own men would have died?"

Seeing a flash of uncertainty cross her face, he continued. "I thought not. None of us are perfect, Royale. We all make mistakes, and I honestly believe that Henry would not have chosen the course he did if he had thought the Spanish clergy would truly be slaughtered by their own people. Spain and Britain may have signed a peace treaty, but this is war. You should have realized from the start that you weren't setting out on a pleasure cruise.''

Royale flushed guiltily and looked away from the penetrating pair of ebony eyes that seemed to bore into her soul. She took a step away from him, wary of her own response to his nearness.

''I realized that quickly enough in Puerto Principe. I'm no longer blinded by girlish dreams.'' Royale's voice was tight with pent-up emotion as she glared up at El Diablo. She fought to keep her wrath alive even as she realized he spoke the truth. Anger was her only defense against her traitorous body. Even as she spoke she longed to reach up and brush the dark curl from his brow, to feel its rich texture beneath her fingers. The breeze shifted in direction, bringing his masculine scent to her. Her nostrils flared as she inhaled the odor of him, and she quickly turned away in agony.

''Just leave me alone, El Diablo. Go back to your elegant Spanish ladies. I don't want you here.''

Royale tensed as his arms went around her and pulled her back against his lean body. His breath was warm against the side of her neck, sending a tiny unwanted tingle along the curve of her throat. He brushed his lips against the sensitive spot beneath her ear before murmuring, ''You ask too much of me, Royale. Had you requested the moon and the stars, I might have granted your wish, but I can't leave you alone.''

'' 'Tis over,'' she said in an agonized voice, fighting desperately against the devastating current of fire that raced through her veins at his touch.

''No, my beautiful Royale. I will accept your curses, but I'll not accept the fact that what we feel is over. It is only beginning,'' he said softly, turning her to him.

''No, El Diablo. What happened between us was only a

mistake made by a young innocent girl,'' Royale said, drawing strength from deep within her to deny him.

Suddenly furious, his desire and her refusal to admit her own feelings for him gnawing away his patience, Bran pulled her against him, his lips descending upon hers before she had time to resist. His mouth was hard and demanding, searing away her words of protest even before her mind could form them. He felt a shudder rack her body as if she had fought a battle with herself and lost. Her lips parted to his probing tongue, and her hands crept up the silk ruffles upon his chest to his neck, her fingers entwining themselves in his dark hair.

Feeling her surrender, he abruptly thrust her away from him. He wanted Royale, but he did not want to take her by force. He wanted her to come into his arms willingly, to give her love as he longed to give his. With another woman it would not have mattered if he had to seduce away her resistance to appease the ache in his loins, but with Royale it was different. He wanted her love as much as he wanted her body, and until she came to him freely he refused to satisfy his desire, no matter how much it pained him.

''Tell me that what you just felt in my arms was a mistake, Royale,'' he said, his own hurt making his voice harsh. ''You want me just as much as I want you, but you're too stubborn to admit it. You'd rather pretend that I have done some great wrong so that you won't have to accept your desire for me.'' With that parting thrust he turned and strode away.

Stunned, Royale leaned against the cool stones, her hand touching the lips that still tingled from his kiss, her breasts rising and falling rapidly as she breathed deeply in an effort to steady her quaking limbs. Uncertainty filled her as she watched him go before she turned once more to stare moodily out across the dark landscape.

She felt torn between her earlier resolve and her need for El Diablo. She knew what he said was true. It was not over between them, no matter what she told herself. Her own response moments before had made that fact startlingly clear to her. She had boastfully pronounced that she was finally seeing things as they truly were, but after his kiss she knew that she loved him with an intensity that made her heart pound against her ribs.

She could accept the fact that he was not responsible for the horrors perpetrated by Morgan, but that did not ease the doubts she still felt where El Diablo was concerned. He was a pirate—a rogue of the seas whose lifestyle she detested. She admitted that she loved and wanted him with a passion that burned through every sinew in her body, but were her feelings strong enough to sustain her in the future? She was young, but she was wise enough to understand that you love a person for who they are and not for what you hope they will become once you've made a commitment. She loved him, but could she live as his mistress and give up her pride and dreams? Could she leave behind the heritage that she had been so determined to regain? And could she survive if he chose to cast her aside once his desire for her began to wane?

All her problems would be solved if he loved her, but he had never uttered one word of love. He had spoken only of his desire and without love to sustain it, that desire would fade as time passed. With a certainty that made her ache, she knew she would be willing to give up everything to have his love, but it was possible that he might never give it to her.

Still pondering the conflicting emotions that assailed her, she descended the stone steps to the drill yard and walked toward Morgan's headquarters. She hoped that while they remained in Puerto Bello she would be able to reconcile her feelings one way or the other about her masked pirate, and then she could decide what to do with her life.

A loud burst of laughter made her pause in the shadows of the arched entranceway that led into the main chamber of the privateer's headquarters. She instantly recognized Morgan's voice and then heard El Diablo's as he answered the English leader. At that moment she had no desire to confront either man, and she pressed herself further into the darkness, hoping they would soon return to their revelry so that she could look for an unoccupied room where she could sleep for the night. Wishing fervently that the two men would leave the chamber so she could find the rest her tired body craved, she paid little attention to their conversation until she heard her name. Her curiosity quickened, and she strained to hear what they were saying about her. As she listened her eyes widened in dismay and the color drained from her face.

"Damn it, Henry, it's not a laughing matter. Because Royale refused me is no reason to think the field is left open to you," El Diablo said.

"I see no reason why not. You just admitted that she said it was over between the two of you. Now I may have a chance with our lovely Madame Captain. You've known all along that I desire her, and since she won't have you, perhaps she'll have me. I intend to do my damnedest to see that she does," Morgan said, and he drank deeply of his wine.

"Henry, I'm warning you to stay away from her. She's not for you."

Morgan cocked one dark brow at El Diablo as his eyes took on a predatory glint. "I believe, my friend, that you take too much upon yourself. What right do you have to say me yea or nay in the matter of our beautiful comrade?"

"I have more right than you know. Just take my word for it and stay away from Royale."

"The hell I will. Just because you've bedded her doesn't make her your private property. You're only jealous because she's refused you." Morgan refilled his glass with wine and then downed the contents in one gulp. "I've known since Cuba that you wanted the girl as much as I did, and I'm about fed up with your interference. You've hovered over her like some great protective bird, and it's damned time you realized she doesn't belong to you."

"Henry, she's my responsibility, and I won't tolerate you using her just for a moment of pleasure."

"You're not her father or guardian, El Diablo. You have no rights where she is concerned," Morgan growled, an angry flush darkening his swarthy features to a deeper hue.

"You're wrong, Henry," Bran said, knowing it was time to reveal his identity to the man who had befriended the pirate El Diablo. "Royale Carrington is my ward by edict of King Charles." Bran watched as Morgan's face registered surprise and then doubt.

"Damn you say!"

" 'Tis true, Henry. Have you never wondered why I've kept my features masked even from you all these years?"

"Aye, I wondered, but at sea we meet many men who have strange habits."

"That is true, but mine was born of necessity. Since I am Sir Bran Langston and am in service to King Charles, it would do our monarch little good if I was recognized as El Diablo." Bran paused and watched as Morgan comprehended the import of what he had just learned. "Now you can see my position where Royale is concerned."

"Aye, and that explains your strange behavior toward the wench all these months. For a while I had begun to believe you were falling in love with the chit. I now see your ploy, and it was a wise one indeed. You kept her close by to protect your own interests. You *are* a devil,

Bran Langston,'' Morgan said, and then he threw back his head and laughed.

Bran smiled and settled back in his chair. He'd let Morgan believe what he would about his motives as long as it kept the privateer away from Royale.

"Aye, Henry, Charles would not look kindly on my not fulfilling my duties. It would not be a wise move on my behalf to let her get herself killed. She is my responsibility, and I have to guard her against any danger, which includes you, my friend.''

"What about yourself?'' Morgan asked, and he chuckled at the look of discomfort on his friend's face.

"That's in the past. When I first met Royale I had no idea that she was my ward. After I found she had joined your expedition and learned the reason behind it, I had to do what was necessary to keep her near me so that I could see to her welfare.''

Morgan shook his head in wonder. "Here I thought you were turning into a guardian angel, but you're still the devil I've always known. Does the minx know?''

"Nay, and if I have my way, she won't find out until I get her back to Good Fortune safe and sound. You know her feelings about Charles making her a ward of the crown. That's what sent her out on this harebrained mission in the first place. Can you imagine what she might do if she learned the truth before I get her back to Witch's Cay? She might take it into her head to sail off to where I'd never find her. As we both know from experience, she has one hell of a temper and reacts before thinking.''

"Aye, you're right about that. I learned that quickly enough yesterday when we found her already gathering men to meet the President of Panama.'' Morgan chuckled at the memory and shook his head. "I don't envy you your position. I hope Charles is planning to reward you for your sacrifice.''

Bran gazed up at Morgan thoughtfully, knowing the reward he wanted to claim from his King. If he had his way, Royale Carrington would be his prize. At the earliest opportunity he intended to ask Charles for her hand in marriage.

"Aye, Good Fortune and its mistress should not be too much to ask. I intend—"

Before anyone heard her, Royale managed to stifle the gasp of protest and indignation that rose to her lips. She did not stay to hear the rest of their conversation but bolted out into the night in search of her crew. She intended to be far away from Puerto Bello before Sir Bran Langston even knew his ward was missing.

Royale paused at the fort's gates and glanced back over her shoulder at the stone structure where Bran and Morgan sat discussing how clever they were. The vendetta that she had thought to lay to rest rose achingly once more and made her face tighten with anger as she narrowed her eyes speculatively. Bran Langston thought he had outwitted her by using her emotions to keep her a prisoner to him, but he was in for the biggest surprise of his life. He wanted the King's favor and a reward for the services he had rendered, but if it was left to her, the King of England would not look kindly upon Sir Bran Langston's deeds in the future. She would see to that.

A cold, calculating smile curled her lips up at the corners as she turned her back on the fort and began to search for her men among the revelers in the streets. Luck was with her. She managed to find Fishbait first, and together they collected the rest of her crew. They growled and grumbled about being taken away from their pleasures, but because their pockets were already full of booty taken from the residents of Puerto Bello they did not refuse to obey their captain's command to follow her to the beach.

At daybreak they were once more back on the *Raven*,

yet Royale was not quite ready to set sail. She stood on the deck, silently contemplating the *Wicked Mistress*, which lay anchored only a short distance from her own vessel. Like all the rest of the ships in Morgan's fleet, it was manned by only a skeleton crew while most of its sailors celebrated in Puerto Bello.

Eyeing the ship's great black hull in the gray light of dawn, Royale smiled to herself. Today El Diablo—or Sir Bran Langston—would learn just who he had thought to manipulate. In swift order she had assembled a boarding party, and they were rowing toward the pirate ship, intent upon taking what booty lay in her hold as well as the supplies that he would need to set sail in pursuit.

Royale called to the watch on duty as they neared the *Wicked Mistress*, "Ahoy, there. Captain Carrington asking permission to come on board."

"What business do ye have on board?" the watch asked as he leaned over the rail, eyeing the group in the small boat warily.

"I've just come from Puerto Bello with a message for your first mate from your captain," Royale said, and she held her breath to see if her ruse would work.

"Well, ye can give it to me. I'll relay it on to 'im."

"I've strict instructions to speak only with your first mate. Now lower the ladder, damn you. We don't have all day," she demanded with all the bravado she could muster.

"Ain't got no order to let anyone on board. Now give me the message and then be off with ye and your scurvy-looking crew."

"Damn you, sea swine. I'll see that El Diablo has you strung up on the yardarm, and then I'll be the one to cut you down and feed your rotten carcass to the fish when he's through with you for not obeying me."

Seeing the flicker of uncertainty flash across the man's ugly countenance, Royale pressed her point. "You're costing us precious time. Our men could be dying at the hands of the Spaniards. Now lower that damned ladder and be done with it, man. El Diablo needs your help.''

Royale heard several of her men give low chuckles and flashed them a quelling look. If they were to succeed in taking the *Wicked Mistress*, they had to lull its crew into believing that they meant no harm. The pirate vessel was manned by only a few crewmen, but unless the crew of the *Raven* were prepared to attack them from the frigate and attract the attention of those on shore, their ruse would have to work.

The rope ladder thumped down the side of the *Wicked Mistress*, its end splashing into the blue water. The watchman called to them as they began to ascend the steep side of the ship, ''I'll go get Mr. Barton.''

Royale chuckled as she stood on the deck of the *Wicked Mistress* surrounded by her men, armed and ready to meet the first mate and any other member of the pirate crew who came to greet them. Her ruse had worked, and now all that was left was to collect their purchase and be on their way.

With swords and pistols drawn, she faced the surprised first mate of the *Wicked Mistress*. He was still rubbing the sleep from his eyes as he stepped from the hatch and out onto the deck to come face to face with Royale and her men. He halted abruptly, his sleep-cluttered mind clearing instantly at the dangerous situation in which he found himself.

''What in hell is the meaning of this?'' Barton growled.

''The meaning should be quite clear to you, Mr. Barton. I've come to collect on a debt owed to me,'' Royale said to the first mate before glancing over her shoulder at Fishbait. ''You take several men to the forecastle and secure the rest of the crew. Then check out the hold to see what baubles El Diablo has concealed there. After that, clean out their stores. We'll have more need of them than they will.''

"By God, woman! You'll rue this day once El Diablo returns and finds what you have done," Barton threatened, but he made no move toward the captain of the *Raven*. At that time in the morning he was not prepared to die, and from the expressions on the faces of her men it seemed that would be his fate, if he put up any resistance.

"I rued the day I first set foot on this ship and am now only recouping a little of what I lost. Be thankful I don't sink this blasted vessel to the bottom of the ocean, as I once planned to do. Now I've listened enough; lead me to your captain's cabin," she ordered, urging Barton to do her bidding with the tip of her blade.

Begrudging every step he took, the first mate led Royale down the few steps to El Diablo's cabin. He opened the door and stepped inside when she prodded him again with the point of her sword.

"Very good, Mr. Barton," she said congenially, and she smiled. "I suggest you wait patiently in that chair while I leave your captain a message." As if reading the man's thoughts, she slowly shook her head. "No, I wouldn't try anything if I were you. As you already know, I'm very proficient with the blade, and it might cost you your life."

Prudently considering the consequences, Barton settled himself in the chair she indicated with her sword and watched as she strode to El Diablo's desk and picked up the quill. A puzzled frown knit his forehead. He had seen many things through his years at sea, but this was the first time a pirate had ever wanted to leave a message for his victim. He shook his head in bewilderment. The woman had surely lost her mind. That was the only explanation for her odd behavior.

Royale dipped the quill into the inkwell and began to

compose her farewell note to the man she had grown to love and hate with equal intensity.

El Diablo,
  I bid you adieu. I'm sorry I could not stay and help you celebrate your victory, but I thought I would find much richer booty elsewhere, as you will discover when you check the hold of the *Wicked Mistress*. I'm sure your powder and shot will also come in very useful to me in the near future. You have my gratitude as well for the men you selected to fill out my crew. They have decided to remain with the *Raven* under my command.

Royale smiled as she signed her name. There was much more she wanted to write, but for now she would be satisfied with the mental image of Bran Langston's furious face when he returned and read her missive. She would not reveal everything she had learned of him. If he even suspected that she knew he was her guardian, he might sail directly to England and try to thwart her plans to regain Good Fortune before she could secure enough gold to purchase her home.

Taking the Spanish stiletto that lay beside the log, she plunged it through the paper into the shining surface of the desk, pinning her letter in place so that Bran Langston would be sure to find it. She smiled with satisfaction as she looked once more at the first mate and said, "Now, Mr. Barton, 'tis time to see that you and the rest of your men have little chance to cause us any trouble before we are on our way." She once more used her sword to urge him from the cabin and onto the deck.

"Fishbait, is everything secured?"

"Aye, Captain. We cleaned her out. One thing I can say fer El Diablo, he keeps his ship well stocked. He also had the misfortune of leaving several trunks of valuables locked away in the cabin next to his. Our men can't complain about the purchase taken today,'' the quartermaster said, chuckling.

"Good. Now I want you to tie up Mr. Barton and his men and sink the dinghy so that if they manage to get free they won't have a way to alert El Diablo. After that, row me back to the *Raven*. We sail immediately."

"Aye, Captain," Fishbait said as he hurried to carry out her orders.

Alone on the quiet deck of the *Wicked Mistress*, Royale paused at the rail. The only sounds to be heard were the creaking of the great timbers and the cry of a gull overhead. She scanned the rigging and the tall masts as she drew in a deep breath and smiled. A feeling of triumph swept over her. She had bested Bran Langston this time and would do so again in the near future. He would soon learn the mistake he had made by thinking her a weak-minded female who could be manipulated by his honeyed words and seductive lovemaking. Today she had taken only a small taste of her vengeance.

"By God, Henry," Bran swore as he slammed his tankard down on the table in Littleton's Tavern, "do you realize it's been three months since Puerto Bello and I can still find no trace of the vixen? And now, to make matters worse, there's this rogue pirate out there somewhere using my name and attacking British ships as well as any others that cross his path."

"Settle down, my friend," Morgan said, and he waved to the thin, white-haired man who had taken the bald, one-eared barkeep's place after his unfortunate demise soon after Morgan's fleet had returned from Panama. It was whispered that his death had not been easy. His bones had been found staked on a beach that was completely covered at high tide. The waters there teemed with sharks and barracudas, and what they had not consumed the crabs had finished. His skeleton, bleached white by the sun and salt water, remained on the beach as a warning to any who thought to spy for the Spanish to fill their pockets with gold.

"Have another rum. You look as if you are about ready to explode," Morgan said.

"Explode! That's too mild a word for how I feel. I'm at my wits' end where my dear wayward ward is concerned. I've been back to Good Fortune twice with the hope of finding that she had returned, but no one there has seen her. As for the bastard who is impersonating me, I relish the thought of our meeting. He will soon learn who he is dealing with, I grant you that. His actions are doing little to help me. It's becoming harder all the time for Charles to keep telling his captains not to retaliate against the pirate El Diablo and that it is the navy's duty, not the merchantman's, to capture me. Soon he will have to let them come looking for me or reveal that he knows and has approved of my actions all along. It's getting to be a sticky situation—one that could have a serious impact on relations between Spain and England, if the impostor is not stopped soon."

Morgan propped his long legs on the table and leaned back in his chair, tilting it onto two legs as he took a long sip of the dark, rich Jamaican brew. He cocked one dark brow curiously at Bran.

"Well, then, what do you intend to do? Are you going to keep looking for our beautiful Madame Captain, or are you going after the rogue?"

Bran's long hair brushed his velvet-covered shoulders as he shook his head and released a long breath.

"I have little choice in the matter. The man has got to be stopped. It's either that or face the gibbet myself when a British man-of-war captures the *Wicked Mistress*. Even Charles couldn't save me then. He's a good friend, but he is the king of his country first and must see to its welfare before anything else.''

"Then you're giving up on finding Royale?" Morgan asked, his dark eyes thoughtful.

"No, I'm not giving up, just postponing it for the moment until this mess is cleared up. I intend to find her if it's the last thing I ever do. And when I do"—Bran paused for emphasis, his eyes glowing with fury—"she'll regret every moment of hell she has put me through. I'm going to shake her until her teeth rattle, and then I'm going to give her the spanking she's been needing all of her life, and then—''

Bran's words were cut off by Morgan's laughter. "And then, my friend, you're going to make love to her.''

"Make love to her?" Bran said, dumbfounded.

"Aye, that's what's really bothering you. You're in love with the girl, and that's what's worrying you to the brink of madness. I've known it for some time now. I guess I knew it all along, but my own foolish jealousy kept me from recognizing it so that I could hope to sway her into my own bed.''

Bran's attention suddenly centered on the tankard in his hand. He rubbed the smooth surface of the vessel with his thumb as he reflected on his feelings toward Royale.

True, he loved her, but after reading her letter he knew she did not return his love. It had been written without emotion, as if nothing had ever transpired between them. Though it was only a brief note, after their conversation on the night she'd left Puerto Bello it said much more than the few words scrawled across the paper. The note's very curtness told him that she cared nothing at all for him, and he'd be damned if she would ever know how much it had hurt. Slowly, his dark eyes lifted once more to Morgan's face.

"Aye, Henry, I love her, but at the moment my feelings

are of little consequence. My main concern is for her welfare. Right now I don't know if she is alive or dead.''

"I suspect, my friend, that our Madame Captain is very much alive. She's a survivor. You two will meet again, and I hope I'm there to see the fireworks. It should be most entertaining,'' Morgan said, chuckling at the thought.

Chapter 12

The Raven *creaked and groaned in protest as the chain* and anchor slipped into the turquoise water to restrain her. Royale absently tucked a stray curl of reddish-brown hair back beneath her hat as she eyed the buildings clustered upon the hillside of Tortuga. Since her first visit so many months before she had become accustomed to the pirate stronghold, but she still found it distasteful. Since it was her only avenue for selling the booty they captured, however, she had forced her own feelings back and had dealt with the Frenchmen who thought nothing of trading for stolen goods as long as they made a tidy profit.

A wave of relief swept over her as she viewed the crowded quay. This would be her last visit to this ill-begotten place, if the cargo taken from the last galleon brought a high enough profit. During the past months they had amassed a small fortune in gold from the prizes they had seized, and she felt secure enough now to go forward with her plans to regain her home.

She smiled to herself as she turned and scanned the deck of her ship. She had grown fond of the rough seamen who worked at their tasks with the precision learned from much experience, but it would be wonderful to see Good Fortune and Adele again. Royale was weary of her wandering and

wanted nothing more than the peace and quiet of her home
and the comforting presence of her friend.

Often during the months after she'd left Puerto Bello she
had been tempted to sail home for just a few days of rest
from the constant strain of commanding the *Raven*. Yet
she had been afraid to do so. She feared that once Bran
Langston found her missing, Good Fortune would be the
first place he would search for her. Her only hope had been
to keep him at a distance.

She prayed that her ruse of using his name when attacking the other vessels was keeping him too busy hunting the
impostor for him to have the time to search for his ward.
Since she had captured three British merchantmen in his
disguise, he should be too concerned now about keeping
his own neck out of a noose to worry much about her
whereabouts.

Royale's light laughter floated across the deck, drawing
several curious looks from nearby crewmen as she mused
on Bran Langston's predicament. It would not be an easy
task for him to explain to his King that he was innocent of
the crimes. She had made sure of that on each occasion.
Masked and dressed completely in black, she had grandly
informed her victims that it was El Diablo who was claiming their cargo. Beyond her vendetta against him, she also
had another reason for impersonating him when attacking
the British ships. It would be much simpler to thwart any
scheme he had of gaining Good Fortune if he was out of
favor with his King.

Smiling at her own ingenuity in defeating Bran Langston
in a manner as devious as his own had been toward her,
Royale turned and strode from the poop deck to where
Fishbait and several other crewmen waited with the goods
to be rowed ashore. The procedure would be the same as
it had been the previous times they had come into port.
She would go ashore and meet with the French officials.

They would haggle over the price, but in the end she would come away with what she considered just recompense. She had learned early how to deal with the Frenchmen of Tortuga, and they, too, had soon learned that the young captain from the *Raven* was not one to let them cheat him.

That thought brought another chuckle from Royale. The Frenchmen, who boasted of their masculinity and their way with women, still had not realized with whom they had been dealing. After they had purchased her cargo and she had her money in hand, she was tempted to reveal her identity to them just to see the shock on their faces. However, that was only a fleeting, mischievous thought. It could easily cause more trouble than it would be worth.

"We'll go ashore first, Fishbait, while the men bring in the booty. Once that's settled, we're for home."

"Aye, Captain. I'm one of the oldest sea dogs on this vessel and love the sea and this ship like me own home, but it'll be good to see Witch's Cay again. I bet me little old Flora has about wilted away with longing since I've been away so long."

"Fishbait!" Royale said, her eyes sparkling with mirth. "You've never told me you had a sweetheart, nor that it was Flora Tettle."

Fishbait rubbed his nose with the back of his hand as he flushed and looked sheepishly down at his feet. "Ah, I ain't got no sweetheart. Flora is just Flora, that's all. And I guess it wouldn't hurt 'er none to wilt a wee bit. The last time I was in port she near broke me back and legs when she flopped down in me lap." Looking up at Royale, he gave her a wry grin. "Come to think on it, it might be in me best interest if we just stayed at sea. It's a lot less dangerous. That woman could smother a man to death."

Royale burst out laughing. She knew well what her quartermaster meant about his Flora. The woman outweighed him by a hundred pounds if she outweighed him by an ounce. Wiping her eyes, Royale forced herself not to break into another peal of mirth and said, "Well, that's the chance you'll have to take. We're bound for Witch's Cay as soon as we sell our cargo."

"I figured that was what you'd say." Fishbait grinned before he began to descend the rope ladder to the dinghy.

Fishbait's disclosure about his love life lessened some of the tension Royale always felt when she had to venture into the pirate stronghold. Since her first visit and the escapade with the whore in the tavern, she had been considerably more wary of Tortuga and its inhabitants.

Night had descended by the time Royale had finished her business with the French officials to her own satisfaction. She had received more for the cargo of silk, satins, spices, and indigo than she had expected. The cask filled with gold sovereigns would add much to her bargaining power for Good Fortune. Even after she paid her crew their part of the purchase, she would have a tidy profit.

Flanked protectively by her men, she failed to note the tall, thin man who stood smoking a cheroot in the shadows as they descended the steps to the beach where their boat was secured. Nor did she see his dark eyes narrow with malice as he watched her climb into the dinghy before he turned to the heavyset man who had followed close in his wake.

She glanced one last time toward the dark structures from which light glowed through unshuttered windows. Sounds of revelry drifted across the water to her. At that moment she said her farewell to Tortuga, to her life as a pirate, and to the pirate who still claimed her heart. It was over. She was bound for home to collect the booty hidden in the cave, and then she was off to England to regain Good Fortune and put the past year and a half behind her.

As she ascended the rope ladder to the deck of the *Raven*, Royale felt that her world was finally righting itself.

Perhaps she would always love El Diablo, but she knew she could live with that knowledge. During the past months she had learned that well. Even as she had carried out her vendetta against him, she had known deep in her heart that he still had a place there and always would. She accepted it, and strangely her acceptance had made it easier for her to deal with her feelings.

At first the anger and hurt his deception had wrought had obscured her love for him, but time has a way of healing. She still felt anger toward him for using her as he had done to achieve his own ends, but now she was also able to recall the other, more volatile feelings he had aroused in her. Her pride would not let her surrender to the memory of the times she'd spent in his arms, nor would it let her end her vendetta. Yet her heart and the yearnings of her body would not let her forget him. It was much easier to accept how she felt toward El Diablo than to do constant battle with herself over something that she could no more stop than she could the beat of her heart.

She had tried to understand her own actions logically but had come to realize that they could not be analyzed in such a fashion. Emotions were not rational, no matter how hard you tried to make them be so. When she was near El Diablo, she reacted instinctively, throwing logic to the wind.

Stepping over the rail onto the deck of her ship, she glanced up at the star-studded sky. She was grateful once more to her father. He had instilled her with pride, and on soft, sultry nights such as this that was the only thing that kept her from forgetting all else and going in search of her masked pirate. With El Diablo far away, her common sense triumphed over her passions, and she knew it would be lunacy to even contemplate such a thing.

Pushing all thoughts of El Diablo from her mind, she gave the order to make the ship secure for the night and strode to her cabin. With the morning tide they were bound for Witch's Cay.

The midday sun flashed on the brass spyglass as Royale peered at the tiny speck that had been dogging their tracks since they'd left Tortuga. She had changed course several times to make certain that they were being followed, and the vessel had stayed with them like a hound on the scent of its prey.

Royale frowned as she lowered the glass. From such a distance she could not recognize the other ship's colors, but she suspected from the way it kept just out of range that it boded little good for the *Raven*. The ship was holding back as if waiting for the right moment to strike.

Absently tapping the spyglass against the palm of her hand, she considered her options and decided that if the other vessel thought her ship would be easy prey then they would be in for a big surprise. All her hopes for the future lay in the *Raven*'s hold, and she would not surrender it without one hell of a fight. The gold that lay in the leather-bound trunks had been earned with blood and sweat, and no one was going to take it from her as long as she still lived.

Giving the order to her helmsman to stay true to course, she was in the process of telling Fishbait to have the gunners ready their cannon for battle when the watch cried from the crow's nest, "Sail ho, starboard side, due south."

"Damn, that's all we need," she muttered as she turned away from the quartermaster and raised the spyglass once more. She paled. Making full speed under full sails and heading directly toward them was the black pirate vessel that she had hoped never to see again—the *Wicked Mistress*.

"See to the gunners, Fishbait," she snapped as she swung about to view the other vessel. It, too, had moved closer, as if wanting to snatch its prey before El Diablo could wrest it away. Looking from one vessel to the other, Royale suddenly felt like the proverbial fox cornered by hounds.

In one direction lay Bran Langston, a known entity. Swiftly approaching in the other was an unknown danger. But unlike the fox, she would not cower in a hole when the hounds chose to pounce. Her eyes gleamed with anger as she judged each of her adversaries. She'd be damned before she surrendered to either one.

Stiffening her spine and lifting her chin in the air, Royale shouted the order to prepare for battle before striding from the deck and to her cabin. As she had done in the past months, she would meet them dressed in her black garments—the very same garments she had thought to retire forever once she left Tortuga behind.

Slipping out of her clothes she quickly put on the tight black britches and loose silk shirt before securing the piece of black silk over her features to mask them. Coiling her hair beneath her black hat, she briefly appraised her appearance. If luck was with her, Bran Langston would never know that it was his ward who had been responsible for the blame placed upon his shoulders. If she could keep her identity a secret from him, he would not know where to search for her once she escaped the unexpected trap in which she now found herself. Arming herself with short sword and pistols, the stubborn set of her shoulders reflecting her resolve, she strode from her cabin.

Before she reached the hatch that opened onto the main deck a blast rocked the *Raven* and sent Royale sprawling to her knees on the rough wood. She paid no heed to the splinters that embedded themselves in her hands and legs but scrambled up the last steps and out onto the open deck to see what destruction had been wrought by the explosion.

Even before she had time to take in the lazily flapping

sails and the limp rigging, another blast shook the frigate. The foremast seemed to scream in agony as it splintered. The ship trembled violently as the tall wooden beam toppled over, tearing out the remaining rigging. The sound of the falling mast was accompanied by the cry of the watchman. Both ended abruptly as the spar and the man's body crashed to the deck; he lay still, his limbs broken and twisted about him.

"Damn your foul souls to hell," she cursed as she ordered the gunners to fire. The *Raven* was jolted as her cannon responded in kind, but her shots fell far short of their target. Before the crew had time to reload for another round, the guns from the other ship again took their toll on the frigate. The iron shot opened a large hole in her deck, sending splinters and shrapnel flying in all directions, wounding and killing those in its path.

Royale managed to dive to safety behind several large barrels that were kept on deck to catch rainwater. Her protective barrier toppled over as the frigate shuddered like a great wounded beast and rolled precariously toward the starboard side, making her cannon useless against the attacking vessel.

Stunned momentarily, Royale staggered to her feet and looked at the carnage around her. Without considering the tiny cuts that laced her arms and ran red with her blood, she fought her way toward the poop deck, shouting orders to those who were still able to fight. The sound of cannon reverberated again in the air and she tensed, waiting for the final blow to the *Raven*, but she was surprised to see that the *Wicked Mistress* had now come into range and was firing upon the other vessel.

Surveying the damage to her own frigate she saw there was little to be done but to watch the exchange between the *Wicked Mistress* and the ship that had attacked the *Raven*. Their cannon boomed, and the clear azure sky became cloudy with the gray smoke from their guns until at last the vessel that had followed them from Tortuga gave quarter and sought safer water to repair the damage done by El Diablo's guns. The ship maneuvered the *Raven* between itself and the *Wicked Mistress* so that the frigate would protect it until it was out of range of the pirate ship's cannon. The tactic worked. El Diablo ordered his crew to hold their fire because he did not want to sink the object of his search without first making the rogue who had used his name pay in full.

His eyes flashed fire through the slits in the black silk as he assessed the damage done to the vessel he had been seeking. Her name had been completely blown away from her prow by one direct hit, and, in truth, she was crippled to such an extent that he doubted she would remain afloat long enough for him to extract his revenge. It would have given him much pleasure to send her to the bottom of the ocean himself.

Ordering a boarding party to her decks as the *Wicked Mistress* eased alongside her, he saw the captain of the frigate standing on the poop deck, armed and ready for battle and dressed identically to himself. A wave of fury washed over him with such force that it made him tremble as he grasped the boarding rope and swung across the short space that separated the two ships.

Concentrating solely on the man garbed in black, he paid no heed to the few remaining crew members of the *Raven* whom he might have recognized if he had not been so intent on reaching their captain. A cruel smile curled El Diablo's lips as he slowly withdrew his sword from its scabbard and moved toward his victim with the ease of a hunting panther, the muscles that ridged his arms and legs appearing relaxed but actually tensed and ready to strike.

"So it seems the time for us to meet has finally arrived, as you and I both knew it would once you began to impersonate me. How long did you think you could play out this ruse without my hunting you down? If you thought I would stand by and take the blame for the deeds you have done, then you should have found out more about the person you chose to impersonate. That small flaw in your scheme will now cost you your life." El Diablo spoke congenially, but his eyes were fiery orbs behind his mask as he eyed his adversary.

The shapely lips beneath his opponent's mask curled into a snarl to reveal white teeth as she swiftly withdrew her own blade and faced him, bravely defiant.

"Beware, El Diablo. I once made a vow that when we met there would be only one El Diablo left to sail the sea. And I intend to keep that oath," Royale said, deepening her voice so that he would not recognize her.

Behind his black mask, Bran's brows knit in puzzlement at the sound of the smaller man's voice. Its timbre evoked memories of another, but he shook the thought aside, doubting his own sanity for even letting the rogue before him remind him of Royale. No, his mind was only playing tricks on him because of his desire to be searching for the woman he loved rather than having to deal with this sawed-off runt of a man.

"And I intend to see that you keep your vow, though I'm afraid it won't be in the manner you planned. When the *Wicked Mistress* sails away from this sinking wreck, there will be only one El Diablo left to sail the sea, and it will be me," he stated, and he made the first lunge with his sword.

Royale countered, deflecting his blade with a precision much improved during the past months. Experience had served her much better than all the lessons she had taken from her father.

"So you think," she said, and she laughed as she thrust her blade at El Diablo's heart.

He parried. Sparks shimmered in the air as their steel blades slid along each other, bringing the combatants close as the hilts of their weapons met with a loud click of metal on metal.

For a long, tense moment they strained to hold their stance, each eyeing the other through the slits of a mask. Though Royale knew the identity of her opponent, she saw Bran's flash of recognition as his nostrils flared when he breathed in the scent of her and peered down into her unforgettable sea-green eyes.

"Royale?" he breathed, relaxing his guard as a wave of relief swept over him at finding her alive.

Taking advantage of his distraction, she thrust herself from him and raised her sword. "Aye, Bran Langston. How does it feel to meet your ward—the girl you seduced to keep under your control—on equal terms?"

Bran reached up and pulled his mask from his face, letting it fall unheeded to the deck at his feet as he looked at her.

"How did you find out?" he asked, making no effort to defend himself in the event she chose to run him through.

Royale tossed her hat aside and ripped off her own mask in the same swift motion as she gave a harsh laugh. She did not relax her own defenses as she eyed him coldly, her features revealing none of the turmoil that quivered in the pit of her stomach like something alive.

"My dear guardian, you should already know the answer to your question unless you've told everyone about the duty assigned you by our good King—with the exception of the one it affected the most."

"You heard me talking with Morgan?"

"Aye, I heard you and know all about your plans, but I'm afraid you're going to be disappointed because I have no intention of going along with them."

"Is that the reason you left Puerto Bello, Royale?" Bran asked, his voice tight with dread as he awaited her answer.

"Aye. You've known my feelings for a long time, and if you thought they had changed then you were sadly mistaken; they have not. I may have been a fool where you were concerned before, but I'm one no longer. You'll not have Good Fortune nor me."

The hard muscles that banded Bran's chest constricted with pain from the invisible blow Royale had dealt him. His heart twisted as if she had plunged her dagger between his ribs and sliced it in two. She had overheard him tell Morgan that he intended to ask Charles for Royale's hand in marriage, and her hatred of him had made her flee into the night to avoid being forced into such an intolerable situation. She had reacted in the same manner when she had received the King's edict making her a ward of the crown. In both instances she had been placed in positions she had found unbearable.

The realization of how she felt toward him hurt, though he had suspected it since the night in Puerto Bello. He felt the need to creep away and lick his wounds like a cur that had been beaten by a master he loved, yet his pride would not let him. He would not give her the satisfaction of knowing she had trampled upon his heart, which no woman had managed to even touch before.

Wounded pride surfaced through the pain, forcing him to mentally lock the door on his emotions and turn his thoughts back to the duty delegated to him by his King. Royale Carrington might spurn his love, but she was still his ward and would do as he bid, no matter how stubbornly resolved she was to fight him.

"My dear ward, as I see it, you have no choice but to go along with whatever I say. Look around you and realize I speak the truth. Your ship is sinking beneath you. Instead of being so stubbornly determined to disobey me because of some misbegotten idea of being your own person without anyone to say you nay, I suggest you act quickly and get your wounded men on board the *Wicked Mistress* before they go down with the *Raven*. She is already listing precariously, and should she start to break apart you'd have no time to save anyone, including yourself.''

Royale could see the reason behind his words. The *Raven*'s timbers were groaning with the strain, and the cries of the wounded floated up to her from the deck below. No matter how hard she wanted to deny Bran Langston, she could not risk the lives of her men. At that moment they were more important than her pride.

"We'll accept your hospitality on the *Wicked Mistress*, Bran, but that does not mean anything has changed between us. Will you have your men help my wounded on board while I see to the cargo?" Royale said, already turning away, her mind focused on securing the trunks from the hold before the *Raven* sank.

Bran's hand on her arm stayed her steps. "Not so fast, my dear ward. You'll come on board the *Wicked Mistress* now. It's my responsibility to see to your welfare first."

"Damn your responsibility. My duty is to see my men safe and then make sure that my cargo doesn't go down with the *Raven*. I'll not leave my ship until all on board are safe and my cargo is secure."

"Oh, yes, you will!" Bran said, grabbing both of Royale's hands with one of his while he jerked the lacings from his shirt. He tied her wrists securely behind her back before tossing her over his shoulder like a sack of grain. He respected her ability as captain of her own vessel and admired her loyalty to her men, but he could not let that interfere with his seeing to her safety. The *Raven* could sink at any moment, and if that happened with her on board, there might not be time for her to reach the *Wicked Mistress*. Though she might want to fulfill her duties as captain, he would not chance that fate, no matter how much she argued. He loved her too much to lose her to the sea.

"Damn you to hell, Bran Langston. Let me go!" Royale squealed in protest, and she began to struggle in earnest against him.

Bran wrapped one arm about her squirming legs as he grasped the boarding rope and said, "I suggest you keep still. If you don't, you may find yourself in the water. I doubt you would find that too pleasant, since I've seen shark fins surfacing in the area ever since the battle started. They always seem to be able to smell death even before it happens."

Royale's struggles ceased instantly, and she raised her head to look down into the turquoise water between the ships. Her eyes widened at the sight of several large, bluish-gray shapes swimming just beneath the clear surface.

"Good, I thought that might make you see reason," he murmured as he wrapped the boarding rope around his wrist and captured it in the hand that also held her balanced precariously over his shoulder. With effortless grace he swung them across to the *Wicked Mistress* and then dumped her unceremoniously on the deck.

"Now I'll see to your men," he said, and he started to swing back across to the crippled vessel.

"Wait," Royale called as she struggled to her knees.

He paused and turned to look back at her, one dark brow arching in question.

"In the cabin next to mine are four large trunks. The key to the door is in my desk. It's important that you don't let them go down with the ship."

A grim smile crept over Bran's lips. He knew well what the trunks contained; his name had suffered a great deal from her capturing that treasure. "All right, you'll have your booty, my greedy little wench," he said, and he swung back toward the *Raven*.

To Royale the minutes seemed to stretch into endless hours as she waited on the deck of the *Wicked Mistress* while the crews of both ships worked efficiently to bring the wounded across from the *Raven*. They took the seriously injured below to the ship's surgeon, while those with only minor wounds were left on deck. She was relieved to find her quartermaster among the latter. Fishbait had suffered only a gash on the head and was able to see to his fellow crewmen as they were brought on board.

True to his word, Bran also rescued the four trunks that held all her hopes for regaining Good Fortune. From the expression on his face as he had the last trunk hoisted on board, she suspected that he thought her motive for wanting the treasure was her greed. He knew much about her and her past, but he knew nothing of her plans, and if it was left up to her, he would never know until it was too late for him to do anything about them.

Royale's musings were interrupted by a high, piercing squeal that sounded much like a woman's scream as the *Raven* gave her last cry. It was a mournful sound, as if the vessel was accepting her death as her great timbers finally gave way and the ocean began to bubble around her until she filled with water and sank to lie amid the brightly colored coral.

Royale's face reflected her ship's agony as it slipped beneath the turquoise froth to a watery grave. She felt as if she was once more burying a loyal friend who had served her well. Closing her eyes against the sight, she bowed her head and fought to keep the tears at bay. Her throat was tight from the effort it took, and she had to swallow several times and draw a steadying breath so that she would not give way to the urge to burst out sobbing.

Bran watched her from a distance, marveling at the different emotions one small woman could arouse within him in such a short span of time. In a matter of moments his anger at her had changed to pity. His heart went out to her as she sat with her feet curled beneath her, her hands still tied behind her back and her head bowed in grief. The sunlight streaked her chestnut hair with golden glints that seemed to beckon his touch, but he managed to resist the urge as he crossed to where she sat.

"Royale, I'll untie you if you think you can manage to control that hellish temper of yours."

Receiving no verbal response but only a slight nod from her, he bent and sliced through the laces with his dagger. Gently, he pulled her to her feet and looked down into her ashen features. He fought the impulse to take her in his arms and give her comfort. For the moment he could show no compassion if he was to make his ward understand that her adventures were at an end.

"Now it's time we got things straight between us. If you had stayed where you were supposed to in the first place, this could have been settled months ago."

Royale did not look up at him, so he could not read the expression in her eyes. The only indication that she even heard him speak was a slight tightening of her features as she pursed her lips. Noting the telltale sign of her mutinous thoughts, Bran took her by the elbow and began to lead her toward his cabin. She resisted, but the pressure he exerted with his fingers urged her forward.

"No more of that, Royale. Today marks the end of your wild escapades. You have placed your life in danger for the last time. From now on you are going to do exactly what I say, or I swear I'll give you the spanking you richly deserve for acting foolishly." Bran opened the door to his cabin and jerked her inside. He left her standing by the entrance while he strode across the room. Seating himself behind the large mahogany desk, he propped his feet up on its shining surface and pointed to the chair directly in front of it as he growled, "Now sit!"

Unused to taking commands from anyone, Royale eyed him through narrowed eyes. Her lower lip jutted out pugnaciously as she folded her arms across her chest and said, "You can go to hell!"

Bran arched one dark brow as he propped his elbow on the armrest and leaned his chin on his thumb and forefinger. The silence lengthened in the cabin as he gazed at her speculatively for a long moment. The tension mounted as ebony eyes clashed with sea-green ones.

"Do you recall the last time we were in this cabin together, my dear ward? It seems that you should know by now to obey me, or you may find yourself in that same position again," he said softly, referring to his tying her to the chair to make her behave.

Royale flushed a becoming rose, recalling their intimate hour together instead of the moment to which he referred. Begrudging every step she took, she stamped over to the chair and sat down, glaring at her guardian.

A pleased smile spread his shapely mouth as he relaxed back into his chair and folded his hands over his hard, flat abdomen. "Now that you're finished with that little bout of temper, we can discuss your future."

"My future is none of your concern," Royale spat, her eyes sparkling with her ire. "I don't give a bloody damn if King Charles made you my guardian or not. I am my own person, as you should know by now. I don't accept your authority over me, nor will I ever. Nor will I go along with your plans to take Good Fortune. It belongs to me."

"You are a ward of the crown, Royale. Good Fortune reverted back to Charles at Sir John's death. You may not approve of the circumstances in which you find yourself, but you can't change them. You should be grateful that Charles has taken an interest in your welfare."

As if shot from a cannon, Royale came to her feet. She leaned across the desk with her hands flat upon its shining surface as she asked, "I should be grateful for the crumbs tossed to me because I'm a bastard, is that what you mean? No, Bran, I have no gratitude toward anyone who takes what rightfully belongs to me. Sir John may not have sired me, but I carry his name, and he wanted me to have Good Fortune. I now understand his reasoning. He knew that the estate would be all I would ever have because of my birth, and he wanted me protected."

"Royale, that is why Charles sent me to be your guardian. He, too, wants to ensure your welfare."

She gave a harsh, sarcastic laugh and shook her head. "Thinking of my welfare when he sent *you* to be my guardian, El Diablo? Surely you jest. Isn't that like asking the snake to watch the bird's nest? If Charles had been concerned about me, he would not have taken my home from me and branded me a bastard in the eyes of the world. No, it was greed for gold that made him send a pirate to watch over me, nothing more. He didn't care that he was placing an innocent girl in the hands of a lecherous rogue who thought nothing of taking her innocence for his own amusement and profit."

His hurt and anger resurfacing against his will, Bran slammed his feet down on the floor and stood. His face was set, and he eyed Royale through narrowed eyes as he strode around the desk and jerked her around to face him. His fingers bit into the flesh of her upper arms as he glared down into her angry face.

"Damn it, Royale, you know I didn't know you were my ward the night my men brought you on board the *Wicked Mistress*. I didn't know who in blazes you were until I went to Good Fortune and saw your portrait. True, I've not always acted the perfect gentleman toward you, but don't try to place all the blame on me by denying your own part in all that has transpired between us. I won't have it."

"My part in what transpired between us?" Royale spat indignantly. "Did I ask to be kidnapped and brought to the *Wicked Mistress*? Did I ask you to make love to me that first time? No, Bran, the only part I played in your evil scheme was that of the innocent, love-smitten fool." Royale froze as she realized she had voiced the very word she had vowed never to say to him. Paling, she awaited his laughter. She cringed inwardly, expecting his ridicule, but when it did not come she realized that the expression playing over his handsome face was one of bewilderment. Seeking to regroup her defenses before he had further time to think on her slip of the tongue, she said, "But I was soon rid of such foolish notions once I realized what a lying, deceitful bastard you truly are. I might have forgiven you for keeping the fact that you were my guardian a secret from me, but not now. I heard you voice your intentions in Puerto Bello, and I'll listen to no more of your lies."

At her mention of love, Bran's hopes had suddenly sprung back to life, but they died another brutal death as she continued to speak. Fury at himself for wanting her love and at Royale for rejecting him swept over Bran and made him heedless to everything except the need to punish her for the torment that was ripping his insides apart.

"I don't want your forgiveness. I only want you," he said as he dragged her resisting body against his hard frame. His eyes sparkled like shards of black glass as he murmured, "See if you can forget this as easily as you have forgotten all else that has passed between us." His mouth came down on hers, crushing her soft lips, trying cruelly to wipe away the bitter words that had stung his heart and soul with their venom.

What he had intended as a punishment soon turned into a gentle caress as the taste and scent of her filled his senses. His grip on her arms grew slack, and with a moan, he slid his arms around her, pressing her slender body against his own passion-hardened form. He felt her resistance ebb like the tide as his lips began their sensual game with hers, assaulting her defenses at their weakest point.

Royale fought desperately to maintain control over her own volatile emotions, but her instincts were more powerful than her rational thoughts. The intoxicating kiss roused the passionate side of her nature, its heady sensation making her forget their quarrel and everything else except his hot mouth searing hers. She returned his kiss, unconsciously molding her body tightly against his, reveling in the touch of his aroused manhood pressed against her belly.

She savored the feel of the sculpted planes of his chest muscles, taut beneath the black silk of his shirt as she slid her hands upward until they crept about his corded neck, where her fingers entwined themselves in the rich texture of his hair.

The past months dropped away from her like a tattered mantle, and she was once more the young woman on the beach in Cuba who had found the man she loved beyond all else.

"God, Royale, you drive me mad," El Diablo murmured as his lips left hers to trail a path of fiery kisses along her cheek to the sensitive spot beneath her ear. He teased its shell shape with the tip of his tongue before nibbling at the white, silken column of her neck down to the valley at the base of her throat. Again he played an enticing game with his tongue as he cupped her firm buttocks in his palms, pressing her even closer to his own body.

Royale clung to him weakly, her legs unable to hold her as she arched her head back to give his questing lips access to her burning flesh. No words of protest rose to her lips as he lifted her in his arms and carried her to the bunk. She wanted him as much as he wanted her. There was no denying her need nor his as they quickly helped each other disrobe and fell together upon the same bed in which their obsession with one another had begun.

She moaned her pleasure as his lips continued their erotic exploration. She kneaded the firm muscles of his tanned back and neck as his mouth found the dark rose nipples that were already hard with anticipation, and she gasped at the fiery sensation that raced through her as he suckled her breast and his hand slid over her flat belly, down to the hidden glen that was moist with her desire.

Bran feasted upon the taste of the rose-tipped mounds until his craving to know all of her with his lips drew him along the smooth line of her ribs to her concave navel, which he enticingly circled with the tip of his tongue before moving on along the downy trail that led to the secret essence between her thighs.

No longer shocked by this ultimate caress, Royale trembled as she arched to meet his questing tongue and lips. Her breath came in ragged gasps as she reveled in the exquisite torment that flowed in a molten current through her entire being. She moved to the heady song in her blood as he flicked the tiny bud and explored the silken passageway to arouse her until she thought she would die from the pleasure he bestowed upon her.

The desire to know him as he had known her rose within Royale, and she boldly urged him away from her with her hands. She pressed him back on the bed and knelt over him, her gold-streaked hair brushing his chest as she placed her palms over his bulging pectorals, tipped with flat nipples. She smiled as she flicked them with her fingers and watched them respond in the same manner as her own breasts at his touch.

El Diablo lay still, hardly seeming to breathe as she looked down at him, a sultry light gleaming in the depths of her eyes. She gave him a provocative smile as she leaned forward and took his lips, ravishing them with her own before she began to trace a path across the raspy surface of his lean cheek with her tongue. She felt the muscles in his jaw tense as she moved slowly along it to his soft earlobe. She nibbled it teasingly before whispering, "You, too, drive me mad."

She heard his sharp intake of breath and gave a soft laugh as she brushed her breasts across his furred chest before playing the same erotic game with her tongue as he had done. She moved with an agonizing slowness down the dark V of silken hair to his hard belly. She caressed the lean surface with her hands and let her fingers trail along the thick muscles of his thighs before returning to the proud member between them.

Her hair flowed in a fan of silk over his abdomen as she laid her cheek against it and caressed the satiny object of her quest. It throbbed at her touch, sending a thrill of pleasure over her. Wanting to know him as he had known her but unsure even in her new boldness, she raised her head to gaze up into the passion-glazed depths of his eyes. His expression told her all she needed to know, and she lowered her mouth to him, caressing him with her tongue and savoring the heady nectar of his masculinity.

She heard him moan and felt him arch to her; then his hands captured her shoulders and pulled her up across his chest, and he was toppling her beneath him once more. His mouth claimed hers, and she tasted herself upon his lips as she opened her thighs to him and he thrust within her.

The time for arousing caresses was past, and in its place came only the need to quench the inferno that had been ignited by their love play. Their blood burned white-hot through their veins as they soared upward into the heavens ablaze with the blue flames of ecstasy. Their cries of rapture mingled as they touched the blissful shore of fulfillment. There gentle waves cooled their passion until it was only a golden afterglow as they lay intimately joined, their limbs entwined. Satisfaction cradled them tenderly in its warm embrace and lulled them to sleep as they savored their unspoken love within each other's arms.

Chapter 13

The night air was cool upon Royale's naked flesh as she slowly roused from sleep. She instinctively snuggled closer to the warmth at her side as she groggily opened her lashes to meet the dark gaze of the man who rested on one elbow, watching her intently. Before any other thoughts could pierce the hazy mist that still clouded her mind, she smiled at El Diablo and reached up to caress his beard-shadowed cheek. Relaxed and feeling as if she had finally found the place where she belonged, she released a contented sigh.

His expression was tender as he returned her smile and placed his own hand over hers, holding it against his face before bringing it to his lips to place a kiss upon her palm, his tongue bestowing an intimate caress on the soft skin.

"What are you thinking?" Royale asked indolently as she stretched her supple body, aware of the sensuous display of her own nakedness.

"I was just thinking about how beautiful you are and how wonderful you'll look once you are out of those horrendous men's britches and gowned as you should be in silks and satins. Do you realize that I've never seen you in anything except men's clothing, except for that time in Gregory Town when you were dressed like a demure young girl?''

Royale's face clouded as reality descended with blunt force, wiping away the enchanted glow that still lingered from their lovemaking. Instinctively she reached for the sheet and pulled it over her body, as if the action could erase all that had transpired between them.

Pushing herself upright, holding the sheet over her breasts, she brushed her tousled curls away from her face and looked at Bran Langston. Her chin automatically rose in the air, her eyes sparkling with disdain.

''I doubt you will ever see me dressed in anything except my captain's clothes.''

''Oh, but I will. I'll insist that you dress yourself in the finest gown you own once we get back to Good Fortune. And if you have none, then I will buy you one. You're far too beautiful to hide such loveliness in men's clothing, though I have to admit that I admire the way your round bottom looks in britches as you walk about. However, I prefer to be the only one to enjoy that luscious sight.'' Thinking all had been settled between them, Bran sat up, reached for his britches, and began pulling them on over his long, muscular legs.

Royale took the sheet with her as she scrambled off the bed and gathered her strewn clothing. Turning her back to Bran, she managed awkwardly to dress without revealing too much of her nakedness to him. It was not an easy task, but once it was complete she turned back to him, a resolute expression once more on her face.

''Nothing has changed, Bran. I meant what I said before. I will not accept your authority over me.''

Her words slapped the look of contentment from his face, and his own anger resurfaced. His patience was at an end. Trying to fathom Royale's mercurial moods was like trying to grasp the wind and hold it in the palm of his hand.

"You're right about that. Nothing has changed. You are still my ward, and after we meet Morgan at Ile a Vache I'm taking you back to Good Fortune, and that's where you're going to stay. From this moment forward you are going to do exactly as I say, or you'll regret it. I've put up with all of your tempestuous stubbornness for the last time. I don't give a damn about what you want or how you feel in the matter. You're going back to Good Fortune, where you belong. I hope to God that Charles finds you a husband as soon as possible so I can be rid of you."

Royale opened her mouth to protest his high-handed manner but then snapped it shut as his last words jolted her speechless. She stared in wide-eyed disbelief at him. Never during the last months had she considered that the King's plans for her might go further than merely sending his man to oversee her affairs.

"A husband?" she finally managed to gasp out, her voice hoarse with shock.

"Aye, a husband. I feel sorry for the poor devil for having to put up with your temper. You'll make his life hell, but better him than me is all I can say on the matter." Bran strode over to the desk and poured himself a hefty drink of brandy. He gulped the fiery liquor down in one swallow and poured himself another drink before looking over his shoulder at Royale. "After all these months Charles may already have found you a husband, and we could very well find him waiting at Good Fortune when we return."

Royale paled and sank abruptly onto the side of the bunk, her legs no longer able to hold her erect. She stared at Bran as she realized that everything she had done had been for nothing, if what he said was true. All she had worked to gain and all the lives that had been lost in the effort whirled through her mind in sickening images.

She felt suddenly very stupid and naive for not realizing that she was nothing more than marketable goods in the eyes of the King. Women were to be simply passed from fathers to husbands unless, as in her own case, a parent's death made it necessary for a guardian to take charge until a husband could be found.

Sir John had reared her to think herself an equal to any man. He had made her proud and independent and had given her freedom that few of her sex ever knew in their entire lives. She had been infuriated by the King's making her his ward instead of respecting her as a person, as her father had done, but she had never dreamed that his action only presaged a worst fate.

The lantern swayed overhead, casting shadows over Bran's sculpted features, emphasizing their beauty as she stared up at him, her heart twisting inside her breast. Even now, when she knew that he wanted to be rid of her and she strove to despise him for it, reality won over pride. She recognized the reason for her opposition to him as her guardian. It ran far deeper than just her need for independence. She didn't want him as her guardian because she wanted him to be her lover, her husband, and the father of her children. She wanted him to love her for the woman she was and to recognize her as an equal. She didn't want him merely to feel that she was a weight hung around his neck by order of his King.

Taking in his chiseled profile, his thickly-fringed eyes, his sensuously molded mouth, she cringed inwardly at the thought of another man touching her. How could she marry a man chosen by the King when only this one made her blood run like molten lava through her veins? No other man could arouse her to such heights of passion, and the thought of another man's hands so intimately touching her body was abhorrent.

A hysterical bubble of laughter rose in her throat at the irony of her situation, and for one wild moment she thought she was going mad. Less than an hour before, she had lain curled next to his warm, hard body content with the world, and then within a short space of time she had been snarling at him, determined to prove her independence. Now, considering the alternatives, she wished for the dominance she had been fighting against.

"Yes, I'm going completely mad," Royale mused under her breath.

Bran cocked his head to one side. "Did you say something?"

"Nothing of importance," Royale said, shaking her head at the contradictory feelings that rushed through her.

"Then it's settled. We meet with Morgan at Ile a Vache, and then we're bound for Witch's Cay."

Settled, Royale mused as a caustic little smile lifted the corners of her lips. Perhaps it was all settled to his satisfaction, but not to hers. Everything within her rebelled at the thought of being handed over like a piece of meat to the highest bidder. That would never happen if she had any say in the matter. She had fought many battles in the past and would not retreat from this one. It was far too important.

She had known the joy of love, if only fleetingly, in El Diablo's arms, and she would never settle for anything less. All other aspirations paled in comparison. Good Fortune was precious to her, but she would never trade her body and soul to remain there. She had witnessed a deep and abiding love between her parents, and she would give up everything before she would be forced into a loveless union to gain a piece of land.

With a sigh of resignation, she freed her dreams of Good

Fortune from their cage in her heart and said her farewell to her home. Bran had forewarned her of the disaster that might await her there, and she knew she could never return to it. Nor could she go to England as planned. That avenue was also closed to her now. All that was left to her was to find a way to escape Bran Langston before he could bring about the conclusion of the King's plans.

Beyond that point she did not want to consider what she would do. At the moment the only thing she was certain of was that she would not be forced into any marriage without love equally shared by both partners.

From across the cabin, Bran surreptitiously studied the fleeting expressions that played over Royale's face and wondered what schemes were now brewing in her lovely head. She was far too quiet for his comfort. The expected outburst had not come when he had told her the fictitious plans Charles had for her future. He had spoken out of anger, wanting to shake her stubborn resolve and make her realize that she might find a worse fate than himself awaiting her once she returned to Good Fortune.

The look on her face when he had announced that Charles intended to see her married had torn at his heart, but he would not retract his words. She had overheard him tell Morgan of his own plans to marry her, and her outright rejection still stung. He'd let her simmer for a while with this new threat hanging over her head, and perhaps after considering her options she would not be so eager to be rid of him.

Bran looked down at the amber liquor he swirled about in his glass. Yes, he'd let her think it over, and then the alternative of marrying him might be much more appealing to her.

Downing the last of his drink, he turned to the door. He paused with his hand on the latch and looked back at the quiet figure still sitting on his bunk.

"I'll leave you now. You may live in this cabin with me, or you may have the one next to it, if you prefer your privacy. The choice is yours." With that he opened the door and strode from the cabin without a backward glance at Royale.

Bitter tears stung her eyes as she picked up her boots and tugged them on. No matter how much she loved El Diablo, she would not remain in his cabin to be his plaything until he was ready to turn her over to another man. What they had shared had been beautiful, but now there were no illusions behind which she could hide from the fact of how he felt toward her. He wanted to be rid of her, and soon he would have that wish. Until then she would avoid any further encounters with him. It was in her own best interest. If she did not keep her distance, her own treacherous emotions might lull her into staying with him until she found herself back at Good Fortune with no recourse but to marry the man chosen for her by the King.

Royale paused at the door and cast one last glance around the cabin. Here their tempestuous relationship had begun, and here it would end. Stiffening her spine against the pain the thought caused her, she slid back the latch and stepped into the passageway. She closed the door firmly behind her, as if the action could also shut off her feelings for El Diablo.

"She's still with us, Captain," Reed Barton said as he handed the spyglass to El Diablo.

"I suspected she would be, since she's been dogging our heels since the *Raven* sunk."

"Any idea what they've got in mind?"

Bran raised the spyglass and peered at the distant speck on the horizon. He could not recognize the ship's colors but knew from the way it had been trailing them that it was the same vessel that had attacked the *Raven*. He suspected that her captain had a score to settle with the *Wicked Mistress* for stealing his prize. Lowering the glass, he smiled at the first mate.

"If they think to catch us unaware, they're in for a big surprise. We'll reach Ile a Vache this afternoon, if the wind holds fair, and then we'll see what our elusive friend thinks when he finds he's sailed into the midst of Morgan's fleet."

Barton chuckled. "I'd not like to be in his boots when he enters that hornet's nest."

"He'd not be wearing his boots now if it wasn't imperative that I meet with Morgan as soon as possible. We'd already have blown him out of the water." El Diablo handed the spyglass back to his first mate. "I'm going below. If they should gain on us or change course, let me know immediately."

"Aye, Captain," Barton said, touching the brim of his seaman's hat respectfully.

Casting one last glance in the direction of the mysterious ship, Bran strode from the poop deck and went down to his cabin. He had more on his mind than just the shadowy threat on the horizon. It had been three days since he had met up with his impostor and two since he had actually seen her. She had stayed in her cabin, taking her meals alone and refusing through the locked door even to dine with him in the evenings.

Royale Carrington was not the type of woman to accept anything meekly, and he suspected that she was keeping to herself so that she could plan another wild scheme to thwart his taking her back to Good Fortune. But this time it wasn't going to work. He was determined to see to that. He paused momentarily at his cabin door and then strode to the one further down the corridor. He tapped on it but received no answer. Annoyed by her lack of response, he knocked harder, but again only silence greeted him.

"Royale, open this damned door. We need to talk," he ordered, fighting to keep his temper under control.

"We have nothing to talk about. Now go away," came the equally determined reply from the other side of the door.

"Blast it to hell," Bran cursed as he braced his hands on the door frame and kicked the portal open, his action splintering the wood of the door. His face was flushed with anger as he strode into the cabin.

"I think, my dear ward, that we have much to discuss."

"Bran, there is nothing left to say between us," Royale said as she came to her feet and faced him with her hands braced on her hips and her chin lifted at a haughty angle. "Everything has been said. I may be forced to accept your dictates as my guardian, but I don't have to accept your company. Now get out of my cabin."

"You know, young lady, that you'd try the patience of a saint, and, as my name implies, I'm far from being one. Now, I want you to sit down and listen to me," he said. Noting her lack of response to his command, he pointed at a chair and shouted, "Sit!"

She pursed her lips and eyed him coldly, making no move to obey.

"I prefer to stand, and if you attempt to lay one hand on me, I swear to God I'll claw your eyes out. During the past two days I've had a lot of time to think, and I have come to realize that being a ward of the crown merits some respect. I doubt the King would approve of your actions toward me since our first meeting, nor would it be to his benefit to have it known that he was foisting damaged goods on some unsuspecting fool. How long do you think you would remain in his favor if he knew exactly how you have treated the girl you were sent to protect?"

"Are you threatening me, Royale?" Bran asked, his voice dangerously soft. "If you are, I give you fair warning: I don't take threats from anyone, not even you."

Royale smiled. She had found a weak spot in his seemingly invulnerable armor. He treasured his friendship with his King. "No, Bran Langston, it's not a threat but a promise that I will keep if you lay another hand on me. I've been bullied for the last time by you or anyone else. However, I am willing to make a bargain with you."

Curious as to the workings of her mind, Bran raised a dark brow and asked, "A bargain?"

"Aye, I'll give you two of my four trunks of gold if you will agree to let me go free and tell everyone that I went down with the *Raven.*"

"Two of the trunks, Royale? As I recall, you took several trunks of gold from the *Wicked Mistress* in Panama," Bran said, and he smiled.

"All right, damn you, then you can have all the gold. You'll also have Good Fortune, as well as all the wealth that goes with it. You will have fulfilled your obligation to the King and will remain in his favor, in addition to having everything else you desire. All you have to do is to let me go free."

"In all of your scheming, have you ever considered the possibility that I don't need your gold, and that I might desire more than Good Fortune, Royale?" he asked, eyeing her speculatively.

"Damn it, Bran Langston, I doubt you need anything I have to offer if you stand in such good favor with Charles. You will lose nothing by granting me my freedom."

"You're right in your assumption that I don't need your gold or your home, but I do have other needs. Are you willing to agree to my terms in exchange for seeing that Charles does not force you into a marriage with a stranger?"

Royale regarded him warily, suspecting a trap but unable to stop herself from asking, "What is it you want from me?"

"Merely a little thing. I want you to marry me instead. I'm at a point in my life when I have a need of a wife, at least in name. Charles has been hinting strongly of late that it is time for me to settle down and ensure my line. This could settle both our problems with our King."

Royale drew an unsteady breath as she looked at the man before her. She had longed to hear those exact words, but spoken with love by El Diablo—not in the form of a bargain struck between herself and Sir Bran Langston like two merchants haggling over the price of a cow. The pirate and the nobleman might be the same man, but to her they were entirely different. For that reason she could not accept.

"No, Bran, I won't marry you. By accepting your terms I would not be freeing myself from an unwanted marriage, only exchanging an unknown entity for one that I know. When I marry, it will be for love, and not because it is the only avenue left open to me. I will not humiliate nor degrade myself further by becoming your legal mistress, because that is all I would be. There is no honor in your offer. Without love, what you ask is little more than prostitution. I would be selling my body to you for your protection from the King. I want to be free, Bran."

In less than two strides he crossed the cabin and captured her by the upper arms, dragging her up against his lean body. His eyes were like shards of ice as he gazed angrily down at her.

"Humiliation, degradation—you expound greatly upon those feelings, when in truth you know that you want me as much as I want you," he said between clenched teeth.

"No, I don't want you," Royale said, shaking her head

from side to side. "I want no man who does not love me but only uses me for a moment of pleasure, and that's all it has been between us, Bran."

"When will you stop fighting it, Royale? Will you wait until it's too late and you are already bound in marriage to another? When will you admit to yourself that no other man's touch can arouse you as mine can, that no man's kisses can make your blood pound in your veins as do mine? I know the fire that burns between us, but if you're so set against recognizing it, then so be it," Bran said, and he thrust her away from him. "I've offered you marriage and have had it thrown back in my face for the last time. We will arrive at Ile a Vache within the hour, and then I will meet with Morgan. Once that's over, I'm taking you back to Good Fortune and washing my hands of you. If in the future the King finds you a husband, so much the better, but after I leave you at Witch's Cay you'll see no more of me. Maybe then you'll admit to the truth of your own feelings and realize that we have shared something that few find in their lifetimes." With that he strode out the door.

Stunned motionless, Royale stared at the closed portal, her eyes brimming with tears. "My God," she whispered aloud as her knees began to buckle beneath her and she slumped down on the side of the bunk, "what have I done?"

Her hands began to tremble uncontrollably, and she clasped them tightly together in her lap in an effort to still their movement. Her mind replayed everything Bran had said to her over and over as new tears glistened on her lashes and spilled down her cheeks onto her hands. She had gained what she sought and had lost it in the same heart-rending moment. Bowing her head, she wept her misery.

When her tears were spent, she lay back on the bunk,

exhausted. Curling onto her side, she stared at the wooden partition that separated her cabin from El Diablo's. She loved him with every sinew of her body and longed to accept his offer of marriage, but her pride blocked her path. His proposal had been made to solve his own problems as well as hers. It had not been made out of any love he felt toward her. True, he desired her, but there was much more involved in marriage than just the physical side, no matter how pleasurable it might be.

She wanted to give way to the yearnings of her own heart but knew she would find no happiness with Bran beyond their intimate moments, and that she could not bear. It would be a living hell to be near the man she loved and know that he did not return her feelings. It would be far better to do the King's bidding and accept his choice for her husband than to bind herself to Bran Langston and suffer daily from the torment of knowing he cared nothing for her.

Releasing a long sigh, Royale pushed herself upright and brushed the damp tendrils of hair away from her forehead with the back of her hand. She had tried to bargain with Bran and had failed. Now her only alternative was to follow through with her previous plan.

Thinking upon her future, she saw that her life would not be easy, since she could carry none of her booty with her when she left the *Wicked Mistress*. But she would survive. Her parents had seen to her education, and with luck she could find a position as a housekeeper or governess at one of the island plantations. It would be far better to do that than to remain as a pawn of Bran Langston and the King.

The *Wicked Mistress* jolted beneath her feet, and she knew from the sounds coming from the deck above that they had reached their destination and had dropped anchor. Soon Bran would go to meet with Morgan, and then she would make her escape. It would be her only chance. Bran had already informed her of his intention to sail directly back to Good Fortune, and if she failed tonight, she would have no other opportunity.

Settling down to wait until all grew quiet and she could slip away undetected, Royale drew her legs up on the bunk and wrapped her arms around them, resting her chin on her knees. She listened to the men as they went about their duties, some shouting orders, others laughing good-naturedly as they carried them out, because they knew it would not be long before they could go ashore and have a tankard of rum and find a little relaxation with the women of the port town. Their stay might be a short one at Ile a Vache, but she knew they intended to enjoy every moment of their free time to the fullest. That would be to her advantage, Royale mused, and she smiled to herself. While El Diablo's men refreshed themselves in the nearby taverns, she would make her way to freedom.

Her optimism dimmed as she recalled the survivors from the *Raven* that she would be leaving on board the *Wicked Mistress*. She was deserting them but she had no alternative. She knew they would come to no harm under El Diablo's command. For all of his shortcomings, she could find no fault with the way he dealt with his men, and she knew he would also deal fairly with the *Raven*'s crew.

He would allow those who did not want to remain on the *Wicked Mistress* their freedom once they were back at Witch's Cay. It was only her freedom that was at stake when it came to the masked pirate—her guardian. She had to think of her own welfare now. She was no longer in command of her vessel, nor would she have any control over her own destiny if she did not follow through with her plan to escape.

Lulled by the sounds of the *Wicked Mistress*'s creaking

and groaning against her anchor, Royale grew drowsy despite her vigil. Her dark lashes fluttered slowly down over her eyes, and she fell into a light sleep, one part of her mind unconsciously staying alert for any change taking place on board the ship.

She jerked awake with a start in a room filled with the deepening shadows of evening. She shook her head to clear her mind of sleep and rubbed her eyes as she yawned widely. Wondering vaguely at what had awakened her, she stretched her cramped muscles. She froze with her arms raised over her head as the sound came again. She recognized it immediately. It was the thump of wooden oars against the hull of a small boat. Scrambling from the bunk, she crossed to the porthole and peered out into the twilight, her eyes seeking the source of the sound.

The small craft was being rowed toward the forty-gun frigate moored some distance from the *Wicked Mistress*. She knew before she even saw Morgan's colors waving in the breeze that the heavily armed vessel belonged to the privateer. Even as she identified the ship her gaze sought once more the dark-haired figure sitting in the prow of the dinghy.

"Goodbye, El Diablo, my love," she whispered as she watched the craft reach its destination and its occupants climb up the rope ladder to the deck where another tall, dark-haired figure waited. She watched as the two friends shook hands and then turned away, already deep in discussion. For a long moment she stood staring at the vacant deck before turning her back on the scene and brushing at her stinging eyes with the back of her hand. There was no time now for tears or regrets. She had to act swiftly and be safely away from the *Wicked Mistress* before Bran finished his meeting with Henry Morgan.

Pulling on her boots and tucking her black shirt into her britches, she picked up her wide-brimmed hat and secured her hair beneath it. She moved quietly across the cabin and eased open the door to peer out into the dark passageway. Fortunately, the door had not been repaired, so Bran had not been able to lock her inside and thwart her escape. In his own smug fashion he'd assumed there was no need for locks on board his vessel. That was his first mistake, Royale mused as she stealthily moved into the corridor and made her way to the next cabin. She quickly slipped inside and leaned back against the smooth wood of the door. Releasing the breath she had been holding, she scanned Bran's quarters. Knowing exactly what she was seeking and spying it casually tossed in the corner, she moved cautiously across the room. She stepped lightly on the wide pegged floorboards, wanting no sound of her presence to reach anyone that might pass the captain's cabin.

A satisfied smile curled her lips as she bent to pick up the embossed leather sword belt her father had given her when she was sixteen. Strapping it around her slender hips, she felt her confidence begin to return. Now that she was armed, she felt more secure. Turning once more to the door, she halted abruptly at the side of Bran's desk. A wicked gleam entered her eyes as she moved behind it and opened the top drawer.

"I believe I deserve a little bit of recompense for my four trunks of gold, Bran Langston," she mused softly. "Perhaps I may find it here." Rummaging through the drawers, she sought anything of value that she might sell once she reached shore.

She had just reached the last drawer when a loud explosion rocked the *Wicked Mistress* and sent her sprawling onto the floor. The drawer hit her in the stomach, knocking the breath from her.

She gasped for air, her chest burning with the effort as she finally managed to drag the life-giving substance into her lungs. Royale was still collecting her wits when another tremendous concussion shook the frigate, again sending her across the floor. At the last moment she raised her arms to protect herself from the objects flying from the top of the desk, scattering in every direction about the cabin.

Royale lay still, her arms covering her head, waiting for another explosion and expecting the ship to disintegrate beneath her with the next. When it did not come, she raised herself up onto her hands and knees before staggering to her feet.

The stench of gunpowder permeated the air to such an extent that it burned her nostrils as she looked toward the blazing sunset in the distance. Her eyes widened in shock as she realized that it had been over an hour since the last rays of the sun had sunk below the horizon.

''Oh God, El Diablo!'' The agonized cry was torn from her throat as she realized what the flames meant. The powder magazine on Morgan's vessel had blown up. Only one thought was in her mind as she raced from the cabin and out onto the deck. She had to reach the ship and El Diablo. She searched frantically for the crewmen on duty, but to her horror she found none on board to come to her aid.

Breathing heavily, her nails biting into the palms of her hands, she screamed, ''Damn you all to hell. Come out, you bastards, we've got to save El Diablo.''

No one responded to her cry, and she screamed again, her eyes going to the inferno on the other vessel, her cheeks wet with tears. ''For the love of all that's holy, please, I need your help. Where are you?''

''Were you perhaps asking for my help, Madame Captain?'' a French-accented voice said from behind her.

Spinning around, Royale came face to face with Pierre LeCruel. Forgetting in her rush that she was facing her enemy and relieved to find someone on board to come to her aid, she grasped the front of his velvet jacket. "Please, you've got to help me save El Diablo. He's on board Morgan's ship."

"Calm yourself, Madame," LeCruel said as he took a firm hold on Royale's wrists, his fingers clamping them tightly. "It is too late to save anyone on that vessel. I saw to it that my good friend, Morgan, received his fair share of French justice, and as for El Diablo, I have her right here where I want her."

"No, you don't understand. He's on that ship, and we've got to save him," Royale gasped between ragged breaths, LeCruel's words not penetrating her terror-ridden mind.

"Ah, but I do understand. I have El Diablo and have seen Morgan pay for humiliating me in Cuba."

Royale stilled abruptly, the blood draining from her face, her mouth falling slightly agape as the horror of his words finally penetrated her mind. She moved as if in a trance, slowly looking toward the blazing frigate and then back at the thin, evil face of the Frenchman. Then the stupor that possessed her shattered as if hit by a bolt of lightning as she comprehended his meaning, and she suddenly turned into a wild thing with eyes that reflected the red flames from Morgan's ship.

"No! You bastard, I'll kill you for this!" she screamed. The change in her was so swift that it caught the pirate unprepared, and she slipped out of his grip. However, instead of retreating, she launched a vicious attack, trying to carry out her threat. She cursed him with every vile word she had learned from the most hardened of her crewmen as she flew at him, biting and kicking. Her nails raked bloody paths down his cheeks before he could avoid her talonlike claws, and he screamed with pain as he backed away to protect himself from further harm.

"I'll kill you, LeCruel," Royale screamed as she remembered the sword at her side. However, her pause to withdraw her weapon was all the opening the pirate needed.

"You bitch," he growled as he raised his balled fist and swung at Royale's face.

She managed to avoid the full impact of the blow at the last second, but his fist grazed her head with stunning force. For a split second her eyes widened in shock before she sank to the deck and fell into the dark pit of unconsciousness.

Chapter 14

An excruciating pain streaked upward from Royale's temple and made a jagged path across her skull. A bright burst of fireworks shimmered and popped behind her closed lids as she slowly began to regain consciousness. She groaned and raised her hand to her injured head. The movement only served to add to her agony, its keen edge making her stomach heave.

Before gaining enough courage to open her eyes, she drew several deep breaths to settle her quaking stomach and then peeped from beneath her lashes. She quickly regretted the action. The light sent splinters of renewed agony through her head, and she whimpered aloud as the bile rose in her throat. She swallowed convulsively, fighting against the nausea, but the effort was futile. With a moan she rolled to the side of the bunk and hung her head over the edge before she could soil herself or the bedding. Her body jerked spasmodically until nothing was left to disgorge, and she lay helpless, with cold, clammy beads of perspiration dotting her brow as she gasped in ragged breaths, trying to still her quivering insides.

Feeling somewhat better, the pain easing, she pushed herself onto her back. The muscles in her arms trembled violently from the effort. She covered her face with her hands to block out the light from the lantern that swung sickeningly from side to side over her bunk.

For a long while she lay trying to recoup her physical strength and reorient her thoughts. Through the pain that still drummed in her temples something niggled at her mind, but she could not force it to the surface. In the mist just beyond the conscious realm she sensed some terrible memory, but she could not draw it out of the gray clouds.

Her heart pounded against her ribs as she began to make it out: The faint image of red flames accompanied by the scent of gunpowder. But before she could see it clearly, the cabin door was slammed back against the wall. The commotion startled her and jarred the memory back into the recesses of her mind as she bolted upright in the bed. She swayed unsteadily, a new wave of pain ripping across her skull, then sank back against the pillows, unable to sit upright.

"You bitch," LeCruel spat as his gaze swept from the floor to where Royale lay pale and trembling. His nostrils flared in distaste and he raised a silk handkerchief to his narrow nose and mumbled from beneath it, "Get out of that bed, slut, and clean up this mess." His beady eyes raked her body, and he curled his lips back in a sneer. "You're just like every female that's ever been born. You're nothing but filth. You and all your sex are an obscenity." A shudder of disgust seemed to shake the pirate's thin frame as he turned away.

The memory that had been only a glimmer now exploded fully into her consciousness at the sight of LeCruel's malevolent face hovering over her bunk. It was so horrifying that she bolted upright once more, forgetting all else as she sat shaking like a sail in gale-force winds.

"You murdered them," she managed to say at last, her voice hoarse, her throat parched.

LeCruel turned slowly to face her, his thin lips curling

beneath his dark, narrow mustache. "*Non*, Madame, I did not murder them; I merely meted out the justice I promised many months ago. If you will recall, I also made a vow to you that day on the beach, and soon you, too, will have a taste of my justice, Madame El Diablo."

LeCruel's threat had no effect upon Royale, for her entire being was focused on one thought. "El Diablo is dead." Her voice was faint, as if she spoke from a great distance. Her heart seemed to shatter into a million fragments as she realized that she was indirectly responsible for the death of the man she loved. LeCruel's vendetta against her had cost El Diablo his life. The agony in her head was of little consequence compared to that in her heart.

"Perhaps the real El Diablo did die with Morgan, but I have men from his ship on board who will testify that *you* are the true El Diablo in order to save their own necks," Le Cruel said, chuckling.

Still stunned by the impact of her loss, Royale gazed up at the pirate, unable to comprehend his meaning. "Me, El Diablo?" she questioned vaguely. Her mind was too racked by guilt to understand the danger of her own situation.

"You may try to deny it, Madame, but nothing will save you from the hangman's noose. Of that you can be assured."

A frown puckered her brow, and she regarded the pirate as if he had completely lost his wits. "You sea slime. I'm not El Diablo. You murdered him along with Morgan," she spat, her voice filling with contempt as her mind began to clear and her temper to rise. Her need to see the vile creature before her punished pushed the pain of her loss into the back of her mind. She could mourn once LeCruel had paid in full for his evil deeds.

An acrid smile spread the man's lips as he looked at Royale and slowly shook his head. "It is your word against that of my witnesses. You will hang for piracy whether you are El Diablo or not. I intend to see you to that end. My plans are already made, and no denials on your part will stop them from being carried out.''

"What plans, LeCruel?" Royale asked, for the first time realizing her own danger.

The evil sound of the Frenchman's mirth filled the cabin as he folded his arms across his chest and leaned back against the desk.

"I've seen to it, Madame, that you will be taken back to England and tried in your own country. It may not be French justice that puts the noose around your neck, but it will be just as sweet to me. In a way, I've also put Britain on trial. Your king will have to see you hanged or face trouble with France as well as Spain.''

"You're mad, LeCruel. You have no proof beyond the false testimony of the men you speak of. Whom do you think a judge will believe? No jury, French or English, would believe a woman would turn to piracy, much less gain the feared reputation that El Diablo possessed.''

"You think not?" LeCruel said. His tone was congenial, as if they were conversing over dinner about a game of chance they were going to play. "I suggest you do not delude yourself. Justice will be served. As you already know from the explosion on Morgan's vessel, I keep my promises. It may take a while for me to fulfill them, but I always keep them.''

The pirate's confidence was more frightening than his hostility. It took all of Royale's willpower not to give way to the urge to cower, but her anger and her stubborn pride held her once more in good stead. She raised her chin up in the air and eyed him coldly, her face revealing none of her feelings.

" 'Tis you who will feel Britain's justice, you bastard. Morgan was commissioned by Governor Modyford of Jamaica to protect England's interests in the West Indies. The atrocity you committed at Ile a Vache has signed your death warrant.''

"Think what you will, bitch. I'm tired of talking with you. This time you will not be able to spread your thighs and connive your way out of the fate awaiting you once we reach Tortuga. Unfortunately for you, I've no liking for soft female flesh. Tomorrow you will be put on a British merchantman bound for England. Once there, you will be turned over to the authorities."

"No good Englishman would deal with you," Royale spat with more bravado than she felt.

LeCruel sneered, his gentleman's veneer giving way once more to reveal the vicious pirate who had earned his name of "the cruel." "This one is eager to escort you to England. He did not take too kindly to your capturing his cargo less than a month ago and selling it on Tortuga."

"As I said before, you have no proof, nor does he," Royale said, feeling much less assured than she had at first.

LeCruel's thin lips spread to reveal yellowed fanglike teeth. "Like all the rest of your sex, Madame, you take all men for fools. You set your own trap on your last visit to Tortuga. The captain of the merchant vessel you took was on the island and watched your transaction with the French official. He recognized the booty you sold as his own cargo."

"You lie! Had the man been there, he would have come forward then and turned me over to the authorities," Royale said, her heart pounding against her ribs as she recalled the quiet man who had stayed in the shadows as she dealt with the Frenchman. She had not questioned his presence but had assumed he was a minor official who had little to do with the proceedings.

"Ah, you forget that you were on Tortuga; it is governed by the French, who make their living from the booty brought into port, no matter what the nationality of the ship. It would not have been to the English captain's benefit to even try to accuse you of piracy in a pirate stronghold. However, he did pay me well to find you and bring you back so that you could be taken to England to stand trial for your misdeeds. Thanks to you, Madame, I was well paid to seek my revenge." LeCruel smiled as he watched the color drain from Royale's face. Throwing back his head, he roared his mirth.

The room blurred before Royale's eyes as she gazed up at the pirate, who stood savoring his victory over her. A blinding streak of pain raced across her skull, and she swayed. She had to brace herself with her hand against the mattress to remain upright.

"You won't succeed, LeCruel," she said, fighting to keep her voice calm and unaffected by the future he'd described for her. "No one can be as evil as you are and go unpunished. I might meet the fate you predict, but you will pay for all of your vile deeds. Morgan and El Diablo had many friends among the brethren of the coast, and you will not live long once they learn of your treachery. One dark night you will find a dagger awaiting you in a shadowy alley or behind your bedchamber door. Perhaps your demise will come in a glass of wine or a tankard of rum. But it will come, I can assure you of that, and I don't envy you your position. There is a certain loyalty among the brethren, and they don't like it when one of their own turns into a mad renegade."

LeCruel's smile faded. His face was mottled with rage as he lunged across the cabin and grabbed Royale ruthlessly by the arms, jerking her up from the bed. He glared down into her pale face through narrowed eyes sparkling with ire.

"Bitch, you tempt me to mete out my own justice. I would love to hang you from the yardarm and strip every inch of flesh from your body with the cat-o'-nine-tails, but I won't waste the effort. I don't want to lose the reward I've been promised," he snarled as he thrust her violently back onto the bunk.

She slammed into the wall. The blow stunned her momentarily, and she was unable to move for lack of strength and the renewed agony in her head. She lay curled against the rough boards as the pain again took its toll upon her stomach, which heaved with nausea. Concentrating solely on not disgracing herself in front of her enemy, she gasped great breaths of air in her effort to quell the roiling queasiness that racked her insides.

Finally regaining some control over her body, she forced herself onto her back and glared up at the pirate. "You can go to hell, LeCruel," she cursed, her eyes flashing with fiery glints of hatred.

LeCruel clenched his fists at his sides and took a threatening step toward the bunk before he managed to collect a semblance of control over his own rage. A snarl curled his upper lip as he spat, "Bitch, I should have left you to burn with the others." Turning, he strode to the door.

The muscles in Royale's arms trembled from weakness as she forced herself upright. Her throat was tight with dread as she asked, "What do you mean?"

The pirate paused and gave her a mocking grin. "Did I fail to mention that I also had the *Wicked Mistress* set ablaze after kidnapping you? The only men to escape it were the ones who agreed to testify against you." Without waiting for her response, he opened the door and stepped through, slamming it behind him. The lock clicked loudly in the silent chamber, and his evil laughter echoed back to her as he strode down the corridor.

"My God," Royale breathed as the tight control she had maintained over herself in front of the pirate shattered. She rocked back and forth like a small boat on a storm-tossed sea. Her face screwed up in agony as she squeezed her eyes tightly closed and clamped a hand over her mouth to keep back the hysterical scream building within her at the thought of the men LeCruel had murdered. El Diablo, Morgan, and what was left of the crews from the three ships—all had died because of the vendetta he had against her.

She wanted to wail and gnash her teeth in grief and guilt, but she refused to give way to it. LeCruel would find too much satisfaction in her misery if he overheard, and she was determined he would receive no more pleasure from his victory over her.

Lying back on the bunk, she wept out her grief in silence. Her tears flowed freely, seeping from the corners of her eyes to dampen a path down the side of her face to the chestnut hair that framed her pale features. She wept for all of the men who had lost their lives because of her, but most of all her tears were for the man she had loved and lost because of her stubborn pride.

El Diablo's words came back to haunt her. They tortured her more than any physical pain caused by LeCruel. He had spoken truthfully on their last night together. She had waited until it was too late to conquer her own pride and admit her love for him openly, whether he was El Diablo or Sir Bran Langston. Under either name he was the man she loved. He was not perfect, but neither was she. She had been as arrogantly stubborn as he had in expecting to gain everything on her own terms. Instead of being determined to prove herself strong enough to withstand the call of her own heart, she should have accepted him, faults and all. He had been willing to do that with her. She had learned a valuable lesson, but it was far too late.

Royale buried her face in the pillow and sobbed. If only she could summon back their last moment together, she would tell him all that was in her heart. But time could not be recalled nor events changed. El Diablo was lost to her forever, and soon she would meet her own death upon the gibbet.

LeCruel had sealed her fate, and no one could save her, not even the King. However, she would not cower and cringe but would meet her death bravely, as the man whose name she had used would have done if he stood in her stead.

"I ain't so sure about leaving ye with 'im," Scrimshaw said to the man who was bending over the still figure on the bunk. "Ye might just take it into yer head to smother the captain with 'is own pillow."

Wringing out the damp cloth in the washbowl, Fishbait turned on the three men surrounding the bunk. "Damn yer scurvy hides to hell. I don't care what ye think I might do. I won't be a-leaving 'im until he's better or dead. He's the only chance we got to find me captain, so you had best plan on having to kill me if you have any ideas of trying to make me leave this cabin."

"We can see to our own captain," Barton said as he peered down at the unconscious man.

"I suspect that ye could," Fishbait said, and he laid the cloth on El Diablo's forehead. "But ye need every hand ye got to refit this vessel so it'll be ready to sail when he comes around. He won't like it a bit when he learns that LeCruel took me captain and caused all this havoc on the *Wicked Mistress*. Me captain means more to him than either of them lets on, and I'd hate to be the one who tries to stand in his way once he learns what's happened to her."

Reed Barton considered the older man's words and nodded. "Aye, that could be true. But the fact remains that you were one of our prisoners, and we can't just let you have the run of the ship."

"To hell you say. I'd like to know why in the blazes ye can't." Fishbait growled as he straightened up and eyed the three crewmen. His critical gaze swept over them contemptuously. "If it hadn't been fer me, ye'd all be at the bottom right now. I was the one who saved yer lily-livered asses from being burned into cinders. Had LeCruel's men not overlooked us few from the *Raven*, we'd all be dead. We'd all have went down with the *Wicked Mistress* had I not been awakened by the smell of smoke. As it was, we saved El Diablo's ship fer him—and now, if ye'd get out of here, maybe I can save his life."

Unable to put up an argument against what the quartermaster said, Barton glanced toward his two fellow crewmen and shrugged. The man *had* saved them, and they owed him their lives. He could easily have jumped overboard and swum to shore to save his own neck, but instead he had stayed on the burning ship and rescued them from the hold, where the pirate's men had locked them.

It was also fortunate that El Diablo and Morgan had survived the explosion on the Oxford. By the time the crew had managed to extinguish the flames on the *Wicked Mistress*, small boats had come from other vessels and from shore to attempt to rescue those from Morgan's ship.

Few had been saved. Only a handful of men had escaped the inferno with their lives. The first explosion had killed nearly all of Morgan's men instantly. The few survivors had been those men who had been seated at the privateer's table. Strangely, it had been the men who were sitting on the same side as Morgan. They had managed to make their way on deck before the second explosion erupted. The blast had thrown them overboard, and they had clung to the debris floating in the water until help arrived.

El Diablo and Morgan had multiple cuts from the flaming splinters that had flown through the air, and they had been slightly burned, but both would live to fight again if inflammation of their wounds did not kill them.

"You've played fair with us, but I give you a warning.

El Diablo's men will not look too kindly upon you if something happens to their captain. You'd better do your best for him, if you value your life," Barton said, and he turned away.

"Keep yer threats to yerself, Mr. Barton. I have me own reasons fer wanting El Diablo alive. He's the only chance I have of getting me captain back in one piece. Once that's done, ye all can go rot in hell fer all I care."

Barton glanced back at Fishbait. Their eyes met for one brief moment and locked. A silent message passed between them. Satisfied that his captain was in good hands, the first mate looked toward the other two men.

"What in hell are you two standing here gaping at?" he growled at Scrimshaw and Black Jack. "Didn't you hear what he said? The captain will want to set sail as soon as he is able, so get your asses busy and make this vessel seaworthy again."

"Aye, Mr. Barton," the two chorused as they hurried toward the door. They reached it at the same time, their shoulders meeting each other's and the door frame. Shoving at each other, each wanting to be the first to carry out the first mate's orders, they finally managed to make their way out of the cabin.

Reed Barton shook his head in disgust and mumbled to himself as he followed in their wake to make sure they did as ordered. "How those two have managed to live this long," he mused, "I'll never know."

Fishbait chuckled his agreement as he again lifted the cloth from El Diablo's brow and dampened it with cool water. He wrung it out before splashing it with a little brandy and turned once more to place it on the pirate's brow. He came to an abrupt halt as he looked down and found alert ebony eyes staring up at him.

"So you're a-thinking it's about time to wake up? I can't

agree with ye more on that account. I'm tired of acting the wet nurse fer a grown man,'' he said with a wry grin.

El Diablo tried to speak but found his mouth too dry to form any words. He cleared his throat and tried again. He succeeded only in releasing a raspy croak.

"Aye, yer throat is parched,'' Fishbait said as he poured a glass of water and raised El Diablo's head so that he could drink.

Bran greedily gulped down the water and wiped his mouth with the back of his hand. He tried to sit up but found the effort took more energy than he was able to muster. He was breathing heavily from the strain as he lay back, his dark brows drawing together in a frown as he looked up at Fishbait.

"What in the hell's wrong with me? I feel as if I've been on a week-long drunk, brawled in every tavern in Port Royal, and come out the loser each time.''

Fishbait reached for the bottle of brandy and poured it into El Diablo's glass. He smiled down at him and nodded. "I'd liken what ye've been through to a brawl with every sea scurvy in the West Indies instead of just Port Royal.''

Bran's hand shook unsteadily as he raised the glass to his lips and drained it. The fiery amber liquid burned down his smoke-raw throat, but once it reached his stomach it seemed to give him a bit more strength as it warmed his blood.

"Well, are you going to tell me what's happened? And what in hell you are doing here instead of one of my own men?''

"To answer yer last question first, I've been trying to keep ye alive. As fer the other, don't ye remember the explosion on Morgan's ship?'' Fishbait asked as he turned the straight-backed chair toward the bunk and straddled it.

Bran's frown deepened. Tiny lines fanned his eyes and etched the sides of his mouth as he sought to recall the events that had led up to his being bedridden and under the care of the *Raven*'s quartermaster. When the memory surfaced, his face reflected the impact of the shock.

"The *Oxford*! My God, it blew up beneath our feet. All I remember is fighting my way up on deck before another blast sent me head first into the water. After that I must have blacked out."

"Aye, that's what happened. Fortunately fer you, Morgan survived to help ye stay afloat. Ye were only half-conscious when they brought ye back to the *Wicked Mistress*," Fishbait said as he reached for the long-stemmed clay pipe lying on the table. He tapped the used tobacco from it and refilled it before striking the tinder box to get a spark. Once the pipe was lit, he drew on it until a steady stream of blue smoke rose toward the heavy-beamed ceiling.

"Were we the only survivors?"

"Just about. There were only a few who made it through the first blast. The *Oxford* burned to the water line before she sank. You're lucky to be alive."

"What caused it? Did her powder magazine blow up?" Bran asked as he tried to recall all that had transpired but found only vague images to relate to.

"That was what everyone thought at first. It wasn't until they learned that LeCruel had attacked the *Wicked Mistress* while all the excitement was taking place on the *Oxford* that they began to think otherwise. It was too much of a coincidence that both happened at the same time. If that Frenchie had had his way, yer ship would now lie next to the *Oxford* on the bottom."

"Damn," Bran cursed, "I should have known LeCruel was the bastard who had been following us ever since attacking the *Raven*. I never got a clear look at the captain of the vessel, nor did I recognize her colors. So that's why he didn't fly his own flag; he had other things on his mind."

"Aye, he had other things on his mind, all right. He

wanted me captain, and he got her while all hell was breaking loose on the *Oxford*,'' Fishbait growled. ''He blew up Morgan's ship, and then the cowardly bastard crept on board yer vessel. He would have burned it, too, had he been more careful.''

Bran was already throwing back the blanket and trying to sit up as he said, ''LeCruel's got Royale!''

Fishbait pushed him back on the bunk and jerked the blanket over him. ''Aye, he's got her, but ye ain't a-going to be doing her nor yerself any good if ye come down with an inflammation in yer chest. Yer as weak as a titmouse, and it's going to take several days fer ye to regain yer strength. And thanks to the bastard's handiwork, it'll also take that long to refit yer vessel so she can sail again.''

Bran lay back, heeding the quartermaster's advice. He knew he had little choice in the matter because his body was too weak. Dark spots danced before his eyes when he moved too quickly, and his muscles trembled so violently that he felt his limbs would fall off. It seemed to take all of his strength just to draw in enough air to speak.

''Does Morgan know about LeCruel's treachery?'' he finally managed to say after several long moments.

''Aye, he knows, but it does him as little good as it does ye,'' Fishbait said as he settled himself once more in his chair. ''He can't go after him until he gets another ship and crew.''

''By God, the black-hearted bastard will rue the day he ever crossed me. He will pay with his life, and if he has harmed Royale in any way, his death will be long and slow.''

Fishbait grinned in agreement. ''That's why I been trying to keep ye alive.''

With her hands bound behind her back, Royale stumbled ahead of LeCruel up the steps and out onto the sun-drenched deck. The sudden brightness blinded her, and she paused, squinting against the harsh light as she tried to focus her gaze on the blurry image that stood near the main mast.

"Get moving, bitch," LeCruel growled irritably, and he gave her a rough shove forward.

His action overbalanced her, and she staggered to her knees only a few feet away from the man who had paid the pirate to capture her. Hair tumbled about her face, shrouding her features and obscuring her view. Ignoring the pain in her knees, she made an effort to rise but found to her humiliation that her bound hands and awkward position made it impossible.

"So this is the great El Diablo?" the captain of the *Rosemond* asked as he folded his arms across his chest and gazed down at the gold-streaked head bowed before him.

"*Oui*, Captain Hillary, this is the witch who robbed your vessel. She doesn't look so fierce now that she is unmasked and on her knees, does she?" LeCruel said as he grasped a handful of Royale's hair and jerked her head back so that the Englishman could view her face.

Hillary's gaze swept over the perfect features, now flawed by a dark bluish-green bruise that spread from her cheekbone along her temple and up into her hair. For a moment he experienced a twinge of pity for the pain he knew the girl had suffered when the bruise had been inflicted, but he quickly squelched it. This one did not deserve his sympathy, nor would she receive it. She and all of her kind were abominations against all good and decent people. They preyed on the helpless; and, as a God-fearing man, he intended to see that this one never got the chance to carry out any more of her evil deeds against honest people. Glancing from the girl back to LeCruel, he eyed the pirate coldly. He loathed having to do business with the same sort as El Diablo, but he had no choice in the matter.

"From the mark on her face, it seems your name well suits you, LeCruel."

"I do what is required, Monsieur," the pirate said, and he smiled, showing his yellowed teeth. "You will learn soon enough that this one may have the face of an angel, but her name also suits her well. She is a hellcat when cornered. I suggest you remember that, or you may find her dagger between your ribs when you least expect it." LeCruel sneered with disgust and thrust Royale's hair from him. "She's a viper in the disguise of a seductive, beautiful woman, and if you have such leanings, Hillary, you had best beware that you do not lose your life because of them."

"I'll take your advice under consideration, LeCruel, but you have no need to worry that I'd take this one to my bed. I wouldn't soil myself with the likes of her. I have a good wife awaiting my return to England. My only intention toward this she-devil is to see her hanged for her evil ways."

"Just beware, Monsieur. I've seen strong men seduced into doing her bidding, and it is a long way from Tortuga to England," LeCruel said, eyeing the Englishman, assessing his character from his weak mouth and chin, surmising that they indicated the same weakness in his personality.

"This hussy won't work her spell on me," Hillary said as he grasped Royale by the arm and jerked her to her feet. His fingers bit into her soft flesh as if to confirm his statement as he gazed coldly down at her. "Now, my little El Diablo, it is time to bid our friend farewell. We don't want to keep the hangman waiting too long."

With a toss of her head she cleared her hair from her line of vision and glared up at the captain of the *Rosemond*. Her eyes sparkled with fiery glints of ire as she said recklessly, "Hillary, you may spout your piety, but you're no

better than LeCruel. Your desire for revenge has cost the
lives of many men. How can you justify their murder to
God when, in truth, it is only your own greed for gold that
caused it?''

"Hush your vile mouth, harlot!" Hillary shouted, his
ruddy features darkening with rage. "If men have died to
see you brought to justice, then it was by God's will."

"God's will? Nay. It was yours and LeCruel's. I may
hang, but when the King learns of your deeds you will join
me on the gibbet."

"Silence, you devil's handmaiden! I'll hear no more of
such talk. You will not gain your freedom by trying to
threaten me. LeCruel was right—you are a viper in disguise, but you'll not be able to work your evil tricks on
board my ship. You'll repent your sins, or you'll stay
locked in the hold, where you can contemplate your life of
corruption," Hillary said, thrusting her toward a burly seaman. "Willy, take this wench back to the *Rosemond* and
lock her in my cabin while I finish my business with Captain LeCruel."

"Aye, Captain," Willy said, and he grinned down at
Royale as he lifted her in his arms and tossed her over his
wide shoulder.

The sharp impact against her middle knocked the breath
from her, and she hung limply, gasping for air as the seaman swung her over the side and climbed down the rope
ladder to the dinghy below. Her world spun dizzily around
her as the blood rushed to her head, and her long hair
obscured her vision of all but the man's broad back. She
felt him sway precariously and for one frightening moment
thought they would both plunge into the choppy waves. If
that happened, she knew she would drown with her hands
tied. At last she felt him gain his balance, and with a bone-
jarring thump he dumped her into the bottom of the small
craft.

The ribbed wood of the hull bit into Royale's back and bottom, and she gave a cry of pain before she could stop herself. The seaman ignored her outcry as he took up the oars and settled himself on the plank seat. Paying no heed to her discomfort, he dipped the flat blades into the waves and whistled a merry tune as he rowed toward the *Rosemond*, anchored a short distance away.

The prow of the dinghy bumped against the side of the merchantman, and, as before, Willy hefted Royale over his shoulder like a sack of flour and ascended the rope ladder to the deck of the ship that was to be her prison until they reached England.

"Hey, Willy," a crewman called, "I see we got her after all."

"Aye," Willy replied as he flashed a roguish grin at the group of sailors who had come to inspect Hillary's prisoner. "The Captain always gets what he goes after." Giving Royale's round behind a firm pat with his wide, flat-palmed hand, he added, " 'Tis hard to believe this little thing could have caused as much havoc as is blamed on her, ain't it?"

"Get your filthy hands off me, you bastard," Royale hissed, and she squirmed against the indignity. There was little more that she could do in her present position.

"She may be little, but she's got spunk," the first mate said, and he laughed. "The Captain may have bitten off more than he can chew with this one."

"I doubt that. A few days chained in the hold will improve her manners. Before we reach England, Hillary will have put the fear of God into her. I can nearly guarantee that," Willy said, and he gave a sly wink. "Or maybe we can put something else in her that might be more to her liking."

A roar of laughter followed Willy's comment. "That'd be more fun than the Captain's prayer meetings," the first mate said as he nudged the man next to him with his elbow.

"You and your captain can both go to hell," Royale said as she tried to wriggle free of the arms that held her legs.

"Such language from a wench. Tsk, tsk," Willy said, striding toward the hatch that led down to the captain's cabin. "Now, that ain't no way to be talking to old Willy, especially since I've decided that you and me are going to become close friends."

"You'll never be my fr—" Her words were abruptly cut short as Willy jolted her against his shoulder, knocking the wind from her once more.

"Now here we be," Willy said as he opened the cabin door and went in. Dumping her on the bunk, he smiled down at her. He ran his tongue around his thick lips as his gaze swept over her from head to toe before coming to rest upon her breasts. Kneeling at her side, he began to unlace her shirt, loosening it until the deep V opening exposed the creamy tops of her breasts. Slowly he ran his hand along the curve of her throat and down to the firm, rose-tipped mounds. A wry grin curled his lips as he said, "Aye, we're going to be real close friends."

"Never," Royale spat, trying to move away from his exploring fingers.

"Never is a long time," Willy mused as he fondled her through the fabric of her shirt. "A lot of unpleasant things can happen in only a few moments. You'll find that out if you're not biddable. In exchange for a few of your favors, I might be able to convince the captain to go easy on you so that your voyage will be a little bit more comfortable."

"You slimy bastard, you know the answer to that. I'd rather die than have you touch me." Royale drew up her knees and kicked Willy in the side with all the force she could muster in her awkward position. The action served its purpose, and he tumbled backwards off the bunk and landed with a loud grunt. However, her reprieve was only momentary; he clambered back onto the bunk, his face hard with anger.

"You bitch," he growled as he grabbed the front of her shirt and ripped it down the center, exposing the upper half of her body to his hot gaze. "Here I was just trying to be nice to you. Now it's time for you to see that I can be mean, too, when it suits me."

Royale cried out from the excruciating pain as Willy's rough hand clamped down onto her breast and squeezed. The agony of it burned through her and left her panting for air. Perspiration beaded her brow, and dark spots hovered before her eyes. She sought the dark oblivion of unconsciousness, but it evaded her, and she was left to endure another painful squeeze before Willy was satisfied with her suffering.

"Now, bitch, are you ready to be a little more generous with me?" he asked as he bent over her, his face only inches from her ashen features.

Royale drew in a ragged breath, and with it came the scent of his putrid breath. The foul odor made her stomach churn with nausea. "You can go to hell," Royale managed to say over the bile rising in her throat.

"I've been told often enough by old Hillary that I'm headed in that direction," he chuckled as his thick-lipped mouth descended over hers.

Royale gagged as his fingers locked about her chin and forced her to open her mouth to his probing tongue. She moaned her protest as she moved her head from side to side in an effort to tear her lips away from his. Her attempt was thwarted by his fingers, which added more pressure to his already bruising grip.

Lying upon her bound hands, she was unable to do more than whimper as his heavy body came down on hers, crushing her into the mattress. He moved his hips obscenely against her thigh, arousing himself through his clothing as he devoured her mouth and worked his hands down her stomach to the apex of her thighs.

For once in her life, Royale regretted her strong constitution. She wished at that moment that she could faint as easily as other women seemed to do. She knew he intended to rape her and longed to escape from the degradation by slipping into the black void of forgetfulness.

Willy worked at the lacings of her britches, and when he released her mouth so that he could tug them from her hips she screamed. She stopped abruptly when the back of his hand crashed against her cheek.

"Hush your mouth, bitch. We don't want anyone to disturb our pleasure," he growled. His lust-glazed eyes traveled the length of her slender body as he worked his own clothing loose.

As he exposed his engorged member, Royale screamed again. The sound ripped through the cabin as she tried to squirm away from him, but he grabbed her by the ankle and jerked her over onto her stomach.

"Bitch, now I'll show you how we find our pleasure at sea when we ain't got no women on board," Willy said as he again tugged at her britches.

Intent upon his purpose, the seaman failed to hear the commotion in the passageway beyond the cabin door. He was so absorbed in his own desire that he was unaware of Captain Hillary's presence until a stunning blow knocked him onto the floor.

Briefly dazed by the impact, he shook his head to clear his vision, and the sight before him made the blood drain from his face. Hillary stood glaring down at him. Swiftly realizing his own tenuous position, he scrambled to his feet, refastening his britches in the same motion.

"It's her fault, Captain. She tempted me, she did,"

Willy said as he pointed at Royale, who lay curled in a ball to try to cover her nudity.

"You lying bastard," Royale cried. "He tried to rape me."

Hillary's face was rigid with anger. His pale eyes were like shards of ice as he gazed from the naked woman back to Willy. Without a word to the seaman he strode to the door and called several of his men from the deck above. When they entered the cabin, he nodded in Willy's direction and said, "Take him on deck and tie him to the mast. I'll be up directly to see to his whipping."

"Captain," Willy pleaded, "I'm innocent of what she says. It was her that begged me to pleasure her."

"I don't doubt that she seduced you, but you'll still feel the lash for succumbing to her wiles. I'll not have my men acting like a pack of dogs after a bitch in heat. Be thankful, seaman, that I don't have you hanged for the infractions you have committed," Hillary said, and he motioned the men toward the door.

"Captain, please," Willy begged as he was dragged from the cabin.

When the door had closed behind the men, leaving Royale and Hillary alone, he gazed down at her through narrowed eyes that held no warmth or kindness within their pale depths.

"LeCruel was right about you. You are a devil in the disguise of a beautiful woman." His voice was husky as his eyes swept over his captive. He felt his heart begin to pound against his ribs at the sight of her full breasts and the shadows that deepened at the hidden junction of her thighs.

Suddenly realizing that he was falling prey to her loveliness, he tried to focus his thoughts on the wife that awaited his return. That was a mistake, he understood too late. His middle-aged wife was an ugly duckling compared to this beautiful swan. She lacked the girl's slender beauty. Where her hips and breasts were much too large to fit into a man's hand, this girl's softly curved body seemed to beckon his touch. His wife's skin was browned with age spots, and her hair was turning a dull, mousy gray, while his captive's skin reminded him of soft, white alabaster polished to a satin sheen, and her hair was a russet silk highlighted with gold.

Hillary felt himself swell with desire, a response that had not been kindled within him by his wife for several years. "Damnation," he muttered in irritation as he turned away from the lovely sight upon his bunk.

He loved his wife, and his body's response to the she-devil was a sin against all he believed in. With a growl of disgust he strode across the cabin and opened his footlocker. Taking the black gown he had purchased for his wife from it, he came back and tossed it at Royale.

"Clothe yourself, harlot. You may have been able to seduce my crewman, but you'll not play your evil games with me." When she made no response to his command, he growled, "I said put on some clothes."

Royale looked at the gown and back at Hillary. "I would gladly obey your command, but I am unable to with my hands tied."

Uncomfortable at the thought of touching the girl with his blood scorching every nerve in his body, Hillary felt his ruddy complexion deepen in hue as he drew a deep breath and bent to cut through her bonds. Unable to resist the urge to touch the softness of her flesh, he took her hemp-raw wrists within his hand and inspected them as if it was his duty. His own senses were so heightened that the small contact jolted him to the very core, and before he realized his own action he ran a caressing hand along the slender curve of her arm to her shoulder. Engrossed in the satiny feel of her flesh, he began to stroke downward to the rose-tipped mounds.

"Take your hand off of me," Royale ordered as she knocked him away from her and jerked the ugly black gown from the bunk to cover her nakedness from his hot gaze.

Hillary's face darkened with rage as he realized his own immoral behavior. He did not blame himself but laid all the guilt on the beautiful she-devil. It was her fault, as Willy had said. Even without a word she could make a man do her bidding. She was far more dangerous than even the pirate, LeCruel, had warned him. And her name suited her well, "the devil."

Royale quickly slipped on the gown. She suspected that the expression on Hillary's face boded little good for her. At least now she didn't feel so defenseless against the hatred she saw in his cold eyes as he formed his lips into a firm, resolute line and glared down at her.

"You are Satan's spawn, and I'll not let your soft flesh make me forget that I am a servant of God," he snarled as he grasped Royale by the arm and jerked her to her feet. "You'll witness my wrath at those who sin against Him. And if you know what's good for you, you'll repudiate your allegiance to your black master and repent your sins by asking my forgiveness and the Lord's."

Hillary forcibly propelled Royale from the cabin and up to the deck, where Willy had been bound with his hands tied to the main mast. His shirt had been stripped from him, and at the sound of his captain's command to bring the cat-o'-nine-tails the muscles in his back tensed visibly.

Thrusting Royale toward another of the *Rosemond*'s crew, Hillary said, "Tie this witch alongside her cohort and bare her back. A few lashes will make her reconsider her evil ways. She'll not be so anxious to use her wiles on another member of my crew when I'm through with her."

"You black-hearted hypocrite. You blaspheme against

God when you say you are his servant. Your piety is a sham that you use to cover your evil deeds, Hillary,'' Royale said as she struggled against the heavily-muscled arms that held her.

"Hush your foul mouth, witch. You'll not change your fate with your lies against me," Hillary said as he lifted the whip and snapped it against the deck.

"Do I lie when I say that only moments ago you would have gladly taken your man's place in my bed had I not stopped you? Do I lie when I say that your reason to see me hanged is not your wish to see evil purged from the high seas but your own greed? Do I lie, Hillary, when I say you have had men murdered just to have your revenge against me?" Royale shouted, noting the silence that hovered around them as the *Rosemond*'s crew listened to her accusations against their captain. She sensed the disquiet brewing among the men gathered on deck as they eyed their captain, seeing him in a different light, not as the God-fearing man he had presented to them.

Hillary also sensed the uneasy quiet and knew he had to silence the girl before he lost control of his vessel. "Witch, your devil's voice weaves false words well. Were I not a man who tries to live by the rules set forth in the Good Book, I'd have your tongue slit from your head. If I am guilty of any of the sins you lay at my door, I suggest you tell the courts in England and let them decide my fate," Hillary said, and he listened to the murmur of agreement that rose from his men. He knew from the sound that they were once more on his side. They knew no man would ask to be tried for crimes he had committed, and for that reason alone they had judged him innocent.

"Aye, I'll tell the courts all I know and will rejoice when you join me on the gibbet," Royale said, sensing that Hillary had swayed his crew once more to him.

"I wanted to deal fairly with you, witch, but I see that

my generosity had been misplaced. I think a few days in Hillary's Hell will suffice to make you repent more quickly than the sting of the lash.'' He motioned toward the hatch that led down into the cargo hold. ''Use your time there well, and pray for the salvation of your soul.''

As the sailor dragged Royale toward the opening that led down into the bowels of the ship she screamed at Hillary, ''Pray for your own soul, you lying, murdering bastard.''

Royale struggled against her captor as they neared the open hatch. Her resistance earned her little except a light cuff on the chin. The blow dazed her momentarily, and he lifted her off her feet; then he picked up the lantern that had been brought to him to light their way down the ladder to Hillary's Hell.

A golden glow surrounded them as they descended into the black hold. The dank air was heavy with the scent of spices and other less appealing odors that Royale preferred not to contemplate as her captor moved toward a small, boxed-in area where several chains dangled from the heavy beams.

Without warning he dumped her onto a pile of rotting rags and stood holding the lantern high as he glanced smugly around the tiny enclosure.

''As Captain Hillary said, this here will be your home on the *Rosemond* if you don't change your ways. We call it Hillary's Hell because this is where he puts crewmen when he thinks they need to ponder their sins and come back to the right way—Hillary's way, as you'll learn soon enough. Old Willy is getting off light this time with just a whipping.''

Glancing once more about the fetid area, he continued, ''I've seen strong men beg for the Captain's mercy after spending one night fighting off the hungry bilge rats in here. Them rats really seem to like toes.''

Hanging the lantern on a peg, he bent and locked the

iron manacles around her wrists and grinned again as he observed his handiwork. "Enjoy your stay in hell, El Diablo." Chuckling at his own wit, he turned and left Royale staring into the darkness beyond the circle of lantern light.

Alone with only the creaking and groaning of the ship to keep her company, Royale realized with horror that she was totally helpless. Bound as she was, she had no defense against what lay waiting with beady eyes in the darkness beyond the realm of light. The idea of being devoured alive by rats began to chase all coherent thoughts from her mind. Her heart beat furiously against her ribs and her breathing grew shallow as the black void beyond the lantern seemed to reach toward her, pressing down on her chest, stifling her.

Already pale, she turned a deathly white. The purple bruises from LeCruel's blow and her frightened green eyes were the only color in her face as she forced herself to keep her gaze locked on the flame in the lantern. An involuntary whimper escaped her as it flickered and threatened to go out. She knew that if that happened, her death would be imminent, but she had no way to prevent it. Her fear grew as dark and heavy as the humid atmosphere that surrounded the weak circle of light.

Royale cowered back against the damp hull. She could think of nothing beyond the fear that consumed her. It devoured great chunks of her courage and left her spirit shrinking inward as she desperately sought a refuge from the dark fate her mind had conjured up. The valiant young woman who had bravely overcome all obstacles placed in her path now fled before the unreasonable tide of hysteria gripping her insides. A keening wail rose in her throat, as if she were lamenting the death of her valor and signaling her final surrender to the terror engulfing her mind.

Her anguished cry could not be heard on deck. Willy's loud agony as the cat-o'-nine-tails ripped at his flesh drowned out that of the terror-stricken girl in Hillary's Hell. His blood dripped down the gashes opened by the barbed tips and seeped into his britches to mingle with his body's excretions. He had wet himself after the second time the lash had come crashing down against his back.

After twenty lashes, Hillary's own hand was wet with Willy's blood, and he tossed the whip away, a satisfied smile upon his lips. His duty was done, and now he could set their course for England. After giving the order to cut Willy down and put him in the forecastle and wash his back with a bucket of seawater, the captain gave the command to up anchor.

Watching his men scurry about to carry out his orders, he unconsciously patted the sheaf of papers in his pocket. He was well satisfied with the events of the day. He had the confessions of the men who had sailed with the witch as well as his own testimony to ensure her conviction at her trial for piracy.

El Diablo would be sentenced to hang, but it would not be her death that he would savor the most. The fact that he, a poor merchantman, had outwitted the famed pirate and would see that good triumphed over evil would be well worth the price he had paid LeCruel to capture her.

Captain Hillary took a deep breath, swelling with his own self-esteem as he looked toward the blue horizon. Bringing El Diablo to justice would assure his place in the world. He would be a man of importance when he returned to England with his prisoner. He would no longer be just another captain of a merchantman who had tried through the years to come up in the ranks of the British West Indies Company. Finally he would have the respect he deserved. His conscience did not bother him over the accuracy of the witch's accusations. She had been right; he would not have wasted his time or gold to bring El Diablo to trial had it not been for his ambition to further himself. Instead, he would have had her hanged from the yardarm, as was the usual custom when dealing with pirates.

It's fortunate for El Diablo, Hillary mused to himself, that I wish to gain favor in the eyes of my superiors. That's the only reason she will live to reach England.

Turning to the seaman who was coiling thick hemp rope around the base of the mast, he said, "Let the witch stay in the hold for a couple of days just to give her a taste of what will happen to her if she causes us any more trouble, and then have her locked in the cabin next to mine. I'd hate to see her cheat the hangman out of his due by dying down there." Already mentally hearing the praises he would receive in England, Hillary strode from the deck.

Chapter 15

The boats filled with El Diablo's men moved toward LeCruel's frigate as silently as moonbeams creeping across the dark waters of the bay. No sound of oars hitting the sides of wooden hulls came to alert the French crew of their jeopardy. El Diablo's men had wrapped cloths around the blades to muffle any noise that might draw attention to them before they made their attack.

With his dagger clenched between his teeth and boarding ropes looped over his shoulder, Scrimshaw made his way hand over hand up the anchor chain and swung himself agilely onto the deck. He landed lightly on his bare feet, making no sound to startle the watch on duty a few feet away. Creeping stealthily toward the unwary sailor, Scrimshaw slit his throat before the man realized his danger. Easing the limp body over the side of the ship and into the water, he moved quietly toward the second man on watch. A board creaked underfoot, alerting the guard to his presence, but before the man could do more than give a grunt of surprise Scrimshaw had plunged his bloody dagger into the man's throat, stopping the sailor's warning cry before it could be uttered. After disposing of the second guard's body as he had the first, Scrimshaw quickly secured the boarding ropes and tossed them over the side to his comrades.

Within moments the men of the *Wicked Mistress* swarmed onto the deck, and before LeCruel's crew could rouse themselves from sleep El Diablo had the vessel secured and the pirate and his crew as his prisoners.

LeCruel was awakened by his cabin door slamming back on its hinges, loudly banging against the wall. He jerked upright and his eyes widened in shock as El Diablo strode into the cabin with two loaded pistols aimed directly at him. The Frenchman instinctively made a move for the pistol that hung in his belt at the head of his bunk but jerked his hand back as wood splintered from the impact of the ball from El Diablo's gun. It shattered the weapon and opened a hole in the wall.

LeCruel's bed partner and cabin boy pulled the blanket over his head and cowered next to the pirate for protection as a lazy curl of blue smoke drifted upward from the barrel of El Diablo's pistol. The masked pirate tossed the useless weapon away and withdrew another from his belt as he smiled at the man on the bed.

"It seems, LeCruel, that you and I have a little business to finish between us before I blow your head off."

LeCruel's thin face paled as he eyed the tall, dangerous-looking man before him. He dredged his memory, seeking an explanation, but could find none. He didn't think he had ever seen the man before, nor did he understand what he meant when he spoke of business between them.

"Monsieur," LeCruel said as he threw back the blanket and started to rise from the bunk, "I believe there has been some mistake. I have no business with you."

"Don't move, LeCruel. You don't realize how easy it would be for me to put a ball between your beady little eyes. But first I want some information from you."

LeCruel gestured helplessly. "Surely you would let a man dress himself before you kill him?"

"If you were a man instead of a mad animal, I might," El Diablo growled, and he aimed his pistol at LeCruel's head.

"All right, Monsieur," the pirate said, raising his hands acquiescently. "It will be as you wish. Now what may I do for you? You seem to have some misbegotten idea that we've had dealings together, but I can assure you that I've never laid eyes on you before."

"True, we have never met before, nor shall we meet again after tonight. However, we do have business to finish between us."

"Monsieur, I'm sure you have mistaken me for someone else. I have no business with you. Why don't you put your weapons away so we can discuss this matter over a fine glass of wine in a civilized manner? I'm sure we can clear up this misunderstanding."

"There's been no misunderstanding, LeCruel. The matter between us concerns a young woman whom we both know."

LeCruel smiled with relief and waved a hand at the lump beside him. "I knew there was a mistake. I have no taste for female flesh, as you can see."

"Get rid of your lover, unless you want him to see your brains splattered all over the cabin," El Diablo said, and he motioned toward the cringing figure beneath the covers.

Not wanting to antagonize the man further, LeCruel jerked the blanket off the naked boy and shoved him roughly from the bunk. "Get out, you little bastard," he growled. "I have no more need of you tonight."

The boy scrambled to his feet and fled gratefully from the cabin. El Diablo kicked the door closed behind him and turned his deadly gaze back to the French pirate. He smiled beneath his mask, but the gesture held no warmth for the man on the bunk, only malice.

"After tonight you will have no more need for him, LeCruel. Now to our business."

"Monsieur, I've tried to make you understand that I have no dealings with you, nor do I even know you."

"Perhaps I should introduce myself, since I would hate for you to die without knowing the identity of the man who had the pleasure of ending your vile life. I am El Diablo, and I think you should know by now that the young woman in question is the one you took from my ship at Ile a Vache."

El Diablo chuckled as he watched comprehension dawn in the Frenchman's tiny, rodentlike eyes. Beads of sweat broke out across his brow, and his skin turned a sickly gray. His face was tight with fear as his Adam's apple worked up and down, reflecting his growing apprehension.

LeCruel moistened his thin lips with his tongue as he stared at El Diablo. His narrow mustache quivering nervously, like a live caterpillar, he said, "Monsieur, there has been a great error. I have no woman on board my ship. If you do not believe me, then you are free to search it from stem to stern."

"You must consider all Englishmen fools. I already know that Royale is nowhere on board your vessel. If I had found her, you would not be breathing now. I've already questioned the traitors from my ship and hers and know that you turned her over to an English captain. Now I want to know where he has taken her."

LeCruel seized upon the small advantage. "Then perhaps we can make a deal. If you'll agree to release my ship and crew, I'll give you the information you desire in exchange."

"Is that all of your bargain?" El Diablo said, eyeing the pirate speculatively.

"*Oui*, El Diablo. I am not a hard man to deal with about such trivial matters," LeCruel said, and he smiled, the tension easing from his face as he sensed the other man's assent to his offer.

"Agreed, LeCruel. Now, where is he taking Royale?"

Relaxing visibly, the pirate pulled on his britches and stood. "Captain Hillary is taking her back to England to stand trial in your stead," he replied smugly as he shrugged into his shirt.

The tension in the room mounted. El Diablo's ire rose until his blood felt like molten lava as it rushed through his veins. The need to throttle the loathsome creature before him was overwhelming. However, he forced himself to remain calm as he asked, "You knew she was not the real El Diablo. Why did you tell the Englishman that she was?"

"I had a debt to settle with the witch. She caused several of my men to die in Cuba and cost me part of the booty from Puerto Principe. It was a way to even the score and to recoup some of my losses with the reward Hillary offered. You see, she robbed his ship in your disguise and then was recognized when she sold her booty in Tortuga. She'll hang for that."

El Diablo motioned toward the door with his pistol. "Come with me, LeCruel. There is still a matter of business that I need to settle before I can sail for England."

"Most assuredly," LeCruel said, and he swaggered forward, feeling once more in control. His confidence faded, however, as he stepped out on the deck and found his crew assembled and standing in file, well guarded by El Diablo's armed men. From the yardarm overhead hung four nooses. Streaked silver by the light of the full moon, they swayed gently back and forth, their eerie shadows falling across the deck at the men's feet.

Forcing a smile to his lips, LeCruel glanced at El Diablo. He feigned a boldness that did not reach his eyes, which shifted involuntarily toward the nooses as he said, "I see you intend to deal with the rogues who turned against you. I can find no fault with that. If they will turn once, they will do so again. However, I see four nooses. There were only three men who testified against the girl. I can't let you harm any of my men. We do have an agreement, Monsieur."

"I certainly intend to keep our bargain, LeCruel. I will hang none of your men," El Diablo said, his voice shaking with pent-up fury.

LeCruel blanched as his gaze shifted again to the four nooses. "Monsieur, then you have miscounted. There were only three traitors," he repeated, the wild light of fear flickering in his beady eyes.

"I have the correct number up there, I assure you," El Diablo said, his tone softly menacing.

"You agreed to release my crew and ship," LeCruel uttered as he comprehended the reason for the fourth rope.

"Aye, and I will do so once you and the other bastards are strung up. I have no quarrel with your crew, because they only followed your orders."

The pirate shook his head rapidly back and forth. "*Non*, that was not our agreement."

At a slight nod from El Diablo, Black Jack seized the trembling French pirate by the scruff of the neck. The big seaman shook the smaller man roughly before pinning his arms behind his back and tying them securely about the wrists.

"As you will find when you leave this world, I always keep my promises. I told you earlier that I intended to see you dead, and I will not go back on my word," El Diablo said, his dark eyes cold and deadly. "My only regret is that I don't have the time to make your death long and slow, in keeping with the atrocities you have committed against good men and ships. 'Tis a shame that I have to let you off so easily for your vile acts, but my time is limited if I am to try to thwart your evil scheme.''

Non,'' the cowering pirate screamed in fright as Black Jack dragged him toward an overturned barrel beneath the dangling rope. Forcing LeCruel to mount it, Black Jack placed the noose around the Frenchman's neck and, with a nod from his captain, kicked the barrel from beneath his feet. A choking sound followed, and then all was quiet as LeCruel's lifeless body swayed back and forth with the movement of the vessel.

The traitors soon followed the pirate into hell. They were executed in the same manner as LeCruel, and all four bodies were left hanging from the yardarm as a grisly warning.

"Now, you bastards," El Diablo growled as he turned his dark gaze upon the remainder of the pirate crew, "I suggest you learn how to swim, and quickly, unless you want to join your captain. You can return and cut down this carrion tomorrow after the gulls have had their feast.''

There was a desperate rush of bodies toward the railing, soon followed by the sound of splashes as the pirates landed in the water. None stayed to argue with El Diablo. All were too happy at the reprieve he had given them. Even those who could not swim preferred to take their chances in the water instead of with the devil himself.

El Diablo smiled with satisfaction for a moment. He might have stayed to enjoy the spectacle, had he not been pressed for time. He had to set sail immediately for England if he was to save the woman he loved.

Turning to his men, who had gathered to watch the humorous exit of their vanquished foes, he ordered, "Barton, have the men search this vessel from stem to stern and confiscate anything of value. Tell them they may keep all the booty they find on board.''

A cheer of approval greeted his command, and his men

set about their work, tearing LeCruel's vessel apart in
search of hidden treasure. Only one man remained on deck
with El Diablo: Fishbait Jones. He stood silent and somber, his craggy features set as he regarded the captain of
the *Wicked Mistress* through bloodshot eyes that held a
silent question.

Knowing what the quartermaster sought, El Diablo said,
"Your captain has been taken to England on the *Rosemond*."

"What do you intend to do?" Fishbait asked, his frown
deepening the lines in his weatherbeaten face.

"We sail for England on the morning tide. We're only
a few days behind the *Rosemond*, and if the weather holds
fair, we may catch her before she reaches port."

Fishbait eyed El Diablo skeptically for a long moment
before he asked, "Just like that, eh? You intend to sail a
pirate ship up the Thames and dock it in London? Having
you next to 'er on the gibbet won't help me Captain."

"I have no choice in the matter, if I am to save her at
all. I can't waste precious time waiting for a British vessel
to take me there. Royale's only hope is for us to overtake
the *Rosemond*, or at least for me to rescue her once she
arrives in London."

Fishbait gave a sad shake of his head. El Diablo had
suffered much worse injuries in the explosion than he had
first thought if the man was contemplating sailing boldly
into London and rescuing his captain. The blast had completely knocked his wits from his head. Running his fingers
through his hair in vexation, Fishbait knew, too, that his
captain was lost to him. There was nothing they could do
to save her.

A lump rose in the quartermaster's throat, and he swallowed several times to dislodge the constriction. El Diablo
had been his only hope, and now the man was showing
signs of madness. At the thought of the beautiful, valiant

young woman losing her life at the end of a rope, Fishbait felt a muscle begin to twitch in his cheek, and he fought against a burning sensation behind his lids.

He had not always agreed with his captain's schemes, but since that first day when she had boarded the *Raven* and bravely dueled with him she had held his loyalty. And over the last months of watching the anguish she had suffered at the death of her men, she had also found a place in his heart—not the place of a lover, but that of a cherished child who often needed his support and understanding.

He wiped his nose with the back of his hand and cleared his throat, again shaking his head. "I believe you're forgetting one small matter in this great scheme of yers—yer crew. Even if ye've lost all yer wits and are determined to go, they won't follow ye up the steps to their own hanging. They'd be strung up on sight in England with no quarter given."

El Diablo frowned. He had not considered the fact that his men might refuse to follow him. They had accepted his orders in the past but now might think the life of one young woman was not worth their putting their own necks in a noose. Realizing that it was time to end the ruse he had perpetrated for over two years and feeling a sudden relief at the fact, he smiled.

"Ah, yes, my crew. I think I may be able to ease their trepidation about sailing to England with me."

"When the *Oxford* blew up it took all of yer brains with it. Ye can't save Royale. All ye'll do is to get yerself and yer men hanged alongside of her. I doubt yer crew will agree to those terms," Fishbait said, and he watched the smile fade from El Diablo's lips.

"Damn it, Fishbait, I intend to save Royale. You and the rest can go to hell if you're too cowardly to sail with me."

"I ain't no coward, El Diablo, as ye well know. I'd

trade me own neck to save hers. It's that ye're not seeing reason where the rest of yer cutthroats are concerned.''

El Diablo threw back his dark head and laughed. Once his mirth was spent, he crossed to the quartermaster and draped an arm over the older man's shoulders. '' 'Tis time you and my men knew a few things about El Diablo. Gather my crew, Fishbait, and we'll settle this matter here and now, because we have no time to spend arguing.''

Fishbait's frown made his heavy brows knit over his eyes as he stared up at El Diablo. The man was mad, but there was little he could do other than carry out his order. The *Wicked Mistress*'s captain would soon learn the true state of affairs without his trying to drum it into his witless head. With a shrug, Fishbait turned toward the open hatch.

Arms laden with booty, the crew of the *Wicked Mistress* filed on deck, mumbling curiously among themselves at this new turn of events. They regarded the tall man who stood on the poop deck with mixed emotions as they looked from him to the purchase they carried. Each man wondered as he eyed the treasure in his arms if their captain had changed his mind and decided to take his share of the booty. Each greedily begrudged even the thought.

The ship's lanterns at El Diablo's feet cast a circle of light around him while illuminating the faces of the men on the deck below. He wanted to able to see their expressions as he spoke to them. It was crucial that all be settled now. He needed to know their feelings about his next venture, because Royale's life stood in the balance.

His feet were splayed wide and his arms folded across his chest as he gazed down into the group of men. A slow smile curved his lips up at the corners as he read the greedy thoughts upon their weathered faces.

''Since sailing with me for the past two years, you all know that once I have given my word to you on any matter, it is law. Tonight you may keep all the booty from Le-

Cruel's vessel, but you will also be asked to be my judge and jury,'' he said, and he watched as his men stared up at him in bewilderment.

''Ye ain't guilty of nothing, Captain. The bastards needed hangin' and worse,'' Scrimshaw said before realizing he had spoken out of turn. With a sheepish grin he quickly stepped back among the men.

El Diablo smiled. ''Aye, you're right, Scrimshaw, they did deserve their fate, but that is not the reason I've called you all before me. What I have to say will not be easy to understand, and before I tell you, I want to make it clear that if any of you choose not to sail with me again, that is your decision and right.''

A rumble of questions rose from the men, but El Diablo raised one hand to silence them. ''On the morning tide I plan to sail the *Wicked Mistress* to England.'' Another rumble, this time of protest, issued from the group. Again El Diablo quieted them with a wave of his hand.

''If you choose to sail with me, I will guarantee your safety. None of you will be hanged for piracy once we reach London.''

''Now, how can ye be sure o' that, Captain?'' Black Jack muttered from the safety of the shadows.

''Because, my friends, you are not pirates but sailors in the service of King Charles of England.''

Silence greeted El Diablo's announcement. His men eyed him in the same manner as Fishbait had only a short while earlier. All regarded him as if he had lost his mind.

El Diablo chuckled at their dubious expressions. ''After tonight the *Wicked Mistress* will fly Britain's colors.''

''It be some kind of jest ye're a-playin' on me and me mates, ain't it? Ye just wanted to liven up our night with a little fun,'' Scrimshaw said, unable to constrain his wayward tongue.

Withdrawing a piece of paper from the band at his waist,

El Diablo shook his head. "No, this is no jest, and if you need proof of what I say, here it is in the King's own hand." Watching the bemused expressions flicker over his men's faces, he continued. "As of tonight, El Diablo is dead. I am Sir Bran Langston, King Charles's friend. It is now imperative that I ask you to sail with me to England to rescue the captain of the *Raven*. If we don't save her, she will be hanged as El Diablo in my stead."

Bran's muscles grew taut with tension as he forced himself to patiently await his crew's decision. He could hear their discussion of his revelation. Some were in favor of his proposal, while others rejected the idea, still believing him mad. Reed Barton and Fishbait had already joined him on the bridge as the rest of the men finally turned once more to look up at him.

Scrimshaw abruptly found himself the group's spokesman as a rough elbow in his ribs from Black Jack jostled him forward. He moistened his dry lips as he stood in front of the men, the narrow pool of lantern light making him feel as if he faced his captain alone. Nervously, he gazed up at the man he had known as El Diablo, remembering well the heights the man's wrath could reach when he was provoked.

"There be just one question we need answered, Captain, afore some of the others can make up their addled wits, and that is: What will happen to the men who don't want to sail with ye?"

"I'll leave them LeCruel's vessel to do with as they please. However, once they leave my service they will be branded as pirates, and no one will be able to save them if they are captured," Bran said. His voice was calm, but his insides twisted with dread. He needed these men to sail the *Wicked Mistress*. Short-handed, it would be nearly impossible to reach England in time.

Again the men huddled together, arguing the advantages

and disadvantages of their captain's offer. Finally Scrim-shaw grinned up at his captain, his features relaxed. "We sail with ye, El Diablo."

"Captain Langston," Bran corrected, giving the final death blow to his assumed identity.

"Aye, anything ye say be just fine with us." Scrimshaw laughed and then added, "Are we truly in the service of the King?"

"Aye, Scrimshaw. Now I would like one answer from you," Bran said, and he smiled, his curiosity aroused as to the reason behind their decision to stay with him.

A wary look crossed the seaman's face as he asked, "What be ye a-wanting to know, Captain Langston?"

"Why did you all choose to sail with me? I know some of you still don't like the idea."

"Well, it be this way, Captain. There ain't none of us qualified to be the captain of the Frenchie's vessel. So it was either sail with ye or sign up on another ship. We figured we'd get hanged either way eventually, so it really didn't matter which we chose," Scrimshaw said, tucking his thumbs in the waistband of his britches and rocking back on his heels as he grinned up at Bran. "But I convinced 'em that ye'd always been honest and fair with us, so I figured ye was a-telling us the truth about working fer old Charlie."

"I appreciate your support, Scrimshaw, as well as that of the rest of you men. Now, if you've got all your booty, 'tis time to get back to the *Wicked Mistress*. We sail for England with the morning tide."

"Aye, Captain," the men chorused as they hefted their loot and made for the dinghies. However, Scrimshaw blocked Black Jack's path before he could reach the rail to the rope ladder. He eyed the bundle in the larger man's arms and smiled.

"It seems to me ye said at one time ye'd give all yer

booty to know about the Captain. Well, hand it over, cause ye know now.''

"The hell I will, ye little bilge maggot. This here may be the last purchase I can get me hands on fer some time, if what the Captain says is true. And if we're a-going to London, I'll need ever' penny I can lay me hands on to sample the women and the high life of the city,'' Black Jack growled as he pushed the smaller man out of his way and descended the ladder.

"Aye,'' Scrimshaw mused aloud, scratching his head. "I hadn't thought of that afore now. Going to England may not be such a bad idea.'' With that thought in mind, he quickly gathered his own booty and followed Black Jack.

An amused smile played over Bran's lips as he watched his men hurry to follow his orders. As the last one climbed over the rail, he turned and came face to face with Fishbait. He could not read the quartermaster's expression as they stood gazing at one another. At last Bran broke the lengthening silence. "Is there something you need to speak to me about, Fishbait?''

"I've been a-standing here and listening as ye talked, and I've been adding two and two together in me head,'' Fishbait said, eyeing Bran curiously. "I've often wondered why ye always seemed to be keeping an eye out for me captain, but I put it down to her looks and that maybe ye loved her. Now I've pieced the puzzle together and have come to realize that ye're the man the King sent to take Good Fortune from her, ain't ye?''

"If you mean that I'm her guardian, then you're right, but I never intended to take Good Fortune away from Royale. You're also right in your other assumption; I do love her. Now, if that satisfies your curiosity, Fishbait, I suggest we make haste to England. I intend to save her before it is too late.''

Fishbait eyed Bran for a moment longer before a wide,

friendly grin spread his lips, and he saluted. "Aye, Captain Langston," he said as new hope blossomed within his chest and lightened his steps. He descended the ladder to the deck, eager for them to be on their way to England.

With her hands bound behind her back, her hair a wild mass of tangled curls, her eyes wide and haunted in her ashen face, Royale entered London as Captain Hillary's prized prisoner—El Diablo.

She stared numbly at the myriad faces surrounding her, unable to comprehend the reason for their interest, closed in the safe retreat she had found in her mind. Since the first day she had spent in Hillary's Hell on board the *Rosemond* she had built a shield for herself, as if to safeguard her sanity from the nightmare she was living.

The protective mantle that enshrouded her mind kept her sheltered from the events that transpired around her, holding them at a distance, as if she was watching them from a glassed-in room that no one could enter. When the fear became too great, she merely pulled the shutters closed, locking herself inside. The only time the barrier inched open against her will was when someone touched her. It was only then that she responded, fighting like a demon to keep herself locked away in her secure haven so that she would not have to face the reality of the outside world.

The cart jolted over the uneven cobbles and rolled through the gates of the prison, leaving the large procession that followed in its wake vying for a better view of the spectacle from the outside of the thick-walled yard of Newgate. Word had spread rapidly along the wharf about Hillary's captive, and the streets had been lined with people curious to get a glimpse of the famous pirate as Hillary took Royale to prison. Mumbles of surprise rose from the crowd when the oxcart passed and they saw that the figure sitting so still and pale behind the captain was a woman.

That in itself increased the number who trailed behind the cart, jeering and laughing as if the hostage had been brought to London just for their amusement.

A smug grin touched Hillary's lips as he drew the cart to a halt before the heavy, iron-studded doors of the prison. He seemed to swell with self-importance as he stepped down and glanced back toward the gates. He was now a man of distinction. Tonight the taverns of London would be filled with people talking about him and his bravery in capturing such a feared pirate.

Stepping to the rear of the cart, he lowered the gate and grabbed Royale by the arm to pull her down. She flinched at his touch, the shutters in her mind slipping precariously as she jerked back and twisted away from his hand.

Hillary frowned. "Witch, don't give me any trouble. I have no reason now to see that you keep on living. You've served the purpose I intended. The company has already promised me a promotion, as well as a raise in my commission from each voyage. So if you know what's good for you, you'll behave." Grabbing her again, he dragged her from the cart and pushed her toward the guard on duty at the door.

"I've brought you a prisoner, guard," he said as he took a rolled parchment from his pocket and handed it to the uniformed man. "Here are her papers."

The guard scanned the papers, then he looked up at Hillary and asked, "Are you Captain Hillary?"

"Aye, and this is the famed El Diablo."

The guard glanced down at the bedraggled young woman at the man's side as he rerolled the parchment and tucked it into his belt. "She does look like the devil, I have to give her that, but it's hard to believe the rest of what her papers say," he said, and he chuckled at his own wit.

Hillary found little humor in the man's remark and eyed him coolly. "It's not your place to believe in her charge;

it's the judge's. Your duty is to see her incarcerated until her trial. If you are going to continue to stand here discussing the matter, perhaps I should deal with your superior. Maybe then I can get this she-devil off my hands without it taking all day.''

''Ain't no need to take offense at my little bit of humor,'' the guard said, stiffening as he regarded Hillary. ''I know me duty, Captain. There ain't no use in your getting all huffy and disturbing the sergeant. I can take care of this wench right enough.''

''Then do your job. I have more important matters to attend to.'' Hillary thrust Royale toward the guard and turned away.

Royale stumbled against the guard's chest, and he automatically caught her, holding her tightly so that she could not escape. For the first time in nearly two months she uttered a harsh sound of protest at the feel of his arms around her. Revulsion swept over her, rending the numbing veil that protected her. She struggled physically against him as she sought to retain her comforting mental shield. It was useless. The protective cloak that had enshrouded her mind slipped away and let all of the memories resurface, along with their accompanying horrors. She fought wildly to keep them at bay but failed. All she had blocked from her mind came back with crushing force.

El Diablo's death, LeCruel's brutal murder of her crew, her abduction, Willy's attempt to rape her, and being locked away in Hillary's Hell—it was all dredged up from the deep recesses of her mind and thrust into her consciousness with horrifying clarity. The images spun sickeningly before her eyes, whirling about in her head, tearing away the last barrier she had erected between herself and reality. She swayed as if from the impact of a blow, and her knees buckled beneath her. The blood drained from her face, and her thick lashes fluttered closed over her eyes. She sank into the blessed relief of unconsciousness.

"Damnation," the guard muttered in disgust as Royale went limp. He had to lift her in his arms to carry her to her cell inside the granite walls of Newgate.

"Well, brother, how does it feel to have everything fall into place without your having to lift a hand?" James, the Duke of York, said as he crossed the manicured lawn to the tall, dark-haired man who knelt to fondle the head of one of his golden spaniels.

Glancing over his shoulder at his brother, Charles straightened up and with the flick of his bejeweled hand indicated that the trainer should take his beloved dogs back to the kennel. A bemused frown creased his forehead as he slowly shook his head.

" 'Od's fish, James, 'tis too early in the morning for you to be playing your dreadful little guessing games. I haven't the faintest idea of what you are talking about."

"You mean you haven't heard?" James said, his handsome face reflecting his surprise.

"James, do I need to send for the court physician so he can bleed you for fevers of your brain?"

"My God, I thought you would have heard by now, because it's all over London."

Charles drew in a deep breath to stem his impatience at his brother's roundabout way of telling him what was on his mind.

"No, I haven't heard anything, and if you don't tell me exactly what you are talking about within the next minute, I swear that I will hang you up by your heels from the palace wall."

"Calm yourself, brother, 'tis good news for you and Sir Bran Langston," James said with a grin.

"Your time is almost up, brother. I suggest you explain

yourself before I call the guards," Charles said, his dark eyes beginning to sparkle with annoyance.

"Here, this will explain everything more thoroughly than I can," James said, handing the King a sheet of paper from a pamphleteer.

The King's frown deepened as he read, and his swarthy features darkened in hue when he looked once more at his brother. "What's the meaning of this? We both know that the woman accused of being El Diablo is innocent."

"Aye, we know that, but the populace of London and your enemies do not. Don't you see that this can be the answer to the dilemma you have been facing where Sir Bran is concerned? In the eyes of the world and especially Spain, El Diablo has been captured and will be tried and hanged by our own courts for the criminal act of piracy."

"I don't like this, James," Charles said, shaking his head and crumpling the paper in his hand. "The woman is not guilty."

"True, brother, but it will solve your problems. The Spanish ambassador has already been to see me and is demanding a speedy trial and conviction."

"Damn the Spanish and their demands. I won't be a party to seeing an innocent woman die just to appease their blood lust."

"Not so innocent, brother," James said. "There are witnesses that will testify that she is the pirate El Diablo. 'Tis one of our own captains from the British West Indies Company that captured her. He swears she is the one responsible for attacking his ship. He also says she sold the booty from his vessel in Tortuga. He witnessed it himself. So you see she cannot be as innocent as you believe."

Still not completely convinced that he should just let everything proceed and allow the woman to be convicted as El Diablo, Charles turned his troubled gaze away from his brother and stared out across the green lawns. He disliked injustice of any kind, but if what James said was true, the wench was guilty of the crimes laid at her door even if she was not the true El Diablo. She had attacked British vessels and must be punished for her acts against England, no matter who she was. And, as his brother had said, it would be to his advantage as well as to Sir Bran Langston's to let her hang. He could appease Spain that way and bring Sir Bran back to court where he belonged. Charles still needed the gold Bran captured from the Spanish galleons, but of late he felt he needed his friend at his side even more. He would have a few choice words for the rascal when he returned for stirring up so much trouble by attacking England's vessels as well as Spain's, but they would only amount to a slap on the wrist. Bran was much too valuable to him to risk letting him continue as El Diablo, only to end up at the end of a rope, as the woman now held in Newgate surely would after her speedy trial.

"So be it," Charles said as he turned to look once more at his brother. "I would prefer that the woman be tried for her own crimes instead of El Diablo's, but if it will put an end to the mess with Spain and save Sir Bran, then I'll say no more."

James relaxed. He had feared Charles would not let things remain as they were. His brother had suffered too much injustice in his own life to easily accept being unjust to another, even if the person involved was no more than a pirate.

"Good," James said. "I'll notify the Spanish ambassador that we will see that justice is done at once."

Royale's eyes glittered like polished jade as she looked at the guard who had come to escort her into the courtroom. She might be tried for piracy, but she'd be damned if she would accept it meekly. She might be hanged, but she was determined to fight every inch of the way. Before she was through all would know of Captain Hillary's part in the deaths of Henry Morgan and El Diablo.

"Come on, El Diablo, 'tis time fer yer trial," the guard said as he approached her. He grasped her upper arm firmly and pulled her toward the door.

"Take your hands off me. I can walk under my own power," Royale hissed, glaring up into his bearded face.

"Ye might be able to do that, but I remember the fight you put up when ye was brought in here. I ain't a-taking no chance on you escaping." He jerked her into the corridor. "Ye ain't done nothing but cause us trouble since they brought ye to Newgate."

"And I intend to cause a lot more trouble before I'm through," Royale said as the guard led her down the dank hall to a door that opened into the courtroom. He pushed it open and shoved her through. She came to an abrupt halt and her eyes grew round in surprise as she saw the throngs of people who packed the large chamber. A hush fell over the crowd as the guard pushed her toward the barred prisoner's box. An air of expectancy seemed to hover over the spectators, as if they had come to see a play and the first act had just begun.

As if on cue, the black-robed, white-wigged judges filed into the chamber and took their seats behind the high desk. A moment later, drawing murmurs from the crowd, Captain Hillary strode into the courtroom and took his seat in the witness box.

At the sight of the odious man Royale forgot the spectators. All her energy was centered on the thought of making him pay for his crime against the man she loved. Rage boiled anew in her veins at the pious, self-satisfied expression he wore. She longed to claw it off his face but knew that El Diablo would only be vindicated by her testimony against Captain Hillary.

With that thought in mind, she forced herself to remain calm as the clerks read off the charges against her. Mumbles of excitement filled the courtroom and all eyes focused on her as the exaggerated atrocities were laid at her door.

The judge's heavy gavel pounded against the surface of the high desk, silencing the crowd before he ordered, "Prosecutor, bring your first witness to the stand."

Hillary straightened his jacket before taking the witness chair. He cast one smug look at Royale before placing his hand upon the Bible and giving his oath to tell the truth.

For one brief moment Royale felt faint from the hatred that surged through her. Her blood pounded in her temples as the prosecutor began to question him.

"Now, Captain Hillary, would you please tell the court how you so bravely captured the famed pirate El Diablo?"

With the righteous air of one who wants only to serve his country and his God, Hillary began his story. As he professed his desire to rid the world of such vile criminals—whose very existence was a sin against all that was good—Royale's gaze never left his face. She had to breathe deeply to suppress the urge to scream her hatred. Her time would come, and then she would see how Hillary felt when he was placed in the prisoner's box for murdering one of King Charles's courtiers. With that thought Royale suddenly paled. The blood receded from her face as she realized she could never divulge the truth without putting England in jeopardy. Nor could she tell the courts the truth of her own identity. It would have the same effect. She didn't feel any loyalty to the King, who had begun this whole sad affair by taking her home from her, but it would not only be England's monarch who suffered. Innocent men would be sent out to fight a war with Spain. A myriad of emotions whirled within Royale as she realized she could only make Hillary pay by telling of his involvement with LeCruel and the explosion on Morgan's vessel. She would not mention Bran Langston, and she had no defense for herself. With that morbid thought she forced her mind back to Hillary's testimony.

"That evil woman has murdered and—" Hillary's words were cut off as Royale came to her feet, clenching the bars in front of her. The man's lies had sliced through her control like hot steel through wax. "You lying hypocrite! Why don't you tell them of the atrocity committed at Ile a Vache? Why don't you tell—" Royale's words were drowned out by the sound of the judge's gavel pounding on the desk.

"Silence, silence in the courtroom. Guard, gag the prisoner. We've heard more than enough from her."

The guard obeyed the judge and after several moments finally managed to subdue the hysterical prisoner enough to put a dirty rag over her mouth. Royale struggled against the guard as he bound her hands behind the chair. She could do little more than squirm and groan her protest as the prosecutor turned once more to Hillary.

"Captain Hillary, the prisoner has mentioned Ile a Vache. Could you enlighten us as to the events about which she speaks?"

Hillary's eyes gleamed with mirth as he looked at Royale and said, "I most certainly will. It is my understanding that Henry Morgan's ship blew up. Since I wasn't there personally, I have to depend on what has been told to me by people who saw the explosion. It was rumored that it was done by pirates." Hillary gave Royale another smug look. "And from the way El Diablo reacted, I suspect those rumors to be true."

Royale strained against her bonds. The muscles in her throat stood taut as she arched her neck back and screamed into the gag. At that moment she could hear the nails in her own coffin being driven into place.

"Most assuredly," the thin-faced prosecutor said as he cast a baleful look in Royale's direction. The girl's own words had convicted her.

Chapter 16

The gentle motion of the Rosemond *as she rode at anchor* in the river current made the lantern over Hillary's desk sway slowly back and forth. Its movement made long shadows dance across the cluttered surface as he sat hunched over the thick log book, making the last notations of the day's events. Beyond the normal sounds of the ship and the scratch of his quill upon the paper, all was quiet on board. With the exception of himself and the two men on watch, the *Rosemond*'s crew had gone into the city to celebrate their last night ashore.

Hillary smiled as he dipped the quill into the inkwell and wrote:

On this day the pirate El Diablo was found guilty of piracy and sentenced to death. The judges commended Captain Willard Hillary for his brave actions in capturing the enemy of the British West Indies Company and bringing her to trial. They further stated that the execution of El Diablo should be a warning to those men and women who think to use barbaric and criminal actions to enrich themselves. El Diablo is to be taken tomorrow at noon to Tyburn Hill and hanged by the neck until dead. Signed by Capt. Willard Hillary, B.W.I.C. on this day, the 1st of April, 1669.

Releasing a satisfied sigh, Hillary tossed the quill onto the desk and leaned back in his chair. He rubbed absently at an ache in the back of his neck as he reflected upon the day's events.

All had gone as he'd planned. He had gained the respect of his peers and El Diablo would die. His testimony that afternoon had ensured that outcome of the trial. The paper signed by the other pirates had held little merit before the court, but the judges had listened to and believed in his tale of evil perpetrated by the woman sitting in the prisoner's box. By the time he had finished giving his testimony he had already known from their expressions the sentence that would be given to her. The only tense moment he had experienced during the entire proceeding was when she had jumped to her feet, shouting about the explosion at Ile a Vache. However, everything had worked out to his advantage and only confirmed her guilt. The judge had had the bailiff gag the prisoner to silence her screams of protest.

He admitted freely to himself and without a twinge of guilt that he had exaggerated his story. He had not witnessed most of the crimes that he had described to the judges, but he knew that the vixen who had watched him with wide, disbelieving eyes had probably committed offenses much worse than he stated. His slight elaboration had served the purpose; as a man who believed in righteousness, he felt it was his duty to do everything in his power to rid the earth of the evil she embodied, no matter how it was achieved. His minor perjury did not bother his conscience in the least.

Opening the desk drawer, he lifted out a wooden cask and set it before him. Taking the key from his pocket, he unlocked the lid and flipped it open. A smile of pleasure spread his lips as he dipped his hand into the gleaming coins. It was a tidy sum—the reward from his superiors for bringing El Diablo to justice.

Lifting a handful of the gold, he let the coins fall one by one back into the cask, savoring the sound of each clink. He was so absorbed in his greedy play that he failed to hear the click of the door latch. Nor did he notice the intruder's presence until a single piece of paper drifted down onto the shining pile of gold sovereigns.

Startled, Hillary jerked back and stared up into a pair of dark eyes. Nonplussed, he sat motionless, his gaze taking in the dangerous-looking man as well as the pistol pointed directly at his own heart. A lump of fear rose to choke him, and his mouth went dry. Clearing his throat, he moistened his lips with the tip of his tongue and managed to say, "If this is a robbery, you will never get away with it. My men will shoot you on sight."

"I can assure you, Hillary, that I did not come to take your gold," Bran said, a caustic smile lifting one corner of his shapely mouth.

"Then, sir, what is the meaning of this intrusion?" Hillary asked, gaining a small measure of confidence, since he was not to lose his precious coins.

"Read that and you will know why I'm here," Bran said softly, his voice deceptively pleasant as he gestured with his pistol at the paper lying on the gold.

Hillary felt his bravado slip; his hand trembled as he lifted the page from the street pamphleteer. He briefly scanned the paper, already knowing what it said. Earlier in the afternoon he had been proud of the fact that his likeness had been drawn; the pamphlet showed him placing the noose around El Diablo's neck. It also recorded his testimony word for word. Now, looking at the man before him, he viewed the page with an entirely different emotion— fear. He sensed that the pamphleteer's rendition could very well cost him his life.

"Sir, I don't see what a pamphleteer's drawing has to do with you coming on board my vessel, armed as if you intend to harm me, for no reason," Hillary bluffed.

The light from the lantern gleamed on Bran's teeth as he threw back his head and laughed. The sound chilled the man at the desk to the bone. It reminded him of how he had always imagined the devil's laughter would sound. And he knew without asking that this man was no ordinary robber. Every sinew of his lean body issued menace, and it was all directed at the captain of the *Rosemond*.

"Then I will explain it to you, since you don't seem to comprehend what you have done," Bran said as he leaned negligently against the side of the desk, one foot swaying gently to and fro as he propped his pistol on his arm to keep it braced and ready.

"You see, Captain Hillary, you have made a grave mistake. One that will cost you your life if I don't have time to save that woman from the gibbet tomorrow."

Hillary paled and again licked his lips. "I've made no mistake. I've only done my duty to the crown by bringing the famous pirate to justice."

"That was your mistake. *I* am El Diablo, and if I fail to rescue the woman I love, then you will forfeit your life in exchange for her death."

All the color drained from Hillary's face as he braced himself against the back of his chair, trying to get as far away from the pirate as possible but too afraid to rise and flee.

He opened his mouth to speak, but no words would come forth until he had drawn several deep, shuddering breaths. "I only took LeCruel's word that she was El Diablo. I'm innocent of anything else. You can't kill me for trying to serve my country."

"There you are mistaken again, Hillary. If anything happens to her, your fate will be the same as LeCruel's, but you will swing from Tyburn Hill instead of the yardarm.''

''I've done no wrong. No judge would have me hanged,'' Hillary stuttered.

Bran gave him a slow, dangerous smile and said, ''The King will do so when he learns that his ward has died because of the lies you told in court today.''

Hillary's face crumpled, and he covered it with his hands. ''I was only trying to do what was right,'' he sobbed.

''Aye, and to fill your pockets with gold,'' Bran growled as he knocked the cask over, scattering its contents across the floor. ''There's your blood money, you bastard.'' Bran's eyes were cold shards of onyx as he eyed Hillary. ''I've heard you're a praying man, so I suggest you do a great deal of it tonight. Because on the morrow you will die if I can't get a pardon from the King in time to save my love.''

Hillary rose unsteadily from the chair and preceded Bran from the cabin with his head bowed and his shoulders slumped. The tapping of the blunt end of the pistol against his spine urged him up the steps and onto the deck, where Fishbait, Scrimshaw, and Black Jack awaited Bran while guarding the two men who were secured at the base of the main mast.

''Fishbait, you watch this bastard. Scrimshaw and Black Jack will remain on deck to welcome his crew when they return. All of them will answer to me if Royale is harmed,'' Bran said, and he shoved Hillary forward.

''Aye, Captain,'' the three replied in unison to Bran, who was already making his way to the ship's rail and the rope ladder. He had no time to waste. He had to reach Whitehall and Charles to secure Royale's pardon before it was too late.

The night was as black as the horse and rider that raced through the London streets to the palace. As soon as the *Wicked Mistress* had dropped anchor Bran had sent a man ahead to his townhouse to bring his mount to the wharf so that nothing would hinder him after he had finished his business with Hillary.

In his hurry he had taken no time to change into court attire but still wore the black silk britches and shirt that marked him as El Diablo. Those who saw the ominous sight flying past their houses and shops shuddered with superstitious fear. The sparks from the iron horseshoes striking the cobbles, combined with the sinister figure dressed in black, brought forth images of the devil out searching for souls to claim in the night. As he passed, doors and windows were quickly latched and candles were snuffed to keep the demon from noticing the inhabitants cowering inside.

With his mind focused on the woman he loved, Bran thought little about the spectral figure he was cutting. It was not until he reached Whitehall and the palace guards refused to give him entrance that he realized his mistake in not thinking about his appearance.

"Damn you, man, I'm Sir Bran Langston. I'm here to see the King, and I order you to step out of my way," he said in exasperation to the two guards blocking his path.

The guards did not move but lowered their lances across the entrance as they eyed Bran skeptically. "We can't be a-letting just anybody into the palace, no matter who they say they are," the sergeant said.

Bran clenched his jaw and could hear his teeth grate. He fought to remain calm while precious moments slipped by. "If you don't believe me, send a message in to the King that I'm here."

"We can't be disturbing His Majesty on just any whim.

He'd have our heads. Now be off with you," the sergeant ordered, and he waved his lance threateningly at Bran.

"If you don't let me through or send the message this instant, I'll see you both drawn and quartered by dawn," Bran growled, his patience at an end.

"Even if we agree to send in the message, how are we to know you're who you say you are?" the sergeant asked.

Exasperated nearly to the point of madness, Bran jerked his signet ring from his finger and thrust it at the man. The guard held it up and inspected it before handing it to his companion. "Take the message in, private." As the young man hurried to do his bidding the sergeant eyed Bran once more, his face set with anger. "You'd best hope that you ain't just caused me a lot of trouble for nothing."

Bran glared at the man, his features reflecting his own vexation. "And you had best pray that I never have any more trouble from you."

The sound of rattling metal reached them before the young guard came racing into view. He was out of breath, but his entire demeanor had changed, and he gave Bran a brisk salute. "Sir, His Majesty the King is not in residence at the moment, but his brother, the Duke of York, will see you."

Bran felt like tearing both guards limb from limb for wasting his valuable time, but it would take even more to vent his annoyance. He merely gave the private a curt nod as he took back his ring and strode past them, noting that they seemed very glad that they had not used a more violent means to dissuade the late-night visitor to Whitehall.

The soft leather soles of Bran's boots made little noise as he took the wide steps up to the entrance hall two at a time. Seeing James, the Duke of York, he bowed gracefully, his court manners elegant, as if he had not just left a pirate vessel and raced like a demon through the streets of London to reach the palace.

"Sir Bran," James said as he came forward, a warm smile of welcome upon his handsome face, his hand outstretched. "It's good to have you back, even if it is at this late hour." Cocking one dark brow as he glanced at Bran's attire, he chuckled. "Now, I can see why they thought you to be a murderer skulking about in the night. You do look the devil incarnate in that clothing."

"Forgive me, my lord. I fear I thought little of my appearance in my urgency to reach Charles," Bran said as he took the Duke's hand and shook it warmly.

"Well, your haste will avail you nought. Charles is at Buckingham's estate in the country for the first hunt of the season," James said, a smile of welcome upon his shapely lips. "However, let me be the first to congratulate you on being a free man."

"Damn," Bran muttered, thinking only of the disheartening news of the King's absence. With his thoughts on Royale, trying to digest the fact that he could never reach Buckingham's estate and return to London again in time to save her from the gibbet the following noon, he failed to comprehend the Duke's last statement.

"I beg your pardon," James said stiffly.

"I'm sorry, my lord, but it is imperative that I see Charles."

"Bran, I would have thought you would be highly pleased to know that you are now free to return to court and to end this ruse you have been playing for my brother."

Still preoccupied, Bran looked at the Duke, his brow furrowed with a perplexed frown. "I'm sorry, my lord. I don't understand."

"Surely you have heard. You're now a free man, because today a woman was tried and found guilty as El Diablo. It's over—you're safe from anyone who ever suspected the truth about your mission for my brother."

"Then you know?" Bran asked.

"Aye. It is truly a fortunate event for both you and Charles, don't you think? Spain has been appeased, and you can return to court."

"Fortunate?" Bran said as he ran his hand over his face in disbelief.

James frowned as he noted Sir Bran's haggard expression and the look of worry in his eyes. Placing a velvet-clad arm around his friend's shoulders, he led him toward the small audience chamber to their right.

"Bran, I've never seen you look this way before—it's as if you've got the world resting on your shoulders. I think you need a good drink of brandy. That should revive your spirits enough to tell me what's so dire that it can't wait until my brother returns. You should be celebrating, instead of looking as if you're facing your own death."

James closed the door on the footmen in attendance and crossed to an intricately carved table inlaid with mother-of-pearl. Unstopping a crystal brandy decanter, he poured two glasses and handed one to Bran. Taking a long sip of the amber liquid, he regarded his friend curiously for a long moment before he said, "Now, perhaps I can be of service to you even though my brother is absent."

A spark of hope flared to life in Bran's eyes as he said, "Aye, perhaps you can." Downing his brandy, he set the glass aside as he began his story. When he reached the part about securing a pardon for Royale, he saw James give a sad shake of his head.

"Bran, that's the damnedest tale I've ever heard. I would love to help the young woman who has stolen the heart of the man who withstood all the beauties at court. But I'm afraid that Charles is the only person with the power to grant a royal pardon."

The muscles across Bran's chest contracted as the cold hand of defeat gripped his heart and twisted it painfully, squeezing the last life from his hopes. He took a deep breath; then his shoulders slumped as he released a long sigh of remorse.

"I feared as much," he said. His voice reflected the agony welling in his heart. "Time, it seems, has been my enemy since my first meeting with Royale. Now it will steal her away from me again, but this time it will be forever."

James's craggy Stuart features screwed up thoughtfully as he folded one arm across his chest while tapping his chin with a long bejeweled finger. He wanted desperately to help his young friend. Bran Langston had served his brother faithfully and had asked for nothing in return. It was time that he be repaid, if there was a chance at all of saving the girl he loved. After a few long moments James's eyes lit up, and he smiled.

"Perhaps there is a way to save her after all," the Duke said, cocking his head and regarding Bran with a twinkle in the dark eyes that were so much like his brother's.

"How?" Bran asked eagerly. At that moment he was willing to risk anything to save Royale, even if it meant storming Newgate with the crew of the *Wicked Mistress*.

"First I need to know if the girl was convicted of murder along with the charges of piracy," James said, and smiled again at Bran's negative shake of the head. "Good. Then you may be able to save her—if you are willing to marry her."

"Of course I'm willing to marry her. That has been my intention all along, but what has that to do with her situation now?" Bran asked, wondering at the Duke's train of thought.

"You see, my friend, there is an ancient law that is still on the books in England from before William the Conqueror's time. It states that a woman sentenced to hang can be saved from the death penalty if a man of good character is willing to marry her upon the gibbet and take charge of her to see that she does no wrong in the future. The only exceptions to the law are those convicted of murder.''

Bran stared at the Duke, dumbfounded with relief. He relaxed visibly and looked several years younger as the tension and worry faded from his face. He flashed the Duke a wide smile of gratitude and extended his hand to him. ''Thank you, my lord, for giving me back my life, for that is what Royale is to me.''

James shook his head and held up a hand in warning. ''The law is old, Bran, and may not hold up in the courts of today. But at least it will give you time—the time that you need for Charles to return and arrange a proper pardon for your lady.''

''Still, you have my undying gratitude. I had despaired of finding any way to save Royale beyond attacking the prison.''

James chuckled as he refilled their glasses. ''You'd have done it, too, wouldn't you?''

''Aye, I would, if I had no other choice. I love her,'' Bran said as he took the glass the Duke offered.

''How does your lady feel about you? Does she return your love?''

Bran's smile dimmed as he swirled the amber liquid in his glass and slowly shook his head. ''I'm afraid her feelings toward me are not those expected by a future husband. Our last encounter was less than amicable, but I hope that after tomorrow things will change for the better.''

''And if they don't? What will you do?''

Bran tossed down the brandy and enjoyed the burning sensation it created. The feeling offset the more volatile emotions that churned his insides at the thought that he might never gain Royale's love. Setting the glass on the table, he looked at the Duke and shrugged. ''I have little to say in the matter. If nothing changes between us, I will let her have her freedom. All I want now is to make sure that she lives. If in the future I lose her, I will have to accept it. But at least I will know she is alive and well.''

''Can you really let her go if she wants her freedom?''

''Aye, if that's all that will make her happy. It will be the hardest thing I've ever had to do, but I will do it. Royale is too precious to me. I can't cage her against her will. That in itself would snuff the spirit from her just as surely as letting her go to the gallows tomorrow. My lord, I love her too much for that.''

''Aye, I believe you do, Bran. Not many men would be willing to give up the woman they loved for the sake of her happiness,'' James said as he clapped his friend on the back. ''I wish you well in your marriage, and I hope you can set everything in order after tomorrow.''

Bran gave the Duke a wry smile as a mischievous twinkle entered his eyes. ''I'm going to do my damnedest.''

''I never doubted it,'' James said, and he laughed. ''Now don't you think it's time for you to be on your way? I would think you'd have much to do before noon, when you will be a married man.''

''Aye, that I do,'' Bran said as he took the Duke's hand and dropped to one knee before him. ''My lord, I thank you for your friendship and help.''

''Rise, Sir Bran. We are friends, and, as such, each of us knows what is in the other's heart. We have suffered and rejoiced together, and because of that I would see you happy.''

''I am grateful, my lord,'' Bran said as he rose.

James gave him a roguish grin that made the resemblance between him and his brother startling. ''Good. We like to keep our subjects that way. Now be off and rescue your lady. I don't want any more scowls on that handsome visage when I see you again. And remember, I want to meet this angel that drives even the devil mad.''

"You will, my lord," Bran said, arching a provocative eyebrow, "after the honeymoon."

James threw back his dark head and roared his mirth as Bran made an elegant leg and strode from the chamber. The Duke still chuckled as he poured himself another glass of brandy and sat down before the fire. Stretching out his long, silk-encased legs, he relaxed back in the chair, thinking over his conversation with Sir Bran Langston.

It was fortunate that he had become interested of late in the ancient laws of England, or he would not have been able to help his friend save the young woman. A smile again tugged at his lips. Charles would be very pleased with this night's work. The strange turn of events had actually worked in the King's favor.

"Ah, yes, my dear brother. After the honeymoon we shall meet this young ward of yours, and then we'll know for certain," James mused aloud before downing the last of his drink and ringing for the footman.

"All right, ye vixen from hell, 'tis time fer ye to go and meet yer Maker," the guard said as he swung the heavy oak door open and stood eyeing Royale with hostility. He didn't feel any compassion for his prisoner, especially after her trial the previous day. His shins were still sore from the kicks he had received when he had taken her from the courtroom after the judges had pronounced her sentence.

At the man's entrance Royale turned from the barred window overlooking the sun-drenched prison yard. Since the gray light of dawn had pearled the heavens she had remained at her vigil, watching the sun rise in the east and creep much too quickly across the morning sky. On the day of her death she had not wanted to waste her last precious moments on earth staring at the damp stone walls of her cell. She wanted to savor her last hours of life by enjoying the beauty of the warm spring day.

Never one to accept defeat meekly, it had taken her nearly the whole night to come to terms with herself and the fate that awaited her. In the early morning hours she had admitted that no matter how much she raged and fought, nothing would change. All that was left to her was to meet her death with courage and dignity. She had been convicted as El Diablo and would not mar his name by cowering in front of his enemies.

To keep from dwelling upon her execution Royale had forced herself to focus on the happy moments in her past. It was the only way to hold at bay the fear that was twisting her insides into knots. She recalled her childhood at Good Fortune and the loved ones who had shared it with her. Mentally she again sailed the seas with her father, and then later with Tim O'Kelly and Fishbait Jones at her side. She refused to think about the moments of pain and death that had blemished her memories far too often. And last but far from least, she thought of El Diablo, the handsome pirate who had stolen her heart and had made her a woman in soul and body.

The man she loved, her father, her mother, and her friends had already passed over to the unknown realm beyond life, and today she would follow the same path. She hoped that they would be there to welcome her.

Royale raised her chin in the air and stiffened her spine as she looked at the guard and said, "I am ready."

"Well, I'm so glad to hear that, since it wouldn't do ye a bit of good if ye weren't," the guard sneered as he took her arm and led her from the prison.

Again she rode through the streets of London with her hands bound behind her back. This time, however, she was fully aware of the jeering crowd that followed the cart over the cobbles to Tyburn Hill. They joked and laughed at her expense. Many envied her for her daring adventures, while others were glad that she had been the one sentenced to hang instead of themselves. All enjoyed the fair-like atmosphere a hanging brought to the city.

Royale forced her thoughts away from the ugly crowd as they passed through London and moved along the narrow dirt road to the small hill where the gibbet stood. She blocked out the sound of their obscene calls and thought only of the more pleasant sights along the way. She noted the rich green of a distant meadow and the first white blossoms of a climbing rose that clung to a stone wall. She was poignantly aware of the sweet fragrance that drifted from the blooms and the feel of the sun on her skin. All her senses were attuned to everything but the event about to take place.

The cart jolted to a halt, and the crowd roared with mirth as the guard dragged Royale down without giving her time to exit the crude vehicle under her own power. She staggered before regaining her balance and glared up at the man. Her eyes were the color of a stormy sky as she raised her chin haughtily and said, "I can walk, so I have no need of your escort."

"That may be, wench, but 'tis me duty," the guard muttered as he propelled her roughly through the crowd and up the gibbet steps.

As they reached the platform Royale shook the guard's hand from her arm and crossed by herself to the black-hooded hangman. Her action brought a cheer of approval from the spectators. They enjoyed a hanging much more when the condemned made it an interesting event by not meekly accepting his fate.

As the executioner read her death warrant Royale scanned the faces of the crowd, noting the amusement her plight brought them. Determining to give them no more enjoyment at her expense, she stood with her head held high and shoulders back as the noose was placed around her neck.

"Under the authority vested in me by the courts, it is my duty to hang you, El Diablo, by the neck until dead," the hangman said as Royale closed her eyes and said one final prayer, preparing herself to die. He reached for the bar to release the trap door beneath her feet, but a cry from the crowd stayed his actions.

"Halt! I, Sir Bran Langston, demand a stay of execution," Bran said as he urged his mount through the mass of people congregated around the gibbet. A rumble of protest and disappointment rose from the crowd as the hangman turned to stare at the man on the black horse.

Royale's eyes opened wide with shock as she stared down into his beloved face. Her heart began to pound against her ribs, and her eyes misted with tears. She could not believe what her eyes saw. El Diablo was dead; this had to be some kind of sinister plot to make her last moments on earth even more horrible, since she had to die and lose the man she loved once more. Either that or her mind was playing vicious tricks on her in her last desperate attempt to cling to life. Unable to believe what was transpiring, she assumed the latter. In some cruel way her mind had conjured an El Diablo to come to her rescue. Numb with shock, she listened and watched, not daring to believe and hope.

"You have no right to interfere with the sentence passed by the court, sir," the hooded man said as he again reached for the bar. "I have me orders to carry out and will do so."

"Nay," Bran said. "Under English law this woman will go free if there is a man here willing to marry her and be her warden for life."

"I ain't never heard of no such law," the executioner said, his hand on the latch. "And if there was one, I don't see no man stepping forward to take the wench."

The crowd quieted with curiosity at the new turn of

events. They moved silently out of Bran's path as he slid from the saddle and took the gibbet steps two at a time. He shoved a sheaf of papers into the hangman's hands and turned to remove the noose from Royale's neck. "I'm the man who will take her to wife."

The hangman scanned the papers in his hand and scratched his head through the black fabric of his hood. " 'Tis law, all right, but there ain't no minister here to listen to yer vows, so this don't mean nothing. The wench has been sentenced to die, and 'tis my duty to see that she does."

"Sir, oh, sir," a thin, black-robed figure said as he scrambled awkwardly up the steps, his voice raspy from exertion. "I've been summoned to administer the marriage vows to Royale Carrington and Sir Bran Langston."

The hangman regarded his prisoner and the two men uncertainly. Crossing to the guard, he showed him the papers, and they discussed the strange situation for several long, agonizing minutes. At last the hangman turned and shrugged. " 'Tis the law of the land and I ain't one to go against it."

Feeling cheated out of their entertainment, the crowd loosed an angry rumble of hostility. The hooded man turned to them and shouted, "It seems we won't be having a hanging today. This gent has agreed to take the wench to wife, and by old English law he has that right. So instead of a hanging, we're all here for a wedding."

Bran tensed as he warily regarded the rough-looking faces below them. If the crowd chose not to go along with the law, both he and Royale could lose their lives. Sensing the precariousness of their situation, Bran knew he had to do something before someone made the wrong move and the mob turned on them and tore them to pieces. Moving Royale away from the edge of the platform and leading her to the minister for protection, he smiled down at the belligerent faces.

"I know all of you have come to Tyburn for a bit of amusement this afternoon. And as a man who would not ruin such a lovely day for anyone, I insist that all of you enjoy yourselves as my wedding guests. Refresh yourself from the vendors at my expense to celebrate our nuptials."

A murmur rose from the crowd as they discussed Bran's offer. At last a few chuckles emerged, and their merriment began to grow at the strange occurrence they were witnessing. One man stepped forward and called up to Bran, "That's right generous of ye, gov'nor. We'd be most happy to offer our congratulations to the newlyweds."

Laughter greeted the man's words, and Bran relaxed. He had won the skirmish. Turning to the minister, he said, "Let's get on with it before this rabble decides they prefer to see a hanging than to drink my wine."

The minister drew Royale to Bran's side and placed her hand in his before drawing a black Bible from his robes. He read the marriage vows, and the crowd cheered as he pronounced them man and wife.

Royale was in a state of shock at the sudden turn of events. She vaguely remembered saying, "I will," and then Bran gave her a hearty kiss, swept her up in his arms, and ran down the gibbet steps to his horse. He placed her on the saddle and swung up behind her. Drawing a handful of coins from his pocket, he tossed them in the air and he called, "Drink hearty, my friends." Giving his steed a sharp kick in the side, he managed to maneuver the animal through the still-cheering mass of people. At the edge of the crowd he threw out another handful of coins to keep their interest centered elsewhere until he reached the road to London.

He had been so intent on his rescue of Royale that he had failed to speak to her beyond their marriage vows. It was not until he felt her tremble that he realized the tremendous strain the whole affair must have had on her. Wrapping one arm protectively around her, he drew her back against his chest, cradling her tenderly as he murmured against her tousled hair, "It's finally over, Royale. You're free. No one can harm you now."

Royale could not speak. Her relief at escaping the gallows and finding that the man she loved still lived was too great. She clung to him as great racking sobs shook her from head to toe. Her tears trailed down her cheeks and dampened a path over the soft velvet of his jacket as she cried to alleviate all the tension and pain she had suffered during the past months.

Her weeping abated as they entered London. All that remained were shuddering sniffles. She did not try to move out of Bran's arms but lay with her cheek pressed to his chest listening to the comforting sound of his heart beating beneath the hard muscles. She was emotionally and physically exhausted from her ordeal. Her resolve to meet her death bravely had taken more strength than even she had realized. Her mind could contemplate nothing further than the warm contentment she felt at being wrapped once more in his powerful arms. Her tears had washed away the past and the future, leaving her too drained to think of anything beyond the moment. The steady beat of his heart and the soothing motion of the horse's regular gait lulled her into the first peaceful slumber that she'd had since the night at Ile a Vache.

Bran felt her relax against him and knew that she slept. Tenderly, so as not to awaken her, he brushed a tangled curl from her brow and gently placed his lips against her smooth skin. He was still amazed at the depth of feeling she inspired within him, and his heart seemed to do a rapid somersault within his chest as he tightened his arm around her, recalling how close he had come to losing her forever.

He knew that for as long as he lived he would never forget the fear and pride that had coursed through him when he had seen her standing on the platform with such dignity and courage. Even as she faced her death she had shown the valiant spirit that he had grown to admire and love.

As noble and proud as the King himself, she had stood with head held regally, her face calm as she confronted death in the same manner in which she had faced life: without fear. He alone knew the strain such bravery had placed upon her. He had seen it in her eyes and had heard it just now as she wept against his chest. Her tears had cleansed her battered spirit, and now her sleep would renew it. When she awoke and had time to recuperate she would again be the fiery pirate who had captured his heart.

Turning his mount down the gracious tree-lined avenue where his elegant townhouse was located, Bran smiled. For the first time in years he was glad to be home. He had no desire to be back at sea seeking adventure. All the adventure he craved lay sleeping in his arms.

Chapter 17

A warm April breeze wafted through the open window, stirring the velvet drapes as it filled the room with the sweet fragrance of spring. An intricate, changing pattern of sunlight dappled the thick carpet, enhancing the rich russet and gold of the wool. Wrens warbled happily among the gnarled branches of the tall oak tree outside, welcoming the spring with their gentle songs.

It was a lovely morning; but because of the terror-filled dreams of the girl who tossed and turned upon the bed, its beauty did not penetrate her sleep. The songs of the wrens turned into laughter from mocking faces that stared up at her on the gallows; the light breeze that touched her face was the rough hemp rope of the noose as it was placed around her neck.

With a cry Royale bolted upright, flailing the air with her arms as she relived her harrowing experience on the gibbet. She struggled against the strong arms that encircled her and pulled her close to the hard, masculine form at her side.

"Hush, my love, 'tis all over. It's only a dream," Bran murmured soothingly as he held her against his chest and brushed her hair back from her pale, frightened face.

"Hush, love. I'll never let anything harm you again, I promise."

Still befuddled by sleep, yet sensing security and comfort in his arms, Royale snuggled against his lean form as the last vestiges of her nightmare slowly faded and she became more and more aware of her surroundings. Gradually her heartbeat returned to normal; she relaxed as she realized that it had truly been only a dream and that she was in the elegant bedchamber of Sir Bran Langston's townhouse instead of her Newgate cell.

It had been a week since her terrifying experience on the gibbet, but she recalled little of what had happened to her since then. Her body and mind had been so totally exhausted that she had slept the majority of the time. She only awoke to take her meals and to let the maid help her bathe.

Curled within Bran's warm embrace, she realized she had seen little of him in the previous days. She vaguely recalled their first meeting after his rescue of her and his explanation of the events that had transpired to save her from the gallows. Since that time he had paid only brief visits, always using the excuse of her needing her rest to be free of her company after only a few minutes.

Until now, lying next to him in bed, she had felt only gratitude toward Bran for rescuing her. She had not considered the other consequence of the ceremony that had taken place upon the gibbet. They were married, and she now belonged to him. He owned her, as he did any other of his properties, and he could do with her as he chose, according to the law.

Royale's heart seemed to stop as she realized that by marrying her Bran had gained everything he desired. He had a wife to appease his King, Charles's goodwill for his valiant gesture of marrying his ward to save her life, and Good Fortune. In turn she had lost everything, with the exception of her life. She had lost her freedom, her home, and her heart to the man who now held her in his arms. She had admitted her feelings for him to herself long ago and was honest enough to know that if he loved her in return she would willingly surrender everything. But love had not been the reason for their marriage, and she could not let herself accept anything less. She could not live a lie for the rest of her life just to remain near him. Nor could she accept the crumbs of affection that he might toss her way when he was not seeking adventures elsewhere.

A cold chill settled in the pit of her stomach; her insides withered at the thought of what she must do, but she had to make her stand now or she would find herself succumbing to the security and contentment she found in his arms. If she did that, she would lose herself completely.

"What are you doing here?" she asked as she pushed herself away from him and sat up, clenching the sheet to her breast to cover what her thin silk night rail emphasized instead of hiding.

"Where else should I be?" Bran asked huskily. He smiled as he leaned forward and brushed his lips lightly against her bare shoulder.

Royale scooted to the edge of the bed. "I don't know where you should be, but I do know for certain that it is not in my bed."

"I'm your husband, Royale, and I've heard husbands are partial to sleeping in their wives' beds," Bran said, and he chuckled at the dark look she bestowed upon him. "Does that thought shock you?"

"Yes—no—I mean—we may be married, but that does not give you the right to come to my bed. I know it was expedient for you to marry me, and I will always be grateful for your valiant gesture, but I also know this farce will come to an end once the King returns to grant my pardon."

"What do you mean?" Bran asked, his brows lowering over his dark eyes as he frowned at her.

"I intend to ask the King to have our marriage annulled. You have fulfilled your responsibilities as my guardian far beyond what was required. I owe you my life, but I won't remain your wife under the circumstances," Royale said as she slid her feet to the floor and stood.

The sheet remained on the bed as she turned to face Bran. The sunlight behind her filtered through the thin silk of her night rail and made it nearly transparent. It outlined the softly rounded curves of her young body, and Bran tensed as he viewed the lovely sight. The muscles across his flat belly grew taut as his blood began to heat with desire. During the past week he had forced himself to keep his distance, because he knew the effect she had on him. He had wanted her to be fully recovered from her ordeal before he came to their marriage bed. Though he had wanted her with a deep hunger that ate away at him during the long hours of each night, he had remained on the lounge in the dressing room adjoining the master bedchamber in the event she might need him. It had not been easy to stay away from her, and now the sight of her was again setting fire to the passions she stirred within his heart and soul.

"Damn it, Royale," Bran growled as he threw back the sheet and rose from the bed, a bronze image of hard sinew and masculine beauty. With only a few short strides, he came around the bed to face her. "It's time we came to an understanding."

Royale's heart fluttered within her breast as she watched him come toward her. She longed to reach out and caress the strong column of his neck and to feel the ripple of his muscles beneath the tanned skin of his back and shoulders. She wanted nothing more than to feel his hard body pressing hers down into the soft mattress, but she refused to give way to her desire.

"I agree," she said, her own voice husky with emotion. "It's time for you to understand that I'm a woman and not a brainless child who can be manipulated at your pleasure. I admit freely that I've made many mistakes since leaving Witch's Cay with such grandiose and foolish dreams, but I won't continue to make them by remaining your wife. You've made your feelings clear to me in the past. You now have Good Fortune, as you wanted, and I have my life. We are even, Bran."

He grasped her by the upper arms and drew her against him. His hot gaze raked her lovely features as he said, "For all I care, Good Fortune can sink into the ocean. I've never wanted that blasted bit of land you treasure so much. All I've wanted is you, Royale."

"Want, Bran?" Royale said, unflinching under his piercing gaze. "Yes, you want me, but I want more than that from a marriage. That's what you have failed to understand, and that's why I will ask the King for an annulment. You want a mistress, not a wife."

"I have need of both. Every man wants a sensual lover in his bed and a beautiful woman to grace his home. Fortunately, I have found a woman who possesses both the fiery, passionate traits of a mistress and the beauty and charm of a wife."

"No, Bran," Royale said. She tried to shake her head but found that he had wrapped his hand in her long hair and now held her firmly.

"Royale, you are my wife, and I want you. I have a need to feel myself within your warmth, to reassure myself that you still live and that I have not lost you. You don't know the hell I suffered at the thought of your death. I died myself when I saw you standing on the gibbet with the noose already around your neck. My God, Royale, I need you," Bran murmured as he wrapped his arms around her and his lips descended to stay her words of protest.

The touch of his mouth against hers ended the battle
Royale had been waging against her own heart. His words
had been spoken as a plea, not a demand, and she could
not refuse the comfort he sought. Her own desire to feel
him cover her body and thrust deeply within her was as
intense as his. She, too, needed to know they both lived.

Sliding her hands through the crisp mat of hair that furred
his chest and around his corded neck, she clung to him,
giving as well as taking as their kiss deepened. She savored
the feel of his hands upon her back, pressing her against
the swollen length of him before he grew tired of the silk
that separated their flesh. With a rending sound he tore it
down the back and stripped it away from her body, leaving
her naked in the morning sun. She heard his sharp breath
as he gazed down upon her body. The knowledge that she
could stir this powerful man to such passion made her feel
omnipotent as she stood proudly before him. Her hair made
a soft curtain of silk at her shoulders, and a long russet
curl lay upon her breast, emphasizing one impudent nipple
as she took a deep breath, savoring the expression of desire
in his eyes.

"My God, Royale," he breathed as he came to her,
recapturing her lips, devouring their honeyed taste before
beginning his sensual quest. His mouth was a hot brand
that scorched her flesh as he trailed his lips across her cheek
and down the white column of her throat to the rose-crested
mounds his eyes had worshipped a moment before.

Royale wrapped her arms around him, her fingers entwining themselves in his dark hair, pressing his head closer
to her breast as her own head fell back and she arched to
his caress.

"El Diablo," she whispered huskily, her voice heavy
with passion, her knees giving way beneath her as the pleasurable sensations mounted each time his tongue flicked a
hard nipple.

He felt the tremor that shook her and eased her down upon the soft carpet. Spreading her gold-streaked mane about her, he knelt over her, savoring her beauty. His gaze took in her passion-flushed features before moving slowly along the length of her body, pausing on the high-peaked breasts, and tracing the trail of soft blond down to the darker apex of her thighs. His fingers moved with his eyes, tenderly caressing each part of her and stirring deeper needs within himself. He throbbed against her thigh as he ran his hands down the length of her shapely legs and then enticingly back up along the inner surface, begging them to open for him as he lowered his mouth to her.

Her thighs trembled as they spread to welcome his tantalizing caress. She moaned as tiny bursts of rapture sparked her flesh, kindling the flames of her passion to an inferno until she arched to his mouth as a blaze of ecstasy shimmered just beyond her reach. She moaned again, wanting all of him to fill her so that she could know the glory of their love to the fullest. Her nails bit into his shoulders as she cried, "Love me, Bran, love me."

He could prolong their love play no further. His own desires were pounding violently within him. He covered her and they shared the taste of her in a searing kiss as he thrust deeply within her welcoming sheath of love. Their passion was not meek. It rose in ferocity, as if the very power of their lovemaking could wipe away all of the emotional uncertainties that each had about the other.

The ecstasy they shared was as poignant as it was beautiful. For a long while afterward they lay still, not speaking, their bodies intimately joined. Neither wanted to move and tempt breaking the enchantment surrounding them.

At last Bran raised himself on his elbows and peered down at her. His face revealed none of the turmoil that raced through him as he tipped up her chin and gazed down into her sea-green eyes, searching for the answer he longed to hear.

"Royale, will you reconsider your decision?"

Her heart twisted with pain as she gazed up at him. If he only loved her, nothing in the world could make her ask the King to annul her marriage to Bran. But he didn't.

"No, Bran, I can't," she said, her eyes brimming as she shook her head.

Exasperation and hurt mingled within Bran as he pushed himself away from her and rose. He strode across the chamber to where his clothing lay on a chair and dressed in silence. As he finished tying his cravat he looked back at Royale. His face and tone reflected his resignation as he said, "I won't force you to remain my wife. Since you are determined to rid yourself of me, no matter how I feel about you, I'll relay your message to the King. I have an audience with him this morning to discuss your pardon."

Turning to the door, he paused with his hand on the latch and glanced back over his shoulder at Royale, who stood naked and still.

"I know when I'm beaten, and I won't stand in your way. I've offered you my love, and you've refused it. I doubt we will see each other again. The *Wicked Mistress* is ready to set sail. Goodbye, Royale."

With that he left her staring at the vacant space he had filled a moment before. She remained motionless for only a split second before bolting to the door. At the last moment, she realized her state of undress and raced back to the bed to retrieve her dressing gown. Fastening it as she went, she ran to catch him.

"Bran," she called as she ran down the hall and to the top of the stairs. "Bran," she cried again as she saw him stride toward the front door.

He paused and turned to look back up at her. Royale took no time to consider what she would say or do as she ran down the stairs. Her dressing gown was a white cloud about her feet, and her hair flowed down her back in wild disarray. She was breathing heavily as she reached his side and had to take a deep breath before she could speak. "You said I had refused your love. What did you mean?"

Bran's hurt was beginning to reform itself into a protective anger, and his tone was abrupt as he said, "Exactly what I said, but you need not worry over my imposing my feelings upon you again. As you once said, it's over, and I now accept it. You're free of me, Royale." Without waiting for her response, he opened the door and slammed it behind him as he strode from the house.

Royale tried to blink back the rush of tears that stung her eyes, but the effort was useless. Her heart pounded against her ribs as great crystal droplets trembled on the tips of her lashes before running down her cheeks unheeded.

"But Bran," she whispered to the empty foyer, "I love you, too."

The audience chamber was quiet as Charles lounged in his chair, his long bejeweled fingers tapping irritably against the dark wood of the armrest. His swarthy features had deepened in hue as his ire rose, and he pursed his lips into a narrow line beneath his neatly trimmed mustache. His eyes flashed with annoyance as he regarded his young friend.

"Bran, if what you have told me is any indication, it seems I made an error in judgment when I appointed you guardian of my ward. In sending you to Good Fortune I had hoped to ensure her safety, not place her in danger."

"Sire," Bran said, flushing under the King's censure, "under the circumstances, I had little choice in the matter. Your ward had already decided to try and gain her letter of marque before I arrived at Witch's Cay. She is not a simple maid. She has a mind of her own, and when she sets it on something it takes more firepower than even the *Wicked Mistress* possesses to jar her from her course. She was determined to keep her home, and nothing would make her accept me as her guardian once she learned my identity.''

''And you're telling me that she turned to piracy and began using the name El Diablo just to secure her home?'' Charles said, eyeing Bran curiously. He sensed that there was much more to the story than his friend was telling him.

''It was one of the reasons,'' Bran said, shifting uncomfortably under Charles's assessing gaze.

''I suspect there is much more between you and my young ward than you are revealing. But since you have married her, I will not probe that side of your relationship. You have done the honorable thing, and I am satisfied,'' Charles said, and he smiled as he relaxed in his chair. His secret wish had been realized. He had sent Bran to Good Fortune with the hope that a marriage between the two young people might follow, and so it had. Ah, my beloved Elaine, Charles mused to himself, I think you would be proud of how things have worked out for your daughter.

''Sire, I'm afraid that our marriage was only a means to save Royale from the gibbet,'' Bran said, and he watched as the King's face again flushed dark with anger. ''It is only a temporary arrangement.''

''It was my understanding from James that you loved the girl. What is this foolish talk of a temporary arrangement?'' Charles asked as he leaned forward, eyeing Bran with a less than congenial light glowing in his deep brown eyes.

''I do love her, but she has refused to remain my wife. She has requested an annulment.''

''Annulment? 'Ods fish, man. If you love the girl, I see no reason to end your marriage, even if she has requested it. Young girls are fickle things and often don't know their own minds. She'll come around, you'll see,'' Charles said, relaxing once more, thinking the matter settled.

"Sire, Royale is not like other young girls. She's a woman with a mind of her own, and that's one reason why I love her. I will not force her to remain my wife. I have learned from my past experience with her that it would do little good. She would fight me every step of the way. Nor would she find any happiness in such an arrangement. I love her too much for that and would see her happy,'' Bran said, his voice reflecting his brave battle with his emotions.

"Bran, you amaze me. You say you love the girl, yet you are willing to let her go?''

"Aye, Sire,'' Bran told him, unable to say more.

Charles tapped the armrest thoughtfully, considering Bran's words. He, too, wanted to see Royale Carrington happy, but he also wanted the same for his friend. From the expression on Bran's face, that would only come about if he had Royale as his wife.

"Perhaps you're right, but before I make my decision I would like to speak to my ward. Have her come to me this afternoon. I will not grant her pardon or any other request that she has made until I have spoken with her.''

"As you wish, Sire. I will have a footman deliver your message,'' Bran said, and he bowed. He had turned to leave when Charles's words stayed him.

"Bran, don't sail before tomorrow.''

Bran smiled as he regarded his sovereign. "You know me well, Sire.''

"Aye, I know you. I've seen that look in your eyes too many times before and know when you have the itch to be away from England. We are friends, not just monarch and subject, and I would see you happy if it is in my power.''

"I am grateful for your friendship, but I'm afraid that in this matter not even the power of a King can change how

Royale feels toward me. Too much has happened to destroy the bonds that were growing between us before she learned of my true identity,'' Bran said, and he bowed again before exiting the audience chamber.

The King was left to ponder his coming meeting with the daughter of the woman he had loved in his youth.

Tiny lines creased Royale's forehead as she frowned down at the royal summons that had been delivered a few moments earlier by the King's messenger. Tossing the paper upon the dressing table, she slumped down on the padded stool and eyed her reflection in the mirror.

The girl she saw looked much like the young woman who had received another missive from the King many months before on Witch's Cay. The only difference between the two images was that her eyes no longer held the glow of excitement that her grand dreams had created. Now they had a look of maturity in their sea-green depths. Much had happened since the day she had set out to prove herself to the world.

She was no longer a naive young girl; she was a woman who had witnessed death and destruction over a few pieces of gold. She was a woman who had found love within a masked pirate's arms and had recklessly tossed it away in the name of her pride.

Lifting the summons from the table, she reread it before crumpling it into a ball and throwing it to the floor. The King's denial of her pardon until meeting with her should have sunk her spirits, but they could plummet no lower after her encounter with Bran. She was still numb with the realization that she had been too blind to recognize his feelings for her without staunch avowals of his undying love. He had warned her at Ile a Vache that she might wait until it was too late, and she had. He was gone, and all that was left for her to do was to ask the King to annul the marriage that she now desperately wanted to continue.

A heavy, foreboding cloud seemed to hover over her as she rose and began to dress herself in the finery that Bran had purchased for her while she lay recuperating from her ordeal in prison. Her gloomy mood did not improve as she slipped an exquisite gown of gold silk over her head and stood eyeing her reflection in the mirror.

In other circumstances she would have found pleasure in the feeling of the rich material against her skin after so many months spent garbed in her male disguise. But now she found little enjoyment in her rich gown because of the purpose it served. In it she would come before the man who had branded her a bastard in the eyes of the world by denying her rights as legal heir to Sir John's estate.

Strangely, she found that the thought spurred her flagging spirits, buoying them back to life. She stiffened her spine and raised her chin haughtily in the air as she eyed her image in the mirror. King Charles held her life and future in his bejeweled hand, but she would not beg for his mercy. She was Sir John's daughter, and she would meet with the King with all the dignity her position merited.

The afternoon sunlight streamed through the high windows of the audience chamber. It highlighted the golden glints in Royale's hair as she came gracefully forward and sank into a curtsy before the King.

Charles's breath caught in his throat as he looked upon the young woman before him. Only those who knew him well would have taken note of the air of tension that surrounded him, but only he knew the reason behind it. The girl was nearly a replica of her mother, the former Lady Elaine Markham. The sight of her brought vividly back to mind the halcyon days of his youth, when he had been the young exiled royal seeking refuge from his enemies on the Isle of Jersey. There he had met the lovely Elaine.

The long-forgotten memories assaulted his senses with devastating force. They rekindled the love the two young people had shared upon the sandy beaches with no restrictions of class and status to come between them. During their brief time together they had been only a handsome young man and a beautiful young woman in love. They had had three wonderful weeks together in the spring of 1650, and from those treasured moments had come this lovely child.

"Rise, Mistress," Charles said, forcing his voice to remain calm through the onslaught of his memories of Elaine.

As Royale rose the King stood and extended his hand to her. "Will you walk with me in the gardens? I would enjoy showing you my spaniels."

"Yes, Majesty," Royale said, confused by his congenial manner after his denial of her pardon and his abrupt summons.

"Good," Charles said softly as he took her hand and draped it through his arm as if they had been longtime friends. When they reached the graveled path that led through the sculptured hedges he paused and looked down at Royale. For a long moment his gaze swept over each of her lovely features; then he said, "Did you know that you are very much like your mother?"

"I have never thought so, Sire. Mother was fair and small, and as you can see, I am neither," Royale said, wondering at the strange expression in the King's eyes.

"True, your hair is dark, but it has been kissed by the same golden shade that was hers, and your eyes are the same color hers were. As long as I live I will never forget the beauty of your mother's eyes. They were the shade of the sea on a clear day," Charles said as he drew her forward along the path.

"You knew my mother well, Sire?" Royale asked, feeling suddenly uncomfortable. Her stomach began to twist itself in knots as she experienced a sense of foreboding. She had a premonition that more lay behind his conversation than just a casual interest in her.

"Aye, Royale, I knew her well," Charles said as he paused and took both her hands in his own. Seating her on a stone bench beneath a tall, gnarled oak, he asked, "Did she never speak to you of me?"

"I'm sorry, Sire. Mother spoke little of her youth, but my father mentioned you a great deal," Royale said, recalling both Sir John's loyalty to his King and the reason that had brought her to England. Her eyes began to sparkle with golden glints of fire.

Charles did not note the angry light in her eyes as he rose from the bench and gazed off into the distance at the dogs romping with their keepers. He folded his hands behind his back and said, "Sir John was a good man, and he served me loyally through the years. I was sorry to hear of his death."

A frown marred Royale's lovely features as she glared up at the back that was turned to her and fumed silently. Sorry to hear of his death! So sorry that you would not abide by his wishes and instead branded the girl he loved as his daughter a bastard. Clasping her hands tightly in her lap, she forced back the bitter thoughts before they could be spoken aloud. Hot tears of anger burned her eyes, and she blinked rapidly to keep them at bay. She would not cry before the man who had been at the root of all the suffering she had endured during the last year.

Glancing back at the quiet girl on the bench, Charles noted the telltale brightness in her eyes and knew what lay behind her tears. His conversation earlier in the day with Bran had enlightened him on her feelings of resentment, and he could understand them. He would have felt the same in her place.

Charles's heart went out to his beautiful child—a child that he had never been able to recognize legally. He had respected Sir John Carrington too much to reveal their secret while he still lived. And Charles had owed the man a debt of gratitude for the love he had given to this beautiful girl and her mother.

Now with Sir John and Elaine dead, she needed his protection, and as her father he was determined to see to her welfare. The events of the past months had shown that he had waited too long to acknowledge their relationship, and it had come close to costing her life. To think that, unaware of her identity, he had almost let her hang! If that had happened he never could have forgiven himself. Yet now he hesitated to reveal the truth to her. The love he heard in her voice when she spoke of Sir John made him waiver in his decision. How would his spirited daughter react when she learned that he was in fact her father and that everything he had done was in an effort to protect her?

"Royale," he said as he settled himself at her side and took her hand once more, holding it as if to prevent her from fleeing, "I know you were told that Sir John was not your father. Have you ever wondered who your father actually was?"

Royale tensed. The conversation was beginning to cross into areas that she preferred to keep locked away in her mind. Her throat constricted as the pain and humiliation of her bastardy rose up to choke her. She lowered her gaze to the bejeweled hand that held hers as she struggled to remain calm. She felt the need to vent all her anger and resentment upon England's monarch, but finally she managed to control the urge. She moistened her dry lips and raised her eyes to the swarthy features of the King.

"Sire, I consider Sir John my father. For a while after

his death I did wonder who my sire was, but then I realized that it didn't truly matter. It is the man who rears you and gives you his love who is in fact your father. It is not the man who callously conceives you in a moment of pleasure and then turns his back on the child that he sires. Sir John's blood does not flow in my veins, and I am a bastard in the eyes of the world, but to myself I am Sir John's daughter. He is the only man I will ever recognize as my father,'' Royale said vehemently, her eyes again bright with unshed tears.

Charles winced from the pain her words aroused within his heart. He loved his children, all of them, and this one no less, but her avowal had made him reconsider his decision to tell her the truth. He had found her after eighteen years and did not want to lose her again. If he told her that he was in fact her father, her resentment might turn to hatred.

"Is that the reason behind your wild adventures at sea?" he asked softly.

Royale met his gaze levelly. Her chin jutted out at a stubborn angle and her eyes held no fear as she said, "Yes. I foolishly thought that by gaining enough gold to buy back my home I would be proving to the world that I had a right to the name I carried."

"My dear Royale," Charles said as he placed an arm around her shoulders and drew her comfortingly against his chest, "had I but known the grief my concern for you would cause, I swear that none of it would have come to pass. When I made you my ward I thought only to see you protected. I did not mean to harm you in any manner. I had too much love for your parents to want anything but happiness for you. I arrogantly thought you would be like the other young women I have met. I did not realize the strength Sir John instilled in you nor the loving bond you shared with him. I honestly thought you would be grateful for my intervention.

"That is why I sent Sir Bran to oversee your welfare. I had no intention of ever claiming Good Fortune. I didn't make the law that required it to revert to the crown, but I did seek to go around it by making you my ward. Greedy men are much worse than a pack of wolves when an unprotected young woman comes into an inheritance. By sending Sir Bran to Good Fortune I thought to keep your home secure for you until you chose to marry. Can you forgive me for all the trouble I caused you by being so presumptuous?"

"Sire, I understand now that you only wanted what was best for me. It is I who must ask for your forgiveness. I'm sorry I created so many problems. I meant only to regain what I thought to be mine by right of my father's wishes," Royale said as she leaned away from the King and wiped at her damp eyes, a wobbly little smile trembling upon her lips as she looked up at him.

"Then Sir John's wish is granted. From this day forward Good Fortune belongs to you and your heirs to do with as you and they see fit. But I fear there is another small matter that we must discuss. It seems that you are also in need of a royal pardon for piracy," Charles said. He grinned, his lips curling impishly beneath his black mustache.

"Yes, Sire, I have a great need for your pardon, but there is also another favor I would ask of you," Royale said, her voice husky with emotion. Her face reflected the effort it cost her to ask the King to dissolve her marriage to Bran. Her lovely features were pinched with tension.

"Ask so I may grant it. I have done you a disservice in the past and now fully intend to make amends so that we can become friends."

Royale flushed a becoming rose, captured by Charles's innate charm—a trait that few could resist when he chose to use it. "Sire, I ask you to have my marriage to Sir Bran annulled as soon as possible."

"Do you find the match so disagreeable, Royale?" the King asked, his smile fading as he gazed down into her somber face.

Royale lowered her eyes to her tightly clasped hands and shook her head. "No, Sire, but under the circumstances I feel it is only right to release Sir Bran from a marriage that he was forced to make in order to save my life."

"I find this a perplexing situation, Royale. You have no objection to your marriage, yet you ask me to have it dissolved. I will need a reason before I can grant your request."

Royale's eyes were again bright with tears as she raised her head and looked at the King. Her lower lip trembled visibly as she said, "It was a marriage of convenience, not of love."

"Most marriages are arranged in such a manner, and they turn out well," Charles said, watching the play of emotions on Royale's face. "You may not love Sir Bran, but he is young and handsome, and he has enough wealth to give you a comfortable life."

"I do love him," Royale blurted out before she could stop herself.

The King smiled and shook his head at the crooked road love often travels before reaching its true destination. He didn't understand why it couldn't for once find a smooth path. Here were two young people who loved each other but who were determined for some misguided reason to give each other their freedom for the sake of their happiness, when in fact neither would ever be happy if they were separated.

Chuckling to himself, he tipped up Royale's chin and peered into the sea-green eyes that reminded him so of the warm, love-filled days he had spent with her mother.

He might not be able to recognize this child as his own, but her name proclaimed the blood that flowed in her veins, and it was his duty as her father to see her happy.

"If you love him, child, don't let yourself make the same mistake that I made so many years ago and let that love slip through your fingers. There are no guarantees that you will ever find it again. Don't be afraid to reach for happiness."

"Sire, it is already too late. I let my foolish pride drive him from me, and now all that is left for me is to free him of this marriage," Royale said, her voice filled with resignation.

"It seems we're at an impasse here, Royale. You want your marriage, but you're unwilling to stand and fight for it. Where is the bold young woman who was willing to turn to piracy to reclaim her home? You were willing to risk your life for a piece of land, yet you won't sacrifice anything in an effort to claim the greatest treasure of all: love. I did not think you such a coward as to let the man you love sail out of your life tomorrow without attempting to win back what you want most in the world."

The arrow of the King's words hit their desired target, pricking Royale's fighting spirit and startling her out of her moment of self-pity. "He sails tomorrow instead of today?" she asked.

"Aye," was all Charles said, and he smiled to himself as he watched the transformation in his daughter. She stiffened her spine and squared her shoulders as if ready to face a battle. Her actions reminded him much of himself. She had inherited his pride and stubbornness as well as his will to fight against all odds to gain something he wanted. The proof of his own determined nature lay in the fact that he now reigned over the country from which he had been exiled after his father's execution. It had taken years to regain his crown, but he had fought and won.

With her thoughts centered on Bran, Royale came to her feet and had already started to turn away before she remembered with whom she spoke. Blushing, she sank into a low, graceful curtsy. "Sire, may I take your advice and ask your leave?"

Charles feigned a frown, screwing up his face in a thoughtful expression as he asked, "What about this affair of the annulment? Do you still want to proceed with it?"

"Nay, Majesty. If I have any say in the matter, there will be no annulment," Royale said, smiling.

" 'Od's fish," Charles said, laughing. "I believe I perceive the return of our bold and beautiful pirate."

"Aye, Majesty. She is back, and she is determined to capture the greatest prize of all—the heart of Sir Bran Langston."

"Then it seems I must grant you a pardon for piracy in the boudoir as well as upon the high seas, my dear," Charles said, and he chuckled at the blush that tinted her cheeks a lovely rose.

"Thank you, Sire," Royale said, and she impulsively gave the King a quick hug and kiss before remembering her manners. She opened her mouth to apologize for her forward behavior, but Charles lifted a hand to silence her.

"Enough. Go seek your treasure, little pirate, before it is too late."

As Royale turned away she did not see the brightness that misted the King's eyes nor the pleased smile that touched his lips. His hopes for his lovely daughter had been realized.

The seamen and the dock workers paused at their tasks as the shiny black carriage emblazoned with the royal crest rumbled to a halt and the beautiful young woman garbed in gold silk stepped down. Intrigued by the sight of a lady at the waterfront, they watched in amazement as she strode purposefully toward the group of rough-looking men who crewed the sinister black ship known as the *Wicked Mistress*. They were further dumbfounded as one craggy-faced seaman lifted her off her feet and swung her around jubilantly while the other men stood grinning foolishly at their antics.

"Fishbait, put me down," Royale managed to gasp out over her own laughter at the exuberant welcome she had received. "That's no way to treat your captain."

"Aye, Captain," Fishbait said as he set her once more on her feet, "but it's glad we are to see ye again. After El Diablo returned without ye or any explanation as to yer whereabouts, we'd begun to doubt if we'd ever see ye again."

"Then he's on the *Wicked Mistress*?"

"Aye, he's on her, but I don't advise disturbing 'im. He's in an ugly mood. I never seed 'im like this before. He's done nothing but give us black looks and growls since he come on board today. None of us were brave enough to ask 'im any questions once we seen the fit of temper he was in. We thought it best to keep our distance till the storm passed," Fishbait said, grinning sheepishly.

"I know his black moods well, but that's not going to deter me from what I've come to do. There are a few matters that need to be settled between El Diablo and me, and it will take more than his temper to stop me," Royale said. Her resolve was reflected in the obstinate angle of her chin and the fiery light of battle in her eyes. Lifting her skirts, she strode up the gangplank and stepped onto the deck of the *Wicked Mistress*.

Fishbait, Black Jack, and Scrimshaw remained rooted to the spot. They made no move to follow Royale. From the look on her face they suspected it would be in their own best interest to be as far away as possible from the explosion that was about to take place between El Diablo and the lovely Madame Captain.

Royale made her way quietly along the passageway to the captain's cabin. Without knocking she opened the door and paused upon the threshold as it swung back on silent, well-oiled hinges. It had only been a matter of hours since their last encounter, but she felt she had been separated from him for years. As her gaze swept over the man who sat moodily staring down at the logbook on his desk, she wondered how she could ever have imagined that she could live without him if she was hungry for the mere sight of him after such a short time.

The rustle of her silk skirts against the polished floorboards alerted Bran to her presence, but he did not look up as she paused before his desk. He concentrated on the book before him in his effort to avoid seeing the look of triumph that would be in her eyes when she told him Charles had granted her wish to be free of him. Picking up the quill, he dipped it into the inkwell and began to make notations in the log. He forced his voice to remain calm as he asked, "Did you meet with the King?"

Royale's courage faltered momentarily as she gazed down into his set face. His lips were held in a rigid line, and a frown etched his brow. She had come here ready to open her heart to him, but his expression gave her little encouragement. His cool tone gave no indication that he would welcome her offer of love; he might very well laugh at her and throw it back in her face. Her pride balked at the thought, but she staunchly fought to overcome it. Her eyes sparkled with golden glints of determination as she said, "Yes, I met with the King, and he has granted my pardon. He has also granted me Good Fortune."

"Then you have your desire. When will you be returning

to Witch's Cay?'' Bran asked, his throat constricted with dread.

"Bran," Royale said as she swallowed the last of her pride and moved around the desk to kneel at his side, "there is something else I must tell you."

Still unable to look at her, he rubbed his hand wearily over his face, knowing the time had come at last.

"You don't have to tell me, Royale. I already know. When will you have the marriage annulled?"

Hearing the pain that laced his voice, Royale's heart leapt within her breast. He still loved her. Joy mingled with compassion as she took his hand and pressed it to her cheek.

Her action finally made him look at her for the first time. In his dark eyes she saw the anguish that she, too, had suffered. A wobbly smile tugged at her lips as her eyes brimmed with tears of love.

"Never," was all she could say before emotion clogged her throat.

A mixture of joy, surprise, and relief played over Bran's handsome face as he gazed down at her and repeated, "Never?"

"Aye, never, El Diablo," Royale said, smiling up at him. "I fear the devil did steal my soul on that night long ago when he first kissed me. I've been all the things that he has called me: foolish, proud, stubborn. But I know now that he is the only person that can take me to heaven with his caresses, and I pray that I have not waited until it is too late to tell him of my feelings." She paused and brushed her lips against his hand. "I love you, Bran."

For a long moment Bran stared down at her, and her heart contracted within her breast in fear of his rejection. But her apprehension vanished as he stood and pulled her into his arms.

"And I love you, Royale, with all of my heart and devil's soul," Bran said huskily as he swept her up into his arms, threw back his head, and laughed with pure joy in the knowledge of her love. His eyes gleamed hot with passion as the bold pirate emerged once more. He captured her lips with a searing kiss and then strode across the cabin to the bunk where the devil, too, would find his heaven within her arms.

Author's Note

While doing my research on PIRATE ROYALE, I became fascinated with the privateer Henry Morgan and have tried to encompass as much of his actual history within the novel as possible. The events I have described read as fiction, but they were only a few of the adventures in the privateer's life.

He was in fact given a special commission by Sir Thomas Modyford, Jamaica's governor, in the year 1668. Gathering seven hundred buccaneers, some of whom were French, he sailed to Cuba and attacked Puerto Principe, now known as Camaguey, on March 31, 1668. The French contingency would not join his next wild scheme and left him in Cuba after one of their own was killed by an Englishman. That left Morgan's force with only four hundred and fifty men. Unaffected by the French desertion, he sailed on to his next target, Puerto Bello, Panama. He arrived there during July of 1668 and found it undermanned. As I stated, he forced the Spanish religious order to precede his men up the scaling ladders, which led to many of them being shot down. After capturing Puerto Bello, he was faced with a much larger threat from the President of Panama, but his daring saw him victorious against the three thousand men in the President's forces.

After receiving the ransom for Puerto Bello, Morgan sailed to Ile a Vache, off the coast of Hispaniola, to plan his next expedition into Spanish territory. He was sent the frigate *Oxford* by the Governor of Jamaica and decided to use it as his flagship. As he and his captains sat around a table on her quarterdeck making their plans, the thirty-four-gun frigate's powder magazine exploded spontaneously. All but a handful of her crew were killed. Those men sitting on the same side of the table as Morgan survived.

As I have stated, much of Morgan's life reads like action-packed fiction, and that is why I have added this note. Actual events are often stranger than fiction. In this day and age it is hard for us to comprehend the brutalities that took place in the past and were accepted as common occurrences.

Here I have dealt with only two of Morgan's daring missions, but his adventures continued into the early 1670's. After the peace treaty between England and Spain was common knowledge in the Caribbean, Morgan's exploits caused him and Modyford to fall out of favor in Britain. The governor was called home, and Morgan was arrested and carried back to England for trial but was never formally accused of any crimes. In January of 1674 he was appointed Lieutenant Governor of Jamaica, and in 1680 he became acting governor for the two-year interregnum between the governor's departure and his successor's arrival. In the year 1688, at the age of fifty-three, Morgan died, prematurely old from his hard life-style of fighting and heavy drinking. He was buried in Port Royal, Jamaica, but four years later during the earthquake of 1692 his grave slipped into the sea along with nearly all of the town he had helped to build with his defense of the British colony of Jamaica.

ABOUT THE AUTHOR

Cordia Byers was born in the small, north Georgia community of Jasper and lives there still, with her husband, James, and their two children, Michelle and Michael. Cordia likes to think of her husband as being like one of the heroes in her novels. James swept her off her feet after their first meeting, and they were married three weeks later. After twenty happy years together, Cordia is looking forward to at least another fifty.

From the age of six, Cordia's creative talents had been directed toward painting. It was not until late 1975, when the ending of a book displeased her, that she considered writing. That led to her first novel, *Heather*, which was followed by *Callista, Nicole La Belle, Silk and Steel*, which was nominated for a *Romantic Times* Reviewer's Choice Award, *Love Storm* and *Pirate Royale*. Finding more satisfaction in the world of her romantic novels, Cordia has given up painting and now devotes herself to writing, researching her material at the local library, and then doing the major part of her work from 11:30 P.M. to 3:00 A.M.

Cordia enjoys hearing from her readers. Her address is Route 1, Box 63E, Jasper, GA 30143.

A touch of romance... from Cordia Byers